THE
EIGHT BANNERS

Also by Alan Savage:

OTTOMAN
MOGHUL

THE EIGHT BANNERS

Alan Savage

LITTLE, BROWN AND COMPANY

A *Little, Brown* Book

First published in Great Britain in 1992 by
Little, Brown and Company

A CIP catalogue record for this book is available from the
British Library

ISBN 0 356 20663 7

Typeset by Leaper & Gard Limited, Bristol, England
Printed and bound in Great Britain by
Mackays of Chatham PLC, Chatham, Kent

Little, Brown and Company (UK) Limited
165 Great Dover Street
London SE1 4YA

'It was easier to conquer the East than to know what to do with it.'

Horace Walpole
Fourth Earl of Orford

CONTENTS

China at the Time of the Manchus

Jehol

GREAT WALL

PEKING

Tientsin

Gulf of Chih-li

Port Arthur

Hwang-ho

after 1853

THE GRAND CANAL

before 1853

Chin-kiang

Wuhu

Nanking

Shanghai

Hankow

Yangtse-kiang

Hang chow

Ning-po

Foochow

Amoy

TAIWAN

Canton

Hong Kong

Macao

Miles

0   100   200   300

THE BARRINGTON FAMILY

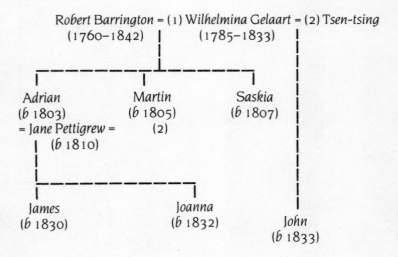

Robert Barrington = (1) Wilhelmina Gelaart = (2) Tsen-tsing
(1760–1842)   (1785–1833)

Adrian
(*b* 1803)
= Jane Pettigrew =
(*b* 1810)

Martin
(*b* 1805)
(2)

Saskia
(*b* 1807)

James
(*b* 1830)

Joanna
(*b* 1832)

John
(*b* 1833)

Historical note: The British squadron which bombarded the Taku forts was commanded by Sir James Hope, and the British army which marched on Peking was commanded by Sir James Hope Grant.

BOOK THE FIRST
Bamboo Empire

'What need we fear who knows it, when none can call our power to account?'

William Shakespeare, *Macbeth*

1

THE POWER AND THE GLORY

'Ten minutes, Mr Leach,' said Captain Gower.

'Aye-aye,' the sailing master acknowledged. 'Hand your mainsail, quartermaster, and make to squadron.'

The topsails had been brought down some time before, as had the fore and mizen sails. Now the great East Indiaman, *Lion*, two hundred feet from stem to stern, sixty-four guns, ghosted towards the shore under jibs alone.

Behind the fleet flagship there were five others, much of the same size. From their mastheads flew the Cross of St George as well as the Union Jack, and the East India Company pennants.

But they were not alone in this vast bay known, according to Mr Barrington, as the Gulf of Chih-li. In front of them, masking the low stone sea-wall, was an armada of junks and sampans, a kaleidoscope of banners, and rising from them, a no less colourful display of fireworks: rockets arced into the sky, Catherine-wheels spun frenetically on the upper decks, hand-held sparklers gleamed and died. 'Had you not assured me these people were friendly, I would assume we were about to be attacked,' Gower remarked, after a particularly loud explosion had scattered the seabirds.

As he spoke, he glanced at the man standing beside him. But Robert Barrington merely smiled. 'They won't attack you if you don't attack them, Mr Gower,' he said. 'The Chinese don't start fights, simply because they don't believe there's anyone important enough to fight against, compared with themselves.'

Gower snorted, and turned away. The fellow was insufferable. It wasn't as if he were a gentleman, or even a sailing master. He held a master's ticket, certainly, but had never been given command of a ship. Barrington would claim that was because he was only thirty-three. Which was all the more reason for his presumption of knowledge to give offence.

Robert Barrington ignored the Captain as he studied the

1

shore. It was as low-lying as he had been told to expect, and the river, the Pei-ho, tumbling over its sandbanks as it gushed into the sea, was as unprepossessing as he had been warned it would be. But it was a relief to feel that thus far his information had been proven correct. Of course, if that approaching fleet *was* bent on mischief ... but then at least the great cannon beneath him in the waist of the ship, and on the gun-deck below that, would have something to do.

Robert Barrington grinned at the thought. His size, six feet two inches in his socks and one hundred and eighty pounds of bone and muscle, suggested that he was a confident man; his blunt, open features confirmed it. Thus he had ambition, and could feel resentment. He knew he occupied a false position in this fleetful of lords and knights, learned scribes and bigoted churchmen. They represented the English establishment; he was suffered to be here because he spoke a foreign language. But if in front of him truly lay all the riches of the earth, he was damned if he would not make some of them his own.

*

'China,' remarked Lord Macartney, standing at the break of the poop. 'The very word breathes empire!'

In this autumn of 1793 his lordship, the Right Honourable George, Our Well-Beloved Cousin and Counsellor, Baron of Lissanoure, Co Antrim and Viscount Macartney of Dervock, Member of the Privy Council of Ireland, Knight of the Most Honourable Order of the Bath and of the Most Ancient and Royal Order of the White Eagle, Ambassador Extraordinary and Plenipotentiary, was fifty-six years old, of medium height, with somewhat placid features and a bald head save for a fringe of hair above his ears. His claret-coloured coat was well worn, and his stockings and cravat sadly needed laundering. He wore his tricorne hat, because of the sun, but had removed his wig, which he carried in his left hand, ready to clap on his head should he encounter someone of importance. He was, however, known to be a man of spirit, as befitted an Irishman who had fought a duel with an erstwhile subordinate, General Stuart, regarding certain differences that had arisen during his governor-ship of Madras. In that duel he had been severely wounded. But he had recovered well, and was now embarked upon the most important mission of his life – and in his youth he had been envoy extraordinary to the Empress Catherine of Russia.

But could Russia truly compare with Manchu China, and all the riches that were there to be found? By repute, at any rate. Now he glanced from the approaching fleet to the big seaman standing beside him. 'Will we be received, Barrington?'

'We will be received, my lord,' Robert assured him.

His confidence was infectious, as there was something undeniably attractive about his personality. Macartney knew there were many people who looked sideways at his choice as chief interpreter for so important a mission. But the choice had been dictated by the importance. Lord Macartney was at once practical and pragmatic. He had been sent to China to negotiate a trade agreement with the Son of Heaven, an agreement which would hopefully benefit both the East India Company and Great Britain ... and leave the Dutch and Portuguese, previous intruders into these waters, far behind.

But he knew almost nothing about the people he was coming to negotiate with. China had been known to the West for some two thousand years; there were scholars in England, their imaginations fired by the recent upsurge of interest in matters of ancient history, who claimed that there had been regular trading missions between the Romans and the Chinese. If that were so, such links had been lost during the Dark Ages. It had been left to intrepid adventurers such as the Venetian Marco Polo to re-create the legend of the Celestial Kingdom of Cathay, so much more huge and powerful than anything known by Christian man.

Much of what Marco Polo had claimed had been dismissed as legend. It was only when the Spanish and the Portuguese, followed by the Dutch, and then the English, had ventured into the Pacific, that the legend had become a reality. There *was* a fabulous nation of yellow-skinned men and women occupying the eastern half of Asia, the most numerous people on earth, and all subject to the will of a single man. Did that also mean they were the most powerful nation on earth? Macartney could smile at such a concept. But perhaps the wealthiest ...

English adventurers had first appeared in the China Seas a hundred and fifty years before, but it was only in the last fifty that the China trade had become important. The British had followed the example and the advice of their Portuguese rivals,

and used the Pearl River, which penetrated South China for
some seventy miles, to reach the great seaport of Canton. Here,
and nowhere else, according to the Portuguese, 'outer barbarians' were allowed to trade with the Celestial Empire, and,
however derogatory that term might seem to a subject of King
George III of Great Britain, France and Ireland, it was applied
without discrimination to anyone from the West. But Viscount
Macartney and his six ships had sailed far north of the mouth of
the Pearl, to reach the Gulf of Chih-li.

*

The noise grew louder as the Chinese vessels approached. The
British were now silently at anchor, but their guns were run out,
and twenty on each ship were loaded with blank cartridges;
the others were double-shotted and primed, just in case.
Captain Gower, commodore of the squadron, was a cautious
man.

But, sailing having ceased, every blue-frockcoated officer on
the six ships was able to level his glass at the approaching junks
and sampans. The junks were surprisingly large, some of three
decks, and surprisingly well armed as well; the mouths of
cannon could be seen protruding from their open ports. No
English sailor was going to be afraid of superior numbers on the
water, for with their superb combination of seamanship and
gunnery they claimed the mastery of the seas, and had done so
for a hundred years, but they could tally up the vast numbers of
men on the decks of each ship, and crowding the sampans
which kept pace with them.

A large proportion of the crews were hard at work. There
was little wind, and that was onshore. It had pushed the Indiamen to their anchorage, but it blew directly into the prows of
the Chinese, and no one could suppose such square-looking
vessels, with their equally square sails, could ever work well to
windward. In fact the Chinese were making no effort to sail to
their objective; they were using manpower. And where a British
ship in such a position would have put down its boats and been
towed, even the largest of the junks was being propelled by
enormous sweeps, handled by fifty men each, which were
dipped into the water through rowlocks the size of gunports,
and then walked forward before coming out, while the oar-crew

marched aft again to resume their labour. 'Have you seen such a procedure before, Barrington?' Macartney asked.

'I have, my lord. On the Pearl. This is a land where labour is the cheapest thing to be had.'

*

Robert Barrington knew the Pearl River well. In the twenty years he had sailed to the East he had ventured up the river on several occasions, as first mate on a trader. But down to very recently he had been one of a select band. The British had been too preoccupied with the great dangling jewel that was India, which had so haphazardly fallen into their clutches with the collapse of the Moghul Empire. India was where a man might make his fortune. Those who found it necessary to risk the additional dangers of the pirate-ridden and Dutch-infested Straits of Malacca in search of Chinese silk had been regarded as over-ambitious.

That had been obtained for individuals. But while the nabobs had begun returning to England with their ill-gotten gains to found a variety of historic family fortunes, the East India Company itself had been sinking into a financial morass. Each battle fought and won, each territory annexed or administered, had cost an enormous sum of money, and such was the venality of the officials that no adequate tax return had ever been forthcoming. It had been necessary to look elsewhere for profit.

To approach China had seemed a brilliant idea – achieved partly through chance. Tea had first been introduced into Europe, by the Portuguese in the middle of the seventeenth century. The leaves had then been a quaint novelty, as often as not spread on bread. It was not until someone had thought of boiling them and drinking the resulting infusion that the beverage had become popular. In a climate such as England it had rapidly been realised that a warming cup of tea could be as refreshing as a mug of ale, yet without in any way impairing one's senses. Over the past half century the demand for these marvellous leaves had grown to immense proportions.

To the tea merchants of England it had seemed that the East India Company had stumbled on a goldmine. Only the Company itself knew better. It required more and more tea to fill its order books . . . but the Chinese who grew the tea apparently

required nothing that the Company could provide in return
– except for silver bullion.

The Company had appealed to the home government for
help, with good reason, as a large number of influential
Englishmen were shareholders. The government had decreed
that, over and above the retail price, tea would be taxed; and
the tax would be used to defray Company expenses. Tea
drinkers in England had had no choice but to pay the tax if they
were to continue to enjoy their favourite beverage. Tea drinkers
in the American colonies had declined to do so, and the
ensuing War of Independence had cost Great Britain half of her
empire – and left the Company precisely where it had been
before. Some accommodation had to be reached with the Son
of Heaven. Hence Macartney, and an embassy which, it was
said, had cost nearly a hundred thousand pounds to mount.

*

The noise was deafening as the junks and sampans came up to
the anchored British squadron, moving to either side, and to
seaward of the tall Indiamen, entirely surrounding them. Drums
beat and tambourines rattled. Bugles blew and firecrackers
erupted. Thin swirls of smoke shrouded the vessels to drift
amongst the fluttering banners, and some of this was incense
rising from the joss-sticks being burned on each Chinese quarterdeck.

Then, at a signal from the flagship, all the noise died, and an
immense silence filled the gulf, broken only by the gentle
thrumming of the wind in the rigging.

'You'll greet these gentlemen, Captain Gower,' Macartney
said.

Gower nodded to his first officer, and the Red Ensign came
down the staff, halfway. The other ships followed the example
of the flagship.

'You may commence, Mr Morley,' Gower said.

The salute rippled down the side of the flagship, to be
followed by those of the rest of the squadron. At the first huge
explosion and gush of smoke, a tremor of excitement and alarm
ran through the Chinese fleet, and for a moment it seemed
almost as if they would return fire. Then they understood that
the guns were not actually loaded, and a fresh burst of fire-

works and discordant cacophony filled the air, while the echoes
of the British cannonfire died away.

Now boats were put down, and commenced rowing to the
side of the *Lion*. 'You'll speak with these people, Barrington,'
the Viscount invited. 'We do not wish more than a few on
board at one time.'

*

For that was Robert Barrington's reason for being with the
embassy at all. He had neither the social pretensions to be
rubbing shoulders with the secretaries and military and naval
officers, nor the financial backing to stand beside the merchant
representatives of the Company. Even less did he belong with
the representatives of the Church of England or the missionary
societies grouped on the quarterdeck. But Robert Barrington
could speak Manchu.

Macartney had been told, in India, that such an asset would
not be necessary. Business in China was conducted in either a
local dialect, or Mandarin, and there were sufficient men in
Calcutta who spoke both Cantonese and the universal
language. 'But will I not be dealing with Manchu officials?' the
Viscount had asked. 'They are the rulers of the country.'

'Quite so, my lord. But they will speak Mandarin.'

'To me and to my interpreters, yes. What will they speak
amongst themselves?'

'Why . . . ah, Manchu, I suppose.'

'Quite. Thus I will have no means of knowing what their
asides may mean. I wish someone able to understand Manchu
at my side, whenever I encounter these people.'

*

Such a man had not been easy to find. The Calcutta government was reduced to advertising, and its worst fears were
realised when the only man to answer that advertisement had
been Robert Barrington.

In the small, tight community that British India still was,
every member of that community was known, evaluated, and
placed in his proper slot; wives joined their husbands at whatever level was allotted to them. Robert Barrington had no wife,

fortunately for her; he had long been placed firmly at the bottom of the social ladder. It was not that he entirely lacked background. His father had been a parish vicar, who had by force of circumstances sent his youngest son to sea at the age of twelve. Many a boy had progressed from apprentice to shipmaster, and higher, in the service of the Company. But over the twenty-odd years that Robert Barrington had made the journey from the Thames to Bombay Roads, it had come to be generally agreed he was unlikely to join that successful progression.

Equally, it was not that he lacked ability. He had earned his master's ticket at the early age of twenty-seven. But he had no money apart from his wages, and he lived too eclectic a life for the nabobs: Robert Barrington was just as likely to be found drinking in some waterfront establishment, engaging coolies and Chinks in conversation, as in the club. No doubt he dreamed of the riches of the East – everyone did that. For the past five years, indeed, he had not made the voyage home at all – his father had died and he did not get on well with his brothers. Instead he had concentrated on the Canton trade.

This had earned him final condemnation from British India. Three years before, Barrington had been taken seriously ill while in Canton, and his captain had felt obliged to abandon him there. No one had ever expected to see him again. But a year later he had reappeared in Calcutta, nursed back to health by the family of a Manchu official in the seaport. Robert had been full of praise for the way he was cared for; others could only see that he had spent several months living like a heathen with heathens, indulging in heaven-knew what heathen practices. It was whispered he even burned joss-sticks to ensure good fortune. As for his insistence on making distinction between the Chinese and the Manchus, when both races were but yellow-faced heathens . . .

But out of that episode had come a remarkable consequence: Robert Barrington was the only white man in Calcutta able to speak Manchu fluently.

*

Wearing his best blue broadcloth, Robert was under no misapprehensions as to the importance of the next few minutes, as he moved forward to stand beside his lordship. Having selected him, Macartney treated him as a friend, however disapproving the glances of his aides. But Robert understood that his lordship, having thus displayed his determination to use his own judgement, would be the more angry were that judgement proven ill-founded.

Barrington stared at the man emerging at that moment into the gangway, and realised that he was no man. He cast Macartney a hasty glance, but the Viscount gave no indication of understanding that anything was different about the Manchu representative. Certainly the eunuch was very richly dressed, in a red tunic over green breeches, both of silk, and soft kid boots. He was unarmed, but carried a lacquered cane. His red hat was round, with four little side points.

The several attendants who crowded on board behind him were hardly less richly dressed.

'My master, Ho-shen, Ruler of the Subject Peoples, sends greetings,' the eunuch said, bowing. His voice was high and brittle. 'My name is Wang Lu-ching.'

Robert bowed in turn. 'My Master, Lord Macartney, responds with greetings to your master, Prime Minister Ho, and brings greetings from his master, King George III of Great Britain, France and Ireland, Defender of the Faith, to his Celestial Majesty the Ch'ien-lung Emperor. My name is Robert Barrington.' He presumed that Wang was sufficiently educated to understand British nomenclature.

Wang bowed again, and waited while Robert interpreted. Then he said, 'Is it possible to sit in the shade?'

'Tell him that it is most certainly possible,' Macartney agreed. 'What do you suppose this fellow might care to drink?'

'We might try him with some rum, my lord.' Wang's eyes moved, and Robert realised that he probably understood at least a word or two of English. But he looked around him with great interest, as a tarpaulin was erected on the quarterdeck, and he sat down at a table with the British officers, several of whom had by now deduced what he was and were clearly scandalised.

The stewards fetched trays of rum punch, and Macartney himself handed a glass to Wang. The eunuch hesitated for a moment, before taking it carefully in both hands while Robert silently cursed his own forgetfulness. Macartney had revealed a total lack of breeding, in Chinese eyes, by offering the drink

with one hand instead of two – his lordship should have been
warned. But there was nothing for it now but to proceed with
the interview.

'You have brought tribute from your King,' Wang Lu-ching
remarked.

Robert translated, and Macartney cleared his throat. 'Tell
him my King pays tribute to no man.'

Robert translated, and Wang smiled.

'All the rulers on earth pay tribute to His Celestial Majesty.
It is true that some of the outer barbarians are remiss in these
matters, but they will undoubtedly be chastised.'

'Upon my soul but this fellow will make me angry,'
Macartney growled.

'I am sure it is but a form the Chinese maintain, my lord,'
Robert suggested. 'The important thing is to gain an interview
with the Ch'ien-lung Emperor, is it not?'

'I suppose that is why I am here,' Macartney conceded.

Wang was looking from one to the other, his great hairless
face blandly lacking in expression.

'Tribute is one of the matters my master wishes to discuss
with yours, to be sure,' Robert said. 'When will it be possible
for us to meet with His Celestial Majesty?'

'It is *not* possible,' Wang said.

'Eh?' Robert's heart sank.

'His Celestial Majesty is presently in Jehol. That is his home-
land, you understand, Barrington. It is from Jehol that the
immortal Nurhachi first led the eight Banners of the Manchu to
assault the Great Wall. The imperial court returns there every
autumn to hunt, and remains there until the first signs of winter.
This year there are as yet no signs of winter.'

'The devil,' Macartney commented. 'Is it not possible for us
to go to Jehol, and speak with the Emperor there?'

Wang looked around him at the fleet. 'Your ships cannot go
there. Jehol is many miles from the sea.'

'But you can provide my master with the necessary transpor-
tation to go there,' Robert urged.

Wang Lu-ching regarded him for several seconds. Then he
said, 'It is good to know that your king is so anxious to pay his
respects to the Celestial Emperor. I will speak with my master,
Ho-shen, and see if it is possible to arrange your journey.'

He had barely sipped his rum. Now he sipped it again, and

set down the mug. 'Your drink tingles the blood,' he said, and rose to bow before taking his departure.

*

'Damned insolent scoundrel,' growled Mr Marjoribanks, one of the Canton merchants who had accompanied the expedition. 'And to send a eunuch ... that is a mark of total contempt.'

'A eunuch?' Macartney inquired, and looked at Robert. 'By God! Why did you not tell me that?'

'Because I suspect he understands a certain amount of English. But, my lord, a eunuch is not necessarily a contemptible creature. Those who are intelligent and worthy are often given positions of great responsibility. This fellow Wang is obviously some kind of secretary to Ho-shen.'

'And he is the prime minister?' Macartney said.

'Well, yes, my lord, in so far as we might use the term. He is the Chief Minister for the Emperor.'

'He is an upstart scoundrel of dubious morals who is hated by everyone in the land,' Marjoribanks commented.

Macartney looked at Robert.

'It is true that Ho-shen is both young and a true court favourite, my lord. It is also true that he is venal and thereby well-hated. But ... we have chief ministers of that reputation in our own past. Surely, from our point of view, the fact that he is the Ch'ien-lung Emperor's favourite is what matters.'

'So long as he remains so. Now tell me, Barrington, why you pronounce Ch'ien-lung as if it were spelt KW instead of CH?'

'That is because of the apostrophe, my lord. The apostrophe makes the CH hard, like a Q. Without the apostrophe, it is soft, and is in fact pronounced rather like our J.'

'A strange language,' Macartney commented. 'Very well, gentlemen. I suppose we will have to kick our heels until this unfortunately bereft fellow returns. Barrington, refresh my memory about these Manchu.'

*

Robert did so. The Manchu's name itself was of recent origin. Originally members of the nomadic Tungus nation, they had, two hundred years previously, been no more than wanderers of the northern steppes. Then there had arisen a great leader who was also a military genius, in the style of Genghis Khan. His name was Nurhachi, and he had organised the Tungus into a fighting nation. His army was based upon the tribes he commanded, and each tribe was given a banner. The first four had been red, yellow, white and blue – yellow being the colour of Nurhachi's own clan. then he had organised four more, in the same colours, but with borders to their flags; these had been known as the Lesser Banners.

With his eight Banners at his back, Nurhachi had swept out of Manchuria to attack the decrepit empire of the Ming, recently bankrupted by a bitter war with the rising island people of Japan. From the very beginning, Nurhachi had dreamed of establishing a new dynasty. He had called his people the Aisin Gioro, or Golden Tribe, and had proclaimed that they were the direct descendants of the T'ang Dynasty, which had reunited China in AD 618 after several centuries of fragmentation, and had been destroyed by the Mongols in 1234. He himself took the title of Chin Khan, and pronounced himself T'ien-Ming, ruler of Manchuria. 'What a relief the Scots never discovered such a leader,' Macartney commented drily, and his staff obediently smiled.

Nurhachi had died of wounds in 1627. It was his successor, Huang T'ai Chi, the eighth of his fourteen sons, who had taken the title of T'ien-ts'ung, as ruler of Manchuria, and then in 1636 had formally proclaimed the imperial Ta Ch'ing Dynasty at his chief city of Mukden, and chosen the name Ch'ung-te, as Emperor of China. 'And this *Ta Ch'ing*, what does it mean?' Macartney inquired.

'Why, my lord, *Ch'ing* means Pure. *Ta* simply means Great.'

The Ch'ung-te Emperor had actually been a rather ineffectual man. Both the pronouncement of the Dynasty and the consequent campaigns against China proper had been the work of his youngest brother, Dorgun, Prince Jui, who had been the real ruler of the Manchus after Nurhachi. It was Dorgun who had led the eight Banners into Peking in 1644, shortly after the last Ming Emperor, Chuang Lieh-ti, had hanged himself.

It had taken another twenty years for the Manchu properly to establish themselves as the rulers of all China. But, commencing with the K'ang-hsi reign of the Emperor Hsuan-yeh, in 1662, there had begun a hundred and thirty years of peace and prosperity, in which only three emperors had ruled. The K'ang-hsi Emperor from 1662 until 1722, the Yung-cheng Emperor from 1723 to 1735, and the Ch'ien-lung Emperor from 1736.

'You mean this fellow Ch'ien-lung has been on the throne for fifty-seven years?' Macartney demanded. 'He must be as old as Methuselah.'

'I believe the Ch'ien-lung Emperor is eighty-two years old, my lord. But the country has never been so well ruled. It is the most prosperous empire in the world.'

Marjoribanks cleared his throat noisily in disagreement. 'What an absurd idea.'

'We are here to negotiate,' Macartney said soothingly.

'Well, my lord, so long as you are not required to kowtow.'

'To do what?' Macartney glanced at Robert.

'Everyone admitted to the presence of the Emperor is required to kneel and touch the floor nine times with his forehead,' Robert explained somewhat apprehensively.

'Bless my soul,' Macartney remarked.

'We'll not have that,' Captain Gower declared.

'I will certainly discuss the matter with Wang Lu-ching,' Barrington promised.

'Explain to me about these Chinese names,' Macartney said.

'Well, my lord, first of all we are actually speaking of Manchu names. Manchu do not have surnames, you see; but the Chinese do. When a Manchu prince is born, he is naturally given a name. In the case of the present Emperor, this was Hung-li. As he grows up, this name is superseded by a title, at least in the case of a prince who will not succeed. When a prince becomes emperor, however, he takes a reign name; in the case of the present Emperor, this is Ch'ien-lung. This name is used for all dating during his reign, and is the only name by which he may be known; his personal name is never used again. It should be noted, however, that this reign name is actually a title. I know it is our habit, but it is incorrect to refer to this current Emperor as Ch'ien-lung. He is *the* Ch'ien-lung Emperor.'

Marjoribanks raised his eyes to heaven.

'When he dies, however, that name is discarded in turn,' Robert went on, 'and he is given a posthumous title. That is decided after his death, so I have no idea what the Ch'ien-lung

Emperor will be called. But his predecessor, who was born Yun-cheng, and ruled as the Yung-cheng Emperor – you will note the difference, my lord – is now known by his posthumous title of Shih Tsung Hsien Huang-ti. Huang-ti merely means 'emperor', as all Chinese rulers trace their title from the Emperor Huang-ti, who reigned before 200 BC. I suppose you would consider it as analagous to our word Caesar. If I may attempt to put it in our terms, it is as if His Majesty, having been known as Prince George before his accession, was thereafter known as, shall we say, the Giver of Great Prosperity, and then, when he dies, is renamed Upholder of the Empire King.'

Macartney cleared his throat, well aware that his interpreter was indulging in some private satire in so describing the king who had lost the American colonies.

'Barbarous,' Marjoribanks repeated.

In the interpretation of that word, Robert realised, might lie the entire success, or failure, of the embassy.

*

After so many weeks at sea, the ambition of everyone on board the ships was to get ashore, and this was managed by requiring fresh water and provisions, but the boats were not allowed to enter the river itself, and had to use the open beach which was dominated by the formidable Taku forts, garrisoned by several thousands of men. Thus their hopes of finding either entertainment or women were dashed. Meanwhile, even if the weather remained warm, they experienced the occasional gale as the year wore on.

'I will tell you frankly, my lord,' Captain Gower said. 'I do not know for how long we can maintain station here on such an unfriendly lee shore.'

'Hm. Barrington, do you still think we are going to be welcomed?' Macartney said.

'I believe so,' Robert said, more in hope than certainty. But a week later Wang Lu-ching returned.

*

'The arrangements are made,' he said.
'My master is most grateful.'

Wang bowed. 'It is my privilege to serve such greatness.'

'Ask him how many of my people may accompany me?' Macartney urged.

Wang Lu-ching looked surprised. He turned to survey the small fleet of sampans which had accompanied him out to the British squadron. 'Why, as many as your master wishes,' he said.

'Bless my soul,' Macartney commented.

*

Captain Gower, being responsible for the safety of the envoy, was even more unhappy than Marjoribanks, especially when Wang informed them that there was little prospect of them reaching the Emperor and returning before winter did arrive.

'Well, you will have to take your ships south to some hospitable harbour, and return here the moment the weather improves,' Macartney suggested.

'And what will happen to you in the meanwhile, my lord?'

'I am sure I shall be very well looked after. Barrington is certain we can trust these people. If I do not believe him, then I might as well sail for home immediately.'

Gower gave Robert the sort of look suggesting that responsibility for his lordship's safety was now entirely in Barrington's hands.

*

However, even Marjoribanks could not complain about the appointments in the sampans which were waiting for them.

Ninety-five men embarked, together with their servants. They were distributed ten to a sampan, and below decks found themselves enjoying the luxury of soft carpets and softer beds, of delicately spiced food and of beer with the texture of sherry – served hot and decidedly stronger.

They were waited on by very young girls and boys, black-haired and doe-eyed, who managed to convey with a glance that they were there to make their temporary masters totally happy.

Sensing this, Macartney warned, 'Remember that we represent

the King's dignity – and that applies to how you behave with
these servants as well.'

*

There was a great deal to occupy any inquiring mind as the
embassy proceeded on its way. Robert Barrington's was such a
mind. Although he had been sent to sea as an apprentice at the
age of only twelve, he had already cultivated the habits of
reading and retention. The Bible to be sure; those verses had
been the tools of his father's trade – and George Barrington
had made sure all of his sons were early acquainted with the
word of God. Robert had found little of godliness as an apprentice on board an East Indiaman, whether it had been going aloft
in a howling gale and a swirl of obscenities from the officer of
the watch, or being held trouserless across the barrel of a
cannon – the gunner's daughter, as his seniors laughingly told
him – either to be caned for some misdemeanour or to satisfy
the sexual requirements of men confined for months at sea with
not a woman in sight.

These two opposing influences, the Word of God and the
requirements of mankind, had given rise to a very personal
philosophy. Invoking the aid of the Deity, when at the mercy of
half a dozen men each bigger and stronger than oneself, was a
waste of time; and in one's teens one simply did not have the
patience to rely on eventual heavenly retribution. While he had
learned to often hate his companions, therefore, he had come
to understand that he could only beat them, not by prayer or
resignation, but by joining them and then surpassing them. It
was his nature to devote his entire strength and intellect to
whatever he determined to achieve. Thus, by outdoing his
fellows, the years had developed his muscles and his stamina,
his courage and his knowledge of his own capabilities – his
anxiety to achieve.

He had learned navigation and seamanship, as he had also
learned the use of his fists and the weapons – pistols and cutlass
– as well as gunnery. It was a fortunate ship that could make the
journey to and from Calcutta without at least one brush with
pirates, while Robert had served through one French war
already – and, judging by the reports arriving from Europe,
another was just commencing, although it had not yet spread East.

As he was serving the East India Company, he had additionally learned Hindustani, and, when the necessity had arisen, Cantonese and Mandarin as well. He had come to mingle with the coolies and the Chinese, to sample their habits while he listened to their talk. He had found such experience both instructive and entertaining. Indeed, there was no master sailing to the East who would not welcome Robert Barrington as mate; equally there was not one who would welcome Robert Barrington calling on his daughter.

This was not a matter that concerned Robert; he doubted there was an Englishwoman anywhere who could equal the pleasure to be obtained from a Hindu or a Cantonese girl who had been paid enough to make her wish to please him. Let the English keep their daughters under lock and key. When he had made his million they would be happy enough to yield their fair maidens to the mercy of his renowned sexual habits. Though he heard himself described as an uncouth rascal, he had to admit there was more than a touch of the truth in it.

It was making the million that taxed his brain. Beginning with Robert Clive, many men had made untold fortunes out of India. But Robert Barrington realised that such men perhaps possessed a touch of genius, and ruthlessness, he lacked. He might be regarded as a villainous lout, but when he made a deal with someone, he carried out his end of the bargain to the letter. The kind of double-dealing which had made Clive both rich and famous lay outside his scope.

Nor was he a soldier, such as Clive. Robert understood that his fortune, if he was to make it, must come from the sea.

When he had opted once to sail as second mate to Canton he had discovered a world which loomed larger than his wildest dreams. In India, for sure, there was great wealth, great elegance, great poverty, great brutality, but also great uncertainty; there was no man, high or low, who could be sure he would see tomorrow's dawn. Robert had discovered that China had all of that same wealth and elegance, poverty and brutality, but there was also an enormous certainty – providing one was friends with the ruling Manchu elite. This possibility appealed to him greatly.

On that previous voyage, when he had the misfortune to succumb to fever and was abandoned by his captain in a communal hospital, delirious and uncaring, he had awakened to find himself in a light and airy chamber, attended by pretty, smiling young women, who had spent the past couple of days immersing him naked in very cold water to bring down the fever. They were slaves, and their master's name was Hui-chan.

Hui-chan was a Manchu of the Yehe Nara Clan, and inordinately proud of it, even if the Yehe Nara flew the Bordered Blue Banner, and were therefore only one of the subsidiary tribes instituted by Nurhachi. The fact that he was even so a Bannerman was enough for Hui-chan. However, he also wore the crystal button denoting that he had passed the examinations to become a Mandarin of the Fifth Rank and, in addition to the silver pheasant badge of his office, he possessed the bear badge of a military commander. He was *Taotai*, or Intendant – one of the Manchu officials who assisted the viceroy in governing the province.

'Why are you interested in a common foreign sailor?' Robert had asked, when he was strong enough to speak.

'It is a man's duty to be interested in other men,' Hui-chan replied. 'Especially when they come from far away. You will tell me of your distant land, and I will be pleased.'

*

Robert was happy to oblige the Intendant, and not entirely out of gratitude for the saving of his life. He was now glimpsing a lifestyle which interested him deeply ... and which he realised was completely unattainable in England.

At home one might acquire a great deal of money and buy a manor, settling down to live the life of a squire. Yet one's behaviour was entirely bounded by the convention of church, and class and custom. Life in China was equally dictated by custom – perhaps even more so – but the customs were so utterly appealing. For in China religious matters were pragmatic, and concerned with duty rather than piety. In China, theoretically, the most humble might rise to splendour through the examinations any would-be mandarin needed to pass. Best of all, social mores seemed to cater for physical desire rather than to repress it, yet all so delicately achieved because of containing no aspect of guilt.

In China a man would spend several hours over a meal, because eating exquisitely prepared food was one of the great pleasures of life, and digesting it equally important; in England a man gorged himself as rapidly as possible, even if suffering violently for hours afterwards. In China a man got drunk quietly and happily, because getting drunk was another of the great pleasures in life; in England a man got drunk aggressively and defiantly, and then fought with his best friend. In China, when a man wished, he beckoned his slave or concubine, who bowed and went before him to his bedchamber; in England a man's desires must be concealed beneath a mass of deceit and hypocrisy.

In England a man, if he would cut a dash, must necessarily enter into debt and spend the rest of his life avoiding his creditors. In China, if one was a Bannerman or a mandarin, one would receive a stipend for life. Inordinate luxury and excessive dress were not permitted by law, save for the Emperor himself, and thus there was no temptation to crippling competition in personal display. Food, silk, women and drink were cheap. Life was easy. True, the Chinese possessed one great vice: gambling. But by living off income rather than capital, and in possessing an income guaranteed by the State, true destitution was difficult to achieve.

Certainly there were beggars and criminals in China. But these all seemed to have been born to that unhappy state. If one was indeed a beggar or criminal, existence was grim. The Chinese held little regard for human life, perhaps because there were so many of them. But to be a beggar or criminal in England was equally grim.

The Chinese themselves were a conquered people, calling themselves the Men of Han to distinguish themselves from their Manchu overlords, but – even though yearning back to a supposed golden age many years in the past – they had the good sense to understand that the Manchu had replaced the chaos of the last of the Ming dynasty with orderly government. That did not stop them resenting subjection to a people who seemed to them as much barbarian as any with white or brown skins. Most of all they resented some of the laws imposed by their new masters, especially those dictating that no Chinese man could marry a Manchu woman, or that all Chinese men must shave their foreheads and wear the pigtail to reveal their inferiority.

They had never accepted this situation in their hearts. They

smuggled and connived and robbed the government in every
possible way while bowing low whenever a Manchu official
rode by. They worked for themselves first, and for the
conquerors last. But they could not gainsay the universal
prosperity the Manchu had brought them.

All in all, the Manchu ethic appealed to Robert Barrington.
When he was fully well again, and Hui-chan had indicated that
he could depart, he had felt some reluctance to do so. 'But no
doubt you will return,' Hui-chan had then assured him.

As lapdog to Lord Macartney, Robert thought now with
bitterness. But at least he was back in China.

*

It was a China even he had not truly suspected to exist, despite
what he had heard and seen in Hui-chan's household that time
before. In the heat of Canton, far removed from Peking, life
had been lived at a very relaxed pace. In the north life was altogether quicker – and harsher. Their sampans were rowed away
from the British squadron and over the muddy, uneven bar of
the River Pei-ho, so different to the Pearl which was navigable
for ocean-going ships. But the Pei-ho was a far busier river with
its constant stream of traffic coming and going, while Tientsin,
some twenty miles within the river mouth, and being the port of
Peking, was very nearly as large as Canton itself: a teeming,
bustling place. But equally such were the river banks to either
side, which lay low and were mostly under wheat.

'I have never seen so many people,' Macartney commented.
'Can our friend guess how many inhabitants there are in
China?'

'At the last census,' Wang told Robert, 'there were three
hundred and nineteen million people in our country. But that
was nearly sixty years ago. It is estimated that the number is
now over four hundred million.'

'Census?' Macartney inquired.

'Every householder is, on a certain date soon after the accession of a new emperor, required to account for himself and
every man, woman and child residing on his property,' Wang
explained. 'Do you not have such a custom in your country?'

'Bless my soul, no,' the Viscount said. 'There was one such
accounting, but that was six hundred years ago, and it was an

immense undertaking, never to be repeated.'

'And as for there being more than four hundred million Chinese,' Marjoribanks protested. 'Why, I doubt there are that many people alive in all Europe.'

'Then China is a greater country than Europe,' Wang suggested mildly.

*

The embassy spent several days in Tientsin, while the expedition into the interior was further organised. Although the Englishmen lived on board their sampans, they were allowed to venture ashore, which for most of them, not least Macartney himself, was a new experience.

He gaped with the rest at the crowded bustle of the streets, the range of things for sale, from food to fortune-telling, from exquisitely painted porcelain to exquisitely fashioned weapons, and at the variety of services as well, from barbering to dentistry, all practised in the most public manner.

His nostrils twitched at the amazing variety of odours which assailed them, from the mouth-watering aroma of frying pork to the stomach-turning stench of human excreta, which lay everywhere – and which was constantly added to as men and women relieved themselves in public without the slightest concern for those around them.

A magistrate himself, he attended a sitting of the local court. He listened to the various prattled arguments of the lawyers, and stared in consternation as the first man who lost his case was immediately stretched upon the ground and held there by four of the court officials, while his pantaloons were yanked about his ankles, and his bare buttocks belaboured with stout lengths of bamboo cane wielded by two more officials – without arousing more than passing interest in those around him, save that some of them paused to jeer at his misfortune.

'Summary justice,' he muttered. '*And* before women. Is there no decorum in this place?'

'Are men not punished also in England?' Wang asked.

'Of course. But when they are flogged, it is done on the back. The victim is not required to expose his all.'

'Where else should a man be flogged save on the buttocks?' Wang asked in surprise. 'Were he to receive a thousand strokes on the back, he would doubtless die; but, flogged on the buttocks, he will probably live.'

'A thousand strokes?' Macartney gasped. 'And you expect him to live?'

'If he was expected to die,' Wang pointed out, 'we would not waste the time making him suffer the bastinado.'

A moment later the Irishman realised what he meant, as the next prisoner also lost his case, involving rape, it seemed, from the anger of the young woman who hurled accusations against him. Again without a moment's delay, this unfortunate fellow was stripped to the waist, and forced to kneel, while two officials held his shoulders and another seized his pigtail to extend his head as far away from his body as possible. Before any of the foreign onlookers truly understood what was happening, one of the waiting executioners had drawn a huge, curved sword, and sliced cleanly through the man's neck.

Macartney turned to look at the magistrate as if he would protest, but the magistrate was already attending to another case. The dead man's body, its trunk still spouting blood, was merely kicked aside from the line of waiting culprits.

'We must leave this place,' Macartney muttered.

'Are criminals not executed in your country?' Wang asked.

'Indeed they are, but after due process of law.'

'That woman's accusation was supported by witnesses.'

'I have no doubt he was guilty,' Macartney agreed. 'But in England, in so serious a matter as taking a man's life, he would have been returned to prison while an appeal was considered, and perhaps the evidence reheard.'

'Perhaps in England there is much time and few people,' Wang suggested. 'Here, there are many people and little time.'

'But to have one's head struck off so carelessly . . .'

'If one is going to die, it is the best way. There are other methods which are worse.' He pointed, at a wooden cage hanging from a tree on the street corner. Inside the cage was a man; as they approached they saw that he was standing on tiptoe, because his head, protruding through the top of the cage, was held there by a circlet of wood under his chin and against the back of his neck. The expression on his face was ghastly, and from the way his tongue protruded he was clearly suffering severely from thirst.

'Now, that man is going to die,' Wang said. 'When he can no

longer support himself, he will strangle – slowly. But it is remarkable how long a man can find strength when he knows death awaits failure. I would wager that should we return tomorrow, that fellow will still be alive.'

'Your master is unhappy,' he confided to Robert, as Macartney hurried past the dying man. 'Is that because he does not like the comfort we are providing on his sampan? Why does he not buy one of those for his comfort?' He pointed.

'What does the fellow say?'

'He suggests you buy one of these girls or boys for your bed, my lord.'

Macartney stared at the group of children which had been pushed into the road in front of him. They numbered a dozen, of both sexes, their ages ranging from ten to about fifteen. They were marshalled along by an older man and a woman, who occasionally clipped one of them with a stick.

Now that they saw the foreigner's interest, they tried to smile, and one of the girls, at the woman's command, raised her blouse to expose her immature breasts.

The embarrassed Irishman looked from right to left, but again none of the passersby seemed the least concerned. 'By God!' Macartney commented. 'Now those two scoundrels should certainly have their heads chopped off.'

'But they are these children's parents,' Wang protested.

'And they are offering their own children for sale?' Marjoribanks cried. 'Can they do this?'

'What else can they do, when they cannot feed them all?' Wang asked reasonably. 'You should buy some. You will find they make good servants, and they will provide much comfort. You can train them, you see, to do whatever you like best.'

Marjoribanks merely snorted.

'If they are not sold for comfort,' Wang went on, 'the girls will be sold for prostitution, and the boys for castration.'

Macartney opened then shut his mouth in consternation as he remembered who was speaking.

'Oh, yes,' Wang said. 'My parents sold me when I was twelve because no one would buy me for comfort.'

'Bless my soul,' Macartney muttered, and hurried towards the docks. But before they reached there, they had to wait for a procession of open litters to proceed down the street. Each litter was carried by four men, and each contained a well-dressed

and attractive young woman, half concealed behind a fluttering
fan and sheltered by a huge parasol borne by a male attendant.
As the Englishmen watched, the procession came to a halt
outside a prosperous looking building, and the litters were set
down. The young women were then lifted from their seats by
their attendants, and carried through the doorway.

'Is that a hospital?' Macartney inquired.

'No, no,' Wang said. 'It is the home of Tientsin's richest
merchant. His daughter must be holding a tea party.'

'For invalids?'

Wang looked at Robert, in question.

'My master is concerned that none of the young ladies seem
able to walk.'

'Well,' Wang said, 'they can walk for a short distance, but it
is not comfortable. The lily foot, you see.'

'The what?' Macartney demanded.

'When a daughter is born to a rich Chinese,' Wang
explained, 'each of her feet is immediately bound very tightly,
the toes being pressed against the heel while the bones are still
soft. Thus when the bones have hardened, they are permanently set in that position.'

'By God! What a barbarous proceeding. And these are
wealthy people, you say?'

'Only wealthy families can practise the lily foot. It is an
indication that the daughters of the house will never have to
work. With a poor family, now, this would be impossible; the
daughters are required to spend too much time on their
feet.'

'By God,' his lordship growled again. 'But this is a strange
land with which we would trade, Barrington.'

*

But he could not argue that it was also a rich one. Their journey
took them from Tientsin up river and past the entrance to the
Grand Canal. This had been cut many centuries before, to facili-
tate trade between Peking and the south, and it stretched all
the way down to beyond the river known as the Yangtse-Kiang,
which Wang assured them was the greatest in the world. Those
of the foreign party who knew of the Nile regarded this claim
with scepticism, but the Canal itself was clearly a marvellous

piece of engineering, even if it had, over the years, fallen into considerable disrepair.

Shortly beyond the Canal, the river bifurcated, the main stream curving away to the north, while the smaller stream, the Han-ho, proceeded more directly to the west. The embassy followed the main stream, between gently rolling hills covered in wheat and barley, and past prosperous little villages where they were watched by cheering children and waving women, and occasionally by a regiment of brooding Bannermen standing on the banks with glittering weapons and lowering glances.

They saw people who wore silk and traded only in silver. They looked full of energy and vigour, and at utter peace.

'Well, 'tis hardly to be wondered at, when the slightest crime is punished so barbarously,' Macartney observed of that.

' *We* hang men for stealing, my lord,' Robert ventured.

Macartney held up his finger. 'The law may be on the statute books, but it is seldom invoked except in the case of incorrigibles. Nowadays we transport them to Australia. That must be a preferable fate to the bastinado.'

I wonder, Barrington thought.

*

At one stage on their journey up river, Peking itself was only fifty miles away, but they did not visit the city. Instead they continued on the water until it became too shallow even for sampans. When they were thus halted, they found a caravan of horses and carts waiting for them.

'Truly you have organised this well,' Robert told Wang admiringly, as they rode to the north.

'It was my duty,' Wang said. 'Is your master pleased?'

'I am certain of it. But there are certain matters which continue to concern him.'

'Tell me of these things, Barrington. It is my duty to make this journey as comfortable as possible for him.'

'I do not think Lord Macartney has any complaints to make about the journey,' Robert said, preferring not to dwell upon the ludicrous efforts of the Irishman and his staff to eat with the ivory foodsticks provided by the Chinese instead of cutlery. 'But he is concerned that he may be required to perform the kowtow when he approaches His Celestial Majesty.'

'Everyone must perform the kowtow,' Wang pointed out.

'My master cannot. He travels as the representative of King George, and whatever he does is done in that capacity. Therefore for him to bend his knee would mean that King George was bending *his* knee. Our King bends his knee to no man on earth.'

'Is Britain so great a country,' Wang asked, 'that your King can assume such an attitude?'

'Britain is not very large,' Robert told him, 'but its people are the greatest warriors in the world. You have seen our ships. Were they not very strong?'

'They were strong indeed,' Wang acknowledged.

'Well, they were not even warships,' Robert said. 'They are merchantmen. Our warships are even larger and stronger. And,' he added, 'we possess more than a hundred of them.'

'You would not lie to me, Barrington?'

'It is not my custom to lie, Wang.'

'I will see what can be done.'

*

The next day the eunuch Wang left the caravan and rode away with a small escort. The remainder of the party continued towards the north, and that evening camped in the shadow of the Great Wall.

'It stretches for hundreds of miles,' Robert told Macartney, as they mounted the battlements. 'It is considered one of the wonders of the world.'

'Was it built to keep the barbarians out or the Chinese in?' Macartney wondered.

*

Beyond the Wall they entered Manchuria. Here the country was far more rugged and there was little cultivation, but instead herds of roaming cattle and horses. Here Wang caught up with them again.

'I have arranged it,' he said. 'Your master need not perform the kowtow. Only your master is excused, mind. The rest of you will have to conform.'

'We will be happy to do so,' Robert assured him.

'You understand this is a great concession,' Wang told him. 'It is secured through the good offices of my master, Ho-shen, Lord of the Subject Peoples.'

'Ho-shen can be assured of our gratitude.'

'I am certain of it. For he would speak with you.'

*

'He will wish some *quid pro quo*,' Macartney mused. 'Well, we shall have to go along with the fellow. But you have done well, Barrington.'

Marjoribanks was looking less happy. He was still faced with the embarrassment of having to crawl into the Emperor's presence.

'Loose breeches,' Macartney said jovially. 'That is the answer: loose breeches.'

'I doubt you do well to trust this slippery eunuch, my lord – or his master,' Marjoribanks warned. 'It is said this Ho-shen is venal beyond belief. Nothing can be done without his receiving large sums of money. What he is going to demand for the privileges he concedes in your case ...'

'That is a bridge we shall cross when we come to it,' Macartney said. 'So far, matters are turning out much better than I expected.' He smiled at his interpreter. 'You have my congratulations, Barrington.'

Next day they came to Jehol.

2

THE MINISTER

Jehol lay some forty miles north of the Great Wall, on the lower reaches of the mountains separating the North China Plain from the plateau of Inner Mongolia. It had long been a favourite summer residence of the emperors, not only because of the coolness of the altitude, but because it was situated on the Je-ho River, a tributary of the Luan-ho. The words Je-ho mean Hot River, and the warm springs were both convenient and well regarded as good for the health.

The city itself was not very large, but was increased in size by the palace complex, which had a circumference of some five miles, and the huge Tibetan Buddhist lamasery which was nearby. The embassy, however, discovered that they were not to be allowed inside the walls. Instead they were escorted to a city of tents on the plain below. Here the appointments were as luxurious as on board the sampans – as Robert discovered when Wang Lu-ching took him on a tour of inspection.

'Is this satisfactory to your master, Barrington?'

'It is perfectly splendid.' Robert eyed the two bowing girls who waited in his tent. 'When will we see the Emperor?' The various gifts brought from England had already been sent into the city itself.

'It will be soon,' Wang assured him. 'You like these girls? Yet you will not take them for comfort. You are strange people.'

'It is the wish of my master.'

'How may a master command what he cannot see?' Wang asked.

*

Robert was too aware that his only hope of advancement lay in remaining in Macartney's good books, so he sent the girls away.

And two days later Wang informed them that the Emperor was prepared to receive them. In fact, since they were still not to be allowed inside the city, the Ch'ien-lung was coming to them.

Macartney hastily assembled all of his staff in their best uniforms, and they saw a huge number of people coming out of the gates to watch the ceremony. They listened to the blowing of bugles and the clash of cymbals, and a few minutes later the imperial procession emerged. It was a long line of palanquins borne by slaves and surrounded by eunuchs and armed guards, which marched slowly round the open space on which the British embassy was encamped, before coming to a halt. Attendants scurried to and fro, extending great lengths of yellow carpet.

'Yellow is the imperial colour,' Wang explained. 'It was the colour of the banner of the great Nurhachi himself, and is the senior colour in all China. Only a member of the imperial clan may wear yellow.'

The carpets now spread, the various palanquins disgorged their contents: a host of officials and princes of the blood who arranged themselves in order of precedence, sheltered by parasols held by their attendants, for the sun was now high in a cloudless sky, and despite the late season it was becoming very hot. The music continued – discordant to European ears because of its constant repetition of one theme – while the centre palanquin remained closed. But now the music stopped, the drapes were drawn, and out stepped the Ch'ien-lung Emperor.

Robert would have liked to look more closely at this man – probably the most powerful man on earth – but he was forced to follow the example of the entire assembly and prostrate himself upon the ground, so caught but a glimpse of a large, bland, thin-moustached face and a plump body, surprisingly tall and well carried for his age, clad in an imperial yellow robe decorated with red dragons, which extended to his yellow kid boots. His round hat was also yellow.

Of the English party, as agreed, only Macartney remained standing, and his lordship bowed from the waist.

The Emperor raised his hand.

'You must go forward,' Wang whispered.

Robert made to rise.

'No, no,' Wang said. 'You must crawl.'

Robert glanced at Macartney. 'Best do as he says,' the Viscount commanded.

It was all very well for him, Robert thought, as he slowly advanced past all the prostrate Chinese and Manchu officials, Macartney walking behind, Wang at his elbow. 'How do I interpret on my face?' he growled.

'You may kneel upright when the time comes,' Wang said.

They had reached the yellow carpet, and again prostrated themselves. 'Who comes to pay homage to the Son of Heaven?' the Emperor inquired.

His lordship had been warned of what the Emperor would say, and by now had had Robert teach him sufficient Manchu to make at least this reply: 'The Viscount Macartney, Minister Extraordinary and Official Plenipotentiary of His Majesty King George the Third of Great Britain, France and Ireland.'

'You have brought tribute to the Son of Heaven from this king?' the Emperor inquired, his voice soft and slightly high.

Macartney looked at Robert, who reared up on his knees. 'My master brings proposals, Your Majesty, for trade between our two nations, which will prove of benefit to both countries.'

'Trade?' inquired the Emperor. 'What has the world of the barbarians to offer us, when we have everything that we desire?'

His lordship digested this, and Robert frowned as he listened to the reply. But he was here to utter Macartney's words, not to interpolate his own. 'There is much that Europe can offer China, Your Majesty,' he said. 'Fine woollen cloth ...'

'What is this woollen? Is it obtained from the wool of sheep? My people make their own woollen clothes.'

'For use as outer garments, Your Majesty. In England wool is worn as an everyday cloth.'

The dignitaries kneeling around the Emperor smiled their contempt. 'In China we wear silk,' the Emperor pointed out.

Robert licked his lips and, on Macartney's instructions, tried again, but this time even more uncertainly. 'In India, whence we have come, there is a marvellous medicine which has the power of ending all pain, thus permitting surgery to be carried out with the maximum of effect.'

The Emperor frowned at him. 'Can there be such an elixir?'

'It is called opium, Your Majesty.'

The Emperor snorted. 'We know of this "marvellous"

substance. It has the property of driving men mad.'

'It induces sweet dreams, Majesty.'

'That may well be so. But it is a drug, and a dreadful one. Do you seek to ruin my people? No, no, barbarian, your country has nothing to offer mine, save tribute. There are well-established regulations governing tributary envoys from the outer states to Peking. The virtue and prestige of the Celestial Dynasty having spread far and wide, the kings of myriad nations come by land and sea with all sorts of precious things. Consequently there is nothing that we lack. Bring tribute to the foot of my throne, as do all the other barbarians – the men of the south and the men of the west, the men of the north and the men who live in the islands to the east. Bring tribute, and you will be allowed to buy of our surplus produce. But our goods must be paid for in silver. This is our will.' He raised his hand again, and his eunuchs hurried forward.

'Withdraw,' Wang Lu-ching hissed.

'He cannot mean to dismiss us so,' Macartney snapped. 'Have I travelled halfway around the globe to be sent off in a few minutes, like some menial?'

To this man, you are a menial, Robert thought.

'Your Majesty,' Macartney protested, as the Emperor was escorted to his palanquin.

'Do not speak,' Wang begged. 'You have been dismissed. To address the Emperor after dismissal means execution.'

Macartney stood there, his face red with a mixture of embarrassment and heat, his hands opening and shutting, as the Emperor's palanquin was closed and the other dignitaries took their places. Then he was politely ushered off the yellow carpet which, with the others, was promptly rolled up. The music had already started again, and the procession moved off.

*

'Outrageous,' declared Mr Marjoribanks, 'that an ambassador of the King should be treated with such contempt.'

'Barrington,' Macartney said wearily. 'I think you should ask Mr Wang what does he recommend we do now?'

'In China, it is said, sometimes the quickest way to cross a river is to wait for a drought, your excellency,' Wang suggested.

'Nonsense,' Marjoribanks complained, characteristically.

'Not necessarily so,' Wang argued. 'When one knows that a drought is imminent. The Ch'ien-lung Emperor, greatest of men, is yet mortal.'

'And he appears to be in the best of health ...' Macartney commented.

'That is so, your excellency. However, His Majesty has already made it known that it is his intention to abdicate his throne in two years' time, when he will have completed sixty years as Son of Heaven. This is because he does not wish to rule longer than his illustrious grandfather, Sheng Tsung Hsien Huang-ti, who ruled for sixty years as the K'ang-hsi Emperor.'

Macartney looked at Robert. 'Can that be true?'

'It is the Chinese way, my lord. To them this is an entirely ordered world, as is their place in it.'

'So this stiff-necked fellow will be gone in two years,' Macartney mused. 'Who will succeed him?'

'The Emperor will be succeeded by his eldest surviving son, Prince Yung-yen,' Wang said.

'And you feel that this prince may be more amenable to change than his father?'

'Are not sons always eager to change their father's ways?'

'By God, but you are right. Two years, though. I cannot remain two years in this heathen land.'

'Indeed you cannot, your excellency. My advice would be to leave China as rapidly as possible, but yet remain in contact with me, and await events. In three years' time it may be possible to return to great profit.'

'Halfway around the world, for ten minutes, and then back again,' Macartney remarked. 'Well, gentlemen, that is the way it is.' He went into his tent.

'He is a sorely disappointed man,' Barrington observed. He was sorely disappointed himself.

'You barbarians despair too soon,' Wang commented. 'But you, Barrington. My master would speak with you.'

*

'He will be seeking his reward,' Macartney commented.

'For what services?' Marjoribanks demanded. 'Did not this Ho-shen know we would be rebuffed? He deserves our contempt.'

'Yet we are in his power until we regain our ships,' Macartney pointed out. 'Where is this meeting to take place, Barrington? Is Ho-shen here in Jehol?'

'As I understand it, no, my lord. He is in Peking. Wang Lu-ching wishes me to accompany him there.'

'Peking, eh? Hm. Well, I think you must go with him,' Macartney said. 'By God, I envy you, Barrington. I would give much to see this fabled city.'

'My instructions, my lord?'

'Why, listen to what this Ho-shen has to say. But of course you can agree to nothing until you have reported to me. By then I anticipate we will have regained our ships, and will be in more command of our situation. Temporise, Barrington. Temporise. That is the secret of diplomacy.'

*

Robert could not overcome a slight feeling of unease as he rode away from the embassy the next day, with Wang Lu-ching and a small escort. He was not afraid; he understood entirely that Wang and his master wanted something from him, or at least from Macartney, and therefore that he was safe with them until and unless they felt they were not going to get what they wanted. It was the concept that he was the guest of this eunuch that was disturbing. Because, for all his studied air of having seen it all before, for the benefit of Macartney and the other members of the embassy, he had never previously encountered anyone like Wang.

He had seen eunuchs enough in Canton. But these had all occupied the most menial of positions, worn the most menial of clothes, carried with them always the rank and distasteful aroma of the eunuch whose bodily secretions too often were offensive. Not one had worn clothes of the richness of Wang's, or been so pleasantly perfumed, or indeed, possessed such an aura of arrogant confidence.

Wang was clearly a powerful man – who travelled in style. When they stopped for the night, they were always given the best accommodation in the village they had chosen, and while they dined off succulent duck and pork, and drank plum wine, Wang would talk at length of the greatness that was China. Equally, he wished to speak of himself.

'In Peking you will reside at my house,' he told Robert. 'My wife has never met an outer barbarian.' He smiled then at Robert's expression. 'Did you not know that eunuchs can have wives? What is to prevent us? I also have children, two sons and a daughter.'

Robert stared.

'They are adopted, Barrington. I am not a magician. But do you suppose I would let a little matter like my being shorn prevent me from enjoying the pleasures of family life? As for possessing my wife, do I not have fingers? In many instances they are superior to what I have lost.' From his travelling valise he took out a sealed bottle and held it up.

Robert gulped again. A penis and testicles were preserved in some kind of spirit, and what sensations did the sight of them conjure up.

'I should have thought that to preserve them would be to perpetuate the memory of your misfortune,' he ventured.

'Perhaps that is so. But a man must preserve his all. For is it not true that only a *whole* man may enter heaven? That is why beheading is such a dreadful punishment, for unless the executioner is merciful, and permits the head to be buried with the body, the soul of the victim must wander forever through the shades. It is the same with genitals. I carry mine with me at all times so that, should I die, they shall be buried with me.'

*

The next day, having passed through one of the gates in the Great Wall, Robert made out a huge purple mass rising out of the plain in front of him. But indeed there was a wealth of distant architecture, on a scale and magnificence he had never seen before. Away to the west there appeared an enormous parkland of trees and lakes, splendid curved bridges and exquisite marble palaces.

'That is the Emperor's Summer Palace, the Yuan Ming Yuan,' Wang explained. 'It is the creation of the present Son of Heaven, the Ch'ien-lung Emperor, and he has spent more than twenty years in perfecting it. It covers more than sixty thousand acres.'

'It must have cost a fortune.'

Wang shrugged. 'What is money to the Son of Heaven?'

There were lakes enough around Peking itself, and the entire city, far larger than London and completely surrounded by high purple walls, was enclosed by a canal, which, Wang said, was actually a branch of the Grand Canal, and which fed all the lakes of the Forbidden City, the walls within walls, where the Ta Ch'ing royal family lived, and from which all lesser creatures were excluded.

Wang's party proceeded south of the city, for only through the southern gate, the Yun-ting-men, could entry be gained. The eunuch presented his credentials to the captain of the guard in the midst of a large crowd of Chinese men, women and children, dogs and goats, cattle and chickens, waiting either to enter or leave. Indian cities such as Calcutta and Bombay were busy enough, but Robert had never encountered such teeming hordes of people before. No one paid the slightest attention to the grinning, rotting heads nailed above the arch.

Within the gate they found themselves on a broad and wide thoroughfare: the Grand Avenue. To their right was the Tien-tan, the Altar of Heaven, set in the midst of six hundred and forty acres, and to their left, the Sheng-neng-tan, the Altar to the Inventor of Agriculture, covering two hundred and twenty acres. These palaces were set in green parkland, but as they crossed the Grand Bridge over the inner canal, they entered the Chinese City, and were again surrounded by houses and people, animals and stenches, in a far greater degree than in Tientsin.

Wang's guards cleared a way through the throng, and the party advanced up to the high inner walls surrounding the Tatar City. This they entered, again after showing their credentials, through the Tsien-men Gate. Now the roadway was even wider and more splendid, as well as less crowded, as few Chinese were allowed within these walls, and in front of them they could see the T'ien-an-men, the gate through yet another high wall into the Forbidden imperial city of the Ta Ch'ing.

'We may not enter there,' Wang said, and the party turned to the right, into a maze of narrow streets which lay in the shadow of the wall. 'My house,' the eunuch said proudly.

*

There was an imposing wall, and a gate which gave access to a

small courtyard, overlooked by a wide porch in which were
stored several sedan chairs. The porch led into the First Hall,
the formal reception room, the centre of which was occupied by
a long rectangular table, while against each wall there was a row
of straight-backed chairs.

From the First Hall, Wang led Robert into the Second Hall,
which was the Ancestral Hall; on one side there was a raised
dais and an altar, on which there was a bowl of incense and a
vase of flowers, while behind these, on the wall, were red and
gold plaques of Wang's ancestors. Here the noise and heat of
the street outside was immediately replaced by a quiet cool, and
they were met by bowing domestics and servants, led by a
small, handsome woman.

'My wife,' Wang said.

Robert bowed in response.

'My children,' Wang said proudly, and Robert greeted the
two boys and the girl who were presented to him. Then he was
shown to his apartment. This was surprisingly spacious and luxuriously furnished, dominated by a huge four poster bed, and it
overlooked a small but delightful garden where, but for the
barking of dogs, the explosions of firecrackers, and the rumble
of the city, it might have been possible to suppose oneself far
away from civilisation. 'This is a splendid house,' he remarked
to Wang, when he joined the secretary in his private dining-
room, where the table was round; in its centre was the silver jug
that Wang's wife would have brought with her when she was
married.

'I serve Ho-shen,' Wang replied, clapping his hands, to bring
servants hurrying forward with trays of tea. 'You know of my
master's reputation.'

'A prime minister makes enemies in equal proportion to his
friends,' Robert countered.

'This is necessary,' Wang agreed. 'But a prime minster's first
duty is to serve *his* master, and none other. Remember this,
when I take you to meet my master tomorrow.'

'And could you serve any other master?' Robert asked.

'No,' Wang replied. 'I would be as meaningless as would you
be, Barrington, without the patronage of your Lord Macartney.'

*

Ho-shen turned out to be only in his middle forties, Robert estimated. His face was thin, as were his moustaches and lips, and
his eyes were hard. His clothes were rich, but his house not
greatly more luxurious than that of his servant. 'It pleases
my master to appear as unostentatious as possible when in
Peking,' Wang had said. 'Do not be misled. There is only one
man more wealthy in all China than Ho-shen – and that is the
Emperor.'

There was a more obvious difference between their places in
the community. Where Wang Lu-ching's house had been
entirely unguarded, Ho-shen's was surrounded by armed men,
apparently lounging in careless conversation, but watching
every movement on the street. Wang was, of course, known to
them, but they stared at the big white-skinned sailor before
being reassured by the presence of the eunuch.

Now Robert was being motioned to his seat by the prime
minister himself. 'Wang tells me you speak Manchu,' Ho-shen
said, in that tongue. 'How is this?'

Robert told him of the illness in Canton.

'Hui-chan,' Ho-shen said thoughtfully. 'He is of small
account. He is of the Yehe Nara clan, of the Bordered Blue
Banner. That is the least important of the eight Banners.'

'Hui-chan told me so himself, your excellency.'

'And did he also tell you that a scurrilous fortune-teller has
said that his house will one day be the greatest in the land? Can
you credit such effrontery? And he believes it. Could you credit
such gullibility? Had not the Son of Heaven laughed when he
heard such a tale, Hui-chan would have lost his head by now.'

'I should greatly regret such a misfortune, were it ever to
happen,' Robert said evenly, 'for Hui-chan and his family saved
my life.'

'Wang has told me also of the ships on which you sail. Of
their strength, and power. Is that true?'

'King George III of England lays claim to the sovereignty of
the seas, your excellency.'

Ho-shen snorted. 'That is a mighty empire, Barrington, if it
can be sustained. I would visit your ships, perhaps.'

'It will be a great honour.'

'And perhaps I will sail in one? I have heard much of India,
where your Company holds power. It would interest me to visit
and see this power which you claim.'

Robert endeavoured not to show surprise. 'You would be welcomed there, excellency.'

'Good. You understand that such a visit will take time to arrange. I have so many duties here. However, it should be possible within the next two years.'

'Whenever you wish, sire.'

'Listen, then, Barrington. Winter will now be upon us at any moment. Then there will be spring, summer, autumn – before next winter. You are aware that the Chinese New Year falls in the middle of winter?'

'I am, excellency.'

'Then after the second Chinese New Year from now, I wish you to bring one of your ships to the mouth of the Yangtse-Kiang. You know of it surely? It is the greatest river in the world.'

'I have heard of it,' Robert acknowledged. 'But I do not know if our ship could enter there. Are there not many sand-banks?'

'The Yangtse is navigable for several hundred miles from the sea,' Ho declared.

'Several hundred ...' Robert did not believe there was a river that long in the world.

'There is a port just within the mouth of the river, known as Shanghai,' Ho went on. 'There you will find a pilot waiting for you. You, mind. No other.'

'May I ask how I will know this man?'

'He will know you, Barrington. Anchor off the mouth of the river, and he will seek you by name. He will guide you up the river to the place where I shall join the ship. Is that under-stood?'

Robert nodded. 'In midwinter 1795,' he said, 'a ship will come for you.'

'1795? I do not understand your reckoning. It will be at the end of the sixtieth year of the reign of the Ch'ien-lung Emperor.'

'I understand.'

'Then here are two more things you must understand, Barrington.' Ho-shen's eyes were hooded. 'This desire of my master to see your King's power for himself is a secret, known but to His Celestial Majesty and myself. And Wang here, of course. And now you. You will convey my request to your master, Lord Macartney. No one else is to know of this. Should word of it come out, my master and I will deny that such a request was ever made, and all further prospect of trade between China and England will be ended, forever.'

'Forgive me, your excellency ... but is there any prospect of trade between our countries, in any event?'

'All things are possible, Barrington. Show me your power, and who can say. But keep the secret. Should you do so, when the ship returns for me, you will be richly rewarded.'

*

'Well, now,' Macartney said. 'What do you think the fellow is at, gentlemen?'

The merchants and officers were assembled in the great cabin of the *Lion*, having regained the squadron while Robert had visited Peking, happy to discover that Captain Gower had so far exceeded his orders as to remain in the gulf despite some very autumnal weather.

Now the Captain spoke his mind. 'No good, I'll be bound,' he opined.

'It's as plain as a pikestaff,' Marjoribanks declared. 'We have already been informed that this Ch'ien-lung character intends to abdicate at the end of his sixtieth year on the throne. Equally do we know that his successor, Yung-yen, will wish his own people in power, and that this Ho-shen is the most hated man in China. What he wants is to be able to get away with his skin, before Yung-yen hands him over to all the people he has swindled these last twenty years.'

Much as Robert disliked Marjoribanks, he had to agree that the merchant's conjecture was more than likely to be correct.

'Well,' Macartney mused, 'if he has sufficient money ...'

'My lord, that is not the point. The point is that the Company will have been seen to help a guilty minister escape his just desserts. This new Emperor will immediately regard us as his enemies, and our hopes of establishing trading relations with this vast country will have been ended forever.'

'Hmm,' Macartney said. 'Hmm. But if your conjecture is wrong, Mr Marjoribanks, and Ho is wishing to undertake this journey with the blessing, and indeed at the command of Ch'ien-lung, as he claims to be the case, then would we be offending the reigning monarch by refusing to humour him?'

'I do not believe Ch'ien-lung knows anything of this plan at all,' Marjoribanks insisted.

'Surely there is a simple way to discover the truth of the matter, my lord,' Captain Gower said. 'This Ho-shen claims to be acting upon the orders of his Emperor, and that this secret mission is a privy matter between the two of them. Why do you not ask the Prime Minister to deliver to you a written request from Ch'ien-lung himself? Then you are covered on all sides.'

'Capital!' Macartney cried. 'Capital. You'll return to this fellow, Barrington, and tell him that we cannot agree to his request without a written confirmation from his master. Oh, indeed, capital. You'll leave tomorrow, and make haste. We cannot remain at anchor here much longer.'

*

Robert explained his instructions to Wang Lu-ching, who looked grave. 'These men doubt the word of my master,' he said. 'Do you also doubt his word, Barrington?'

'Good heavens, no,' Robert protested. 'But ... I must carry out my instructions.'

'Of course,' Wang agreed courteously. 'Let us make haste to Peking, before winter comes.' The weather was indeed most threatening, with clouds tumbling across the sky all day, frequent heavy showers of rain, and chilly nights.

And an even chillier reception from Ho-shen when he heard what was required of him. 'Does this barbarian seek to make a fool of me?' he demanded.

'I assure you, my lord, that my friend Barrington is but carrying out the instructions given him by his master,' Wang said. 'Left to himself, Barrington would straight away agree to your wishes.'

'Is that true, Barrington?'

'Oh, indeed, excellency,' Robert assured him. As he did not possess either a ship or Macartney's ear in this matter, it was an easy promise to give.

Ho-shen was gazing at him most intently, however, which made him feel distinctly uneasy. Then the prime minister smiled. 'I believe Wang is right,' he said. 'You are an honest

man, Barrington. Which is more than can be said for your
master. You will dine with me. More, you will stay here in my
house while I consider the matter.'

*

The meal consisted of a mouth-watering series of exquisitely
prepared dishes, and was accompanied by rice beer, or *sake*,
which had an innocuous taste but, served very hot, soon had
Robert's head spinning. Sitting at table were several other
members of the household, but no women, and not Wang
either. The eunuch was, however, waiting for Robert when he
finally arose, after some hours, and went outside to relieve
himself.

'My master is pleased with you, Barrington. He has great
faith in you. May I offer you some advice?'

'Go ahead.' Robert grinned. 'I don't have to take it.'

'It would pay you to. You are far away now from Lord
Macartney and his strictures. Accept whatever my master offers
you. Serve him well, and you will know riches beyond your
imagination.'

Serve Ho-shen? Robert wondered, as he was escorted to his
bedchamber, a place of rustling silk drapes and a soft mattress,
of gentle fragrance and utter quiet. Nor was he alone. When he
had closed the door and stumbled to the bed, he heard movement, and looking up in alarm, gazed at a girl.

She was naked, somewhat taller than the average Chinese or
Manchu woman of his experience; he estimated her height at
about five feet four inches. She stood very straight, close by the
lanterns which hung at the head of the bed, the better to expose
herself. She was slender, with small breasts and narrow thighs,
but her nipples were erect and the thin pubic hairs were like
silken threads; her legs were long and strong – no lily foot here.
Her hair was black as midnight, and hung absolutely straight
past her shoulders to the curve of her buttocks.

He had never seen such an alluring picture, nor had he ever
seen so compelling a face. It was pretty enough, in that its
features were regular and well-formed, if a trifle large. It was
the eyes and the mouth which were irresistibly attractive. The
eyes were as black as the hair, and deep, and thoughtful,
perhaps even a trifle sad. The mouth was straight and flat. It

was a mouth which suggested endless pleasure – but also a great deal of strength. In a serving girl?

'I am Sao,' she said, softly. 'You are Barrington.' Robert remained on his knees, gazing at her, as she moved closer, until her thigh rested against his face. 'I will make you very happy,' she told him.

He didn't doubt that for an instant. But what of Macartney's stricture? But then he remembered Wang's advice; Macartney could never know what happened in the house of Ho-shen.

He allowed the girl to undress him; clearly she had never encountered European clothes before.

'I am a virgin,' she told him as she exposed him.

He was concerned. He had been unable to stop himself from caressing her breasts and buttocks as she removed his garments, nor was he going to be able to stop himself having her, he knew.

'How is that?' he asked.

She gave a little shrug. 'My Lord Ho buys many girls and boys. Many of us are kept to be given to exalted guests.'

Robert found it hard to believe he was an exalted guest; he realised that Ho must be desperately anxious to get out of China.

Sao had finished, and he was as naked as she. Now she straddled his legs, so that his penis rested against her groin. 'Do you wish to beat me?' she asked.

'Why should I wish to do that?'

'I do not know. It gives men pleasure, so I have been taught,' she added. 'Do you desire the Jade Girl playing upon the Flute?'

'Briefly.' He had imbibed the Chinese literature of love, and knew what she meant. She knelt between his legs to take him into her mouth, watching him as she did so. 'Briefly,' he reminded her, as her sucking became more insistent. 'Come here,' he commanded.

She hesitated, mentally bracing herself, perhaps, for the coming ordeal, and then came up his body without changing her position. Her buttocks brushed across penis and groin and stomach, came to rest on his chest. His body hair was thick, and she gave a little wriggle as it tickled her.

'Do you find me ugly?' he asked. 'Distasteful?'

She looked surprised. 'You are beautiful,' she said. 'You are my lord.'

'Am I beautiful because I am your lord?'

'All lords are beautiful,' she told him, with simple philosophy.

He held her shoulders and brought her down to him. When he attempted to kiss her she was even more surprised, but the feel of her lying on him was entrancing.

'How old are you, Sao?'

'I am fifteen years old, my lord,' she said.

And thus I am a brute and a monster, he thought, *who should be hanged.* But only in England. Here in China, this girl was old for a virgin.

'What is your pleasure, my lord?' she asked.

He searched his memory for the correct phrases in the Chinese library of love. 'I would have the Fish Interlock their Scales.' She inclined her head; he had known of course that that was a favourite Chinese way, and virgin or no, as a girl sold for prostitution she would have been taught the desires of men, and how to assuage them.

Sao pushed herself up, and slid her body back down his until she was sitting on his penis.

'Are you afraid?' Robert asked. He could see the tension in her face.

'You are my lord,' she reminded him, and inserted him into herself.

*

'I have considered his lordship's request,' Ho-shen began the following morning, as he and Robert ate together. 'It is an insult to me and to my master. You will return to your ships, and tell your master that I have changed my mind, and will not visit his ships – or India.'

'I am sorry, your excellency.'

'I believe you. Barrington, are you a man of spirit? A man who would rise in the world, and make a name for himself?'

'If it can be accomplished without breaking the law.'

'Laws, Barrington, are made by men for their own purposes, and therefore may be broken by men when those purposes no longer serve. However, I will ask no law-breaking of you. I asked whether you had the courage to become rich.'

'I would hope so.'

'Then listen to me. Your master fears to agree to my wishes.

He is a fool. But will you not agree to what I wish? I will pay you well.'

'I, your excellency? I have no ship.'

'You will procure one.' Ho-shen snapped his fingers, and two of his servants hurried forward, bearing a small box. This was placed on the floor beside Robert, and one of the servants opened it. The metal inside gleamed. 'That is a hundred taels. It is the purest silver to be found. Do you know what a tael is, Barrington?'

'Yes. It is a measure of weight, and equals one and one-third ounces in our calculations.'

'Therefore what you have before you is a hundred and thirty-three ounces of silver. More than eight pounds weight by barbarian reckoning. That is a great deal of money.'

Robert swallowed. 'Yes, excellency, it is.'

'It is yours. If your master will not send a ship to Shanghai next winter, I wish *you* to bring one, Barrington. That silver is yours. But when you return with your ship, you will receive a thousand taels, and the master of your ship an equal amount. Eighty-three pounds of pure silver for each of you. Will that not make you rich for life?'

'Yes, excellency.' Robert could not believe his ears.

'Then listen. You will come in your ship to Shanghai at the mouth of the Yangtse, as I have said. There my agent will meet you, and pilot you up the river to Hankow, where I will join you. Do you understand?'

'Yes, indeed.'

'Then understand also that this must be a secret between you and me. Especially must Macartney not know of it.'

'Yes, excellency. Is my ship to convey you to India?'

Ho-shen smiled. 'Just bring me the ship. When you do that, I will tell you where I wish to go. But remember: you must be at the mouth of the Yangtse within one month of the end of the next but one Chinese New Year.'

'I understand.'

Ho nodded. 'Then go ... Did you sleep well?'

'Very well, excellency.'

Ho-shen snapped his fingers again, and Sao was led in, fully dressed now, in a red cloak and matching hat.

'Take the girl and enjoy her,' Ho said. 'She will remind you of what you have left behind – and of what awaits you.'

*

Travelling with Sao was a delight. She was so anxious to please in every way, prepared Robert's meals and brushed and folded his clothes, as well as being apparently desperately anxious to satisfy his sexual needs at night.

'Could any other woman be so accommodating?' he asked Wang.

'Not any woman, to be sure,' the eunuch replied. 'When one marries a lady of equal stature, socially or financially, one is probably in for an unhappy time. It is not to be recommended, except for political or financial reasons. But this girl has nothing, save you. Should you cast her out, her only recourse will be the street, which is rapidly followed by disease and death. To avoid that, she will serve you faithfully to the end of her days, and hope that, when she grows old and wrinkled, you will remember enough of what you have shared not to dismiss her. But of course, being a slave, she will never be in a position to carp when you decide to add a younger woman to your household.'

'That is a very happy philosophy – if one is a man,' Robert agreed.

*

Sao exclaimed in wonder when she saw the great ships, riding at anchor in the teeth of a north-easterly gale. Robert was just happy to see them still there.

'I will say goodbye.' Wang clasped his hands. 'I look forward to seeing you again in Hankow.'

'I shall be there,' Barrington promised fervently. What he was going to do might make him the least popular Englishman in the Far East, amongst Englishmen. But it was also his road to more wealth than he could ever dream of obtaining by honest toil.

*

A sampan was hired to take Robert and Sao out to the *Lion*. It danced over the considerable waves, and Robert looked at the girl for signs of alarm but, beyond an occasional smile at him, she seemed unafraid. She was, he thought, an absolute treasure, her small mouth forming an increasingly large O as the ships grew in size, until at last the sampan was bobbing in the lee of the Indiaman, and they were assisted on board, the seamen looking askance at the Chinese girl. The box containing the taels was concealed in the midst of Robert's clothes.

Lord Macartney was waiting on deck. 'About time,.' he declared. 'I doubt we could have remained here another week, so fierce are these winds. Well? Have you the letter from Ch'ien-lung?'

'I am afraid not, my lord. Ho-shen was quite insulted by your demand and decided that he would not, after all, be interested in visiting our ships.'

'Exactly as I prophesied,' Marjoribanks cried. 'The scoundrel was trying to escape his just desserts without the knowledge of his master.'

'Upon my soul, but I believe you are right,' Macartney agreed. 'I must say, this has turned out to be a sorry misadventure.' He gazed at Robert, as if it might not all be his fault. Then he looked at Sao. 'Who is that person?'

'She is mine, my lord,' Robert explained.

'Yours?'

'She has been given to me by Ho-shen, as a token of his appreciation for my efforts on his behalf. Even if,' he hastily added, 'those efforts have now come to naught.'

'Bless my soul,' Macartney commented. 'Given to you?'

'It is quite customary in China, my lord.'

'A heathen land,' Macartney grumbled. 'Truly am I glad to be rid of it. But you'll rid yourself of that young woman, Master Barrington. Immediately.'

'My lord?'

'I have made it plain from the beginning that I will have no immorality on board my ships,' Macartney said. 'I am surprised at you, sir, and disappointed, that you should have sunk so low as to adopt Chinese manners. But I will have none of it. Send the woman ashore, Barrington. We make sail within the hour!'

Robert stared at him in consternation. Though he had only possessed her a week, life without Sao did not seem possible. 'My lord,' he said, 'I would willingly marry the girl.'

'What, marry a heathen Chinese? I have never heard of such a thing. You would ruin your life. I could not permit it. Besides,

I will not have one on board my ship. Send her ashore, or I will clap you in irons and have her thrown over the side.'

Robert was sorely tempted to defy his lordship – to tell him that if Sao went, he would go too. But what would that accomplish? If he was marooned in China he doubted that either Ho-shen or Wang Lu-ching would wish to know him, since he would no longer be of any use to them. His hundred taels would support him for some time, perhaps ... but the money would run out soon enough, even did Ho not have him arrested and executed as knowing too much of his plans.

He gazed at Sao. She was beautiful, and she was willing. Reject her, Wang had said, and she will have to take to the streets, and a life of disease and humiliation. But she would have to find her own salvation, as would he. Only wealth and the power that wealth bestowed mattered in this world. And he still had wealth within his grasp, if he did not fail Ho-shen.

Besides, the situation was not as desperate as it had first appeared. He was still working for Ho-shen, and Wang knew that.

'You must go ashore,' he told Sao.

'I am to accompany you, my lord.'

'You cannot, on this occasion. Listen. Return ashore, to Wang Lu-ching. Explain that it is impossible to take you with me, because my master will not permit it. Say that I make it his charge to keep you safe until I can return for you. He knows when that will be.'

Sao gazed at him, her eyes slowly filling with tears. 'I will never see you again.'

'You will,' he promised. 'Now go.'

She hesitated a last moment, looked from him to Macartney, then turned back to the gangway and the waiting sampan.

'Why so sad?' his lordship demanded. 'You've had the girl, I'll be bound. You'll not want her draped round your neck for the rest of your life. You are a scoundrel, Barrington, but a fortunate one. Now, Captain Gower, let us make sail. I will tell you, sir, I am more than anxious to see the last of this heathen country.'

Robert stood at the rail to watch the sampan being rowed back to the shore. Sao stood in the stern, the wind whipping at her cloak. She did not look back.

3

THE WHITE LOTUS

'Cheng Yi!' Lu Shan exclaimed, bowing very low. 'Welcome to my humble establishment.'

Lu Shan was a small woman. Her black hair stretched towards the floor, and when she bowed, it appeared completely to shroud her head and body. Her eyes were soft and liquid, a description which had been applied to her figure some years before. Only those who had known Lu Shan a long time were aware that she was as hard as steel, as unpitying as fire, as brutal as any beast. She worshipped at a single shrine, that of money.

Or those who could obtain it. Sometimes Cheng Yi was wealthy, more often he was not. But he was always likely to become wealthy. Besides, he was even less a man to cross than she was a woman; Lu Shan intended to die in her bed.

Thus she smiled as she slowly straightened, and took in her customer. There was a great deal to take in. Cheng Yi was a very big man for a Han Chinese. He stood six feet tall in his kid boots, and had shoulders and chest to match; they filled his red tunic as he breathed, deeply. Cheng Yi always breathed deeply, as if about to embark upon a challenge to the world. Often enough he was. He threw several silver coins upon the table. 'I have been in the mountains.'

'And prospering,' Lu Shan suggested. She preferred not to speculate at what. 'I have some new girls. Very attractive. They will make you forget the mountains.'

Cheng Yi followed her into the inner room, where several young women lolled on divans wearing pantaloons and nothing else. Lu Shan snapped her fingers, and a goblet of plum wine was brought for her customer.

'Now this girl,' she said, gesturing one of the prostitutes to her feet, 'is a Khitan. The Khitans are so sinuous. You will think you are in the arms of a snake.'

Cheng Yi sipped his wine and regarded the girl who had brought it. She was taller than the average, with longer than usual black hair, and eyes which seemed to suck him towards her. But her stare was hostile.

'Or what about this one,' Lu Shan was saying. 'She is from far in the south, from Vietnam. She is small, but no one knows the art of pleasure more.'

The girl with the tray lowered her eyes, and backed away.

'I will have that one,' Cheng Yi announced.

Lu Shan turned her head in dismay. 'You wish Sao? She is a menial. She was a creature of Ho-shen.' Lu Shan's voice was almost a wail.

Cheng Yi grinned, a brief widening of the tight lips. 'That will make me enjoy her the more.'

'He threw her out,' Lu Shan said. 'After she had been whipped with canes. A hundred strokes. You can see the marks.'

'I will look for them,' Cheng Yi agreed.

'She walked the streets. She came to me pregnant.'

Cheng Yi's eyes narrowed. 'She has a child?'

'It was aborted. It was a botched job. Now she hates everybody. But principally men.'

'Then tell me this, Lu Shan, why do you keep her if she is of no use to you?'

Lu Shan hung her head; her reputation for toughness was at stake. 'Her father was a good man, who fell on hard times.'

'He was your husband?'

'He was my brother.'

'Then no doubt this girl will be as good as you were, in your youth.'

*

'Tell me of Ho-shen,' Cheng Yi said as he removed his clothing in the privacy of the bedchamber.

Sao gave a little shiver. 'He is a devil.'

'You dare to say that of Ho-shen?' Cheng Yi made a gesture, and the girl let her pantaloons drop to the floor.

'He destroyed me,' she said. 'What more can he do now?'

Cheng Yi turned her round and thrust her across the bed, to look at her buttocks. Definitely there were unseemly scars upon the otherwise smooth flesh. Scars which might put many a man off, as Lu Shan had feared. Many a man – but not Cheng Yi. He held the tight mounds, one in each hand, pulled them apart, and let his fingers trickle between. 'Did he possess you?'

Sao snorted. 'I lack an appendage his excellency most wishes in his victims.'

'And why not?'Cheng Yi asked.

Sao looked over her shoulder in dismay.

Cheng Yi gave his tight-lipped grin, and made his entry. 'In the mountains a man must accept whatever he can find.'

Sao waited for him to climax, made suitable noises herself, and collapsed on to her face, his weight still pressing her into the mattress. 'Are you a bandit?' she panted.

'Do you find it necessary to speak all the time?' He rolled off her. 'I understand why Ho-shen had you flogged. I have a mind to flog you myself.'

'Ho-shen had me flogged because I did not please the outer barbarian.'

Cheng Yi frowned. 'An outer barbarian has been in Nanking?'

'It was in Peking. The man was a member of the embassy from the King of Engrand.'

'Tell me of this embassy,' Cheng Yi said.

'I know little save that it came in great ships.'

'I have seen the barbarian ships in Canton,' Cheng Yi said. 'Have you ever been to Canton?'

Sao shook her head, her long hair floating to and fro. 'These ships were greater than any in Canton.'

'All women lie,' Cheng Yi observed. 'It is their nature.'

Sao climbed on to his stomach. 'I do not lie. I have been on board these ships. They are very great.'

Cheng Yi held her shoulders. 'You have been on a ship belonging to the outer barbarians? Tell me how.'

'There was business between Ho-shen and this Barrington, but Barrington's master was against it, and I was set ashore.'

'Business,' Cheng Yi said thoughtfully, his eyes closing. 'Will these outer barbarians return?'

'Barrington said he would return for me.'

Cheng Yi's eyes opened again.

'But who can believe a long-nosed, red-haired outer barbarian?' Sao asked. 'And if he does return, having forced me on to the streets, I will personally shear him to his groin.'

Cheng Yi made her sit astride him. When he was satisfied a second time, he smiled at her. 'You have pleased me, woman. I shall buy you from your aunt, and take you with me.'

'Take me where?' Sao asked suspiciously.

'When I leave Nanking, I will go up the river to Hankow. I have friends there. Then I will go into the mountains of Shensi. I have friends there, too.'

'Are you a bandit?' Sao asked again.

'You ask too many questions. I shall beat you every day.'

'I cannot go with a man when I do not know what he does.'

Cheng Yi frowned at her. 'How old are you?'

'I am sixteen years old.'

'And you care what a man does, so long as he feeds you and fucks you?'

'I care,' Sao said, refusing to lower her eyes.

'Because you hate all men. Lu Shan told me that. Well, you may think of me as a *chianghuk'o*.'

Sao stared at him. The phrase *chianghuk'o* could be translated as a man of rivers and lakes. But it meant far more than that. A *chianghuk'o* was essentially a knight errant without any concept of chivalry, who took life, money, women and allegiance as he found them.

And he wished her to accompany him. To the mountains, where they would shiver from cold and be chased by vengeful Bannermen when they robbed to live. And in the course of time – but by the very nature of his existence not too *much* time – he would be killed, and she would again have to fend for herself.

But she had fended for herself just about ever since she could remember. It might please Lu Shan to pretend that her brother had been a man of substance who had fallen on hard times; the fact was that he had captained a sampan trading on the Grand Canal, and had continually got drunk and gambled away whatever money he had possessed.

Sao did not resent this. She understood that gambling and drinking with friends were the great pleasures of the Chinese masculine existence – women were not supposed to have any pleasures outside the home. She only resented the fact that he had not earned more money, and thus had some to leave to his family.

Yet he must have been a man of some intelligence, simply

because she was a woman of more intelligence than most. When the inevitable had happened, and she and her brothers and sisters had had to be offered for sale, she had never doubted that – according to the rules of Yin and Yang, that the universe is governed by two sides of the same coin, so that there can be no peace without war, no love without hate, no success without failure, and no misfortune without fortune – she would progress.

As she had, even if briefly. She had been one of a selection taken before Ho-shen by his eunuchs. And she had been one of the few chosen, after a searching physical examination which had left her feeling like a stranger to herself. Then she had set her eyes on the Prime Minister herself, only to discover that he seldom took any girl to his bed. She had been left in a kind of limbo, performing menial tasks about the house, until some useful position could be found for her.

That such a position would have to be in subservience to a man had always been obvious; that the man should have turned out to be an outer barbarian had frightened her at first. But Barrington had been a curiously gentle man, even if bigger than anyone she had ever seen before. He had not wanted to hurt her. The life he had promised her had been terrifying, but exciting as well. She had felt sure that he would protect her from all the miseries which had disrupted her girlhood. But he had only been a man, after all, who had discarded her the moment she became inconvenient.

So she had resolved never to trust a man again. She did not intend to trust Cheng Yi, certainly. But if he was not as big as Barrington, he was by far the biggest Chinese she had ever seen. And he would take her away from the drudgery of Lu Shan's establishment, the hateful presence of Lu Shan herself. Lu Shan might be her aunt, but the harridan had insisted Sao could not have her child. That had been bad, but the butcher whom Lu Shan had called in to perform the abortion had been a nightmare. By all the rules of the universe, she was due some good fortune, and perhaps it could be provided, even by a *chianghuk'o*.

'Tell me where we shall go,' she invited.

'We go to find the White Lotus,' Cheng Yi replied.

*

'I do not like it, Master Barrington,' declared Captain Petersen. 'I do not like it one little bit.'

He had been saying this fairly regularly for the past three days, as the brigantine *Alceste* had fought her way into a steadily increasing north-easterly wind.

'What do they call the great storms they experience in these parts?' the Captain demanded, peering at the huge grey walls of water surging past, their crests torn into white shreds by the breeze. Reefed down, *Alceste* was handling them comfortably enough, waddling up each slope and then plunging down into the trough beyond in a flurry of spray, her timbers creaking, but no more than was normal. But the Captain, small and red-bearded, with hunched shoulders and quick movements, was a worrying man.

'They call them typhoons,' Robert Barrington told the shipmaster. 'But this is not the season for such storms.'

'We should've put into the Pearl,' Petersen growled. 'Macao, at least. This wild goose chase ...'

Robert sighed. This theme had also cropped up more than once in the past few days, even though Petersen knew exactly why they had not put into the mouth of the Pearl, or at Macao. No one must know of their intention.

The fact was that Joshua Petersen did not possess the steadfastness of purpose Robert would have liked, nor did he own the sort of ship Robert would have preferred – there was some considerable difference between the great 64-gun Indiamen *Wang Lu-ching* had so extolled to his master and this narrow little cockleshell, with her twelve guns and her limited accommodation. But Petersen was the only shipmaster Robert had approached who had been prepared to risk the wrath of the Manchus, whatever wealth might lie at the end of it.

Besides, if *Alceste* entirely lacked the power or comfort of *Lion*, she might well serve their purpose better, because of her speed and manoeuvrability. The brigantine, known amongst English seamen as an hermaphrodite brig, was an attempt to compromise between the square rig and the schooner. Where a brig proper was merely a smaller version of a square-rigged vessel, with two masts instead of the conventional three, in a brigantine the mainmast set a fore-and-aft sail, instead of a square one; even if still square-rigged on the foremast, this, allied to her several jibs, enabled her to work to windward far more efficiently than other rigs. The brigantine had indeed been invented by the West Indian pirates, seeking speed both on and off the wind. Robert personally thought he had never sailed a better ship – but he could hardly expect a land-limited Manchu to appreciate that, until they were actually at sea.

*

It had been a difficult year. The return voyage to Calcutta last November had been dismal. Not only had Robert Barrington served his purpose, and that purpose been unsuccessful into the bargain, but Macartney had made it plain that he felt his interpreter had let him down by attempting to 'make off', as he put it, with a Chinese woman.

Macartney's moral and mental condemnation had naturally been aped by the other members of the embassy. The days when Robert Barrington had taken his meals with Lord Macartney and been made to feel almost a social equal of his staff were very rapidly forgotten. On the return voyage he had been required to mess with the mates, who had *not* forgotten that he had been unnecessarily elevated above his station on the voyage north, or that he had no specific employment on board the ship.

Their backbiting, no less than his resentment at his rejection by Macartney and his cronies, had simply hardened Robert's resolve. He had still possessed his hundred taels, securely hidden at the bottom of his sea-chest. With that to fall back on he could treat his equals with contempt, at least in the short term. Of course he understood that to a man like Ho-shen, a hundred taels carelessly given away was like a penny from Robert Barrington to a beggar, just as two thousand taels spent to secure his life and family and wealth for his old age was an irrelevancy. But all things were relative in this life.

Had he also been able to install Sao in his hammock he would have had his shipmates' envy as well. Sao was gone, presumably either back to Ho-shen, to be given to some other client, or on to the street: in either event she was lost to him – whatever his message to Wang Lu-ching, he had little hope that in so pragmatic a society the girl would be kept for his return. But there were, as Wang had reminded him, many other Saos in China, just as there were a thousand taels waiting for him when he fulfilled his side of the bargain. Sufficient money to enable him to spit in the eye of these contemptible seamen, even if he could never hope to equal Macartney himself. And replace Sao? She remained an entrancing memory. But it had to be the money which mattered.

*

He had not touched it. For a year, he had preferred on occasion to starve rather than offer an ounce of silver for sale. That way lay questions, and investigations.

But a hundred taels, even a hundred taels, had not been sufficient wealth actually to purchase a ship. Returning to China he had to depend upon his eloquence, his salesmanship. It had not been easy. Great Britain was now engaged upon a full-scale war with France, and although it was an inflexible British rule that nothing should be allowed to interfere with the Indian trade, there were inevitably less ships available for private ventures. Those shipmasters, and their agents, who had been prepared to pass the Straits of Malacca into the South China Sea, were not prepared to look beyond Macao and Canton. That trade contained risks enough, but at least it also contained the merit of proof; much of what went on in Canton was illegal, by Manchu law – but it worked, through the venality of Cantonese merchants and officials: the mere permitted existence of the Portuguese enclave at the mouth of the gulf was proof enough of that. There was no proof that further north, closer to the centre of Manchu rule, any profit would be commensurable with the risk.

Robert Barrington had had to paint vast canvases with words. In this he could draw upon his personal experiences. He did not have to invent the wealth and teeming prosperity of North China, of Peking and Jehol, of the distantly glimpsed splendour of the Summer Palace; discerning men could tell that he was remembering rather than creating.

His task had been complicated by the need for secrecy. He could openly dream about attempting a forbidden trade route, and be smiled at by those who knew how impossible his dream was. But had Macartney, or any of the high officials of the East India Company, learned what he was truly about, he would have found himself in irons and on his way back to England, banished from the East forever as a troublemaker. Thus he had had to play the disappointed drunk, his brain filled at once with the enormous wealth that was China, and with resentment at his treatment by Macartney. These things were fact; from the point of view of his superiors he had become simply a failed Englishman – there were enough of them about – who would now drink and talk himself into an early grave.

Often enough he had supposed them right. But his dream, of that thousand taels, and perhaps of another Sao, had kept him sane. And eventually found him Joshua Petersen.

*

Robert took his noon sight beside the Captain, and carefully packed away his sextant. 'Thirty-one degrees, ten seconds, North latitude,' he said as he entered the reading in his notebook.

'Thirty-one degrees, *twelve* seconds, sir,' Petersen corrected.

'As you wish, sir,' Robert said. 'It is sufficient. Your course should be west by north.'

Petersen glared at him, and then at the still surging waves. 'That will mean beam seas, sir.'

'The wind is dropping, Captain Petersen, and the seas will diminish as we close the land.'

He remained on deck all day, as the *Alceste* approached the land under shortened sail, the leadsman calling the depths, and anchored in four fathoms of water. The drooping sun rendered identification difficult, but they could make out islands fronting a low-lying shore, and in the distance, well inland from the shoreline, the pagoda roofs of a town.

'You spoke of a river,' Petersen remarked.

'It lies beyond the islands.'

Petersen continued to stare through his glass. 'I see breakers. Do you expect me to take my ship into that deathtrap?'

'Someone will come out to us,' Robert promised.

That they had been seen was certain; through their glasses they could observe a large number of people clustering on a stone sea-wall to the south of the islands, gazing at them. But the sun was now setting fast, and within half an hour it was dark.

'Now we can expect to be murdered in our bunks,' Petersen complained.

'I think it would certainly be a good idea to keep a sharp lookout,' Robert agreed.

'We could have been snug in Macao,' Petersen grumbled, as he gave the orders. And indeed during the night several boats approached them, but as they came with their lanterns burning and their people calling out, they could hardly be considered pirates. To their shouted questions Robert made the reply that they sought fresh water, and asked if it was possible to enter the river.

'Oh, yes,' the men on the sampans called back. 'You can enter the river. You come now? We will guide you.'

'Tomorrow, when it is light,' Robert told them, and that seemed to satisfy them.

*

When the sun rose out of the ocean behind the *Alceste*, the bay was empty. The seas had now gone right down, and the brigantine hardly moved; the offshore wind – it had backed during the night to become a land breeze – was light.

Captain Petersen wiped sleep from his eyes and stroked his beard. 'I had not expected to see this day, and that's a fact,' he remarked. 'What now, Master Barrington?'

'We wait.'

As the day developed, the brigantine again attracted much attention from the shore, and was again surrounded by sampans. Several of these obviously had been there last night as well.

'You come in to the river, now?' their crews called.

'Do you know my name?' Robert countered.

'Name? Name? How are we to know your name?'

'I will wait for the man who knows my name,' Robert said.

Petersen grew more and more surly as the morning wore on, while his men muttered amongst themselves. It was just on noon when a strange sampan emerged from between the islands and was sculled straight at the brigantine.

'Man your guns!' Petersen called.

'Hold your fire until I have spoken with them,' Robert commanded, and stood at the rail.

The sampan slowed its approach as it came nearer, and Robert watched a very well-dressed man, resplendent in blue silk, coming up to the bow. 'Who is Barrington?' this man inquired.

'I am Barrington,' Robert called back.

'I will come aboard.'

Petersen reluctantly gave the command, and the sampan surged alongside. Robert went to the gangway, and watched the man in blue climbing up.

'I am Yun Kai-lu.'

'Tell me the name of your master,' Robert said, aware that he was addressing a Han Chinese rather than a Manchu.

Yun Kai-lu bowed. He was a little man, with drooping moustache but lively eyes. 'My master is also your master: Ho-shen.' He glanced left and right. 'This is the ship he expects?' He had obviously had the Indiaman described to him.

'This ship will do what is required,' Robert assured him.

Yun looked at the mainsail; even furled, it was clearly not a squaresail. 'I have never seen a sail like that.'

'It gives us great speed,' Robert promised him. 'Where is our master?'

'Our master is in Peking, serving the Emperor. You were not expected so soon.'

'I thought it best to be early. Where do you wish me to go?'

'You will enter the river, and ascend it to Hankow.'

'How far is that?'

'Fifteen hundred li.' A li was roughly a third of a mile.

'Fifteen hundred,' Robert swallowed. 'This is possible?'

'Of course. But it is good that you are early. The journey will take time. Your ship has no sweeps.'

'She can be towed,' Robert said. 'Who will be our pilot?'

'I am your pilot,' Yun Kai-lu said.

*

Joshua Petersen nearly had a seizure when he learned that he had to take his ship into the very heart of China. 'But think of it,' Robert told him. 'You will be venturing where no European vessel has ever been before.'

The crew was even less happy, especially when they discovered that a large part of the journey might consist of towing their vessel. In fact, this was not often practical. The Yangtse ran very fast, and to attempt to breast it by muscle power would have been useless; Yun recommended that in the first instance they follow the example of the considerable Chinese river traffic and anchor out of the stream to wait for the tide, which flooded up the river for several miles.

Now they were inside the coastal defence, or sea-wall, that protected the vast plain which apparently stretched for hundreds of miles to either side, although so deeply had the river cut into the earth over the centuries that all that could be seen from the deck of the *Alceste* were the embankments. On the southern side of the river, however, a tributary emerged. This was called the Whang-poo, and it was some miles up this smaller stream that the city of Shanghai was to be found; its pagoda roofs could be seen in the distance.

Next day, when the tide had turned, the boats were got out and the brigantine was towed upriver. It was hot work, but the English seamen found themselves surrounded by sampans and junks being propelled by sweeps, and were not about to give best to a bunch of yellow-skinned youths. When, in mid-afternoon, the sea breeze sprang up, the *Alceste* took in her boats and surged ahead, leaving the sampans behind, but still was kept company by the junks, some of which made even better speed. By the time they anchored for the night, however, Petersen was in a good humour. 'I'd not supposed this river work could be so simple,' he remarked.

'All that is required is patience,' Yun said in reply.

*

Patience was not Joshua Petersen's strongest characteristic, and his humour soon faded, as the following day there was no wind at all, and *Alceste*, now beyond the reach of the effective tide, had to remain at anchor while the sampans and junks forged steadily onwards.

This became the pattern of the succeeding weeks. When the wind was in the east, progress was good. When it dropped or was in the west, the ship remained anchored. The weather indeed became very important as they moved further inland, to their surprise. At sea, once there was room, a ship, and especially a brigantine, which could work to windward, could always make some progress. On the other hand, most seamen supposed that the weather at sea was far more dangerous than it could ever be in the centre of a huge landmass. They quickly learned different. Tremendous gales would spring up across the plain without the least warning, and more than once the crew were taken unawares and the ship driven on to a sandbank before an anchor could be put down, to be laboriously kedged off when the storm had passed. Even when already apparently securely anchored, the wind could drive the brigantine sideways.

Then there were amazing electrical storms, when forked lightning would slash down to the water. On several occasions the masts were struck and the entire ship would tremble. Worse yet were the dark, triangular-shaped clouds which seemed able to bounce; and where they descended to the earth, whole villages could be destroyed in an instant.

Weather and delays apart, their journey was pleasant enough. At Yun's recommendation they flew the pennant of Ho-shen from the main masthead, and this enabled them to obtain all the fresh water, fruit and vegetables they wished at every stop. Meat was seldom available, and the seamen grumbled, but it was easy to see that they were healthier than they had been for years.

They were also very well provided for, as invariably there were young women on board the sampans which came out to them. Captain Petersen was himself a sober and God-fearing man, but he had no means of maintaining the strict discipline of an Indiaman, especially when there was so much invitation to indiscipline available. The sailors regularly accompanied the sampans ashore, while their Captain strode the quarterdeck and muttered under his breath . . . but they were always back by dawn, sated and happy, if in no very good shape for a hard day's work.

More serious was the pilfering which resulted from these amorous adventures. The seamen soon ran out of money, whereupon they discovered that their female friends were willing to trade sex for European articles, and particularly guns and bullets. Arms formed a principal part of the brigantine's cargo, on Robert's recommendation; although their business was not to trade, it had to be made to appear so. Now it appeared as though there would be no profit left.

'Another musket gone,' Petersen growled. 'What's to be done, eh, Master Barrington? What's to be done? You guaranteed me a thousand taels profit from this voyage. I shall be lucky to return with my ship.'

They were by now lying off the great city of Nanking, some two hundred miles from the sea. Robert thus felt that there was no risk of Petersen at this stage abandoning the enterprise. 'You will receive your thousand taels,' he promised. 'Sit down, sir, and I will tell you how.'

Petersen listened in growing consternation, a mixture of apprehension and avarice, to the real reason for the voyage. 'By God!' he commented when Robert had finished. 'But you have hoodwinked me, you rascal.'

'Would you have come if I had told you the truth?'

'Indeed not. I have no wish to become mixed up in politics. That is a quick way to lose your head.'

'And you have no use for eighty pounds of pure silver?'

'By God!' Petersen got up and strode to and fro.

'As far as anyone, including the Chinese, knows, we are here to trade,' Robert told him. 'When Ho-shen and his family are ready, they simply board our ship, we sail downriver, a good deal faster than we have come up, and deliver the prime minister wherever he wishes . . . and sail away, wealthy men.'

Petersen gazed at the bank, from where they were being overseen by a band of armed and mounted Bannermen. These were often visible, and often they rode for some time abreast of the ship. But Yun assured them that as long as the *Alceste* flew Ho-shen's banner, they were safe. 'Very simple,' the Captain growled, and went below.

'He is too frightened to be of value,' Yun remarked. He might not be able to speak English, but he could discern the Captain's demeanour.

'He will fulfil his part of the bargain,' Robert promised.

*

But for the underlying anxiety at the immensity of what he was attempting, Robert would have enjoyed the voyage enormously. Venturing into strange places and seeing new sights was the salt of life to him.

As ever, he was astounded by the development of the society with which he was surrounded. The huge plain was principally under rice, the extensive necessary irrigation being drawn from the river itself and its several tributaries, but it was also dotted with many more ancient aspects of Chinese civilisation.

Shanghai itself had been a sizeable town; only a few miles upriver, on the north bank, was Tungchau, which was hardly smaller. Opposite Tungchau was the fortress complex of Kiancyin, for here the river began to narrow, and the fort was there to prevent any unauthorised vessel from ascending beyond this point. Once again, Ho-shen's banner carried the brigantine safely past the muzzles of the guns, although the battlements were crowded with Bannermen, gazing at this strangest of craft.

From Shanghai to Kiancyin, a distance of some fifty miles, the river had proceeded generally north; at the fort it began a long, slow bend to the west before turning north again to the city of Chin-kiang, situated at the point where the Grand Canal debouched into the river. This was not the terminal of the Grand Canal; it continued to the south, past Suchau to Hangchau, another hundred-plus miles away, but viewed, as it were, from both ends, it created an even bigger impression of the enormous manpower controlled by the Son of Heaven.

From Chin-kiang a journey of some forty miles had brought the *Alceste* to Nanking, which several times in the past had been the capital of the empire. Here was a really huge city, only smaller than Peking itself, surrounded by similar enormous walls. Although more than two hundred miles from the sea, Nanking had the feel of a seaport, as it was the main trading centre on the river east of Hankow. Here again the rice-covered plains stretched north and south of the river, and here there was a viceroyalty which was virtually independent of the capital.

Thus here Ho-shen's banner carried less authority. Yun had to go ashore and seek an interview with the viceroy, and he invited Robert to accompany him; the pilot had decided that Robert was the driving force behind the expedition, and indeed, the two men had become good friends. Yun had a dry sense of humour, but he was also, for all his sang-froid, more tense about the situation than he allowed most people to see. But in Nanking, and especially after the viceroy, having invited himself on board *Alceste* and inspected the ship from her hold upwards, had pronounced her free to continue on her way, Yun announced, 'Tonight we will get drunk. The most difficult part of the journey is over.'

He did not invite Petersen, but Robert reflected that the Captain would probably not have wished to indulge anyway. So he accompanied Yun ashore, to a very high-class brothel. 'I'm afraid I am a little short,' he confessed, still not prepared to delve into his sea-chest.

Yun gave him an old-fashioned look, to indicate that he probably knew about the hundred taels, and then smiled. 'You will repay me when you have received your reward from Ho-shen.'

'You have my word,' Robert said, and held out his hand.

Yun looked at it curiously for a moment, then grasped it, and his smile broadened. *I am making friends*, Robert thought. *I could be happy here.*

*

It was the Chinese New Year, and Nanking was *en fête*. Multi-coloured lanterns were strewn the length of every street, equally multicoloured fireworks screamed into the sky: walking through the city was like making one's way through an unending battle. But everyone was so good-humoured. Robert decided these had to be the happiest people on earth.

The madam welcomed them with deep bows, and obviously liked the look of the huge white-skinned sailor. She was in fact an extremely attractive woman, and although she was surrounded by nubile girls, she stood out on her own with her sleek black hair, her mature figure, and her bedroom eyes.

'You wish the old one?' Yun asked, as they were fed sake and roast pork.

'Is she available?'

'Lu Shan is always available, at a price.'

'Which you are going to lend me,' Robert suggested.

'Of course, if that is what you wish.'

Robert decided that it was. The sake was playing its part, and none of the young girls matched Sao in looks or, he was sure, in sexual capability. Lu Shan clearly would do, and he was not disappointed. Lu Shan was a mistress of the art of love, exclaiming with joy when she removed his breeches. 'I have heard of the size of barbarian men,' she confided.

'Who has told you?' Robert asked, concerned. He did not know of any European vessel trading on the Yangtse before.

Lu Shan smiled. 'My niece has told me of them.'

An encounter in Canton, no doubt, Robert thought with

relief. Nor was she concerned by his peculiar western tastes; she presented her lips to be kissed and seemed to enjoy it when he played with her nipples. He did not doubt she was at least fifty, but there was nothing wrong with her figure, while her interest was centred on his by now enormous member. When she finally came down on him he realised that she had made even Sao seem a naive girl – which, of course, she had been.

*

But thoughts of Lu Shan were soon forgotten as they proceeded on their way in a long slow sweep to the west which brought them to Wuhu. Here was another sizeable city; and the main rice-shipping port on the river. It teemed with activity, and with prosperity as well, fronted by the inevitable suburb of moored sampans. Robert was beginning to wonder just how many cities of this size, every one larger than London, there were in this fantastic country. In Wuhu they learned that the Ch'ien-lung Emperor had abdicated.

*

'How far are we from Hankow?' Robert asked.

'We are about halfway,' Yun told him.

'Then our mission is a failure.'

'That is not necessarily so,' Yun said. 'The Emperor may have abdicated, but he has not given up his power.'

Robert frowned. 'I do not understand you.'

'It is simply that, whilst he has fulfilled his vow not to reign longer than his grandfather, he intends to continue *ruling*. There is a difference, my friend. Prince Yung-yen has ascended the throne, and is now the Chia-ch'ing Emperor, but his father will continue to make the decisions. And one of those decisions is that Ho-shen shall continue to be prime minister. So you will understand that we are yet in good time. Ho-shen will make arrangements for his departure when he is ready.'

Robert stroked his chin. But already other anxieties were replacing the one just allayed. 'And just how long do you suppose it will be until he *is* ready to leave?'

'I do not think it will be very long. The Ch'ien-lung Emperor, who is to take the name Kao Tsung Shun Huang-ti, is very old.

He could mount the Heavenly Chariot and make the ascent to his ancestors at any moment, and Ho-shen is aware of this. I would say that within a year his plans will have been completed.'

'Within a year?' Robert cried.

'What is a year, when great matters are at stake?'

A very Chinese point of view, but it was difficult to estimate Petersen's reaction to the news that they might have to kick their heels in Hankow for a year. Robert decided that it would be best not to tell the Captain the truth; once he was in Hankow there was little chance of his being allowed to leave again without Ho-shen.

*

Yun had been over-optimistic. The *Alceste* had ascended the river one hundred and eighty miles to reach Wuhu; it was another two hundred and seventy from Wuhu to Hankow, and their progress was slowed by the rise in the river, as the first thaws began in the mountains. Sometimes, indeed, they spent several days riding to three anchors while the brigantine bucked and heaved in the fast-flowing water.

Their way took them past the cities of Kiukiang and Wusu, before they finally reached the bifurcation where the Han Kuang flowed down from the hills to the north to join the Yangtse, which rose many hundreds of miles away in the mountains of Tibet. It was at this junction that a huge city complex had arisen, Hankow on the north bank, Wu-chau on the south, and on the triangle of land where the rivers came together, the fortress town of Han-yang. The three were dominated by the walls of Hankow, a city not greatly smaller than Nanking, and like Nanking, a provincial capital. Here Yun was apparently well known, and here too, to Robert's immense relief, Wang Lu-ching was waiting for them. 'Is all well with our master?'

Wang gravely bowed his head.

'When will he join us?'

'He is presently in Peking. But he knows you are here, and he has commanded me to attend to your every want.'

'That is good news. But ...' Robert warned the eunuch not to let Petersen know what was happening, but to give the impression that Ho-shen would be arriving any day.

'Of course,' Wang agreed. 'But there is no need for your Captain to become agitated. Why do you not just remain here, and trade with the local people, and grow rich. My agents will keep you supplied with food and fresh provisions. It would be best to keep your ship ready to depart at a moment's notice. When our master decides to leave, it will be in haste.' He looked around him. 'This is not a very big vessel.'

'It is all I could procure. Do not worry, it will take your master wherever he wishes to go.'

'And his family? He has a large family.'

'And his family,' Robert assured him. 'Tell me about Sao.'

'Sao?'

'The girl our master gave me.'

'And whom you turned away. Ah, yes, I remember.'

'I was forced to let her go, Wang. Lord Macartney would not allow her on board the ship.'

'He was a strange man,' Wang agreed. 'Born never to taste the fruits of happiness.'

'But what of Sao?'

'I cannot say. She is probably dead.'

'Dead?' Robert cried.

'It is hard for a young girl on the streets. If she does not become diseased, she stands the chance of being murdered for whatever money she may accumulate. And if she does not accumulate any money, then she starves. It is hard.'

'But ... did she not go back to Ho-shen's employment?'

'She attempted to do so. She persuaded me to take her back to Peking, and I, fool that I am, agreed. But Ho-shen considered that she had debased his word by not remaining with you. He ordered her to be beaten with rods and thrown on to the street.'

'My God! Could you do nothing to assist her?'

'I was beaten with rods as well,' Wang said severely. 'For taking her back in the first place. But why do you still think of that girl? Did I not tell you that there are many such as she in China?'

*

Petersen seemed content with the story he was given that Ho-shen would appear, as would the money, at any moment, and that in the meanwhile he was free to empty his ship of its entire cargo. Before departing back to Peking, Wang Lu-ching made a public announcement that the British ship had been allowed up to Hankow to trade. Yun also went ashore; apparently he had family living outside Hankow whom he wished to visit.

This left Robert to do all the interpreting, as next day they were boarded by several merchants who examined the cloth goods with great care, but did not seem overly impressed.

'It is the muskets that will earn us our profit,' Petersen decided, and that very afternoon they received a visit from a man named Sen Tu-kan, to inspect the weapons. 'Your ship is a veritable arsenal, Barrington,' he commented.

'We arm our own soldiers with these muskets,' Robert assured him.

'I will pay you five hundred taels,' Sen said. 'For everything you have.'

'Everything is for sale. We retain the ship's weapons.'

Sen bowed. 'I understand. Your ship must remain armed.'

'Then it is a deal.' He held out his hand, and as with Wang the first time, Sen looked bewildered for a moment before clasping the proffered fingers.

'I will come tomorrow, with a sampan, and remove the goods.'

'And you will bring the money,' Robert reminded him.

'I will bring the money,' Sen agreed.

*

Petersen was jubilant. 'Forty pounds of silver. There is our profit. With the rest to come. Master Barrington, I apologise. I have doubted you, from time to time. Now I see that this is a great venture. 'Tis a pity it cannot be repeated.'

Because once they had helped Ho-shen to escape his just desserts, they would be *persona non grata* to the new regime.

Yun returned the following morning, reaching the ship just as Sen, having loaded the muskets and ball into his waiting sampan, was pushing off. 'What business have you done with that man?' Yun demanded.

'Very good business. We have sold him all our munitions.'

Yun stared after the sampan. 'He must be arrested. I will go ashore and inform the Bannermen.'

'Arrested? Is it illegal to sell arms?'

'It is illegal to sell *him* arms; he is a revolutionary.'

'A revolutionary? I thought this the most peaceful and settled of countries.'

'No country is ever entirely peaceful and settled, Barrington. We are a conquered people. You know this.'

'Well, yes. But I had supposed you were content to be so.'

'All sensible men, all true men, are content to be so. It is the law as written by Confucius, that when the opposition is too strong, a true man surrenders to it and awaits better times. But there are many in my country who are not true men. In particular, in these parts, there is a society known as the White Lotus. You have heard of that society?'

Robert shook his head.

'It is a very ancient society. And very evil. Its members call themselves the only true Chinese. Ha! They say it was through their efforts that the Mongols, the Yuan, were expelled from the Middle Kingdom four hundred years ago, and the Ming installed in their place. The White Lotus prospered beneath the Ming. But then the Manchu came, and swept the Ming away. The White Lotus fought against the Manchu, and were defeated. It was supposed that they were destroyed. But during the past fifty years they have begun their activities again. They are to be found to the north of the river, where they hide in the mountains, recruiting followers, attacking Manchu units whenever they can. Their leader is a man called Cheng Yi. The man Sen is one of his agents. Now I must make haste.'

'But if you know this, then surely the authorities here in Hankow know this. Why was Sen not immediately arrested on entering the city?'

'Bribery and corruption,' Yun said darkly.

He hurried off, while Robert told Petersen what had happened. 'He will not confiscate our money?' the Captain asked anxiously.

'He knows we were unaware of Sen's identity. In any event, we are still Ho-shen's only hope of survival.'

*

Yun did not succeed in arousing the local Banner commander to take action against Sen, and the event seemed to be rapidly forgotten. Robert and Petersen and the crew settled down to wait. In Hankow their surroundings were even more pleasant than on the river, for as Wang had promised, they were supplied with fresh food and water, free of charge, and if they had largely run out of tradable items, this no longer appeared a handicap in the matter of obtaining women, for Yun was prepared to advance them what was called 'cash' or small denomination paper money which apparently circulated freely, for their daily needs.

While for their free entertainment they could follow the example of the Chinese and attend the very popular theatre, although it took them some time to understand what was going on, for the Chinese indulged in no sets, and everything was fantasy and stylised, with each prop or costume always meaning the same thing. Thus a man carrying an oar was on a boat, one carrying a fan was a scholar, and if he was standing on a table while the other actors ran round him he was invisible. Additionally, all the actors – there were no women involved – had heavily painted faces, and each line and colour denoted some characteristic of the part, well known to the audience.

When all of this became too confusing, there were daily public whippings or executions to be watched, or they could join the crowds tormenting those unfortunates confined in their cangues, and forced to submit to whatever amused the laughing, jeering spectators. 'It's enough to make the blood run cold,' Petersen commented.

More attractive were the gambling dens, in which the seamen very rapidly lost all of their 'cash'.

But as winter began to drift into spring the sailors became restive, and started to wonder aloud if they were ever going to get home. Robert kept reassuring them, but he began to feel uneasy himself, because Yun was suddenly uneasy. 'There is fighting in the mountains,' he said. 'Our master has been sent against the White Lotus.'

'Is our master also a general?'

'Indeed. He has campaigned against the White Lotus before.'

'And they are still there.'

Yun gave a twisted smile. 'There are those who have accused our master of using the money allotted to the campaign for his own purposes, instead of destroying the rebels.'

'Has it never occurred to you, Yun, that our master is a scoundrel?'

'He is our master,' Yun said angrily.

*

Robert went ashore to watch a detachment of the local Bannermen march out to join Ho-shen's army. These were of course all Manchu, big, strong fellows, at least when compared with the Chinese. They wore a variety of clothes rather than any uniform, but were well if antiquely armed with swords and halberds; there was one platoon of musketeers. They marched under a red banner, and made a splendid show.

But they were back again, some of them, in three days, hurrying into the city to shout that Ho-shen had been defeated, and that the rebels were swarming out of the mountains.

'I think we should leave this place,' Yun said.

'And go where?' Petersen inquired.

'We can drop down the river, out of the reach of these bandits.'

'And will your master know where to find us?'

'We will send a messenger.'

'Who will never get through. Here is where Ho-shen knows we are to be found. Here is where he will come, probably very quickly, if he has truly been defeated.'

'But the White Lotus may come here first.'

'Will the city not be defended by the Bannermen?'

Yun looked at Robert. Robert was surprised by the Captain's sudden determination. But he was none the less pleased. 'I think Captain Petersen is right,' he said. 'We should remain here, where our master knows he can find us.'

'It is all your fault,' Yun grumbled. 'For selling those guns to the rebels.'

*

Next day, some of the reasons for his agitation became evident, when the Bannermen boarded sampans and fled from the city. This left the garrison in the hands of the Green Flags, irregular troops. There were a great number of them, but as Yun pointed out, somewhat dolefully, it was generally accepted that they had been infiltrated by the White Lotus, and without the government soldiers to stiffen them were of little account.

'You don't think we'd do better to forget the money and concentrate on our skins?' Robert asked Petersen. 'Everyone knows we're Ho-shen's people. These bandits are his enemies.'

'They'll not take my ship,' Petersen declared. He gave orders for the *Alceste* to be cast off and anchored in the stream, some hundred feet from the shore on either side. The guns were loaded and run out, and the muskets were also loaded and placed in stands on the deck.

'If we're attacked, we'll fight our way downriver,' Petersen told his men. 'If they have the sense not to attack us, we'll see what happens.'

Robert realised that he had misjudged this man's character. He had begun by deciding Petersen lacked the steadfast determination to carry out a mission like this; now he realised that the Scot was so stubborn he might be endangering all of their lives. But he found himself admiring the old curmudgeon.

*

By next day it was obvious that the rebels were approaching the city, and that it was not going to be defended. White Lotus badges began to appear on the streets, just as the green flags of the garrison disappeared. The men on board the *Alceste* watched large numbers of people taking to the river in junks and sampans, obviously either Manchu or Chinese supporters of the government.

That afternoon, the first of the rebels entered the town. Their appearance was marked by a huge noise from the landward wall, a great deal of screaming and shouting, cheering and exploding fireworks, mingled with gunshots. Within an hour they appeared on the waterfront, staring at the brigantine, and soon a sampan put out and approached the English ship.

Robert mounted the rail to watch them, while beneath him the crew lit their matches. 'You, barbarian ship!' someone shouted. 'You surrender to the White Lotus. This is the word of General Cheng Yi!'

'We surrender to nobody,' Barrington replied. 'If the General wishes to speak with us, let him come to us, or send an accredited envoy.' The sampan was close now, the men on board staring at the gun muzzles protruding from the brigantine's ports. 'If you come any closer, we will fire into you.'

The sampan immediately backed off. 'We will tell the General what you say,' said the spokesman.

Petersen and Yun stood beside Robert as he came down. 'It is my opinion,' Robert said, 'that the moment the wind shifts to the west we should get out of here. There is no chance of Hoshen coming to us now.'

'Aye, you're right, even if it goes against the grain to flee these monkeys,' Petersen said.

'The wind will shift,' Yun said.

*

The guns were manned all afternoon and into the night, while Hankow throbbed with the sounds of the triumphant revolution. Some of the sounds were distinctly unpleasant, and Robert guessed that not all the Manchu, or their Chinese collaborators, had been able to get away in time. By sunset, sampans had swarmed across to the south bank, and the rebels were also apparently in control of the arsenal, from the explosions to the west.

No one slept on board the *Alceste*. There was a good deal of activity in the river, both above and below them, with multi-coloured lanterns darting in every direction. But an hour before dawn the wind shifted to the west. Instantly Petersen and Robert alerted every man. 'We sail at first light,' the Captain told them. 'Blast anyone or anything that attempts to stop us.'

It was one of the longest hours of Robert's life. But at last the darkness turned to grey. 'Make sail,' Petersen shouted, himself taking the helm. 'Raise the anchor.'

The windlass creaked, while as the sails filled the brigantine began to override the chain. But the anchor came free, and the ship surged forward, round the half bend in the river ... to find itself facing a barricade of sampans, roped together and strung right across the passage.

'We're done!' Petersen yelled, and instinctively put the helm up, so that the *Alceste* immediately came about, and lost way through the water; she continued to be carried downstream towards the waiting sampans by the current.

Robert thrust the Captain aside as he grabbed the helm and

put it down again. 'We must smash through them,' he shouted.

But he was too late. The brigantine had lost too much speed, and her sails were all taken aback. She only half came round, and then drifted sideways into the boats, which were secured together by stout rope cables.

'Fire!' Robert shouted, as he realised they were going to be brought up. The starboard guns responded, but in the half light they had not been properly aimed, and none of the sampans was hit. Seconds later wood crunched against wood, and the Chinese came swarming over the gunwales, waving their swords. Robert and Petersen had each earlier armed themselves with cutlasses, as had Yun, and they attempted to hold the poop, but now men were coming over the stern as well. The morning was filled with a cacophony of shrieks and yells, exploding pistols and muskets, and the inevitable firecrackers. Robert swung his sword to and fro, felt it crunch into bone and blood spurting over his arm, clanged the blade against another, and was then overwhelmed in the huge body of men who were flooding the deck.

He went down, and his sword was torn from his hand. His arms were seized by several men and he was dragged back to his feet, winded and gasping, but otherwise unhurt, to gaze at his captors, and their leader – who was a woman.

For a moment his astounded gaze could only take in that fact, the long black hair, the heaving bosom, for she was dressed like her men. Then he realised that it was Sao.

4

THE REBELS

Robert blinked at the apparition in front of him. Sao wore trousers, a loose blouse, boots, all in flaming red. Her head was tied up in a red kerchief, from the back of which her black hair floated in the breeze. Her figure had undoubtedly filled out, but it was the face which had changed most. The lips were more firmly compressed than he remembered, and the eyes had lost their servile expression, and were now darting black coals. And she was armed with a sword, which was dripping blood!

'Sao?' he muttered, and was struck a blow across the head with a stick, which sent him back to his knees.

'My name is Cheng Yi Sao,' Sao said. 'You will address me as Lady Cheng. Who are these men?'

Petersen and Yun, as well as Tommy the cabin boy, had also been made prisoner. Robert shook his head to clear his brain, dimly recalling that the leader of the rebels was named Cheng. Was it possible? 'My Captain, Joshua Petersen,' he began.

'I do not like his face,' Sao said, and raised her hand.

The two men holding Petersen dragged him forward. A third seized his hair to pull his head away from his body. A fourth swung his sword, and the head fell free, leaving a spout of blood behind it as the men holding the Captain dragged his headless trunk to the rail and threw it into the water.

It had happened so quickly it was obvious Petersen had no idea he was about to die.

'For God's sake!' Robert shouted. 'Sao ...' There was another blow on his head and again he collapsed to the deck.

'And this one?' Sao inquired.

'I am Yun Kai-lu,' Yun declared; if he was afraid he did not show it.

'You are a traitor to your people,' Sao told him, and repeated her gesture. Yun's head rolled across the deck, coming to rest against Robert's knees as he tried to regain his feet,

74

staring at his erstwhile slave and mistress. 'And him?' Sao turned her gaze on Tommy.

The boy was on his knees as well, tears streaming down his face. 'Our servant,' Robert gasped.

Sao smiled. 'He amuses me. Bind him.' She looked down at the waist, where the surviving dozen of the crew had been accumulated; Robert observed that Armstrong the boatswain was there, but Johnson the mate was not. 'Bind them all,' she said, and turned back to Robert. 'Bring him – and the boy.'

*

Robert's arms were tied behind him very tightly, and he was thrown down the ladder to the waist. Tommy landed on top of him a moment later.

'What will happen to us, Mr Barrington?' one of the crew called.

'Pray,' Robert advised him, as he was hurled off the deck of the brigantine and into a waiting sampan, as if he were a sack of grain. It was a miracle he had not broken something. Certainly blood was dribbling into his mouth from a cut lip. Once again Tommy landed beside him. 'Lord above, Mr Barrington, I'm scared,' the boy whispered.

'Yes,' Robert agreed, and tried to think as some of the red pain haze began to fade from behind his eyes. Sao, waving a sword and leading the rebels into battle ... and claiming the name of Cheng. And in total control, it seemed. She had herself now boarded the sampan, and was standing above him, her bloodstained sword thrust through her belt.

'Barrington,' she said, and he had a vision of a large cat standing above a helpless mouse. 'You abandoned me.'

'I had no choice,' Robert said, hating himself for begging.

'Man can always choose,' she told him. 'But now you have come back.' She smiled, and without warning the smile changed into a snarl. 'To help the monster Ho-shen escape justice.'

Robert understood that lying to her might be the biggest mistake he could make. 'I came back for the money,' he said. 'And to find you.'

'You are lying,' she spat, and kicked him in the ribs. She then stalked off to stand in the stern of the boat as it made for the shore.

Here there was a crowd of people, all armed and excited, shouting curses at the two Englishmen. Robert was more interested in the man who strode through the throng towards them, people darting left and right to get out of his way. He was big for a Chinese, also dressed in flaming red, with a high forehead and a thick moustache. To signify his rebellion against the Manchu he had cut off his pigtail. 'Cheng Yi!' the people shouted. 'Cheng Yi!'

The rebel leader reached the dock, and looked at the two captives, and then at his wife. 'Who are these men?'

'They are my prisoners,' Sao told him. 'This is the barbarian I spoke of.'

Cheng Yi gazed across the harbour at the *Alceste.* 'You spoke of a ship as big as the greatest junk. I will inspect it.'

He boarded the sampan, while Robert and Tommy were hurried away. People spat at them and poked at them with sticks as they were marched along the streets, staggering and stumbling and gasping for breath, until they reached the viceregal palace. This had been thoroughly looted, but men and women scurried about, endeavouring to tidy the place up and arrange such of the furniture as had not been wrecked.

The room into which Tommy and Robert were thrust, however, was devoid of furniture, nor was there the slightest chance of their escaping, as two men, armed with the fearsome executioners' swords, entered the room with them, stood by the door, and stared at them with folded arms and fierce expressions.

'Are we going to die, Mr Barrington?' Tommy asked, his voice quavering.

'I think probably yes, Tommy,' Robert said. 'So you must prepare to be very brave, and remember that you are a Christian.'

Tommy gulped, and stared at the swords. 'I am so very thirsty, Mr Barrington,' he said. 'Do you suppose they will give us any water?'

'We can try,' Robert said. It was difficult to accept that it was only mid-morning. So much had happened since that so-confident attempt at departure; his mind was still filled with the memory of his comrades' heads rolling across the deck.

But was his own not soon to join them? Unless Cheng Yi Sao had some more unpleasant fate in store for them. He had a rather unhappy feeling that she did. But he was as thirsty as the boy. 'Water,' he said. 'We need water.' Their guards' lips curled in contempt.

The minutes ticked by interminably, and with each one their thirst seemed to grow. Tommy began to cry again, great tears rolling down his cheeks, while Robert lost all feeling in his bound wrists, and even began to contemplate getting up and hurling himself at the guards – that would at least ensure a quick end. He had not yet made a decision on committing suicide, however, when the door opened and Sao came in, accompanied by several eunuchs. He was relieved to see that she had discarded her sword.

She stood above Tommy, who shivered with fear, and said to the guards, 'Amuse yourselves. But leave him whole. I will instruct you later.' She turned to Robert. 'Bring this one.'

Barrington was grasped by the shoulders and dragged through a succession of corridors, before being hurled into a high-ceilinged and airy chamber where stood a low table on which a meal waited, with cushions to either side. Sao followed them and seated herself, gestured Robert to sit opposite. One of the eunuchs cut the cord round his wrists, and then joined his fellows in a respectful group at the far end of the room. Robert rubbed his hands together and winced in agony as his circulation returned.

'Eat,' Sao commanded. 'Are you not hungry?'

For all his churning stomach, Robert could not resist tasting the sake. Or asking, 'What is to be my fate?'

'Ho-shen's creature,' she said contemptuously.

'I wished the money,' Robert told her. 'Amongst my own people, I am a poor man. I sought wealth. Is that so very contemptible? I had no share in Chinese politics.'

'And me?'

'My master made me abandon you. You were there.'

Sao delicately picked up a single small morsel of meat in her foodsticks and conveyed it to her mouth. 'You exposed me to much hardship.'

'This I know. Wang Lu-ching told me of it.'

'Wang Lu-ching,' she sneered, 'His head will roll, together with that of his master. But Ho-shen will lose more than his head. He made me suffer the bastinado. Do you understand that?'

Robert swallowed, at once from a vision of this exquisite creature stretched naked on the ground to be beaten by rods, no doubt in public, as in an understanding that his personal danger was far from over. 'I have seen it.'

'Should I not have you also given a hundred strokes?'

Robert gazed into her eyes. 'It is in your power to do so.'

Sao's nostrils dilated. 'Then he threw me out into the street. I was forced to sell my body, to live.'

'Do you not think I dreamed of you every night?'

'Do you know what I dreamed of?' she asked him. 'I dreamed of having you bound naked before me. That is what I dreamed of, while I submitted to every insult a woman may suffer.' She smiled, but it was not a pleasant smile. 'Am I not fortunate? At least a part of my dream has come true.'

'You have surely been fortunate in more than that,' Robert said. 'I see you famous and powerful.'

'Am I not the most beautiful woman you have ever beheld, Barrington?'

'Without question.'

'Others also believe this. Cheng Yi saw me, and bought me, and loved me so much he made me his wife. He is a *man*, where you are a crawling thing.'

'And with him you sought revenge on all China.' He was desperate to keep her talking, because he did not dare suppose what might be going to happen when she stopped.

'On all the Manchu,' Sao corrected. 'And those who support them. The White Lotus will be the salvation of China. You have eaten enough.' Before he could move, his arms were seized by the eunuchs. 'My dream was to hear you scream as I cut away your manhood,' Sao told him.

'My God! Sao . . .'

She waved her hand, and he was stretched on his back, on the floor beside the table, and held there by eight of the eunuchs, two to each arm and each leg. They grinned at him in anticipation as two more stripped him of his pants.

Sao got up to stand above him, one leg on either side of him as she looked down at him. 'It is the custom, in China,' she said. 'That before a man is cropped, he is allowed one last hour of pleasure. I extend this privilege even to you, Barrington. I will enjoy you one last time.'

Sao's eyes seemed to shroud him, as she looked down at him.

Despite his fear, he had an erection, and he was sure he remained the biggest man she had ever seen.

She smiled. 'You understand that I must milk you dry, Barrington.'

'I understand,' he gasped, as she let her clothes fall to the floor.

One of the eunuchs hurried away and returned with a loudly ticking clock; the others watched her with interest – what emotions the sight of a naked woman might arouse in their breasts was impossible to suppose. Again she stood astride him. 'Am I not still the most beautiful of women, Barrington?'

'You are more beautiful than I remember.' Which was no lie. She was a mature woman, with heavy breasts and welcoming thighs.

'Then make me wish to receive you.' She knelt above his face, and he responded with all the vigour he could summon, endeavouring not to think of the eunuchs. Sao sighed her pleasure. 'I am remembering, too,' she murmured, and slid back down his body, to sit on his thighs and take him into herself, moving up and down. Pinned to the floor as he was, he could do little himself.

Her orgasm was as tumultuous as he recalled as well, especially as he was deliberately holding back as long as possible. This was partly to prolong his manhood, and partly to give himself time to dissuade her. She had not yet made a final decision about him, he was sure. Equally she had not yet made a final decision about the remainder of the crew ... He remembered Cheng Yi's keen interest in the ship.

Sao gave a last sigh, and subsided, shoulders bowed, hair trailing on his belly. Then she dismounted to sit beside him, and looked at the clock. 'Ten minutes,' she remarked, 'and you have dwindled. I must restore you.'

'You have done this before?'

'When I walked the streets I was often paid to give a man his last hour of pleasure. But they were mostly boys who knew nothing, and they were afraid. Are you afraid, Barrington?'

Her fingers began to slide over him. 'Yes,' he said.

'What is there to be afraid of? Oh, the knife is sharp, but you will be given opium to smoke before the cut. Then there is a difficult period, admittedly. You swell, you see, so that you cannot piss. This means you cannot drink, or your bladder would burst. But, unless there is some infection, the swelling should go down in three days.'

'And if there is an infection?'

She shrugged, daintily. 'Then you die. But it is pointless to consider that. Once you can piss, the wound will heal, and you will then be able to remain for the rest of your life in my personal employ. Your last sexual memory will be of being in me ... Now, you will soon be ready again.' She continued to play with him, her fingers gently insistent. 'Tell me what you are thinking of, Barrington.'

He was running out of time. 'I think of you and me on my ship, sailing across the ocean.'

'You promised me that once before,' she reminded him, her strong hands closing suddenly to cause him to gasp.

'I have my own ship now,' he told her. 'I can take you anywhere in the world.'

'What of storms, and rocks, and sea monsters?'

'The *Alceste* sailed to the East all the way from England. That is many thousands of miles. She has sailed through many storms already. As for sea monsters, I have sailed the oceans since the age of twelve, and never seen one capable of destroying a ship.' Sao had stopped manipulating him. 'But I could scarcely command such a vessel to your satisfaction, if cropped,' he added.

'What use have I for your ship?' she asked. 'Are there not junks for me to use?'

'The *Alceste* can outsail any junk,' Robert claimed. 'And under my command, it can outfight any junk as well. What will you do when the Emperor sends his armies against you?'

'Has my husband not defeated all the armies in Shensi?' she demanded.

'Provincial levies. You may be sure that when he learns of the fall of Hankow, the Emperor will throw the full might of the Banner armies against you.'

'Then we will defeat them also.'

'You cannot be certain of that, Sao. And if you are defeated, and taken before the Emperor, or Ho-shen, what do you suppose your fate will be? The death of a thousand cuts – no doubt after you had been given to every man in his army.' Sao bared her teeth. 'While, should you be victorious, will you not then wish to advance down the river, to Nanking and the sea?

For that you will need a fighting ship, an admiral. You will *need* me, Sao.'

Her expression was difficult to fathom, but he was sure he had made some impression. 'You could be my admiral in more than that,' she murmured. Then she waved the eunuchs away.

*

He had won a respite – for himself and for Tommy and the rest of the crew. How much more than that, he could not at that moment be sure. But even if he had saved them all from the knife, their position remained precarious. All of his dreams had come tumbling to the ground. Far from collecting a thousand taels, he had lost his hundred: his sea-chest had been thoroughly looted by the rebels who boarded the brigantine. He had also tied his fate to a woman whose beauty was only equalled by her bloodthirstiness. He could not doubt that if they were defeated by the Manchu, his execution would hardly be less slow and painful than her own.

More even that this, it had been the Manchu realm which seemed destined to make his fortune, not this chaos that lurked beneath. But at least he was alive – and intact. He was allowed to return to the ship, with Tommy, and make her ready for sea under orders from Sao. The *Alceste* was now permanently garrisoned by some twenty White Lotus soldiers, and the crew's own weapons had all been removed, save of course for the cannon, which the Chinese regarded with suspicion. They had never seen any guns so large, for although Chinese armies had long used artillery, these had always consisted of light field-pieces. However, Barrington abandoned any idea of attempting to regain command and make a break for freedom; even had he succeeded, the White Lotus army had spread some miles down-river, and would recapture him the first time he stopped. Although he had taken careful note of Yun Kai-lu's pilotage on the ascent, he still knew that without a pilot the descent would prove a slow business.

*

But once he had reconciled himself to the fact that he had inadvertently become a rebel, Robert's natural ebullience reasserted itself. He had grown to know Hankow quite well during his wait for Ho-shen's arrival, and where before the Chinese had looked at him askance, as being a creature of the hated prime minister, now that he was in the service of the White Lotus, and General Cheng Yi, he found himself welcomed with smiles. The people of Hankow, he quickly understood, did not expect their present good fortune to continue – after all, life was but a catalogue of misfortune – but they were prepared to enjoy their freedom from governmental control as long as it lasted.

Hankow and the area around it had degenerated into anarchy, but it was a happy anarchy. The people had had their moment of savage euphoria, when the Manchu and any Chinese suspected of supporting them had been hacked to pieces – men, women and children, their bodies horrifyingly mutilated. Then they had settled down a bit. The White Lotus might have ideas on forming a government, but for the moment they seemed too elated by their triumph to worry about things like laws and taxes. True, Cheng Yi strode the streets of the city frowning, and he harangued his fellow generals at every opportunity. But though he might have led the final assault on the city, he remained only one amongst several leaders, and any one of his equals could countermand his orders.

Cheng Yi was indeed an interesting character. In his middle thirties, he was therefore hardly older than Robert himself. The son of a wealthy merchant who had also been a soldier, he had grown up with bitter enmity against the Manchu ruling elite. Chinese philosophy had set the pragmatic principle by which these people lived: when an adversary proved too strong, all sensible men submitted, because the conquerors were obviously favoured by the gods; but equally, when a government proved weak or corrupt, it was the duty of all true men to rise against it and replace it, because the gods had abandoned that government. The White Lotus Society insisted that with the abdication of the Ch'ien-lung Emperor the Ch'ing were no longer capable of ruling, and had thus forfeited the Mandate of Heaven. In fact, Cheng Yi did not seem to care much for any philosophy save his own. Undoubtedly he saw himself as the creator of a new dynasty, once the Manchu were destroyed, and with his dominating personality he was well fitted for such ambition. But he simply had no idea how to turn this triumphant rabble into an army, much less organise it into a nation.

Fortunately for all, the tradition of the Chinese civil service, created centuries before and carefully handed down from examination to examination, was capable of withstanding any number of shocks and upheavals, as it had so often done in the past. Thus taxes continued to be collected – on a diminished scale since any landlords convicted of supporting the Manchu had their properties razed – and laws continued to be administered, save where they had been inflicted by the Manchu. For instance, most of the male inhabitants of Hankow followed the example of the rebels and promptly cut off their hated pigtails.

But Cheng Yi knew as well as did Barrington, that a mere continuation of the status quo was not going to secure the day when the full might of the Banner army was eventually launched against him. Thus he fretted, and consulted with his wife. For Cheng Yi Sao never doubted that her personal star would remain in the ascendant. Her confidence was infectious. It was also so practical and earthy that it offended many of her fellows. The leading members of the White Lotus Society were genuine patriot fathers, who believed in the purity of the Confucian ideal, often confused by a leaning towards Buddhism which had been the mainspring of the original secret society many centuries before. Thus, to be led into battle by a woman waving a sword seemed a negation of all they held valuable, and they suspected that the very tenets of their rebellion were being undermined. Their sense of Confucian discipline was outraged by her colourful presence.

But Sao could do no wrong in the eyes of the common people who ran behind her banner. She was the embodiment of the spirit of anarchy which lurks deep in the subconscious of every Chinese, more than in any other people – perhaps because their surface lives had to be lived to so rigid a code.

More importantly, Sao could do no wrong in the eyes of the Society's leading general – her own husband. One had to look no further than her flashing eyes, her swelling breasts, her tumultuous thighs, to understand why Cheng Yi had plucked her from the street. But to understand why he had raised her to such visible eminence, when a woman's true place was in the home, one had to study the personalities of the pair. Cheng Yi was an ambitious revolutionary, but was bedevilled by a streak of realism which left him prey to moods of pessimism and depression, when the smallest task became for him a huge mountain to be laboriously scaled. He had apparently suffered from this problem all his life – until Sao had come to his rescue with her bubbling, often angry confidence. Thus she had largely inspired the revolt, as she now inspired its continuation. But Sao valued little the teachings of Confucius. For her, life had been a struggle from birth. She sought only two things now: revenge on those who had wronged her, and all the wealth and pleasure she could obtain.

In these ambitions she was encouraged by Cheng Yi, content to draw his strength from her. Thus he offered no objections when she summoned Robert to her bed, time and again. Or when the boy Tommy was similarly honoured. But Barrington knew exactly how precariously their lives hung – by the desire of this woman.

But what desire! Did she not surpass his wildest dreams in her eroticism, which combined the subtle seductiveness of the Chinese character with the willing obscenity of the prostitute? He attended her only when she called for him, and left promptly when she dismissed him. He had never thought to find himself in so dangerously humiliating a position. Yet it did not take him long to realise that Sao, however humble her origins, was more intelligent than her husband, and more far-seeing. She knew only too well that the success of the rebellion was a fleeting moment. And she had every intention of escaping the calamity she could see looming, in order to continue successfully her own personal career. In suggesting one way to do this, Robert had touched a very responsive chord.

But Cheng Yi Sao was also a woman. She was not yet twenty years old, but she had the instincts of maturity surging in her veins. Above all, she wanted a child – and this was the one ambition she could not realise. Perhaps it had to do with the abortion she had been forced to undergo while a prostitute, in order to keep earning. Now she made a not uncommon mistake and assumed that Robert, because of his phallic size, must necessarily be able to impregnate her. But he could not accomplish the impossible, no matter how many evil-tasting herbs Sao consumed, and no matter how outlandish the positions she tried in the belief that could he but penetrate far enough, impregnation was certain.

As she never lost faith in eventual success, he supposed that there had never been a captive who enjoyed more physical pleasure than himself. He was given the best to eat and drink, and his only duties were to keep his ship ready for sea or to repair to his mistress's bed when she summoned him. His only anxiety was the possible anger of her husband, but Cheng Yi regarded his wife's foibles with benevolent unconcern.

*

Yet Robert could not help but wonder what the future held, as spring bloomed into summer, and summer once again into winter, until it was over a year since the *Alceste* had cautiously entered the Yangtse-Kiang with Yun Kai-lu in command. Presumably in Calcutta they had long been given up for lost.

Well, he thought, were they *not* lost, just as surely as if they had gone to the bottom in a typhoon? He had little hope of any of them again seeing England. Indeed, his seamen had entirely abandoned that prospect. Several of them had taken native wives, and they spent more time ashore than confined on the brigantine – but no one objected. While Tommy had entirely fallen into the ways of the palace; Robert sometimes wondered if Sao was grooming him as a replacement for himself, should he grow old and feeble. Only Armstrong the boatswain kept himself aloof from Chinese ways, since he seldom left the brig, and brooded continually on their situation. For them all, only survival mattered, and this remained precarious. It seemed even more so in the summer of 1796, when Sao, having held what was virtually a slave market, chose a six-year-old boy named Bao to adopt as her son.

'Then I am a failure,' Robert said.

Sao smiled. 'Never a failure, Barrington. You warm my bed as no man has ever done. But I must look to the future.'

Robert was not absolutely sure what she meant by that, but shortly afterwards the news they had all been waiting for arrived: the Ch'ien-lung Emperor was dead.

*

The death of an emperor was an event of enormous significance throughout China quite apart from the change of ruler. No emperor could be buried until a day decided by the court astrologers, and this day could be as much as a year in the future.

Then the period of mourning lasted twenty-seven months.
Throughout this period no one was allowed to marry; the dead
were interred with less than proper ceremony; no babies could
be named.

No one seemed to know the appropriate law in the case of an
emperor who had already abdicated, but in any event the
people of Hankow were not inclined to take much notice of
what was happening in Peking. Cheng and his associates were
merely relieved that the man they had feared more than any
other was now dead. Only Ho-shen remained. But then news
arrived that Ho-shen had been dismissed from all his offices by
the new emperor, and in addition had been forced to commit
suicide. 'Now is our revolution triumphant,' Cheng Yi declared.

'It is a pity,' Sao said wistfully. 'I had dreamed of cropping
him with my own hands.'

Cheng continued, 'And now that the Ch'ien-lung Emperor is
dead, we are surely safe. This new man lacks the strength of
purpose of his father. The Manchu empire will collapse, and we
will create our own empire here in Shensi. I do not think we
have any further need for the barbarian ship.'

'I will consider what is best to do,' Sao said.

*

Robert tried to influence Sao's thinking one last time. 'If you
have no further need of us, will you not permit us to return to
our homes?' he ventured.

'Ha,' Sao commented. 'We will see.'

He had to be content with that for the time being, but within
another month the entire situation changed again, as news
arrived in Hankow that a vast Banner army was being assembled by the Chia-ch'ing Emperor, to march on Shensi
Province and deal with the White Lotus once and for all.

'You said we would now have several years of peace,' Sao
reminded her husband.

'I do not understand it. Kao Tsung Shun Huang-ti is dead. The
Chia-ch'ing Emperor has long been known as no more than a
sot and a womaniser.'

'He is also a fool,' Sao declared. 'We will defeat him, even as
we defeated his father.'

'His father's troops were commanded by Ho-shen,' Cheng

pointed out. '*This* will perhaps be someone who has the stomach to fight.'

'Bah,' Sao commented. 'Then,' she grinned. 'But now we shall go to war!'

Her confidence made Cheng Yi again a happy, confident man. War and bloodshed were all he really understood. Sao, for all her bold words, became more reflective when she regarded her adopted son.

'Why do you not remain here, and let the men do the fighting?' Robert suggested..

'No, I must be there.' Sao glanced at him. 'And you must be there as well, Barrington.'

'Me? I am a sailor, not a soldier.'

'It will be of value to you to learn how also to be a soldier. Besides, I wish to be sure your ship remains here, just in case we need her.'

'I will be here, Sao.'

She smiled. 'You will be with me, where you belong.'

*

'There is nothing I can do,' he told Armstrong. 'However, I believe our captivity may be coming to an end. The White Lotus are confident of victory. Should they win, the Chengs will have no further use for us.'

'And will then chop off our heads.'

'I do not think they will do that now. It is the event of their being defeated that we must consider. Jim ... I want you to listen to me very carefully. Every man capable of bearing arms is to be conscripted; that includes the guards on our ship. I want you to keep the ship ready for sea, but make no move until I return, or until you receive news of the defeat of the White Lotus. Should you receive such news, you will leave Hankow immediately, and slip down river. I wish you to move no more than five miles a day, for a week. You have the cannon, and I am going to see that your hand weapons are returned to you. Drift down for five miles each day, and then anchor. I will find you.'

'What about the women?'

'Let the men take their wives, certainly.'

'And if you do not return within that week?'

'If I have not come to you by the end of the week following news of a White Lotus defeat, then make sail and leave China. The ship will be yours.' He clapped the boatswain on the shoulder. 'But I have every intention of returning.'

*

With his usual determination to live life to the full, Barrington found himself quite looking forward to accompanying a Chinese army to war. But it was not an euphoria that he retained very long. Discipline was entirely lacking in the White Lotus army, which merely advanced in the direction indicated by its generals. As there were no uniforms, it was impossible to distinguish the soldiers from the camp followers who surrounded them, varying from women of all ages to young boys proudly swaggering behind the multicoloured banners which fluttered in the breeze.

Accompanying the humans was an army of animals, with dogs and pigs predominating, but the presence of food on the hoof did not prevent this host from absorbing any living creature encountered on its march. There was no sense of order or justice. Thus a sergeant might strike off the head of a soldier he found raping a woman, but only to obtain the use of the woman for himself. The women thus savaged came mainly from the gentry class, for whom the White Lotus seemed to find no ill-treatment severe enough; there was something singularly obscene about a woman with a lily foot, and all the refinements accompanying her status, being ravished in the mud by a group of filthy louts.

Most of the army marched on foot, but horses were provided for the generals, and for Sao. No horse was supplied for Robert, so he walked beside Sao, splashing through the mud of the winter rain, staying close to his mistress because it was the safest place to be. 'Will these people fight?' he asked, when they camped for the night, surrounded by a cacophony of shouts, screams, bellows of anger and wails of despair, barking dogs, bleating sheep, lowing cattle and squawking chickens, exploding fireworks and dripping rain, all of which spread across an area several miles in extent.

'That is what they are here to do,' she pointed out. 'Are you anxious, Barrington? Do not be afraid. The White Lotus never loses.' Even by Sao's standards that was stretching the truth a little. But confidence continued to run high, even as the conditions grew worse. The advance continued.

Robert attempted to ascertain what, if any, were the differing components of the army, but that proved futile. There were some small cannon, for sure, but they were not organised into batteries. There was a sprinkling of muskets, but again these were not coordinated into regiments or companies. Most of the men were armed with swords or spears, but they all followed whichever of the generals took their fancy. It was at least reassuring to see that so many wished to march beneath the banner of General Cheng, but whether on his account or that of his wife, Barrington could not be sure. He could only feel increasingly certain that the moment that rabble found itself opposed to any disciplined force, it would be destroyed.

*

The campaign, if it could so be called, continued into the spring, and then the early summer. This was because both armies moved so very slowly. The White Lotus might flood forward like an irresistible wave for two or three days at a time; then it necessarily came to a halt as it foraged for food, or systematically looted a town, or simply stopped from exhaustion. Each halt could last a fortnight.

The imperial army had obviously been commanded not to give battle until it was concentrated, and this was a long and slow business, as the Banners needed to be assembled from garrison duty all over this vast country. Yet it was clear that both sides meant to destroy the other. Barrington had no idea what the Manchu feelings might be, but the White Lotus forces were motivated by a confidence which he continued to suspect was wholly unfounded.

There was no one to whom he could convey his fears, for he was regarded entirely as Sao's creature, almost as her toy. But to suggest to her, during their increasingly rare moments alone together, that this huge unwieldy mass might trip over its own feet, would either make her laugh or make her angry, and he was in no position to risk antagonising her.

At last, during one of their interminable halts, some foragers hurried back to where the main White Lotus army was sprawled, to report having sighted a forest of banners some ten miles away. Thus close had the Manchu army been able to approach undetected; for the White Lotus had no cavalry to reconnoitre with, nor any idea of how to utilise one.

Instantly there was a great deal of pugnacious enthusiasm. Bugles blew, firecrackers exploded, men scurried to and fro, women chattered in high-pitched voices.

'Call them out!' Cheng Yi was shouting. 'Call them out, and let us destroy the enemy.'

Robert realised he intended to fight there and then. 'Sao,' he yelled, grasping her arm as she was about to swing into the saddle. 'You must at least make a reconnaissance.'

She looked at him. 'What do you mean?'

'You must send people to inspect the enemy position, to estimate his numbers and dispositions, and his weaponry.'

'Bah!' Cheng Yi declared. 'We have come here to destroy them.'

'It will be easier done if you know his dispositions, Great Cheng,' Robert insisted.

'I think he is right,' Sao said. 'I will go and see.'

'You?' her husband demanded.

'Who else will know what to look for. But Barrington will accompany me. Find him a horse.'

A mount was brought, and Robert, who was not an expert horseman, clung on for dear life as Sao cantered away from the seething mass of the White Lotus army. Only then did he realise that they were the only two in the reconnoitring party. But there was nothing more to be done; there were insufficient horses to mount any adequate protective force.

The weather was dry, although the river alongside which they rode had not yet fallen to any great extent, Robert noted with some satisfaction. He had no doubt they were going to need it, and very shortly. They saw little in the way of people or animals; although they rode through two villages, these had already been looted and destroyed – the stench of death was everywhere. Some very extensive fields had not even been planted.

'Will this land ever recover?' Robert asked, when Sao drew rein before a low rise.

'This land always recovers.' She glanced at him. 'Are you still afraid, Barrington?' Laughing, she kicked her horse, then tugged on the rein again. On the hill in front of them had appeared half a dozen horsemen. Even at a distance they could make out lances with red pennons.

'Bannermen,' Sao growled, loosening her sword in its scabbard.

'We had better get out of here,' Barrington protested. They both carried pistols and swords, but he did not like the odds.

Sao hesitated, always spoiling for a fight, then wheeled her horse and rode off. The Bannermen did not give chase, and as soon as they were out of sight, Sao reined again. 'Do you suppose they are from the main Manchu army?'

'Yes,' Robert said. 'Listen!'

Even over the heavy panting of their horses they could hear a tremendous *seethe* in the distance. 'That rise,' Sao decided, and set off at a gallop. Robert followed more slowly, expecting to see further Manchu troops at any moment. But they gained the hillock unmolested, and gazed down on the plain. It was almost obliterated beneath the moving banners: blue and bordered blue, white and bordered white, red and bordered red, yellow and bordered yellow. Beneath the banners themselves rode thousands of horsemen, advancing in squadrons. Skirmishers rode perhaps half a mile before the main force, and behind the mounted Bannermen followed the masses of conscript infantry, marching beneath their green flags.

Robert glanced at Sao, who stared at the approaching mass with her mouth slightly open. Suddenly she shed her aura of battle-tried sophistication and become what she actually was: a very young, startled woman.

'That is the power of the mightiest empire on the face of the earth,' he remarked.

'How many?'

He levelled his glass, brought with him from the ship. Even at this distance he could just discern some of the faces, and isolate the huge multicoloured pennants that flew above the commanding general and his staff. He moved the glass to and fro, identified musket regiments and pikemen, swordsmen and artillerymen ... 'I do not believe there are less than a hundred thousand. Have you any idea how many men we muster?'

'At least as many.'

'But you do not know for certain.'

'Does it matter? We will sweep them aside like chaff.' She

wheeled her horse and set off back down the slope.

Robert galloped alongside her. 'Sao ...' His knee brushed hers as he reached for her bridle and brought both their horses to a halt.

'You are afraid!'

'Yes, I am afraid. Those are professional soldiers.'

'Bannermen!' Her voice filled with contempt.

'Men who know nothing *but* fighting.'

'We will destroy them.'

'Perhaps. But not by marching straight against them.'

'What would you have me do?'

'You must let them come to you. You must make adequate preparations. There is just time. They are committed to attacking you. That is your strength. If you were to set your people to work, and dig a ditch and build a barricade, and remain behind it, and let the Bannermen assault you and be driven back, then you would have a chance.'

'Is this how outer barbarians fight?' Her tone was even more contemptuous.

'Outer barbarians are concerned with winning. That is how they would fight in these circumstances.'

'We will fight as we have always fought.' Her tone softened. 'We have no choice, Barrington. If I put my people behind a barricade, they will simply run away. They can only go forward. Thus we will go forward. We must win, or we will die. It is as simple as that.'

5

THE DRAGON LADY

With a huge hurrah the army of the White Lotus surged forward. It was unlike anything Robert Barrington had ever heard of, much less seen. Cheng Yi merely pointed his sword in the direction indicated by his wife, and the army advanced. There had been no real reconnaissance, no attempt to determine tactics, no orders save the simple one: 'Charge!'

Even more amazingly, in the early stages, the sword-waving men were accompanied by their women and older children and dogs. The women and children soon dropped out as the pace became faster. The dogs continued, barking and snapping.

The rebels topped the rise, and checked for just a moment. This was partly because they were blown from the rapidity of their ascent, but also because of what they now looked at. Their charge had been observed by several enemy mounted patrols, and the Manchu general had had the time to make his dispositions. The Banner army fought as tribes, but each banner floated above a complete division. The spearmen stood in line, with bodies of musketeers at each end – but there were also companies of archers. The cannon – small field pieces – were emplaced before each body. The horsemen waited behind the infantry.

It was a very old-fashioned disposition, and a very static one; the Manchu general had apparently discarded, or not considered, any of the tactics of warfare revealed in Europe by Frederick the Great: the use of masked flank marches or the concentration of superior forces at a given point in the enemy position. No doubt the general knew enough of White Lotus tactics to be sure of his victory. And with reason. As the rebels charged down the slope, firing off their muskets and sending up their fireworks, the guns roared in response. Elevated as high as possible, they sent their shot over the heads of the front ranks, to smash into the thick masses behind. Screams and shrieks

93

filled the air, and soon the firecrackers died away.

The front ranks were now fast approaching the Manchu muskets. But the rebels had long fired their own, and there had been no time to reload. The Bannermen, well disciplined, waited until the enemy were within effective range, a hundred yards, then loosed a volley which proved almost as devastating as the cannon shot. The bullets were accompanied by arrows, in an immense medieval cloud. It seemed one man in three tumbled to the ground, although Robert was sure that only about half were hit, and the remainder were taking evasive action. He felt like doing the same, as he ran beside Sao's horse, his mount having been retrieved by one of the rebel leaders. Now he seemed to be surrounded by a hot wind.

Suddenly Sao's horse sank to its knees, and then collapsed totally. Leaning forward behind her sword, she was pitched from the saddle, and Barrington had to leave the shelter of the fallen beast to seize her by the armpits and drag her back.

'We must advance!' she muttered.

'Would you go to your death?'

He raised his head at the sound of a great roar, and watched the Bannermen advancing at the double, still in ranks, their swords and halberds gleaming in the sun. The rebels had been halted by the volley; now the entire army seemed to tremble, before starting to move backwards. Then the rebels unashamedly turned and ran for their lives.

'Cowards!' Sao shrieked at them, regaining her feet.

Barrington was more concerned with survival. One of the White Lotus generals nearby was still trying to rally his men. Robert swung his sword and cut the fellow from the saddle, then bundled Sao into it and climbed up behind her. The Manchu were very close, but for the moment they had expended their shot. Robert kicked the horse and sent it galloping through the fleeing rebels, bowling men over, left and right. Sao screamed and shrieked imprecations at her erstwhile followers, but she did not object to being rescued.

On the rise Robert drew rein to look back. The Bannermen had swarmed over the first ranks of the rebels, and there stopped, their swords swinging as they decapitated dead and wounded alike. Clearly they had orders to take no prisoners.

He then looked down the reverse slope, where the defeated army was streaming towards the hills in a huge disorganised mass. Perhaps they would rally eventually, but he doubted they would be allowed the time – for the Banner cavalry was now moving forward to take up the pursuit.

Nearer at hand a group of horsemen were approaching. 'It is Cheng Yi,' Sao said with some satisfaction.

'Cheng Yi Sao,' Cheng Yi called out with equal satisfaction as he neared her; even if he seldom visited her bed, he valued her as his ever-faithful support. There were a dozen men at his back; all were mounted although none of them were generals, so Robert had to suppose they had all followed his own example and unseated their superiors to ensure their escape.

'Those fellows have gone to the mountains. We will follow,' Cheng said as he came up.

'With what in mind, excellency?' Robert asked.

'Why, to rally them, and lead them back to battle.'

'Even if they followed you after such a rout, would they not be defeated again?'

'I believe Barrington is right,' Sao said. 'The revolution is over, at least with those people. We must save our own lives.'

'And how do we do that, if we do not go with our friends?'

'We will go to Hankow.'

'Hankow? That is the first place they will look for us.'

'But when they come, we will no longer be there.' She looked over her shoulder and smiled at Robert.

*

Robert had not confided his plan even to Sao. For one thing, he did not know if Armstrong had been able to carry it out; for another, he was sure these people would be far more impressed by his organisation when it was revealed, than if they were made aware in advance. He suggested that the quickest way to return to Hankow was by proceeding along the riverbank, and the Chengs did not argue with this.

It was still necessary to make haste, however, especially as Sao naturally insisted upon returning to the encampment to regain Bao. If the main Manchu cavalry had gone in pursuit of the fleeing rebels, this group of horsemen on the hill had been spotted, and a squadron of mounted men was already moving towards them. Bao was found deserted by his attendants, which drove Sao into a fury. While she was threatening vengeance,

Barrington hunted around and found half a dozen rockets which had not been discharged; he tucked them into his belt. Then they kicked their mounts and forced them on.

*

For the next few days they played a kind of hide-and-seek with their pursuers, being seldom more than a few hours ahead of them.

'We are lost,' Cheng groaned. 'While we are trying to escape, they will have already sent horsemen direct to Hankow. They will have taken your ship by now.'

'Trust me,' Robert told him.

Wherever they were forced to ride, he regained contact with the river at least once in every day. It was on the fourth day after the battle that he came upon the *Alceste* anchored in a bend, out of the mainstream, and off a sandy beach. He was alone at the time; his companions were sheltering in a burned-out village. Robert headed down to the water's edge, and waved his tricorne. After a few minutes a boat put out and came towards the shore.

'Thank God!' Armstrong himself was at the tiller. 'We had all but given up on you.'

'There are a dozen of us,' Robert told him. 'I will fetch them now. Prepare to raise anchor. Are your guns loaded?'

'My guns have been loaded from the day you left, Mr Barrington.'

Robert nodded. 'I will return at dawn tomorrow morning. I'll signal my approach with a single rocket. When you see that, put down a boat for us. But you yourself remain on board to command the guns. Make sure they are loaded with grape. Aim them at the top of that embankment, then depress them to cover the slope beneath it. Open fire when I wave my sword. You understand?'

Armstrong nodded. He looked unhappy about having to delay another night, but he and his men returned to the ship, and Barrington made off to find the Chengs' party.

They listened in consternation as he told them the ship was only a few miles away. 'You have tricked us,' Sao snarled.

'How so? Had I meant to trick you, would I not just have boarded my ship and sailed off down the river, leaving you to your fate?'

'Why, that is true,' she smiled. 'You are my very faithful Barrington. Let us make for your ship.'

*

As they walked their horses through the darkness, they could hear the whisper of the water as the black night turned to dawn. Then also could be heard the jingle of harnesses.

'Halt!' Cheng snapped.

They waited in silence, and saw the shadows of some forty horsemen proceeding beside the embankment.

'We are lost,' Cheng muttered.

'We wait until they are past,' Sao said.

'We cannot,' Robert pointed out. 'They will see the ship, and either attempt to seize her, or remain between us and her. We must charge through them.'

Sao hugged Bao against her breast. 'It is too risky.'

'Twelve against forty!' Cheng pulled his moustache.

'Twenty-four,' Robert said. 'There are twelve men on board the ship, and they have cannon.' He lit the rocket, and a moment later it arced into the steadily lightening sky.

The Bannermen saw the flaming projectile, and turned in their saddles. But the Chengs were already charging, swords drawn, screaming their defiance, Bao hanging on for dear life with both arms round his foster-mother's waist.

Taken by surprise, the Bannermen had barely the time to draw their own swords before the Chengs had burst through them. Two men fell from their horses, but none of the rebels was hurt. Then they were sliding down the embankment towards the beach. It was daylight now, and the ship was clearly visible. So was the boat – which had put out the moment the rocket was sighted – manned by six men, and it was already close to the beach.

'It cannot take us all,' Sao gasped as she dismounted.

'Not this time. You go first, with the boy.' Robert was relieved to observe that Armstrong had remained on board, in accordance with his orders.

'You must come, too,' Sao insisted.

Robert looked at Cheng. Behind them the Bannermen were regrouping to charge. 'We will be quite safe,' he promised, and waved his sword, as the Bannermen urged their horses down the slope. The six cannon in the starboard broadside exploded; as Robert had instructed, they had been loaded with grapeshot, and the hail of bullets swept into the Bannermen, scattering them left and right. Sao gave a shout of joy, as she boarded the boat, with Bao and six of her followers.

Cheng and Robert and the remaining four men faced the shore. This was actually the most dangerous moment. The cannon had been fired, and although at least half the Bannermen had been struck down, the rebels were still outnumbered three to one.

But the Bannermen had suffered enough, and withdrew to the shelter of the embankment. One or two had muskets, but the range was too great to be effective. Within ten minutes the small boat was back, and five minutes later they were all safely on board.

'A west wind,' Robert said. 'What more could we ask for.'

*

From his point of view, nothing. Because *he* was now in command. The Chengs knew nothing about ships and the sea, or even the river. They gazed in awe at the way the brigantine was handled as she slipped downstream, urged by both wind and current. They shrieked in terror as inevitably she ran aground in mid-morning, and gasped their admiration as two boats were put down to tow her off. Equally did they stare at the cannon which had rescued them, so much larger than the field pieces used by the Chinese armies.

'Barrington?' Sao asked. 'Are we safe?'

'Safer than we were,' Robert told her.

*

There remained a very long journey ahead of them, but they were well in front of the Banner army, which was still engaged in pursuing the fleeing rebels into the mountains; and it was some time before any effective force tried to follow them. By then they had a start of several days.

The news of Ho-shen's fall was of course known the length of the river, and there was no longer any welcome for them on that score. They still encountered villagers sympathetic to the

White Lotus cause, but even so, haste was imperative. Only one serious attempt was made to stop them before the Grand Canal, when they anchored for the night just upstream from Nanking. During the darkness several sampans, filled with armed men, put out from the shore. But luckily there was a moon, and Barrington and Armstrong saw them coming. The guns were run out, and two of the boats were hit, causing them to capsize, throwing their crews into the water amidst a chorus of shrieks and yells. The remaining sampans quickly withdrew.

*

It was necessary to buy food from various villages they passed, but Cheng had a saddlebag well filled with silver coin, so this presented no difficulties as long as the money lasted. If a local mayor refused to sell, he could always be overawed by the guns; a single roundshot directed at the nearby houses invariably brought capitulation. They also experienced the usual problem of grounding with monotonous regularity as the summer drew on and the river fell. There were windstorms and thunderstorms, dragging anchors and leaking seams, days and sometimes weeks when the wind blew from the east – but going downriver it was worth towing the brigantine even into the wind. Nothing stopped their progress, and the Chengs daily grew in admiration for the way the English seamen coped with every mishap, enthusiastically assisted by the nine Chinese wives who had elected to accompany them.

Meanwhile every day took them closer to the open sea. 'Where do you wish to go?' Robert asked Sao, who stood beside him on the poop to watch the pagoda roofs of Chinkiang rising out of the plain, with the entrance to the Grand Canal on their left.

'Where can we go, Barrington? We are outlaws.'

'Well ...' He checked as Armstrong came up the ladder.

'Begging your pardon, Mr Barrington,' the boatswain said. 'But what do you make of that fellow?'

Robert peered at the large junk which had been sheltering in the Canal, and was now being propelled out into the stream by its sweeps. Its masts were covered with banners and pennants, its decks were crowded with men, while there were some twenty guns in its broadside. 'That is a war junk,' Sao said.

Cheng came hurrying up. 'We are lost!' He was a most confoundedly pessimistic fellow, Robert thought.

But Sao was also alarmed. 'What are we to do, Barrington?'

'Run out the guns, Mr Armstrong,' Robert commanded.

'You mean to fight it?' Cheng was concerned.

'We have no alternative.'

'But it is so much bigger.'

'We have the wind, and the speed. Take the helm, Mr Armstrong.' He went down into the waist to check the guns. He had to judge their elevation blind, as he did not yet possess a target. But he could envisage the height of the junk at the moment of passing. 'You had best go below,' he told Cheng and Sao. 'They will certainly fire into us.'

'I wish to stay and watch,' Sao said, but she sent Bao below. Cheng felt obliged to stay on deck with his wife, although he was clearly very nervous.

Robert sent up the topsails, as the wind was fair. He knew he was risking everything; if they went aground carrying full canvas they would probably lose their masts, which would finish them. But his nerves were tingling with excitement, and confidence ... this was his element, where he had not known what he was about, on land. And more than that: if he won now, the Chengs would be eating out of his hand.

The *Alceste* gathered speed and, for all the weed trailing from her bottom, was making several knots through the water, and considerably more than that over the ground, as she was urged on by the current. The war junk, still stationary, was held facing upstream, against the current, by her sweeps, but unable to manoeuvre with any ease. More than twice the size of the brigantine, her captain seemed to feel that her mere presence would bring the barbarians to a halt.

'Stand by,' Armstrong called, and Robert checked his sights once again, before looking over the bulwarks. There was a great deal of activity on the junk's decks, but this seemed more agitated than positive, as the brigantine bore down on her.

The slow matches were burning, and Robert, peering through the forward of the ports, saw the bulk of the Chinese ship come into view. 'Hold your fire!' he bellowed, as the junk's guns belched smoke. Where the Manchu balls went he had no idea, but they were clearly aimed too high. Although the mainsail took a couple of rents, no damage was done on deck.

And now the whole ship was in his sight. 'Fire!' he yelled. The *Alceste* rolled away from the explosion, but the iron balls were already speeding on their way to smash into the timbers of the junk. One of the Chinese guns was dismounted, and another ball sent the helmsman and his mate sprawling on the deck, their heads taken off. Two more smashed sweeps, which were abandoned by their panic-stricken oarsmen, and the junk, now out of control, turned broadside on to the stream.

The *Alceste* was now well past her, but the river was broad and deep at this point. 'Bring her about, Mr Armstrong!' he shouted. Armstrong hesitated a moment, then brought the helm up, while the crew manned the sheets.

'What are you doing?' Cheng screamed, as the brigantine turned in almost her own length to face upstream.

Robert and Tommy were running to and fro the length of the deck, making sure the port guns were properly sighted; Robert wanted them depressed to aim at the waterline. 'Settling that fellow,' he panted.

The crew of the junk had realised what was happening, but drifting sideways as they were, and with both the helm and the sweeps unmanned, only their empty port broadside was available. Some of them were trying desperately to reload the guns, others were fleeing to the starboard side in terror.

Round came the *Alceste*. 'Steady,' Robert called, summoning the seamen back to man the slow matches. 'Steady.' The brigantine seethed through the water, close-hauled, until she was as well ranged as Robert could estimate. 'Helm down!' he roared.

Armstrong responded immediately, and the *Alceste* came about again. As she did so, Robert gave the order to fire. The six balls smashed into the hull of the junk, just on the waterline. Instantly the big ship began to list, while the shrieks of the crew were echoed by the watchers on the shore.

'It is sinking!' Sao cried, jumping up and down.

'Man your braces,' Armstrong bellowed, and Robert himself freed a sheet to loose the mainsail as the brigantine gathered way downstream. Then he could stand at the taffrail, with Cheng and Sao, to watch the junk slowly settling, while her crew leapt into the river.

'Barrington,' Sao observed, 'you are the victor.'

*

There were no further attempts to stop them, and only a few days later they spied the roofs of Shanghai, and then the islands. Robert opted to drop anchor overnight and wait for the dawn land breeze to make their final escape. The Chinese were all on deck as the anchor was raised and the brigantine left the estuary – and exclaimed in terror as, for the first time in their lives, they gazed at a stretch of water which had no visible far bank. 'Where is the other side?' Cheng inquired.

'Roughly eighteen thousand li away,' Robert told him. Cheng stared at him in disbelief. 'So tell me where you wish to go.'

Sao leaned on the rail to watch the receding shore. 'How will you know where we are,' she asked, 'when you have lost sight of land?'

'I have my sextant to give me my latitude, and my chronometer to give me my longitude, and also my charts. The charts are not very accurate, to be sure, but I can manage.'

'It is wonderful.' She pointed. 'Are those junks pursuing us?'

They could see a small squadron of ships making north; the wind was still south-west and offshore. 'No, no. They are merchantmen. They are probably bound from Canton to Shanghai.'

'Not Peking?'

'Their cargoes may be bound for Peking, but most likely they will be transhipped in Shanghai or Chin-kiang and taken up the Grand Canal by sampan. Nearly all of China's trade is water-borne, you see. It is quicker and cheaper than trying to cross the mountains. But north of the Yangtse the weather is less certain, which is the reason for the Grand Canal.'

'Could you capture those ships, Barrington, with all their goods?'

Robert frowned at her. 'That would be an act of piracy.'

'It would be most effective in continuing our struggle against the Manchu, would it not? For a country lives by its trade. So if we disrupted that, we would be striking at the Manchu far more severely than merely fighting with their Bannermen.'

Robert scratched his head; he had not supposed to hear such devastating logic. 'I had thought you meant to escape from China,' he ventured.

'So that you could return to *your* people? As what? You would be penniless. This way you can grow rich ... and *then* return to your people.'

Robert stared at the laden junks. He had never thought to become a pirate ... but that had been in Western terms, with the Royal Navy breathing down his neck. There were no Royal Navy ships in these waters, and he was already a rebel in the eyes of the Manchu. He would have been a rebel even if he had succeeded in the original plan of helping Ho-shen to escape. Only then he would have also had a thousand taels in his sea chest.

Sao watched his expression changing, and knew she had won. 'Those ships must not all be sunk,' she said. 'I wish to preserve at least one of them for our use.'

*

Robert gave the orders, and the brigantine altered course towards the merchantmen. These clearly had no idea what was about to happen, and maintained their way until the *Alceste* was close enough to fire into one of them. Robert aimed for the decks, and swept them with roundshot with devastating effect, bringing down two of the three masts, and leaving the junk a hulk, drifting helplessly.

The others now realised their danger, and attempted to scatter, but they had neither the speed nor the manoeuvrability of the brigantine; and, besides, they had been taken entirely by surprise. Barrington went about to present his port broadside to his second victim, this time using grape, so that she was also left drifting, her masts and sails intact, but her decks heaped with dead and dying men. By then his starboard broadside had been reloaded, the Chinese and the women working as hard as any of the seamen, and this time Robert again used grapeshot. His third victim's decks were raked with the flying bullets and those who survived scurried below. In an instant Armstrong had put the brigantine alongside; ropes were carried across and made fast, and the Chinese crew were met with swords and pistols when they attempted to regain the deck.

Sao and Cheng led the boarding party. It was easy to identify the Manchu on board; they did not wear the pigtail. These were unceremoniously thrown over the side. Robert watched this happening with mixed feelings, but they were fighting a war, and they had no facility for taking prisoners.

Sao addressed the Chinese survivors. 'Are you slaves to the Ch'ing,' she demanded, 'or are you prepared to fight like the Men of Han, for the freedom of our country?'

As they could have no doubt as to their fate if they opted for the former, the sailors gave a great shout of acclaim for Madame Cheng.

The other three junks were racing to the north as fast as they could, so Barrington left Armstrong with six of his seamen and six of the Chinese on board the prize to make sure no one changed his mind, and then he sailed the *Alceste* back to the drifting hulk, and hailed the crew, telling them to abandon ship; he no longer had the strength to board.

There was of course a risk that they would open the seacocks before leaving, but they were still terrified by the earlier gunnery, and swarmed down the sides into the boats, where-upon Robert put the *Alceste* alongside. He lacked the men to sail this ship as well, even if he had the time to repair her, so she was thoroughly looted of everything she possessed, including all her powder and any shot which would serve the brigantine's guns, and was set on fire.

He then sailed over to the second junk. She had already been abandoned by her surviving crew, who were rowing for the distant shore as fast as they could. Robert took her in tow, and went after the boats, forcing them to come alongside. Sao made her usual speech, but this time she made the Chinese sailors execute their Manchu masters, so as to involve them fully in the crime. Then the three ships were brought together, and the second junk was looted before being cast adrift, blazing from stem to stern.

*

The success of the action was staggering. Quite apart from the hugely valuable cargo taken out of the three junks – jade, porcelain and even a considerable amount of silver – they had in one afternoon doubled their fleet, and quintupled their forces. 'Now you have a ship of your own,' Robert said.

'Now we have two ships of *our* own,' Sao pointed out. 'It is your ship that matters, Barrington.'

He was snared. Perhaps this was the life he had always dreamed of, and there was more to be made fighting for the Chengs than for England against France, and with less risk.

*

A fortnight later they attacked another northbound group of junks. With Robert in command of the captured junk, and Armstrong of the *Alceste*, they cut out five of the seven, and this time kept two of them, again to double their forces, while again they found a willing response amongst the captured seamen.

The Manchu on board died to a man – or should have done. Having led the boarding party to secure the second vessel, Robert was turning away as usual from the butchery about to take place, when he was checked by a shout. 'Barrington. Have mercy, Barrington!'

He swung back, to see one of the Manchu being dragged to the side by his captors. 'Barrington!' the man screamed.

'Avast there!' Robert roared, recognising the face.

The Chinese checked at his voice, and a moment later he was amongst them, scattering them as he seized the victim from their hands. 'Hui-chan, by all that's holy.'

'Barrington!' His old friend clung to him. 'Save my life.'

'What is this?' Sao demanded, coming up to them. 'You have Manchu friends, Barrington?'

One of the Chinese pointed excitedly. 'He is Hui-chan, Intendant of Kwantung. He has executed many of our people.'

'And he will now die for his crimes,' Sao declared.

'No,' Robert said. 'I have told you of a man who saved my life once in Canton. This is he. Consider the workings of Fate, Sao. Had this man and his family not nursed me back to health, you would not be here now, mistress of the seas.' He knew of Sao's belief in Fate. 'Are your family with you, Hui-chan?' he asked.

Hui-chan pointed to another group of Manchu waiting to be thrown over the side, which included several women and a young boy. Two of the women Robert recognised as being Hui-chan's wife and his eldest daughter. 'I demand the lives of these people, Sao,' he said firmly.

Sao hesitated, then nodded. 'So be it, since they gave you to me, Barrington. Put them in a boat,' she told her sailors.

Hui-chan seized Robert's hands. 'I am forever in your debt.'

'And I am repaying a debt,' Robert reminded him.

'I will never forget this, Barrington. There is a prophecy, as I have told you ...'

'That one day your family will rank the highest in the land.' Robert smiled. 'I should be careful who you say that to, old friend. It could be interpreted as treason.'

'It will happen,' Hui-chan said stubbornly. 'For it has been told in the stars. And when it does, you will be honoured above all other men, Barrington. I swear this upon the souls of my ancestors.'

Robert stood at the rail to watch Hui-chan and his son pulling on the oars as they directed their boat at the shore, while his wife and concubines and daughters prayed in the stern.

*

Their store of shot, at least for the brigantine's guns, was now all but expended. They could secure powder from the captured ships, and ball for the smaller weapons carried by the junks, but these would not fit the *Alceste*'s 24-pounders. Robert was forced to abandon his ship-smashing tactics and depend upon sweeping the decks with charges made up of any scrap iron he could find. But this was effective enough. Over the next month they attacked two more junk squadrons, and captured five more ships. Cheng Yi now commanded a fleet of nine ships and a thousand men. 'This is my destiny,' he told Robert. 'For am I not descended from Cheng Ch'eng-kung, he who the barbarians called Koxinga? Have you heard of him?'

Robert had certainly heard of Koxinga, who had supported the Ming cause against the Manchu in the previous century, refusing to surrender even after the final Ming collapse, and seizing the huge island of Formosa as a principality of his own, before dying in battle. But this was the first time he had heard of his Chinese name. On the other hand, Cheng was a fairly common name amongst the Chinese, and he doubted that Cheng Yi was really a descendant of Koxinga's, even if it was very good propaganda for him to claim that amongst the Chinese.

But in fact, Cheng Yi needed no propaganda beyond the terror of his own name, which was now being whispered from waterfront to waterfront as his raids became more and more successful – enhanced by the presence of the beautiful, blood-thirsty wife always at his side. Sao indeed devised the pirates' banner; where the imperial flag was a red dragon upon a yellow background, the Chengs sailed beneath a yellow dragon on a red background. Soon the very sight of the dragon flag was sufficient to persuade ships to surrender.

Robert was content that it should be so. He was busily accumulating money, which was now his main aim in life. He was also, however, thinking ahead. The Manchu could not submit indefinitely to having their wealth drained through piracy. He knew they were not in themselves a seafaring people, but he also knew they would have to make an effort, for there was no other way for them to come to grips with the Chengs. The pirates had the entire immensely long coastline of China at their mercy. In between raids they would lurk in one of the hundreds of available bays, whether on the mainland, or on one of the many offshore islands. There they careened and repaired their ships; undoubtedly their presence was always quickly discovered, but most of the peasants were their supporters against the hated Manchu, and were more likely to give them information of shipping movements than to betray them to the local governor.

Even when a force of Bannermen was sent against them, they merely raised their anchors and sailed away. When they needed substantial replenishment they would enter a sizeable port and take it over, looting it for whatever they needed, then departing again before the Bannermen could be mobilised. And everything they did enhanced the name of Cheng.

It was during their resting periods that Robert trained them as fighting seamen. Nearly all of them were, in any event, seamen; now Robert taught them how to load and fire their guns, how to take advantage of wind and current even in their unwieldy junks. Above all, he imbued them with the confidence that when the time came they could take on and defeat an imperial fleet.

Cheng and Sao were as enthusiastic pupils as any, and Sao in particular revealed an ability quickly to grasp the principles of seamanship and sea warfare. Soon she was commanding her own ship, with an expertise that almost equalled Robert's own. 'Now you have no further need of me,' he remarked, half in jest.

'I will always have need of you, Barrington,' Sao assured him. But now that was in a purely professional sense. Though she still occasionally summoned him to her bed, there were so many other handsome young men to choose from.

*

The expected clash with a fleet of imperial war junks took place off the mouth of the Yangtse – the pirates' most lucrative hunting ground – in the summer of 1801. It had taken the Manchu over a year to concentrate sufficient ships to hope to gain the day, and Barrington had to confess to a slight feeling of doubt as he saw the imperial squadron, some twenty large vessels, emerging from the mouth of the river. But Cheng Yi's fleet now numbered forty, and several of these were war junks themselves, captured when sailing singly.

More important, the pirate fleet was led by the *Alceste*, and the brigantine had gained a legendary reputation. The battle was won even before it had been properly commenced, as the pirates loaded and fired their cannon at twice the speed of the Manchu gunners. Each pirate ship had been crammed with eager men, and when any two vessels closed, the Bannermen, unused to fighting on the water and fearful of it, were no match for the swarming Chinese.

That night there were great celebrations, as half of the imperial fleet had been taken or sunk, and the rest had gone scuttling back into the river. 'We control China,' Sao declared.

*

It was no idle boast. Within six years, Cheng Yi's pirate fleet had virtually brought all sea-borne trade to a standstill, forcing the Manchu to use the overland routes, which quadrupled the length of any journey and the cost of all goods.

Indeed it seemed as if the entire empire might be about to crumble, for reports from Peking spoke of the Chia-ch'ing Emperor being lost in debauchery and sloth. Now Cheng began to dream of taking his fleet up the Pei-ho and attacking Peking itself. Fortunately Sao possessed a more level head.

'We are winning,' she pointed out, 'by doing what we are doing so well. It is simply a matter of continuing as we are, and waiting for the Manchu to collapse into the dust.'

'And how will we feed our men, expand our conquests, replenish our powder and shot?' Cheng demanded. 'For the number of trading ships using these waters diminishes week by week.'

'We shall go further afield,' Sao told him.

'Ha! *You* will go further afield. I will remain on the China coast, wife, for this is where our future lies.'

'As you wish,' Sao agreed. For however much she might respect her husband, she no longer feared him, and was glad to get away from his moods of alternating confidence and depression.

There was no point in sailing north. That way lay bad weather and an empty ocean, for the Japanese Shogunate had forbidden trade with the outside world, and only a single Dutch ship was allowed into the harbour of Nagasaki every year. But to the south, more and more European ships were appearing on the route to Canton.

'Are you afraid to attack European ships, Barrington?' Sao asked him.

'Providing they are not English ships,' Robert replied. 'And providing you promise there will be no indiscriminate murder. *These* people are not your enemies; they are merchants trying to earn a profit.'

'You have my word that all who surrender will be spared.'

'But they will fight stoutly,' Robert brooded. 'We must change our strategy.'

He took ten ships, including that commanded by Sao, to the islands south-west of Macao. This was where vessels coming up from the south began to close the coast, either for the Portuguese colony or to make the entrance of the Pearl estuary; equally, ships leaving the river mouth passed close by the islands before reaching their offing. Cheng Yi was reluctant to let the *Alceste* accompany them, but Sao insisted, and Cheng was still not capable of withstanding his wife's requirements. Then it was just a matter of waiting, for both the right ship and the right weather. Thus a Portuguese ship was let by, and an Englishman, because the wind was from the east. Robert would have let the Englishman go in any event, but the crews began to grow restive. Robert refused to budge, however, until he sighted a large ship southbound from Macao before a north-westerly wind.

The stranger was several miles off. Although her flags could not be identified at that distance, she was clearly a European vessel, from the cut of her sails, and in the fair light wind she was carrying all the canvas she could set. She was a big ship, too. 'Laden with silk and tea, I'll be bound,' Robert said.

And also, no doubt, fully armed. As he wanted her intact, he had already discussed his plan of campaign with Sao, and she seemed to understand it to perfection. Now the brigantine put to sea, crammed with heavily armed men, but under reduced canvas; this meant she would take longer to be sighted by the stranger, and also that she would not be able to travel very far from the islands – yet when she was sighted, there would be no indication where she had been sheltering.

As their victim came more positively in sight, Robert dropped his sails and allowed his ship to drift to the south, while he waited for the stranger's flags to come into view. He was prepared to abandon the attack should he see the Union Jack, but instead soon identified the Dutch tricolour. He knew that, although Holland had been overrun by the new French Republic, the Dutch East Indies were endeavouring to stay independent. The vessel remained, in his eyes, a legitimate prize.

Now began the most dangerous part of the operation. He had emptied the inflammable material from a large number of fireworks on to his deck, and added to it some oil. This was now fired, carefully monitored by Tommy and the crew. Immediately it produced a huge column of thick black smoke, which rose several hundred feet into the air, and would be easily visible from the approaching ship.

Robert had his people scurrying around as if attempting to dowse the fire. The captain of the approaching Dutchman would see that the apparently burning vessel was European, and he was not likely to leave her to her fate in such inhospit-able waters. He stood on, shortening canvas, and using a minute gun to indicate his intention of effecting a rescue.

The *Alceste* had now drifted some miles south of the islands, and thus, when the pirate junks emerged from the shelter of the land, they were upwind of the stranger and sailing, as junks did, very fast indeed when the wind was free. But the merchantman's sailors did not notice them as they prepared to approach the English brigantine, which still seemed to be burning furiously.

Soon enough she was within hailing distance. 'Ahoy, there!' her captain shouted through his loudhailer, in English. 'Will you abandon ship?'

She was also now within effective cannon range. 'Now's your time, Mr Armstrong,' Robert snapped.

Instantly the fake fires were doused, the gunports were opened, and the six cannon in the broadside run out, to be fired almost on the instant. Loaded as usual with smallshot, the victim's decks were swept, men tumbling about in every direction. No real damage was done, and Robert did not suppose more than half a dozen men had been seriously hurt, but the merchantman was taken by surprise, and before her crew could recover, the last of the smoke had disappeared, the sails had been set, and the *Alceste* was forging ahead to come about.

Robert's aim was to get alongside as soon as possible, not only to allow his superior manpower to count, but to make sure of preserving such a large, powerful ship undamaged. But before then he had to take a broadside, for the merchant crew responded as soon as they had realised they had been hoodwinked. The *Alceste*, by then very close, suffered heavily as the iron balls smashed through her bulwarks, and with a huge crash the foremast went overboard, leaving her unmanageable. But Armstrong had already put the helm over to bring the two ships together, and the victim, whose name could now be discerned as the *Jan Pieter*, out of Amsterdam, was too close to avoid the wreckage, and ploughed into it, coming to a standstill.

Instantly Robert was leading his men over the fallen foremast to gain the forward shrouds of the larger vessel. Sword in hand they climbed on board, while the Dutch sailors hurried to resist them, armed with cutlasses and pistols.

But now they were distracted by shouts from aft, as the captain discovered that ten war junks were bearing down on him. Desperately some of his people began hacking at the cordage with which they were surrounded, but it was far too late. The pirate junks, on Robert's instructions, had also loaded with smallshot, and this raked the Dutch stern, shattering the windows in the after cabin, sweeping the poop clear of living men.

Those defenders in the bow now fell back, and more and more of Robert's men gained a footing. Aft, the junks came alongside as well, so that the beleaguered merchantman was entirely surrounded. The sailors retreated into a little knot by the mainmast, and there faced their foes.

'Who commands?' Robert demanded. He had picked up some Dutch during his earlier voyages to Canton.

'I am the Captain,' said a bearded man.

'Then tell your people to surrender. Their lives will be spared. I give you my word.'

'What word?' the Captain sneered. 'I see you, a Westerner, leading these savages . . .'

'You mistake the situation, Captain. These people at my back consider *you* to be the savages. Now, surrender and live – or fight and die.'

The Dutchman hesitated a last moment, but he had only one choice. He threw down his sword, and his men followed his lead. By now Sao had come on board, and the captives stared in consternation as they understood into whose hands they had fallen. 'The Dragon Lady!' the Captain muttered in Mandarin.

Sao smiled. 'Is that how they call me, Barrington? I think that is splendid.'

'Indeed, Sao. Now, Captain, break out your boats, and take to them. Macao is twenty miles away.'

The Captain gulped. 'I have passengers below.'

Robert turned to some waiting pirates. 'Fetch them up, but do not harm them.'

They had been cowering in the great cabin. Here the aft windows had been shattered by the junks' broadsides, and several passengers had been cut by flying glass, but none seriously. Now they emerged into the waist of the ship, blinking uncertainly in the brilliant sunlight. Four were women, three were men; there were also two children. They were sufficiently well-dressed to indicate that they were prosperous merchants; the women, wrapped up in redincotes and their heads concealed by vast bonnets, were all but invisible. They stared at the pirates with enormous eyes.

'You may take them in the boats with you, Captain,' Barrington said.

'What of our belongings?' demanded one of the women, bolder than her menfolk. Her voice was young and strong.

'Those are forfeit,' Robert told her, and he turned away to inspect his prize. And she *was* a prize – a mere glance at the 32-pound cannon mounted in the waist, far heavier than anything in the brigantine, convinced him of that.

But to his distress he then discovered Tommy among the few dead; he had been shot through the head as he had gained the Dutch deck. Robert gazed upon the shattered features as sorrowfully as if the boy had been his son.

His grief was suddenly distracted by what was happening at the gangway, where Sao had barred the women from leaving the ship. 'It is time you had a wife from amongst your own people, Barrington,' she announced.

Robert was as surprised as anyone. 'You gave me your promise.'

'And I am keeping it. For I promised their lives, but I said nothing about giving them all their freedom. Now come, will you make your choice, or must I do so for you?'

She was speaking Mandarin, yet many of the passengers – who had clearly lived some time in Macao before choosing this unfortunate moment to return home – could understand her. 'You cannot permit this,' protested the same woman who had spoken earlier.

'I would not choose *her*,' Sao remarked. 'She is a shrew.'

Robert moved closer to them. Sao's suggestion had aroused his interest. Did he not indeed wish a wife? So far he had not taken a Chinese woman because he had feared Sao's reaction ... but now she herself was urging him. After today's work, he could never again hope for a Western bride. These people would brand him a pirate from Canton to London. His place was now here, forever, and now Sao was actually inviting him to abandon her bed ...

'You scoundrel!' the Captain exclaimed, as Robert closely studied the women.

They gazed back at him with expressions of fear and loathing. The eldest of them was in her forties, with a softly pretty face; but she was clearly married to one of the three merchants, and shrank against him, clinging to the two children who buried themselves in her skirts. A second was also entering middle-age, and plainly married.

The other two women were both much younger. As Robert stared at them, he realised they were sisters – perhaps daughters of the eldest woman. Though neither could be described as beautiful, both possessed regular features; they were quite tall and, as far as be could discern beneath the redincotes, were strongly built. There seemed a considerable difference in their characters, however, for whereas one looked on the point of fainting, the other – the previously outspoken one – had a jutting little chin and met his gaze without flinching.

Sao came to stand beside him. 'You may take them both, if you wish.'

'No,' the mother cried. 'Please, sir, as you are a Christian ...'

'Do not beg, Mama,' snapped the defiant girl.

Robert gazed at her, aware of a sudden desire to possess, and at the same time to conquer. This girl would be a challenge for her strength of character.

Sao had been watching his expression closely. 'You will have to beat her,' she pointed out. 'But she will bear you strong sons.' Her face twisted; that was her own only failure.

'What is your name?' Robert demanded of the girl.

She raised her head to return his gaze. 'Wilhelmina.'

'Wilhelmina Gelaart,' her father said resignedly, speaking for the first time in a low voice. 'Will you use her well, sir?'

'I will use her as my wife, sir,' Robert told him. 'You, Captain, perform the ceremony now.'

The Captain looked uncertainly at the Gelaarts.

'If it must be,' Gelaart said. He knew there was now no choice.

Sao clapped her hands. 'It will be sport.'

*

It was, Robert supposed, the most remarkable wedding that ever took place. It was early afternoon, and the sun was beginning to slowly decline into the west. The waist of the Dutchman was a mass of watching men, some wounded. Although the dead had been thrown over the side, there were still bloodstains everywhere; even the breeze had not been entirely able to sweep away the odours of battle. And, in the midst of it all, a girl and a man being wed, the bride's reluctant parents at her side.

At the bidding of the Captain, Wilhelmina Gelaart placed

her hand in Barrington's and repeated the words after him. But she did not look at her future husband, gazing only at her parents. Her mother wept openly, as did her older sister. Her father's face was a picture of helpless distress.

They will never forgive me for this, Robert thought. But he was more concerned with the physical nearness of the girl, and the thought of what lay ahead.

'There is no ring,' the Captain complained.

Mevrouw Gelaart pulled a ring from her own finger, and handed it to Robert. He placed it on her daughter's.

'I pronounce you man and wife,' the Captain said at last.

Robert looked down at his bride, and for the first time she looked up at him. He lowered his head and brushed her lips with his; she made no response.

'A strange ceremony,' Sao commented, fascinated. 'Now, away with you, barbarians. Away with you.'

'May we be allowed a moment alone with our daughter?' Mevrouw Gelaart asked.

'One moment only,' Sao agreed.

As briefly the Gelaarts whispered together and exchanged last hugs, the other Dutchmen and their women were forced to the side and into the boats. Wilhelmina Gelaart, now Barrington, remained on the deck, gazing after her family and friends. She had not yet shed a tear. As Sao had predicted, she would give Robert strong sons . . .

'Let us inspect this ship,' Sao interrupted his thoughts. 'Or are you impatient to deflower your bride?'

'Let us inspect the ship,' Robert agreed.

'Well, then, have her sent below to the cabin, and watched, carefully. She may wish to kill herself.' Sao laughed. 'I have heard tales of these coy barbarian maidens.'

*

As he took Sao on a tour of the ship, he grew more and more delighted with every ladder they descended. Not only was the *Jan Pieter* crammed with fine stuffs and porcelain but, far more important, she had a dozen of the 32-pounders in each main-deck broadside, long-ranging 24-pounder carronades mounted in her bows, and a score of swivel guns for close work. Besides sufficient powder and shot to fight several battles.

'You understand,' said Sao, looking after the boats which were pulling away north for Macao, 'that because of your generosity that strategem of appearing to be on fire will not work again. Those people will alert every ship out of Macao.'

Robert slapped the breech of a 32-pounder. 'With this ship we no longer need strategems.'

She kissed him. 'Once, I cursed the day I met you. Now, I praise that day to my ancestors. Go, and enjoy your bride.'

*

Robert escorted Sao to the gangway, and saw her on board her own vessel. Then, after the guns were removed from the *Alceste*, hoisted on halliards and winched across to the *Jan Pieter*, the crippled brigantine was scuttled. Robert stood with Armstrong on the poop to watch her slowly sink beneath the waves.

No seaman can watch the sinking of a ship in which he has sailed without considerable emotion; but when one has lived on board for several years, and fought a dozen actions in her, that emotion is considerably increased. Both men saluted, before turning to each other and shaking hands. 'May this one do us as proud, Captain,' Armstrong said. 'What will you name her?'

'I think *Dragon Lady* would be most appropriate,' Robert decided.

'It'll please the little girl, that's for certain,' Armstrong agreed.

*

They then set sail to follow the rest of the pirate fleet back to the islands. As Robert went below, his mood was mixed: sombre because of the scuttling of the *Alceste* and the death of Tommy; elated because he had replaced the brigantine with a ship so much more powerful; and now sexual? No man fights, risking his own life and taking others, without feeling some welling-up within him of all those components which make up a man. He had drunk deeply and eaten well, and now . . .

He opened the cabin door. He had ordered food to be taken to his bride as well, and the remains of the meal lay on the table; so Wilhelmina had not lost her appetite. Two Chinese stood to attention as he came in. He waved them outside, then closed and locked the door.

His bride had taken off both bonnet and redincote. She had very pale yellow hair, long and absolutely straight, with pale blue eyes and a fresh complexion. Her gown was blue silk, conventional enough in having a wide collar but some *décolletage*, although not in the least immodest. A large bow secured a wide waistband, and the skirt was hemmed in white. She grew even more attractive as he gazed at her.

There had been wine in the hold of the ship, and he carried a bottle with him. Now he filled two goblets and offered her one. She hesitated a moment, then took it.

Robert raised his. 'To a happy marriage.'

'Can that be, sir?'

'That is up to us. Or rather, up to you.'

She raised her head in her now familiar chin-jutting pose. 'I have always realised I might one day have to marry a man twice my own age, whom I personally would not have chosen. That he also happens to be a pirate is yet one more burden I am obliged to bear.'

You will have to beat her, Sao had said; she is a shrew. But Robert thought he would not wish to alter one aspect of this vibrant personality. What she said had struck home: he had never considered his age before. He felt as strong and vigorous as at any time in his life – yet he was forty-one years old. 'And how old are you?' he demanded.

Wilhelmina tossed her head. 'I am seventeen, sir.'

'Ah. Well, then, my dear Mina, I fear you are indeed wed to a man more than double your age.'

'Mina?'

'Has no one ever called you that before?'

'Why, no, sir.'

'Then that shall be my special name for you. I like that. Now, Mina, I wish to bed you.'

For the first time she lost some of her composure. 'Now, sir? It is the middle of the afternoon.'

'The heat but excites me more.'

She licked her lips, a quick and nervous movement. 'Then, sir, if you insist upon it ... will you kindly withdraw?'

'I wish to watch you undress, Mina.'

She had risen as she spoke. Now pink spots filled her cheeks.

'Will you then humiliate me?'

'No, that's how I will love you more, Mina.'

They stared at each other for several seconds, then she came to a decision – and started to take off her gown. It was a very long time since Robert had had anything to do with Western feminine underclothes, but Mina seemed to be wearing a great number, including even drawers. No doubt fashions had changed since last he had been in England.

But he was even more interested in what was now being uncovered; Wilhelmina Gelaart might be only seventeen, but she was quite the most voluptuous woman he had ever seen naked – with swelling breasts and buttocks, strong legs, and a prominent, well-covered mount. In later years she might well become ample, but for the moment she was a woman to be held, and caressed, and indeed cherished.

She stood bathed in a glow of sweat and embarrassment as she gazed at him.

'Lie down.' He gestured at the bunk.

She obeyed, lying absolutely straight, legs pressed together. But he found her staring at him as he in turn undressed.

'I shall endeavour not to hurt you,' he promised, sitting beside her and cautiously touching her breasts.

Mina gave a little shiver from her shoulders right down to her toes.

'And I will endeavour not to hate you, sir,' she said.

She entirely lacked the cunning arts of Sao, yet she was not afraid of him. And, however innocent of the ways of love, she accepted how it must be, for a wife. He longed for some response, but reminded himself that she was very young – and that he had time.

*

'Well?' Sao demanded, when the pirate fleet reassembled at its anchorage. 'Are you pleased with your bride, Barrington?'

'I am well pleased,' he assured her.

*

Adrian Barrington was born in 1803, Martin two years later, and Saskia in 1807. Robert had no objection to Mina choosing

Dutch names for his children; he had fallen in love.

But, then, so had she, however much she disguised it under a veneer of composure. Only when, lying naked in his arms, she would sometimes gently kiss his ear, or herself timidly initiate some love play, did she betray herself.

*

With every year, Cheng Yi's fleet grew. By 1805 he commanded a hundred war junks, with a host of auxiliary vessels. Barrington remained his most active commander, sailing the *Dragon Lady* the length and breadth of the China Seas in search of prey. Mina might have longed for a house ashore, but she never complained, and the great cabin of the Dutch East Indiaman was turned into as comfortable a home as she could create.

Mina could never come to terms with attacks on Dutch shipping, but as the war with France intensified following Napoleon Bonaparte's assumption of supreme power in continental Europe, Holland became ever more an enemy, however unwilling, of England. Truth to tell, the pirate fleet had grown to such a size that Robert himself could no longer exert control over it, and several British ships were also taken as they endeavoured to trade with Canton. Because of such regrettable incidents, Barrington knew that more than ever he would be regarded as a renegade and an outcast. He had always sought fame and fortune, and now no doubt possessed both – and was anathema as well, to his own people.

The Manchu government was at its wits' end to find some means of coping with this unceasing scourge. The Chia-ch'ing Emperor could only pray to his ancestors for a miracle ... which arrived, as he supposed, without warning. In a skirmish between Manchu junks and a pirate squadron off the mouth of the Huang-Ho, the Yellow River, in North China in 1807, Cheng Yi fell overboard, and was drowned before he could be rescued.

*

The news was conveyed to Cheng Yi Sao and Barrington at their station in the south. They sailed north immediately, to find the pirate fleet in disarray. 'What is to be done?' asked Cheng's vice-admiral, Hung Lo-feng. 'The great Cheng was our leader in all things. Now he is dead, what is to be done?'

Sao looked from face to face among the captains gathered to receive her. '*I* will be your admiral.'

The captains exchanged glances in disbelief. A woman as admiral?

'Yes, I am a woman!' Sao faced them, hands on hips. 'But I have slain more men in battle than did my husband, or any of you. I have pointed my sword, and men have followed. Am I not the Dragon Lady? Where I lead, you will follow. And in front of me will sail my own *Dragon Lady*, with Barrington in command.'

*

Inspired by her words, the pirates took on new courage – raiding, capturing, looting and burning with twice the energy of before.

However, news of Cheng Yi's death also encouraged the Manchu. For Cheng Yi had always been assumed the true leader of the pirates. If his widow attempted to hold together his criminal empire, well, then, she must be dealt with. All the ships the Manchu commanded were slowly gathered in the mouth of the Yangtse, until a fleet of more than a hundred junks was assembled; then the sweep south commenced.

Cheng Yi Sao was aware of what was going on, through her network of spies. She summoned Robert to her war junk, the *White Lotus*. 'They seek now to destroy me,' she told him. 'This is a challenge we must meet. Will we defeat them?'

'If *you* will it, Dragon Lady.'

Sao glanced at Bao, who sat patiently by her side. Every man in the fleet knew that she slept with her adopted son, just as every man in the fleet knew *that* was about the sum of Cheng Bao's abilities. 'I am tired, Barrington,' she said at last. 'Do you realise that I am thirty-one years old? And what have I to show for it?'

'Wealth, fame, immortality?' he suggested.

'I wish only to spend my old age in peace,' she insisted. 'But I cannot let those achievements be destroyed. We must first win this battle. And then we must consider the future.'

*

Robert insisted that Mina and his children be put ashore before
the pirates confronted the imperial fleet. It was the first time he
ever saw Mina weep. 'But we have sailed with you for many
years,' she protested.

'This will be a fearsome battle,' he told her, then showed her
the contents of his treasure chest. 'If we are victorious, I will
return for you. If we lose, I will die, and you will return to your
own people. There is enormous wealth here, so you will live in
splendour for the rest of your life.'

'What is splendour without my husband?' she sobbed.

He ruffled her hair. 'Mina, you are but twenty-four years old.
You have a long life ahead of you – and a prosperous one.'

*

The battle took place some miles south of the Yangtse. The
Manchu had by now learned a great deal from studying the
pirates' strategy and tactics. They had also hired Dutch and
British mercenary seamen to man their ships and guns, and
Barrington had hardly any of his old crew left – even
Armstrong having died the previous year.

But the pirate fleet possessed 'The Dragon Lady'. Sao herself
was rowed through her ships in a sampan, allowing her people
to see her in all her splendour: red robe, sword in hand, hair
floating in the breeze. And she did this in full sight of the
approaching Manchu navy.

When the clash came, the pirates were inspired. As with all
Chinese naval battles, this was fought with the tactics of land.
The two fleets made straight for each other: those downwind,
the pirates, using their sweeps; those with the weather gauge,
the imperial navy, making no attempt to capitalise on their
advantage, anxious only to come to grips with their foes.

Then it was a case of courage and gunfire. Neither side
lacked courage; but, as before, the pirate guns were served at
twice the speed of the Manchu. Robert had sailed *Dragon
Lady* close-hauled in front of the pirate fleet, tacking to and fro
to maintain his station. He had acted thus as a kind of bravado,
and so found himself amidst the imperial ships several minutes
before he could receive any back-up.

But his gunners were so well trained that they gave more than they got; and gradually the rest of Sao's ships came into action, pounding away at the Manchu. First one ship flying the red dragon banner fell out of the fight, and then another. Several more were soon on fire, and several more were then boarded by swarming pirates.

By nightfall the remnants of the imperial fleet were in full flight. The cost to the pirates had been heavy in dead and wounded as well as shattered ships. But of the completeness of their victory there could be no doubt.

'Now are the oceans truly mine,' Sao declared. 'My late husband had once the ambition of taking his ships up the Pei-ho, and forcing the abdication of the Emperor. Is that such an impossible dream, Barrington?'

'Yes. Because your ships could never ascend that river. And should you leave the ships to face the Manchu on land, you would only be delivering yourself into their hands.'

'Then how am I to capitalise on my victory?'

'Be patient,' he advised. 'After such a great victory, I have an idea that the Emperor may well come to you.'

*

He was proved correct a month later. The pirates were gathered in one of their favourite bays, south of the Yangtse, still recuperating from their battle losses, when one of their outer guard ships hurried into the anchorage with the news that a war junk, flying the imperial banner but with all her gunports closed, was approaching from the north.

'As I predicted, Dragon Lady, the Emperor has come to you.'

*

'What is your ambition, Dragon Lady?' asked Sen-ching, the Manchu admiral.

'To drive all Manchu from the land of Han,' Sao replied without hesitation. She had elected to receive the envoy on the poop deck of the *White Lotus*, with her admirals gathered around her, and her fleet gathered beyond that. It was an impressive sight, and to make her point Sao had dressed herself in a yellow robe, the colour reserved for members of the imperial clan.

But Sen-ching was not to be overawed. 'That you can never do.'

'Have I not driven them from the China Seas?' Sao demanded.

'The sea is an empty province, Dragon Lady. Has it not beaten upon the shores for all eternity, yet the shore remains?'

Sao looked to Barrington, as she invariably did when out of her depth.

'Then *why* are you here?' Robert intervened.

'Ah, the great Barrington,' Sen-ching observed. 'My master has sent me to ask you if you understand exactly what you do. Your piratical raids cause my master no harm, but they have brought untold harm to the people of China. Your own people, Dragon Lady. The men of Han, their wives and children are starving because there can be no trade. They are bankrupt because there is no trade. They hate the name of Cheng Yi Sao because there is no trade. Do you not care for your own people?'

Breath hissed through Sao's nostrils. 'Do you then expect me to surrender and bare my neck to the sword?'

Sen-ching spread his hands. 'My master recognises the magnitude of your victories, your achievements on the sea. But now he asks why do you, like the waves, batter yourself against his impregnable shore, and cause so much hardship to your own people – when you could combine with that shore to increase your greatness.'

Again Sao glanced at Robert. 'What does your master propose?' he asked.

'The Son of Heaven offers an amnesty to all those in arms against him. More, he wishes this pirate fleet to be incorporated with the imperial navy. All officers in your fleet would take equivalent rank in the imperial navy, with appropriate stipends.' Sen-ching paused for a deep breath. 'And the Dragon Lady would be appointed Admiral in Chief of the whole imperial navy.'

Sao gazed at him in consternation.

'Obviously such a proposal needs serious consideration,' Robert murmured.

*

'It would be a betrayal of all my husband fought and died for,' Sao declared, once the envoy had withdrawn.

'You must think of yourself now, Dragon Lady,' Robert urged. 'Would not Cheng Yi himself have accepted such an offer? Would it not be the greatest achievement of your life?'

'Admiral of the imperial navy,' Sao muttered, her eyes gleaming.

'If the Emperor can be trusted,' Cheng Bao remarked.

'Where the Emperor pledges his word as Son of Heaven, he dare not break it,' said one of the other captains.

'What is your will?' Sao looked from face to face.

'I believe the envoy is right: the sea can never overcome the land,' said Hung Lo-feng. 'We have achieved our apogee. I believe we should now make peace with the Manchu, and restore our country to prosperity.'

Sao bowed her head. Then turned to Robert. 'And you, Barrington? Will you continue to sail at my right hand? Or will you now return to your own people?'

He gazed at her. It was seventeen years since he had first beheld her, and what a seventeen years they had been. He had come to China searching for wealth; he had achieved that, and much, much more. But in doing so he had severed his roots. To the Western world he was merely a pirate.

Besides, did he wish to return to the grime and hypocrisy of London? Could he not create a place for himself here, where he had loved and conquered – where he was already famous rather than infamous? 'I would do neither, Dragon Lady,' he said at last.

'Explain.'

'I would remain in China, if the Emperor permits it. But I would no longer fight. All I ask is the right to trade on the Yangtse-kiang.'

BOOK THE SECOND
The House of Dreams

'And the end of the fight is a tombstone white with the name of the late deceased,
And the epitaph drear: A Fool lies here who tried to hustle the east.'
Rudyard Kipling, *Naulakha*

6

THE DEN OF INIQUITY

With a thudding of drums and an explosion of firecrackers, the huge junk moved slowly towards her anchorage beneath the walls of the city of Nanking. The *Yangtse Queen* had entered the river after which she was named before a fresh easterly wind, which had carried her upstream beyond Chin-kiang. Then the wind had dropped, but after so long a voyage, to be so close to home called for a special effort, and Martin Barrington had made his men get out the sweeps. The Chinese seamen responded with a will: Nanking was their home as well. But they would have responded in the middle of the ocean, Martin knew; to sail for the House of Barrington was a privilege and an honour.

He stood at the break of the poop as the mooring came in sight, a tall, strong figure, cast in the Barrington mould, his prominent features softened only a trifle by the smooth lines inherited from his Dutch mother. This morning he wore the loose tunic and baggy pantaloons of a wealthy Chinese merchant; his boots were softest kid, and his hat broad and flat in the summer heat. In the burgeoning British colony of Singapore, whence he had just come, he wore blue broadcloth and a peaked cap, to remind him, and others, of his heritage. Even so, the British thought him a renegade.

Yet he enjoyed his visits to Singapore. They enabled him to see his sister Saskia, who might be a renegade's daughter but was happily married to an army officer, and they also enabled him to keep his pulse on the European trade which was the mainspring of the House. If he knew he aroused hostility, he felt it was more for what he represented than for what he was; as no European ships were allowed north of the Pearl, all of the House of Barrington's trade was carried in Chinese junks. The English shipmasters and their employers could not help but be jealous, and dream of opening up that vast coastline and that

127

even vaster Yangtse river to their own ambitions.

As far as the House of Barrington was concerned, that dream was going to remain a dream: whatever the politics circulating in Britain and India, they intended to allow no rivals, and this determination was well known in Singapore.

*

The junk glided up to its buoys, where a sampan waited, its crew delegated to pass up the warps to the seamen. There were other sampans waiting to begin the unloading of the cargo. As the first came alongside, Adrian Barrington climbed on board.

The brothers shook hands. Adrian, thirty-two years old, was the elder, although Martin, at thirty, was somewhat the bigger man. Their facial resemblance was very obvious, but there were differences. Adrian Barrington's expression was composed, almost severe. If no one had ever doubted either his fairness or his honesty, he had early earned a reputation for being a hard man, and a difficult customer. Martin's face was more open and relaxed. But, then, he had none of the administrative responsibilities of the House, however much he was required to deal with the day-to-day business. 'Well?' Adrian asked.

'We've a full manifest,' Martin answered. 'So?'

Adrian shrugged. 'He still lives, if that is what you mean.'

'And Jane? And the children?'

'Oh, they are in splendid shape,' Adrian said. 'Did you not know that we Barringtons are blessed with good fortune?'

*

The unloading commenced, the brothers went ashore, entering the city by one of the gates in the water-wall. Nanking was the most famous city in China. For centuries it had been the capital, sitting as it did both in the centre of the country and astride China's greatest waterway. And if, since the Manchu conquest, Peking had bidden to replace it, both in size and importance, the people of Nanking were not disposed to regard the usurpation as more than temporary.

Within the city the streets teemed, and these were mostly happy Chinese. Many remembered the terrible days of more than a quarter of a century before, when all trade had been dislocated by the activities of the pirates, led by Cheng Yi, and then by his widow Cheng Yi Sao. No doubt they remembered that their principal merchant, Robert Barrington, had been the Dragon Lady's sailing master. But they also remembered that Robert Barrington, respected nowadays by the Manchu hierarchy, had yet struck a blow for the Men of Han; that he had prospered because of that blow did not lower him in their esteem any more than did the prosperity of Cheng Yi Sao herself ... Sao had not set foot on the deck of a ship since becoming Imperial Admiral, but lived in splendour on the estates granted her by the government, with her adopted son and lover, Cheng Bao.

The important fact to the pragmatic Chinese was that peace and prosperity had been restored, whatever the vagaries of the Son of Heaven. They might still feel relieved that the Chia-ch'ing Emperor had died early, in the year 1820 of the Christian calendar, struck down, with awful symbolism, by a lightning shaft. His life had been a long catalogue of disaster, of which the pirate triumph had been the greatest. His personal uncertainty had been illustrated for all in 1816, when a second British trade mission, this time headed by the Earl of Amherst, had left China without even seeing the Emperor, because the Chia-ch'ing had stood so firmly on his prerogatives that he had insisted every member of the embassy, including the Earl, should bang their foreheads nine times upon the ground if admitted into his presence.

The Barringtons might privately have been relieved at that fiasco; had Amherst been admitted there was no saying what privileges might have followed, with what consequent cost to the House of Barrington. Yet they, like everyone else, had breathed a sigh of relief when the Chia-ch'ing Emperor had been gathered up on the Heavenly Chariot and conveyed to his ancestors as Jen Tsung Jui Huang-ti. He had been succeeded by his eldest son, a sufficiently rare incident in Chinese history; but then, for all the meaning of his name, High Felicity, the Chia-ch'ing Emperor had only had five sons, unlike his immortal father, who had sired fifteen possible heirs to the Throne of Heaven.

The new Emperor, Min-ning, who had taken the reign name of Tao-kuang, or 'Glory of Right Principle', had at once proved himself a stronger personality than his father. Over the past

dozen years China had rediscovered what it was to be ruled by
a young and vigorous monarch rather than by either a voluptu-
ary or a venal chief minister. Yet the Tao-kuang Emperor had
broken none of his father's promises; rather had the privileges
of the House of Barrington been extended, with permission to
trade the entire length of the river, and even to send their
sampans north along the Grand Canal to Peking itself. They
fulfilled the only criteria in which this new emperor was interested: they earned a great deal of money and thus paid a great
deal of taxes, and they were subservient to the rule of the
Manchu. That way lay prosperity and happiness for all.

*

Thus the original dwelling-house Robert Barrington had
secured for Mina and himself and their young family had been
added to time and again, much as the warehouses on the waterfront had been expanded time and again. Now the house was a
palace of marble floors and lacquered façades, surrounding a
magnificent garden in which birdsong competed with the
babble of flowing water, and, when there was a wind, the
equally loud sighing of the giant willows which drooped beside
the miniature lakes and streams, and over the ornamental
bridges.

In the outer porch, the family waited to greet Martin.
Adrian's two children, James and Joanna, aged respectively five
and three, their yellow hair tinted with red, were anxious to hurl
themselves into their uncle's arms. Behind them, Jane advanced
more slowly. Her hair was auburn, and curled around the
creamy white complexion of her face. No doubt, Martin
thought, as he often did, her body would possess a similar
whiteness. Her features were bold, almost Barringtonian, and
wore an air of defiance, but Martin had never been certain
whether they reflected her true personality, or the character she
had felt called upon to assume in the unusual circumstances of
her life.

She was, he supposed, a prize of war just as much as had
been his own mother. Only the war fought over Jane Pettigrew
had been a commercial one, and her Calcutta-based father had
chosen to sacrifice one of his daughters in the hopes of gaining
some advantage thereby. Certainly the match had seemed an

attractive one: Adrian Barrington, eldest son and heir to the House of Barrington; and Jane Pettigrew, eldest daughter of one of India's most prominent merchants, a man who sought new financial empires to conquer. Whatever the Barrington background, surely an alliance between the House of Barrington and that of Pettigrew must result in a consortium which might well one day challenge the East India Company itself.

The disappointments had been general. Robert Barrington had determined that he would retire once Adrian was married and had produced an heir; to this end he had welcomed his daughter-in-law. It had been sheer misfortune that in the year following the marriage Wilhemina had been taken fatally ill.

Perhaps Robert's life had soured before then. His dream had always been to return to India, and thence England, with all the fame and wealth he had envied in others. To this purpose he had put out feelers, through his sons and his trading captains, and most of all through his new in-law, John Pettigrew – always to be met by rebuff. The East India Company could not forget that the ships of Cheng Yi Sao had occasionally preyed upon their own. More important, they could not overlook the fact that Robert Barrington had secured the trade routes they most desired. It had been intimated that should Robert Barrington set foot upon British soil he would be hanged as a pirate.

Robert's frustrated anger had perhaps hastened Mina's journey to her grave. And driven by both grief and frustration, he had changed his mind about handing over the rule of the House to his eldest son. This had embittered Adrian. And that, in turn, had made Jane's life a misery.

Which did not seem to concern Adrian. Perhaps, born and bred in China, Adrian had become too thoroughly Sinicised, believed too completely that when a woman married she forsook her own family, entirely, whatever differences might arise between it and that of her husband. But Jane had refused to abandon her heritage to such an extent, and now found herself isolated. The fact that she had given her husband two children, and thus appeared to meet all of her father-in-law's requirements, was negated by the widening gulf between John Pettigrew and Robert Barrington. For Pettigrew found himself powerless to assist Barrington towards the goal he sought, and Barrington refused to admit Pettigrew into any share of the Yangtse trade.

Now it was too late. Since Mina's death, Robert Barrington had turned his back upon his dream – and his daughter-in-law.

And Adrian? Martin did not know what went on in the private apartment of his elder brother and his wife. He spent so much time away from Nanking on family business, he did not see as much of them as he would have liked. He was only aware of that constant expression of defiance upon Jane's face. And also, disturbingly, that she only ever smiled when greeting him.

Now she came forward for an embrace. 'Welcome home, brother,' she said.   'Oh, welcome home.'

He held her close for a moment. 'There are letters ...'

'Father is waiting,' Adrian said impatiently.

'You'll excuse me,' Martin said to Jane, and placed the satchel of mail on the table.

*

Adrian was already striding along the marble-floored corridors, past bowing servants, towards Robert Barrington's apartment. Here the door was opened for them by Tsen-tsing, her babe in her arms. This was an invariable act of policy, as irritating as it was clearly important to the Chinese girl. She was nothing more than that; since Mina's death Robert Barrington had sought to regain at least one of the glories of his famous past, and Tsen-tsing might have been a reincarnation of the immortal Sao, doe-eyed and apparently subservient, beautiful and seductive – and hardly less ambitious.

And she had achieved something of which even Sao had been incapable: she had mothered a son. John Barrington – an incongruous name for a half-caste Chinese – was only two years old, so Robert Barrington would be long dead before the little boy could compete for power within the House ... But Tsen-tsing was clearly intending to make his path to that power as smooth as possible while her doting master still lived. 'Say greetings to Uncle Martin,' she cooed.

'Uncle Martin,' the little boy lisped.

Martin obligingly stroked his head, and then kissed Tsen-tsing's hand: she had all the airs of a great lady, and almost looked like one, in her pale blue satin tunic, and with her hair upswept and coiled on her head, held in place by a gold band.

Then he looked past her at the divan on which his father lay.

At seventy-five, Robert Barrington had put on a great deal of weight, and his arthritic hips allowed him little comfortable movement. That he had become, only two years before, the father of a child was no doubt a tribute to Tsen-tsing's ability as a lover. But the massive features, shrouded in white hair and beard, could yet smile at his youngest legitimate son. And he could still raise a hand to be squeezed.

'Tell me of Saskia.'

'She is well, and sends you her best love, Father. She would visit you, but the children ...'

'You mean that rascal of a husband will not permit it,' Robert growled. 'Is there news?'

'There is a change of government in England. Peel has resigned, and Lord Melbourne is Prime Minister.'

'That is news?' Robert remarked. 'Tell me of the Company.'

Martin sat beside his father. 'It is as we were advised would happen, Father: the East India Company's trade monopoly has been abolished. Already there are independent merchants sending ships into Bombay and Calcutta and Singapore.'

'And further east?' Adrian asked.

'To Canton. Yes.'

'And further north, no doubt.' Robert Barrington commented.

'I have seen no evidence of it, Father. Yet.'

'But we have known for some time this day would come. Sit down, boy. We are proposing an expansion.'

Martin waited with interest. The House had two centres: Nanking – and Shanghai at the mouth of the river. He was not convinced that a third was necessary, but he was very much the junior partner.

'We wish you to set up a warehouse in Wuhu.'

Martin raised his eyebrows; Wuhu was hardly more than a hundred miles upriver from Nanking.

'We believe it is important for the future of the House that we control the whole of the Yangtse,' Adrian explained. 'Especially in view of the news you have just brought.'

'Well, then, Hankow is surely the place to start.'

'Wuhu is where we will set up the next warehouse,' Robert declared. 'It is the centre of the rice-growing district south of the Yangtse. And rice is one of our principal exports. More important, it is a place where we will, at this moment, be welcomed. Do you remember my telling you of the Manchu who saved my life, oh, nearly fifty years ago?'

'The Intendant at Canton,' Martin said. He had heard the story often enough. 'And then you saved his life in turn?'

'Hui-chan – that is right. His son, Hui-cheng, has just been appointed Intendant for South Anhwei, and has taken up residence in Wuhu. Now is the perfect time to expand there.'

*

Martin could follow his father's reasoning; even for the House of Barrington, expansion, and indeed business, was dependent upon the goodwill of the local Manchu officials, and an Intendant was an important personage. It was a disappointment, however, to be told to leave again so soon after returning from a voyage of several months. But Robert Barrington, as always, was in a hurry.

'You go so soon,' Chun-wu complained. Chun-wu had just turned twenty-eight, and was inclining to plumpness. She had been given to Martin when he had been eighteen and she no more than sixteen. Perhaps Robert had not anticipated that they would become so very fond of each other. Had Chun-wu ever become pregnant, Martin might well have married her. But in that he had no doubt been fortunate. However irregular his own past, in his old age Robert Barrington had become a stickler for 'right behaviour', or '*li*', as the Chinese would have it: one did not marry a slave girl. Robert had naturally hoped that Martin would follow the example of his elder brother, and seek a bride in Singapore or Calcutta. Adrian had also been presented with a Chinese mistress at an early age, and had demonstrated that marriage need not in any way interfere with one's domestic arrangements. Another cause, no doubt, for Jane's defiant misery.

Martin was unable to envisage marriage to anyone, even if he knew that his love for Chun-wu extended no further than the bodily comforts she provided for him. As now, when Jane herself was announced, Chun-wu skipped from his bed in dismay.

He wrapped himself in his robe and went to the sitting-room where his sister-in-law was waiting. 'You'll forgive this intrusion,' she said, pink spots filling her pale cheeks.

'I am flattered at your presence.'

Jane waited while the maidservants hurried in with the tray of tea, and withdrew, then she rose and roamed about the room. 'I had hoped you would be home for a few weeks.'

Martin poured tea. 'So had I. But business is business.' He made her sit beside him. 'Tell me what is troubling you, Jane.'

She gazed at him for several seconds – then got up and departed as abruptly as she had arrived, her skirts rustling. He inhaled the scent she had left on the air.

Chun-wu stood in the inner doorway. 'She wishes to be your lover,' she remarked.

Martin's glance was astonished, yet he had to shroud it in anger. 'Is that all you can think of?' he demanded.

'I know what is in a woman's mind,' Chun-wu told him.

*

Wuhu, like Nanking, was on the right or southern bank of the river, and, again like Nanking, was a walled city, although not more than half the size of the erstwhile capital. It contained the same suburb of moored sampans, some of which traded, the majority of which were floating homes, providing every entertainment from prostitution, through gambling, to food.

Like all of Manchu China, since the suppression of the White Lotus revolt, it was a place of peace and prosperity – at least for those who served the government and obeyed the laws. This peace was in the general care of the Intendant, who was responsible only to the Viceroy. As Anhwei province covered a considerable area, it was split into two for administrative purposes, but even so each Intendant had a large area to supervise, and Martin was relieved to learn that Hui-cheng, the Intendant of the southern half of the province, was actually in the city when he arrived.

He found the Manchu to be a dapper little man with a fussy manner, and clearly very conscious of his responsibilities, which was both rare and reassuring. Since most Manchu civil servants handed on their positions from father to son, as Hui-chan had done to Hui-cheng – for members of the Manchu élite were excused the more exacting aspects of the Civil Service examinations, such as the Five Essays, and thus found entry into the Mandarinate all the more easy – the general tendency was for efficiency and administration to weaken with each generation, until an excuse could be found for dismissing the incumbent and bestowing the post upon a new family. Then the whole cycle started again.

But Hui-cheng was surrounded by male secretaries, to whom he issued a constant stream of instructions, in between times studying various scrolls – mostly petitions – presented to him in the hopes of obtaining some form of justice. 'Martin Barrington!' he exclaimed with apparent pleasure. 'I am honoured.' He gestured Martin to a seat, watched appreciatively as Martin's servants brought in a succession of boxes of presents, and then listened carefully to what the Englishman had to say. 'The House of Barrington in Wuhu! I think that would be very acceptable. I will recommend your petition to the Viceroy. You will dine with me, Barrington.'

*

Hui-cheng lived in a surprisingly modest house, which indicated that he might just be an honest man; for most government officials saw the accumulation of wealth – by demanding the maximum bribes they estimated each petitioner could bear – as more important than administration of justice. Here Martin met Hui-cheng's children, two small boys and a girl, but not his wife.

'I am soon to be the father of a third son,' Hui-cheng explained happily.

*

Then it was a matter of waiting, but only for a short while, during which Martin firstly explored the waterfront and chose a site for the warehouse. Then he returned downriver to Nanking, to report to his father and brother. At the end of the year he went back to Wuhu, to find Hui-cheng wreathed in smiles.

'Your permission has been granted, Barrington.'

'I am delighted, as I know my father will be,' Martin said. 'My felicitations upon you and upon your family, Hui-cheng. May I ask if you were blessed with a third son, as you anticipated?'

Hui-cheng sighed. 'It was not the will of the gods. My wife

was delivered of a daughter. Can a man be more unfortunate
than to have *two* daughters?'

'But you also have two sons,' Martin reminded him.

'Four sons would have been better,' Hiu-cheng declared. For
by Confucian law only a son could perform the sacrifice to
heaven on his father's death; a man without sons was doomed
to die without proper ceremony. But then his ready good
humour reasserted itself. 'Now you will dine with me, and see
my child. We have called her Lan Kuei.' It meant Little Orchid.

'Then you anticipate that she will be a great beauty,' Martin
suggested.

'One must hope,' Hui-cheng said, sad again.

*

The following year the House opened a warehouse in Hankow;
and Martin became as well known on the river as he already
was on the coast. On every voyage he naturally stopped at
Wuhu to oversee the operations there, and invariably he dined
with the Intendant. Hui-cheng became a close friend, and
Martin delighted in watching the four attractive children
growing older. Soon there was a fifth, but to Hui-cheng's
disgust this also proved to be a daughter. 'How may that
prophecy of my family's future greatness come true if I have
nothing but daughters?' he wailed.

'Perhaps it were better did it not come true,' Martin
suggested, ruffling Lan Kuei's hair. She was his favourite, just
as the little girl obviously adored the big barbarian. 'Have you
not everything you can desire already, old friend?'

*

But Robert Barrington's brain was still active. 'Now the river is
secure,' he said, 'I wish to open a warehouse in Canton.'

Even Adrian was taken aback by this idea. 'It will be like
dangling a red rag before a bull,' he protested.

'So? As long as we are bigger and stronger than the bull,
what is there to be afraid of? Nearly all the trade in and out of
Canton is illicit. It has grown up by custom, and with the
connivance of the Cantonese officials. It has never been
acknowledged as legal by Peking. But our other trading centres

have indeed been legalised by the capital. Where you have a large number of people trading illegally, one more illegal act is not going to trouble them overly.'

Robert then looked at Martin. 'Are you afraid of being set upon by a bunch of rascally Dutchmen and Portuguese?'

'By no means, Father. But what of rascally Englishmen?'

Robert grinned. 'If they should attack you, boy, then they are indeed rascals, and need to be treated as such.'

*

'You go virtually to war,' Jane complained, as they walked in the garden.

'I doubt that. I believe Father is right, and they will be too aware of our power to fight us openly.'

'Then what of a dagger in the dark?'

'It is not such an easy business – even were it easy for the conscience.' Her anxiety made him recall Chun-wu's words, and he gave her a sidelong glance. 'Would you then mourn me, Jane?'

She stopped walking. 'Yes, I would mourn you grievously, Martin.'

He, too, stopped, and faced her. Amidst the heavy-clustered blooms of the Barrington garden, they were out of sight of the house. 'Then be sure that I will come back.'

Her tongue stole out and circled her lips, quickly and guiltily. Her cheeks shone pink.

'Does he treat you so badly?' Martin asked gently.

'He does not "treat me", as you put it, at all.'

Martin frowned. 'You do not sleep together?'

She shrugged. 'We have not done so since Joanna was conceived.'

'That's unbelievable. Tell me why.'

'Perhaps I have spoken my mind too often.'

'Yet you remain his wife.'

Her voice was suddenly brittle. 'I live in a world controlled for me by the name of Barrington. I have two children. What would you have me do?'

Suddenly she was in his arms – and he was kissing her mouth and nose, her eyes and cheeks. He swept her from the ground and carried her to one of the stone seats, where he sat her down and kissed her again.

'I love you,' he panted. Did he mean it? He desired her, most certainly. But love, with all that entailed! Another man's wife. His brother's wife!

'Martin,' she whispered. 'Oh, Martin!' Her kisses were as passionate as his own. Then suddenly she stiffened. She wanted, too – but she dared not. He could see it in her eyes.

'What would you have *me* do?' he asked.

'Go to Canton, brother,' she begged. 'But ... please come back!'

*

Surely, to cuckold one's own brother was the greatest moral sin one could commit. The very thought left Martin feeling breathless. But he knew it was bound to happen when he returned to Nanking. And how could he avoid returning to Nanking?

But first Canton. The huge junk entered the wide gulf which led up to the Pearl River, piloted through the many sandbanks and shoals which encumbered the mouth, and saluted the Bogue Forts which guarded the seaway. The garrison, having ascertained that the *Yangtse Queen* flew the pennants of the House of Barrington – a silver dragon on a blue background – returned the salute. Earlier, Martin had been more interested in the white houses and the steepled churches in the Portuguese colony of Macao, on the south side of the gulf. To the English and Dutch who also used the staging-post – barbarian women and children were not allowed in Canton, and those merchants who had set up establishments in the city had needed to build their homes in Macao – the ship entering the river would seem nothing more than a large Chinese vessel. But they would learn about her ownership and her purpose soon enough.

*

'Barrington,' said Wen Cho-su, Governor of the city. He was tall and thin for a Chinese, with a very long moustache and bowed shoulders. Surrounded by his aides and secretaries, he received his visitor in the porch of his palace, looking out over the harbour and the river.

'I have letters from the Viceroy.' Martin handed the wallet to one of the waiting men.

'You will build a godown here in Canton,' Wen observed.

'That is certainly my father's desire, your excellency.'

Wen turned his hands outwards. 'Everybody else has a godown in my city. You will trade between Canton and the north?'

'And with the south as well.'

Wen wagged a finger. 'You must be careful, Barrington. The Viceroy will disown you if you are caught.'

'Caught, excellency? Do you suppose I intend to deal in contraband?'

Wen's eyes were hooded. 'Are you not English?'

'I am a citizen of the Middle Kingdom,' Martin declared.

Wen smiled sceptically. 'There is too much opium in Canton already. I wish no more. Now go with Sung Tang-chu, and he will prepare the papers for you to sign.'

*

Martin accompanied the secretary into his office. 'What is this talk of opium?' he demanded. 'Surely the trade is forbidden?'

'There is an imperial edict against the importation of opium,' Sung agreed, after giving instructions to his own secretary, a young man, to copy out the necessary papers.

'Which is ignored?' Martin suggested.

Sung shrugged. 'Peking is many hundreds of miles away, and there is much profit in opium. Our people foolishly wish to indulge in the habit, and your countrymen are anxious to trade.'

'And it is good for business?'

'Of course. My master takes his cut, as do we all.'

'And now he grows afraid of what he is doing?'

'It is the fault of the English,' Sung said angrily. 'They have no sense of moderation. For years the East India Company imported six thousand chests of opium into Canton every year.'

'Six thousand chests?' Martin cried in consternation.

'No more, and no less. They were very precise. But then, as you no doubt know, four years ago your government took away from the Company the monopoly of trade in these waters, with the result that *any* English shipmaster could sail up the Pearl. Do you know how many chests of opium were imported into Canton during this last year? *Twenty thousand!*'

Martin was aghast. 'And Wen permits this?'

'I doubt he could stop it, even if he wished,' Sung remarked. 'Besides, as it is all illegal, it means more profit for him, eh? Every shipload has to pay its way.'

'And now he is afraid,' Martin said again.

'We have more opium than we can handle. The price is being forced down.'

'But who buys such a treacherous substance?'

Sung shrugged. 'Everybody. Should any man not be able to dream?' He smiled. 'Or a woman? Are those papers ready, Hung?'

The boy spread them on Sung's desk. The secretary scanned them. '*There* is a mistake ... and *there*. Start again, stupid lout, and quickly, or I will have you caned.'

The boy bowed as he gathered up the papers and returned to his own high table. Martin looked at him for the first time. With his shaven forehead and long pigtail he looked like any other Chinese youth, but Martin was struck by the glow in his eyes. Anger, certainly, at his dressing-down, but there was more than just resentment behind the visible fury.

'I don't know what I will do with that halfwit,' Sung growled, clapping his hands to have tea brought in. 'He aspires to enter the civil service – and do you know how many times he has already failed the examination? Thrice.'

*

'Have you ever smoked opium?' Martin asked Kang-ju, knowing that the mate had sailed up the Pearl before.

Kang-ju smiled. 'My wife would beat me, Barrington.'

Martin nodded. 'I suspect mine would also, had I one.'

He surveyed the waterfront from the poop of the *Yangtse Queen*. Save for some of the cities of the remote interior, Canton was as far removed from the centre of Manchu authority as it could be. It was a different world down here in the south, as was typified by the numbers of white men to be seen in their frock coats and tall hats. They were not allowed into the old walled city, but had created quite a colony for themselves in the area around the waterfront. Several of them were clearly interested in the big ship, and its captain who was far too large to be Chinese or Manchu, however he chose to dress.

Besides, the name of the *Yangtse Queen* was well known in Singapore. 'The House of Barrington,' one of the men on the dock remarked, loud enough to be overheard.

'The devil! What does he do here?' said his companion.

Martin looked down at them. 'The same as you, gentlemen.'

'We'll not have it, sir. We'll not have it!' declared the first speaker. 'Governor Wen shall hear of this.'

Martin made no reply, and watched them disappear into the throng, outrage evident in their gait.

'Those people do not seem to like you,' Kang-ju remarked.

'They will like me even less after they have spoken to Governor Wen,' Martin remarked wryly.

*

Still, he decided against going ashore to sample whatever pleasures Canton might offer. As Jane had reminded him, a knife in a dark alley was something not even he could confidently protect himself against.

In the middle of dinner a visitor was announced. 'Some rascally clerk named Hung Hsiu-ch'uan,' Kang said.

Martin frowned. 'Sung Tang-chu's secretary? Show him in, Kang. But stay with us.'

Kang admitted the Chinese boy. Hung looked furtively from side to side as he entered, taking in the luxurious furnishing of the cabin.

'You have a message from Sung Tang-chu?' Martin asked.

'No, excellency.' Hung licked his lips. 'I would speak with you, sir.'

'You are doing so.'

Hung glanced at Kang.

'I have no secrets from my mate,' Martin advised him.

Hung drew a deep breath. 'Sir, this afternoon, I sensed that you were a good man.'

Martin raised his eyebrows. 'There are not many on this river would agree with you.'

'That is because most on this river are evil,' Hung said, his voice filled with a strange anger.

'That's a point of view. Does your master know you hold it?'

'My master is as evil as any.' Hung stared at Martin. 'If you tell him that, he will have me caned.'

'I will not tell him,' Martin promised. 'But why have you told me this?'

'Because you are Barrington, and so you have the ear of the Son of Heaven.'

Martin glanced at Kang-ju, who made an effort to keep his face straight; the poor boy did not know that there was scarce an intact male in all China, save for the imperial councillors, who had ever seen the Son of Heaven – much less some outer barbarian, however privileged. The Tao-kuang Emperor kept himself secluded even more than had his Ch'ien-lung grandfather.

'You must warn the Son of Heaven of the evils that are ruining the south,' Hung continued urgently. 'They will, in time, ruin the Empire.'

'You mean the trade with the barbarian nations?'

'I mean the trade in opium! That's evil!' Hung insisted. 'Do you know what harm it does to my people?'

'It gives them dreams. Some say the dreams are sweet?'

'You cannot live on dreams, great Barrington. Come with me, and I will show you these dreamers, so that you may understand. Then you may act – and tell the Emperor of the evils being committed in his land by men like Wen Cho-su. Then he, in turn, may end this horror.'

Martin looked at Kang-ju.

'At night? That's inviting murder. This rascal could have been sent by your enemies.'

'I seek your aid,' Hung begged. 'But you are right to be cautious. Night, day – it makes no difference. The dens never close. Choose when you will come. But come!'

'I will come with you tomorrow,' Martin decided. 'And, until then, you must remain here on my ship.'

*

Even in broad daylight, Martin took an escort of armed sailors. They went ashore just before noon. By now most of the population of Canton knew that a ship owned by the House of Barrington was in the harbour. A crowd had gathered to stare.

Hung led them away from the waterfront – and soon away from the more prosperous parts of the city. They headed into mean streets where little of the prevailing prosperity seemed to have reached. Dogs snarled over scraps of food, children played games knee-deep amid sewage, men and women urinated openly as the party hurried by. Martin warned his men to be on the lookout for any attack by robbers. At least they were not interfered with; but somehow the people they passed gave knowing smiles.

Eventually Hung stopped before a larger, more solid building than the tumbledown shacks they had been walking between. He knocked on the closed door. It was immediately opened by a young Chinese man blinking at them. Their nostrils were assailed by a sickly-sweet stench.

'Barrington to see Sun Wong-li,' Hung announced.

The boy bowed, and Hung gestured Martin to enter. 'It would be best if your guard remained on the street,' he said.

'Just remember, Hung – at the first sign of treachery it will be your head that rolls,' Martin told him, slapping the sword that hung at his side. It was a Chinese sword, slightly curved, perfectly balanced, sharp as a razor.

'I wish you to see,' Hung said.

Martin ducked to enter the building. He was immediately surprised and relieved at his surroundings. It could have been the front room of any decent shop in Nanking or Wuhu, with attentive and quietly-dressed young women hurrying forward to usher him to a seat.

Supervising them was an elderly Chinese man who rubbed his hands together as he bowed. 'I am Sun Wong-li. It is a great honour, Barrington. Will you have one pipe, or two?'

Martin glanced at Hung, standing beside him. 'Great Barrington wishes to inspect these premises before smoking,' Hung said.

Sun turned his hands outwards. 'My establishment is at your command.'

At the clap of his hands, one of the girls hurried forward.

'If you will accompany me, sir.'

'Come with me, Hung,' Martin said.

She ushered him into a corridor where the strange scent was stronger, then opened a door to their left. Here the sickly smell was so strong that Martin found difficulty in breathing; and the fumes were so thick it was difficult even to see. But as he followed the girl into the room, he was again surprised – and began to wonder what Hung was getting at.

He was in a room some thirty feet square, filled with comfortable-looking divans. Beside each divan there was positioned a low table, and on each table there was a bowl in which rested a pipe. Each divan was also occupied by a single reclining figure. To his consternation, Robert perceived that there were several women present. Men and women lay on comfortable cushions, smoking. There were occasional words, but others seemed just content to stare at the ceiling; a large number had their eyes shut. Most were very respectably dressed. Among them circulated other pleasant young women, smiling and talking, who carried off finished pipes to be refilled, while the customers reached for a replacement waiting in the bowl.

'We call this the Room of Dreams,' Martin's escort explained.

'It seems very pleasant ...'

'There is an empty divan. Will you recline, sir? I'll fetch your pipes.'

Martin looked at Hung. 'I'm afraid I do not understand your concern, Hung. So these people have drugged themselves into dreams – perhaps, when they awaken, they'll find life more pleasant.'

'They never truly awaken,' Hung declared. 'Come, there are other rooms.' He stepped back into the corridor.

The girl followed. 'Do you not wish a pipe?' she asked in bewilderment.

'Down here.' Hung hurried along the corridor.

'You cannot go in there!' the girl almost shouted.

But Hung had reached another door – and this he threw open. Martin checked in dismay. Now the sickly-sweet odour of opium was overlaid by the ripe stench of unwashed bodies and human excreta. The smoke was thicker, as he peered into the gloom.

'You must come out of there,' the girl was shouting behind him. 'It is not for you.'

Martin ignored her, and blinked away the smoke. The room was no larger than the one he had just left – but there the resemblance ended. Here there were no divans, no tables, no pretty girls. It was a mass of bodies lying on the floor or sitting against the walls or propped against central pillars. All were in varying stages of stupor. Every one had a pipe – which appeared to be the most precious thing in the world to them. They inhaled ... and perhaps they dreamed. Otherwise, their mouths drooped open, dribbling saliva. Several were totally naked, stained with their own filth. But, more disturbing were those who still wore the remnants of once fine clothes. Again the sexes were mixed; some even were coupling without arousing much interest in their neighbours.

'We had better leave,' Hung recommended. 'The girl has gone for help.'

They stepped back into the corridor, and closed the door.

'What drives them into such a place when the other fine room is available?' Martin asked.

'It's still the lust for opium – where there is no money. Maybe all of them began in that other room. But for smoking the pipes they have sacrificed all – sold their homes and shops, given their wives and families to starvation, their children for prostitution. All for a pipe! And when their money runs out, they are thrown in here, and allowed to smoke until they die. Since they do not eat, that is a quick business. Yet many of these people were once leaders of the community – before taking to opium.'

'By God!' Martin muttered, genuinely shocked.

'There are one hundred of these dens in Canton alone,' Hung informed him. 'And thousands in the south as a whole.'

Several men had appeared in the corridor. 'You! Out!' They carried sticks.

Martin drew his sword. 'Stay close,' he told Hung. 'We must go,' he said, and pushed his way through. They gained the street and the protection of Martin's seamen. At last they could breathe clean air.

'Now, will you tell the Son of Heaven?' Hung asked.

'I will tell someone, I promise you,' Martin said.

7

THE ANGRY LION

The following January – 1839 of the Christian calendar – the *Yangtse Queen* waited at anchor off the city of Chin-kiang, at the southern end of the Grand Canal. Martin was now acting on instructions from Peking itself; instructions he had not even shown to his father or brother. Because these instructions commanded him to keep everything secret.

That he had obeyed such a distant command, under the seal of the Emperor's brother Prince Hui, was a measure of how far he had already mentally distanced himself from his family. Easy to say that Father and Adrian would not have understood what had motivated his report to the Viceroy without themselves having seen the degrading effects of the opium, and that in their desire not to become involved in the affairs of other barbarians they would have brought pressure on him not to make a report at all.

Equally was it easy to say to himself that he had not expected a report made by a barbarian, even a Barrington, to have been acted upon. However much he had wanted to assuage his anger, and perhaps his guilt, at what he had seen, he had supposed that, like so many memoranda, it would have found its way into the dusty archives of the viceregal palace, and there been forgotten. That it should have been forwarded to Peking had taken him entirely by surprise. And that Peking should have determined to act upon it had surprised him even more. The Tao-kuang Emperor was not one for violent action, as a rule. As opposite in character to his father as could be imagined, his sole aim in life seemed to be to save money, rather than spend it on vast schemes – he had even abandoned the annual visit to Jehol to hunt, because he regarded it as too expensive.

Martin did not regret what he had done. Quite apart from what he had seen, he found it extremely distasteful that his own countrymen should be flooding a nation with such a debilitating drug, simply because they lacked the money to trade honestly.

Nor did he have any sympathy with officials such as Governor Wen who were growing rich upon the cravings of their people. And if he was involving himself – as Father and Adrian would see it – in the affairs of others, he was also surely looking to the future; if the imperial government determined to end the illicit trade in Canton, it would also end the encroachment of barbarian traders, and that could only benefit the House of Barrington.

That was a point that could well have been put to his father and brother. But he had not done so, because he was involved in secrets of his own. To commit adultery in a world where beauty was for sale on every street corner had to be condemned by every right-thinking man. To have done so with his own sister-in-law put him beyond that pale of decent behaviour.

But how could a woman be resisted, when she was of his own race, and so beautiful, and when she had appeared so very unhappy thanks to her ill-treatment by his own brother . . . and when she had wanted him so very badly? When he had returned, they had merely looked at each other and their mutual desire had been sealed: within forty-eight hours she had found her way to his bed.

Now he lived on a knife-edge. Chun-wu knew of the liaison, indeed, she had encouraged it – had willingly stood guard while her master and his sister-in-law had committed their crime. Perhaps because as she herself grew older and less attractive, she considered it her responsibility to cater to her master's needs. But equally did she intend to safeguard her own future, and what better way could that be accomplished than to hold her master's secrets in the palm of her hand.

But what mattered knife-edges, when *he* had held that tumultuous pink-and-white body in his arms, known the passion of those lips, the sheen of that auburn hair?

*

The sampan was as richly furnished as Martin Barrington had ever seen, from its red silk centre tent with its matching drapes, to its highly polished oars which flashed in the sun. Yet the man who climbed on to the gangway of the junk was clearly Chinese rather than Manchu. He was a small man, both short and thin, with a thin face, and very hard eyes. His smile was brief.

'Barrington,' he said. 'I am Lin Tse-hu. I am the Imperial Commissioner for the restoration of order in the south. You will take your orders from me.'

*

The *Yangtse Queen* entered the wide mouth of the Pearl at the beginning of March, and made her way up the river. It had been a rough voyage down from the Yangtse, with the winter gales still howling across the China Sea, and Lin and his men had been mostly prostrated by sea-sickness. But they recovered very rapidly once the calm waters of the river were reached, and Lin was standing on the poop as the pagodas of Canton itself came into sight.

'What are your instructions, your excellency?' Martin asked.

'I am here to end the opium trade,' Lin announced.

'Yes, but how to you propose to do this?'

Lin looked surprised. 'I will end the trade by destroying all the opium in Canton, and all of those who prosper by it. You will accompany me, with a dozen of your best people.'

*

They went ashore, Lin and his twenty soldiers, Martin and his dozen well-armed sailors. The junk had been recognised on her way upriver, and was undoubtedly expected in the city, but no one had anticipated having an Imperial Commissioner land. Crowds gathered to stare, as Lin marched straight for the Governor's palace. Messengers ran in front of him, and Wen Cho-su was in the porch to greet his illustrious visitor.

'Lin Tse-hu, your excellency.' Wen bowed low, and then glanced at Martin. 'May I inquire the reason for this visit?'

'I seek opium,' Lin said.

'Opium? Why, your excellency, in that case you have come to the right place. Oh, yes, we have opium here.'

'So I understand.' Lin walked past the Governor and into the antechamber where several officials were waiting, amongst them Sung Tang-chu, Martin observed. 'Where is this opium?'

'It is stored in safe places, excellency.'

'You have none, here in your house?'

'Oh, well . . .' Wen was wringing his hands.

'Have it brought to me.'

Lin sat down in Wen's official chair, and surveyed the room, from which two of the secretaries had hurried; his escort arranged themselves behind him. Wen clearly had no idea whether to be frightened or pleased at Lin's appearance and request. 'Does your excellency wish to sample a pipe?'

'I wish to see this opium,.' Lin told him.

Wen looked at the inner archway, whence the secretaries had returned, accompanied by four slaves bearing trays upon which there were several small boxes. Now he beckoned, and the trays were brought in.

'Barrington!' Lin summoned. 'Is this opium?'

Martin went forward, opened one of the boxes, untied a sachet, and sniffed. 'Yes, Commissioner. This is opium.'

Lin surveyed Wen, who was commencing to shiver. 'Was this purchased by you from the barbarians? Or given to you as a bribe to permit them to land their goods?'

Wen stammered in confusion.

Lin turned to the waiting secretaries. 'How many chests of opium are there in Canton at this moment?'

The secretaries looked at the Governor.

'He is certainly guilty,' Lin said. 'Execute him.'

It happened with the invariable Chinese rapidity. Wen's head rolled across the floor, an expression of bewildered horror on its features.

'Now,' Lin said. 'How many chests of opium are there in Canton at this moment?'

'Very many, excellency,' Sung said hurriedly. 'Perhaps as many as twenty thousand.'

'You know where these chests are to be found?'

'Most of them are in the warehouses of the barbarian merchants.'

Lin nodded. 'You will muster your soldiers and accompany me to these warehouses.'

*

The waterfront was turned into a shambles of broken doors and terrified people. Chinese clerks fled in every direction as Lin and his men systematically looted every warehouse of its contents, piling the chests of opium at the dockside, scattering precious lists of customers and accounts into the wind and water.

'You rascals!' shouted the first British merchant visited, as he watched his profits being torn apart. 'What is the meaning of this? Are you bandits?' He glared at Sung, who now marched at Lin's side. 'Where is the protection promised us by your Governor?'

'The Governor is no more,' Lin told him sternly. 'And you are under arrest!'

The merchant's eyes found Martin. 'Is this your doing, you scoundrel?'

'Why, yes,' Martin said. He could see no point in dissembling, even if he could not but suppose Lin's intemperate actions would likely end in catastrophe.

'Arrest that man,' Lin commanded. Immediately his soldiers seized the merchant and bound his hands behind his back.

'By God, sir!' the Englishman shouted. 'You'll not treat me so!' He was dragged away, still shouting.

'He may be placed on board my ship,' Martin suggested, 'and I will convey him downriver to Macao.'

'He will be imprisoned,' Lin declared. 'Every barbarian in Canton will be imprisoned, until His Majesty decides what is to be done to them. Were it left to me, I would strike off their heads here and now.'

'That would make the British very angry,' Martin protested.

'Am I afraid of outer barbarians?' Lin demanded. 'Are you?'

*

Lin carried out his threat. Every Englishman in Canton was placed under arrest. One or two ships managed to get away; the rest were seized and impounded. Meanwhile, plans went ahead for the destruction of the opium. Huge ditches were dug along the waterfront, and into these the drug – there were actually 20,283 chests – was emptied, and then sluiced into the Pearl River.

The Chinese watched in silent consternation.

*

Martin was aghast at what had happened, and the more so when he visited the imprisoned Westerners. He understood that in China criminals of any description were regarded as worthy only of contempt and ill-treatment, even before they were adjudged guilty; he had never supposed he would see his own countrymen so reduced. But the dozen British merchants who had been arrested, most of them men of middle-age and some prosperity, had been crammed into a single Chinese cell, entirely below ground save for a small barred window which looked out upon a courtyard where executions were daily carried out. In the cell itself there was not even a slop bucket, the floor was of mud and seething with insects. The only food for the prisoners apparently consisted of watery soup in which odd lumps of raw meat floated. They still retained their spirit, however. 'By God, Barrington,' one shouted. 'I saw you at that scoundrel's side. You will pay for this!'

However unsympathetic he might feel about their trade, Martin could not but be sorry for them. 'I shall try to have you released,' he said.

'What of our goods? Do you know the value of what he has destroyed? More than two million pounds!'

'As I have said, I will endeavour to procure your freedom. I will not assist you in resuming your filthy trade.'

This brought a fresh chorus of execrations, in the midst of which there was one reasonable voice. 'Mr Barrington, can you at least tell our families that we are alive,' the man said. 'You know this country, and the rumours which will already have travelled down the river.'

'I will do what I can,' Martin promised. 'Your name, sir?'

'Josiah Barnes. I have a house in Macao, where my wife and son and daughter reside.'

'I will see that they are informed,' Martin promised. He wondered what the young man, Hung – he who had caused this to happen – thought about it all. But Hung was not to be found.

*

'Release the barbarians?' Lin snorted. 'So that they may then resume their nefarious trade? Let them sit there and rot.'

'There will be repercussions,' Martin warned him.

'I believe you *are* afraid of the barbarians,' Lin said contemptuously. 'No doubt because you are one yourself. What do you suppose they, so many thousands of li away and with such puny resources, can possibly do against the mandate of the Son of Heaven? I wish to hear no more of this matter, Barrington.'

'When will you be returning to Peking, Commissioner?'

'I shall remain here until I receive further instructions from His Majesty. The place needs ruling until a new governor is appointed.'

'But you will, I hope, permit me to leave with my ship?'

Lin nodded. 'You may go about your business. When I have further need of you, I will send for you.'

*

Martin went to see Sung Tang-chu. 'You have the effrontery to visit me?' Sung demanded. 'After you have destroyed our livelihood?'

'I came to inquire after Hung Hsiu-ch'uan.'

'That crazy young fool!' Sung snorted. 'Tell me straight, Barrington: was it not he put you up to sending the memorandum which brought this calamity upon us?'

'He showed me the evils of the opium trade, certainly.'

'He is a devil,' Sung growled. 'I will not have him back here. Because of him, Canton is ruined.'

*

Martin wished he could be as convinced as others that the barbarian presence was finished. Deporting British merchants and sealing up the port was one thing, and it might well work of itself, especially with Great Britain fully occupied at home, with such things as a girl queen and a bedchamber crisis. But to imprison British citizens in appalling conditions ... when news of that reached London, he did not care to think how the British lion, so proud and so powerful, was going to react.

He left Canton the next day, dropping down the river to Macao, and there bringing up in the middle of a considerable number of vessels. Their crews were in a state of high agitation, swept by rumour, and by the news brought down the river by escaping ships. 'I did not breathe freely until I had passed the forts,' Captain Morrison declared.

Martin was besieged by questions when he went ashore, for if no one yet knew of his part in the affair, it was known that Commissioner Lin had reached Canton on board the Barrington ship, and that the House of Barrington occupied a privileged position in China.

'I'm afraid, gentlemen,' he told them, 'that the days of un-limited importation of opium into China are finished.'

'By God, sir, you sound like a Chink yourself,' someone snapped.

'I am an honest man, sir. What would be your response were the Chinese to import opium into England?'

'Why, sir, that is an entirely different matter. These poor devils have nothing else to live for, save sweet dreams.'

'And will they have anything at all to live for when they wake up from their dreams to find their homes sold, and their wives and children offered on the street corner?'

'Fine words,' sneered Morrison. 'Do they not merely cover your resolve that no Englishman shall trade with China save the House of Barrington?'

'Why, sir, since your trade with China has involved such irres-ponsibility, I do feel it would be best for us all for you to take your ships and yourselves out of here, not to return.'

His words provoked such a clamour of protest that he felt compelled to wrap his right hand the more tightly around the handle of his cane.

'You, sir,' Morrison declared, 'are the son of a pirate, a scoundrel, a renegade, and a traitor to our race and colour!' He paused, understanding that he had said too much. But, equally, he knew that he had the support of the other men present.

Martin drew a long breath. But as he had no real hope that these people would withdraw from the China trade, he must expect to deal with them for the rest of his life; therefore his position had to be maintained. Besides, he was angry. 'I must ask you for an apology, Captain Morrison.'

Morrison glanced from left ro right, and received only encouraging nods. 'You'll not have it, Barrington.'

'Then I must ask you for satisfaction.'

'Have you a second? An English second?'

'No, I have not. My mate . . .'

'This is an English matter, sir. What does your yellow devil of a mate know about honour?'

'Then I must be my own second, it seems. I have challenged you, sir. Name your weapon and your chosen place.'

Again Morrison looked left and right. No one knew enough about Martin Barrington, of what he was capable – that was the trouble.

'If you will permit me, gentlemen,' said a somewhat younger man than the rest, who had hitherto taken little part in the discussion. 'It seems to me that we have a difficulty here, as Captain Barrington may not be familiar with European usage. May I suggest that it were best for you both to forget your differences and shake hands like men . . .' He paused, looking from one to the other.

He was a handsome fellow, and his features were vaguely familiar, although Martin was sure they had not met before.

'All I require from Captain Morrison is an apology,' Martin persisted.

Morrison licked his lips. 'Damned cheek,' said someone in the crowd. 'You'll not apologise, Morrison.'

Morrison hesitated a last time, then threw out his chest. 'I'll not apologise, Barrington. If the cap fits, wear it.'

Martin looked to the young man – who sighed. 'Well, gentlemen, we must hope that saner councils prevail. Will you allow me to organise this for you, as Captain Barrington has no second? I would say tomorrow morning at dawn? It is the usual time. An exchange of fire?'

'As you wish, Mr Barnes,' Morrison said, and turned away, heading for the nearest bar.

'I thank you, sir, for your endeavour,' Martin said. 'Do I understand your name to be Barnes?'

'Indeed it is, sir. Donald Barnes.'

'And your father is at present in Canton.'

'He is, sir. I was hoping you might have word of him.'

'I spoke with him but last week. He asked me to inform your mother that he is well.'

'I would have you tell me of it,' Donald Barnes said. 'And tell my mother as well. Will you dine with us, sir?'

*

'Have you ever fought a duel before?' Donald Barnes asked, as the two men walked towards the Barnes residence.

'It is not a custom in China. When men fight, it is without such formality.'

'As I told Morrison, there is always the chance that, with a twelve-hour cooling-off period, saner thoughts may prevail. We must hope for that in this case.'

Martin found himself warming to this young man, and had to remind himself that, as his father's assistant, Donald Barnes was just as guilty of growing wealthy on the import of opium into China. But it was difficult to remain offhand when eventually they arrived at the Barnes' house. This was quite palatial in what was becoming known as the Colonial style; all three storeys were protected at the front by a high porch roof supported on marble pillars.

'My father has been trading with Canton for more than thirty years,' Donald explained. 'He reminisces, indeed, of once being chased by one of *your* father's ships.'

'I can assure you that if your father was flying the British flag, then my father would not have been his pursuer. But where he was not present, the pirates unfortunately made war upon *any* foreign vessel.'

'I but mentioned the matter to let you know that this house of ours was not built overnight. Now you must meet my mother.' A gracious lady in her middle-fifties, whose strong face was etched with worry lines. 'And my sister Catherine.'

The girl, in her early twenties Martin estimated, had inherited her looks from her mother. She was handsome rather than pretty, tall with a mature figure, and possessed the most splendid straight dark brown hair, worn long and without any attempt at elaborate dressing; perhaps she had not anticipated her brother bringing home a guest.

'Captain Barrington!' Alice Barnes exclaimed. 'We have heard so much about you.' She glanced at her son, uncertain how to proceed.

'Captain Barrington has news of Father,' Donald explained. 'I have invited him to dine.'

'I will tell Wong to lay another cover,' Catherine volunteered, and hurried off. Meanwhile Martin informed Alice Barnes and her son what was happening in Canton.

'You say my husband is well?' Alice Barnes asked.

'As well as can be expected,' Martin told her. 'The conditions of imprisonment are harsh, but I intend to write to the Viceroy requesting that they be ameliorated, and indeed for the release of the prisoners. Unfortunately these things take time, so I must ask you to be patient.'

'You said *all* the Englishmen in Canton were arrested, Captain Barrington,' Catherine Barnes remarked, having returned to hear the end of the conversation.

'I'm afraid that is so, Miss Barnes.'

'But *you* were not?'

Her brother coughed uneasily.

'I am a Chinese citizen, Miss Barnes,' Martin said equably.

*

It was a somewhat difficult meal, with Alice Barnes and her son attempting to make polite conversation, and Martin very aware of Catherine's hostility.

'Now you must excuse me,' he told Mrs Barnes the moment it was polite to do so. 'I must have an early night and a clear head tomorrow.'

'Do you put to sea?'

Martin looked at Donald.

'Captain Barrington has been challenged,' Donald said.

'Oh!' Alice Barnes looked quite shocked.

'I'm sure you will do very well,' said Catherine.

*

'We sail now, Barrington?' Kang-ju inquired.

'Tomorrow's tide.' Kang-ju waited. 'I am to kill a man,' Martin told him.

'Can you not do it now?' Kang-ju was bewildered.

'It must be done tomorrow.'

'Let me do it for you.'

'I will do it,' Martin promised him.

*

Kang-ju insisted upon coming ashore with Martin at five, when darkness was just beginning to fade. He wanted to make sure his friend and master's back was protected; for this purpose he had equipped himself with a blunderbuss.

Donald Barnes was waiting for them. 'You understand the form,' he said. 'An exchange of shots.'

'Does he intend to apologise?'

'I doubt it. But once you have exchanged shots . . .'

'We then shake hands? I'm afraid I do not understand that way of doing things, Mr Barnes. My family and I will still have been insulted. Besides, what would be the point in drawing on a man and not shooting him down?'

'By God, sir, but this will not go down well with the community.'

'I do not belong to this community,' Martin reminded him.

*

They left the docks for the beach, where most of the gentlemen from yesterday were already gathered, besides several additional onlookers.

'Well, Captain Morrison,' Barnes said, 'it is my duty again to invite you to apologise to Captain Barrington, that we may conclude this matter without bloodshed.'

'I have said that I will not,' Morrison insisted.

'May I advise you most strongly, sir,' Barnes begged. 'Captain Barrington will have satisfaction.'

Morrison gazed at him. It was now quite light, and some of the colour could be seen to fade from his face. 'If you apologise now, you'll announce to the world that you are a coward,' said the man at his elbow.

Morrison hesitated, but only for a second.

The distance was paced out, while the onlookers gathered to either side. The pistol case was presented, and Martin allowed Morrison first choice. He felt perfectly cool and totally confident. Early as it was there was alcohol on Morrison's breath – not that it altered his resolve for a moment.

Did Martin mean to kill his adversary? He had been taught the use of weapons by his father at a very early age; and had been taught that weapons should only be used to destroy an opponent. As he had told Barnes, he knew nothing of duelling codes. Nor did he have any certainty that Morrison would follow any code in dealing with someone he regarded as a renegade. The sooner it was done, the better. Barrington was not seeking popularity, or even acceptance, from these people.

The two men faced each other on the sand, and Barnes held his handkerchief high. 'As I release it, gentlemen,' he called.

The wait seemed interminable, though it was only a few seconds, and then the white cloth fluttered downwards. Martin raised his pistol, and was taken by surprise as Morrison moved the more quickly. For a moment his brain froze, and then he was aware of a jar and a sense of shock, although there was no immediate pain.

Someone clapped, and others ran forward, but Barnes waved them back. 'Captain Barrington is still on his feet,' he shouted. 'You'll stand your ground, Morrison.'

Morrison, who had also started to move, checked, his face the picture of consternation, the smoking pistol trailing from his fingers. But now the pain was starting, and Martin realised he was shaking, and that, indeed, he had only a few moments of consciousness left. He raised his right arm with an immense effort, and sighted along the barrel. Morrison had turned side on to him, no doubt in the hopes of presenting a more difficult target, but he could not stop himself from looking at his adversary. Martin gazed at the face, white in the morning, almost round like a target itself. He made a tremendous effort to hold his hand steady for one moment, and then squeezed the trigger. It was the last action he remembered for some time.

*

When Martin awoke, he was between silk sheets in a cool, shaded room. He inhaled the scent of flowers, and listened to soft movements. And he looked up at Catherine Barnes, who was placing a vase on the table beside his bed, unaware that he was watching her. When it was arranged to her satisfaction, she glanced at him, and started. 'Oh,' she said. She hurried for the door.

'Don't go.' His voice seemed very faint, but she checked.

'I must tell my brother you are awake,' she said.

'I should like to look at you for a moment. A man's first sight should be of beauty, do you not think?'

She hesitated, then came back across the room, cheeks flushed. 'Beauty? Me?'

'Has no one ever told you of your beauty before? But you have a mirror.'

She stood by the bed. 'You are badly wounded,' she explained. 'You have lost a deal of blood.' It was as if her words had released a spring in his mind, which had hitherto been restrained. Immediately he was aware of pain, and weakness, and a great thirst. Catherine saw his change of expression and laid a cool hand on his brow. 'You must not agitate yourself,' she told him. 'I will fetch my brother.'

'And some water,' he begged.

*

Water was brought; and a surgeon arrived. The sheets were pulled back and the wound unbandaged. 'The bullet struck a rib and broke it,' the doctor said, replacing the bandages. 'And then penetrated the abdomen. I was fortunate to be able to remove it, and you are fortunate to be alive. The broken bone robbed the shot of its force, you see.' He did not look the least pleased.

'And Morrison?' Martin asked.

'Why, sir, Captain Morrison is dead.'

*

'You shot him through the head,' Donald Barnes told Martin. 'It was a pretty shot, but to most people an unnecessary one. I had some difficulty in saving you from further harm. Indeed, but for your man Kang-ju and his blunderbuss, I doubt I would have succeeded. But I am afraid you must now be about the most unpopular man in this whole community.'

'Then why did you assist me? You do not approve of what I did more than anyone else.'

'I could hardly stand by and see an unconscious man beaten, or left to bleed to death. Besides ... well ...'

'I am the only hope of attaining your father's freedom.'

'You believe in plain speaking, Barrington.'

'It hardly makes sense to do otherwise, Barnes. But I am grateful for your help, and I will do all in my power to assist you, in turn. As soon as I can leave this bed.'

'I'm afraid that may not be for some time yet.'

'What of my ship?'

'She lies in the roads, and awaits your coming. Do not fear. There is no one going to attack a ship of the House of Barrington. But I must warn you that the strongest represent- ations are being made to the Governor-General in Calcutta, demanding vengeance upon Lin. And upon all those who are associated with him. You must certainly try to be well enough to depart by the time a reply is received.'

*

Martin was concerned that there was no means of letting his family know what he was doing. Rumours of what had happened in Canton, if not in Macao, would certainly have reached the Yangtse, and they would wish to know his part in it. His part in it! He had killed a man, and very nearly lost his own life, though neither had been intended. He had meant to hurt Morrison – to make him regret his words. It had never crossed his mind that he might be in danger himself. He wondered how bold he would be the next time he faced an armed man.

But now he had no choice other than to rest and wait both for his wound to heal and his strength to return. He knew it would be virtual suicide to put to sea in his present condition, with the risk of tearing his stomach lining open again. And waiting at least meant that he could see a great deal of Cath- erine Barnes, for her mother had the house to manage, and her brother the office – ships kept arriving from India filled with opium for the Canton warehouses, only to be forced to remain in Macao until the situation was resolved, to the great dissatis- faction of everyone. Thus Catherine was left to do both the entertaining and the nursing of their guest, and, as it was Donald's sound advice that Martin should not leave the garden even when his strength did start to return, they spent a good deal of each day together.

Catherine was a somewhat silent, moody girl, but Martin found himself liking her more and more. There remained an immense gulf between them, however. 'Why did you do it?' she asked one day, as they walked slowly up and down the lawn.

'Morrison insulted my family and myself.'

'Not him. Why did you bring that dreadful man Lin to Canton?'

'I brought him because I was commanded by the Emperor. If you mean why I protested about that vile traffic, have you ever seen an opium den?'

'No one forces them to smoke,' Catherine objected.

'There is not a lot of difference between that and offering something very tempting to essentially simple people.'

'And the House of Barrington has never imported a single chest of opium into China?'

'Not one.'

They gazed at each other. 'My father is suffering terribly, because of you,' Catherine said at last.

'I'm afraid I am bound to say that he brought it on himself,' Martin replied.

'But you still intend to help him.'

'Yes. That does not mean I approve of what he has done.'

'Then no doubt the sooner you set about helping him the better, so that you can forget all about us.'

'I should hate to do that,' he said quietly.

He wondered what he was doing. He loved Jane. He did not think there could be any doubt about that. But he did not know if she loved him. They had not spoken in such terms. After the first fatal step had been taken, it had been a matter of touching, not speaking. Equally, they had never discussed the future. When he had left her last she had merely said, 'Be sure you come back, Martin.'

To renew their immoral liaison put them both on a collision course with calamity. Whereas this girl, so innocent ... Would he be betraying Jane – or making sure they both regained the path from which they had strayed?

'You amuse yourself, sir,' Catherine said.

'I wish I had that art,' he told her.

A moment later she was in his arms.

*

'It is good to be going home.' Kang-ju smiled.

There was so much to be done. If Martin's mind was filled with Catherine, there were a hundred and one other matters to be resolved as well. But Catherine loomed largest. She was the lynchpin which connected everything else.

He had, of course, immediately approached Donald and his

mother, and found them reassuringly warm to his request for Catherine's hand. However, they had pointed out that the decision was not theirs to make. Catherine had also felt that any betrothal would have to be blessed by her father.

Almost had he sailed back up to Canton. But he realised that would accomplish very little. It was Josiah Barnes's freedom that was required. Thus, to regain Catherine's arms, meant an interview with the Viceroy. The Viceroy of Anhwei might not be able to dictate to the Viceroy of Kwantung, much less an Imperial Commissioner, but they were certainly able to exchange views and request favours.

As soon as the entrance to the Yangtse was negotiated, the sweeps were brought out to propel the *Yangtse Queen* upriver to Nanking, where Martin called on the Viceroy before heading home. 'Release them?' Shung-wong asked. 'But are these men not the guilty ones?'

'Indeed, excellency,' Martin said. 'But they have been punished enough by having their goods destroyed and their warehouses burned.'

'If they are criminals, they must suffer for it.'

'I fear for the vengeance of the British.'

'What can these British do?'

'They have the mightiest fleet ever known.'

'If they send their fleet against us, they will be defeated, and scattered to the four winds. However, I will again forward your memorandum to Peking, then act upon their instructions.'

There was nothing more to be done. So Martin went to the House of Barrington, and faced his father and brother, who by now had accumulated every rumour which had seeped up the river.

'Are you mad?' Robert Barrington demanded.

'The fortunes of this House have been based upon refusal to become involved in the affairs of others,' Adrian reminded him.

'The importation of opium is forbidden,' Martin insisted.

'You acted hastily,' Robert growled. 'Now, God knows what will happen.'

8

THE ADMIRAL

Having seen the Viceroy, Martin's thoughts were now centred on his private meeting with Jane. She could tell that he was not in the best of favour with his brother and father, and naturally hesitated to take the slightest risk that might exacerbate this situation. But equally she could show herself totally shocked at the news of his wound, and the risk he had taken in fighting a duel to uphold the good name of the House.

How lovely she was in her colouring, her spirit, her determination not to be subjected by her husband. Martin began to have second thoughts about his projected engagement when she finally managed to visit him on the third day after his return.

'Oh, my darling,' she said. 'Can I touch you?'

'I am perfectly healed.' He showed her the scar.

'I can scarcely believe you survived that.'

He held her close, kissed her hair and her forehead, her eyes and her cheeks, then her mouth. She lay across his chest to kiss him in turn, her red hair flopping on to his face. But he was engaged to be married!

'Tell me the name of the family who nursed you back to health,' she said. 'I wish to be grateful to them.'

He told her about Josiah Barnes, and Donald's part in the duel, and of his mother Alice, and the welcome he had received.

'They sound nice people,' Jane remarked.

'There was also a daughter of the house.'

'Whom you bedded the moment you were well enough,' Jane joked.

'As a matter of fact, I did not. But I proposed marriage.'

Jane gazed at him for some seconds, then rolled aside and sat up. He caught her hand. 'It can make no difference to us. You know you can never make Adrian divorce you.'

She gave him another long look, then reached for her shift. 'Even if he should find out about us?'

'Then he would probably kill me – make me kill him. Do you suppose I could marry my brother's widow?'

'It has been known.'

'Not where one brother has killed the other. Jane, he must never find out. No one must ever find out. And the only way to make sure our secret remains a secret is for me to marry.'

'And our relationship must end?'

'I have said that need not happen.'

Jane fastened her gown. 'You are greedy with us, Martin.'

*

He told himself that she was no more than piqued. For the next few weeks Jane remained no more than conventionally polite, as befitted a sister-in-law, but Adrian and Robert were delighted to hear that he had become engaged to an Englishwoman. Chun-wu was less happy, and Martin strove to convince her that the arrival of Catherine Barnes would make no difference to their domestic arrangements. He was becoming increasingly aware of treading a tightrope of feminine outrage. Meanwhile, Catherine knew nothing of either Chun-wu or Jane, except in so far as she knew there was a sister-in-law.

During these weeks Martin remained in Nanking, and he left the *Yangtse Queen* in the care of Kang-ju, who was perfectly capable of mastering her; his wound was still sufficiently painful to suggest it was not entirely healed. Besides, he wished to keep behind Viceroy Shung-wong, to make sure that something was done about the British prisoners in Canton before the British decided to do something about them themselves.

In the event, the British did act first. All three of the Barringtons were summoned before the Viceroy at the end of the summer. Shung was at once grave and angry, and gestured towards the official letter on his desk. 'The barbarians have dared to declare war upon the Celestial Kingdom,' he announced.

'War?' Robert, who had been carried to the interview in a litter, was horrified.

'It amounts to that. An ultimatum has been delivered to Commissioner Lin, demanding the immediate release of his prisoners, and in addition the payment of total compensation for the opium which has been destroyed. Failing this, a British fleet will sail up the Pearl River and take what is demanded at the point of a gun. Have you ever heard of such effrontery? A British fleet sailing up the Pearl! Have we not forts to command the entrance? Have we not fleets of our own?'

'May I ask what was Commissioner Lin's reply?'

'Why, he dismissed the barbarians with contempt – and had one executed.'

'My God!' Adrian exclaimed. 'Then there *will* be war.'

'The barbarians will be destroyed,' Shung declared.

'Your excellency,' Robert said, 'you were but a boy forty-five years ago, yet I am sure you remember the great ships which brought Lord Macartney to China.'

Shung smiled. 'And you, too, Barrington. But there were only six ships. His Celestial Majesty commands hundreds of war junks.'

'Excellency, those ships were merchantmen, not half as powerful as a British warship, and the King of England commands at least a hundred of them, any one of which could destroy ten Chinese war junks within minutes.'

Shung frowned at him. 'You expect me to believe that?'

'It is the truth. I beg you to inform his Celestial Majesty of what I have said, and suggest to him it would be better to recall Commissioner Lin and release the prisoners.'

'That would mean surrendering to the barbarian threats.'

'I doubt they are mere threats.'

*

'Will he act, do you suppose?' Adrian asked his father, as they returned to the House of Barrington.

'I believe he will. Shung is an intelligent fellow. As to whether anyone else will do so ...'

'What course do you wish us to follow?' Martin asked.

'Strict neutrality,' Robert said. 'And that particularly applies to you, since you stirred up this hornet's nest in the first place. We will recall all our ships from south of the Yangtse until this crisis has been resolved.'

'I must at least send a message to my intended.'

Robert nodded. 'You must do that. But your marriage must also wait upon the outcome of this matter.'

*

Catherine was overjoyed, judging by her letters, at the thought that 'something was being done'. Her only fear was that Lin might order the execution of his prisoners, should a British battle fleet appear in the Pearl. Martin knew this was a real possibility, but did his best to reassure her; and to promise her that the most likely outcome would be the release of the prisoners, and thus their marriage could take place.

Jane continued to hold herself aloof. Meanwhile the House of Barrington concentrated upon its Yangtse trade. As soon as he was again fully fit, Martin went upriver to Wuhu, and visited his friend the Intendant there. Hui-cheng was far more concerned about the crisis than Shung had been; he had spent his boyhood in Canton and seen barbarian ships at close hand, even if, like all Manchu, he had never actually seen a British man-of-war.

'Lin is a madman to have acted so,' he declared. 'This is what comes from employing a Chinese in a position of authority.'

'But all is well on the Yangtse,' Martin reassured him. 'And with you, I hope.' That he could see.

Hui-cheng still refused to enrich himself at the expense of his clients, but his family was well; and despite the preponderance of girls, he was encouraged by the prognostication of a new fortune-teller, who reinforced the earlier prophecy by assuring him that one of his daughters was destined for greatness. Certainly Lan Kuei, the Little Orchid, was a black-haired delight as she approached her fifth birthday. As she had been born towards the end of 1835, by European reckoning, she was of course only three and three-quarters years old – but the Chinese custom was to date one's years from the previous New Year's Day, thus Lan Kuei, born within six weeks of New Year's Day 1836, had appeared in the world at virtually two years of age!

They were a happy, rumbunctious family who always made Martin feel good within himself, and he returned downriver in the best of humours – to find awaiting him a summons to the Viceroy's presence.

'I forwarded your memorandum to Peking, Barrington,' Shung-wong told him. 'And, as before, His Celestial Majesty was impressed by your honesty and your perspicacity.'

'I am greatly flattered, excellency.'

'It is an honour,' Shung agreed. 'Now, as to what is to be done! His Celestial Majesty is agreed with you that Commissioner Lin exceeded his authority and acted in a high-handed and arrogant manner that is unbecoming for a representative of the Throne of Heaven. He is thus to be dismissed from his post.'

Martin gave a smile of relief.

'However,' Shung went on. 'His Celestial Majesty regards this as simply an act of justice. It is not a surrender to the barbarian demands.'

'But, if Commissioner Lin is considered to have exceeded his authority, then the prisoners will be released?'

'It is possible that if the barbarians withdraw their ultimatum and make a suitable apology, the prisoners may be released. However, there can be no question of any compensation being paid for the smuggled goods which were destroyed.'

'Your excellency, the barbarians will not accept that.'

'It is suspected that they may not,' Shung agreed. 'His Majesty has commanded his viceroys to prepare for war, so that the barbarians may be taught a lesson once and for all. I have here' – he tapped a parchment on his desk – 'a letter under the imperial seal, authorising you to proceed immediately to Canton.'

'Me?'

'His Majesty is of the opinion that since you began this business, you too had best finish it. You will place Commissioner Lin under arrest. He is not to be executed, Barrington, but is to be returned to his estates, and told to stay there until His Majesty comes to a decision about his future.'

Martin nodded. He thought this task was going to be a pleasure. And besides ...

Shung seemed able to read his thoughts. 'You will not release the barbarian prisoners until instructed to do so.'

Martin sighed. But at least he could surely alleviate the conditions of their imprisonment.

'Having arrested Commissioner Lin, you will then take command of the imperial fleet in the South China Sea. You have the power to requisition ships and men as you choose. With this fleet you will destroy any barbarian ships which may attempt to enter the Pearl River. Is that understood?'

Martin stared at him in consternation. 'I have never commanded a fleet of war.'

'It is well remembered how your illustrious father commanded the fleet of the immortal Dragon Lady. Were he a few years younger, he would have been given this command himself.'

'You are asking me to fight against my own countrymen?'

'You are a Chinese citizen, are you not?'

Martin swallowed. 'Excellency, as my father has explained, this is impossible. No fleet in the world can defeat the British.'

'His Majesty discounts such an absurd suggestion. Your instructions are to destroy the barbarian ships. See that is done.' Shung looked at him very directly. 'The future of the House of Barrington depends upon it.'

*

'You have brought it on yourself,' Robert remarked.

'But what am I to do? I have never fought a ship at sea.'

'There is nothing you can do save obey the Emperor's command – and then hope to escape with your skin.'

'I will sail with you,' Adrian said. 'And I *have* fought a ship at sea. Do not worry, Martin. I shall not encroach upon your prerogatives. *You* are the Admiral. You may appoint me your second-in-command, or your sailing master ... whatever you will.'

'By God, to have you at my side ...' Martin's heart swelled, but with self-disgust as much as with pride. He had shamefully betrayed this man who was now prepared to fight beside him. 'Will Shung agree?'

'Why should he not? He will still hold Father, and Jane and the children, and all the wealth of the House of Barrington. He will know we intend to return.'

Martin looked at his father.

'Oh, go, both of you,' Robert growled. 'I but wish I could come with you. Just be sure that one of you, at least, comes back.'

*

'Are you mad?' Jane cried. 'You and Adrian going off to fight a war against your own people? A war you are bound to lose? Are you *mad*?'

'We must hope to lose with honour, at least,' Martin said.

'Anyway, we have no choice. The Emperor has decreed it.'

She was not reassured, and came to his bed that afternoon for the first time since he had told her of his engagement. But it was a frenzied, unhappy love-making. Clearly she supposed she was about to lose both husband *and* lover.

*

'Will you stop at Macao?' Adrian asked, as they stood with Kang-ju on the poopdeck of the *Yangtse Queen* and watched the headland rising out of the ocean.

Martin had been considering the matter. 'I think not.'

'You are supposing Catherine will not take kindly to the knowledge that you are to command a Chinese fleet against the British.'

'I am certain of it. My only hope is a *fait accompli.* If I can turn up at Macao with her father safe and sound, then she will forgive me anything.'

Adrian made no comment, but clearly he was of the opinion that his brother was being optimistic.

Martin stayed on the north side of the estuary, and dropped anchor off the Bogue Forts guarding the entrance to the Pearl River. There he went ashore to see Teng-go-lin, the Manchu garrison commander. Teng inspected the commission with great care. 'This places me also under your command, Barrington.'

'Our business is to hold the river, and defeat any force which may attempt to sail up it.'

'Oh, we will do that,' Teng asserted. 'There is no warship can pass beneath my guns.'

Martin hoped he was right. Next day the *Yangtse Queen* began the ascent to Canton itself, and four days later was moored alongside the quay. Martin went ashore immediately, and called on the Commissioner.

Lin was all smiles. 'It is good to see you again. I heard of your wound. Now you have come to help defend us against these barbarian threats?'

'I have come to command you,' Martin told him, and showed him his own commission.

Lin frowned as he read it. 'Am I to die?'

'You are under arrest, and will be returned to your estates to await the judgement of the Emperor.'

'I am thus rewarded for carrying out his instructions?' Lin said bitterly.

'For exceeding his instructions.'

'You think so? Well, now you have received your instructions, too, Barrington. We shall have to see what reward *you* receive for carrying them out.'

Lin was a shattered man. But Martin could afford to think only of the future. When he went to visit the British prisoners, he was appalled. The conditions under which they existed had deteriorated with the coming of the winter rains; their clothes were in rags and they themselves were emaciated and weak; several were suffering from fever.

Martin commanded them to be removed from their cell and taken to rooms in the viceregal palace, where they were bathed and given decent clothes to wear. He then summoned Josiah Barnes to his presence. 'Have you heard anything from Macao?' he asked.

'Nothing more than rumour.' Barnes had suffered as severely as anyone, and found it difficult to stop his hands from shaking. 'Why are you doing this?'

'Should I not? I am in command here, now.'

'But you will not release us.'

'I am forbidden by the Emperor. However, you *will* be released, whatever the outcome of the war.'

Martin told him of the British ultimatum, and the Manchu response. 'By God,' Barnes muttered. 'And you say ... whatever the outcome?'

'Should the British win, it will certainly be their intention to obtain your freedom. Should they be defeated, His Majesty will certainly order your release. He is not an unjust man, or a cruel one; he simply will not be browbeaten.'

'And you are confident of victory.'

'On the contrary, I have no doubt of my defeat.'

'You are a man of character, Mr Barrington.'

'I would hope to be more than that, sir.' Martin then told him of what had happened in Macao.

Barnes stroked his freshly-shaven chin. 'I suppose there is not a deal of difference between character and effrontery,' he commented. 'Or do I endanger my life by saying that?'

'Do you then consider me unworthy of your daughter's hand?'

'You are a renegade and the son of a pirate, who now intends to fight against his own people.'

Martin bristled. 'I am endeavouring to end a criminal business which does your people no credit, sir.'

'The importation of opium is an enterprise sanctioned by the British Parliament,' Barnes declared.

'And is the British Parliament the supreme arbiter of what is right and wrong upon the face of this earth?' Martin demanded. 'In this instance it is most terribly wrong, and the Chinese are right to resist such a pernicious trade. I know enough to realise that the Royal Navy may well gain the day against us, but I most fervently hope I am proved wrong.'

'And you wish to marry my daughter!'

'Can we not differ in politics and yet be friends?'

Barnes gave him a cold stare. 'I doubt that will be possible, Barrington. Now do your worst.'

*

Martin sent him back to his room. He was angry, because he had supposed Barnes at least would understand his situation. Now it had to be settled between Catherine and himself.

He had in any event to return downriver and begin accumulating ships, and training their crews. Only half a dozen junks capable of serving in battle were alongside in Canton, and although two British ships had been seized, he did not have the time to train Chinese seamen in the method of handling such vessels, although he appropriated their guns and powder and shot.

By now his purpose in Canton, and his commission, were well known, and there was no one dared refuse his command that they place themselves under his orders, but he could tell they were reluctant – and he had no means of knowing if they would actually fight when the moment came. They were all he had, however, so he instructed them to follow the *Yangtse Queen* downriver when he sailed next morning.

That evening, as he and Adrian sat in the after-cabin with their meal, Kang-ju came in to announce that there was someone to see him. 'That boy,' the mate said disparagingly, 'who first took you to the opium den and caused all this trouble.'

'Hung Hsiu-ch'uan!' Martin murmured, and went to the door. 'Come in, Hung.'

The young man had certainly deteriorated in appearance since last they had met. His clothes were threadbare, his hair lank and uncombed, his eyes wild. Martin had to wonder if Hung had himself succumbed to the temptations of opium smoking.

'I had heard you were unwell,' he said.

'I am well.' Hung looked over at Adrian.

'My brother, and vice-admiral,' Martin told him.

'You serve the Manchu.' Hung's voice was bitter.

'We have always served the Manchu.'

'I would speak with you in private, Barrington.'

'He is a rebellious lout,' Kang-ju declared.

'Leave us,' Martin said. 'And you, too, Adrian, if you would be so good.' Adrian looked as if he would protest, then changed his mind and went out, closing the door behind himself.

'Some sake?' Martin offered.

'Strong liquor is the stuff of the devil,' Hung growled. Clearly he had become even more intense since his illness.

Martin poured some sake for himself. 'What did you wish to speak with me about?'

He sat down, and after a moment Hung also seated himself. 'I have heard there is to be war between the Manchu and the British, and that you are fighting for the Manchu?'

'They are the government of China, Hung. And you are attempting to preach treason to an imperial admiral. That I do not arrest you is because of your ideals – ideals upon which the Manchu have acted, and which condemned your own people.'

'My people,' Hung sneered. 'I am a Hakka, not a Chinese. The Chinese despise the Hakka. Yet I will save them from themselves, because they are at least more acceptable than the Manchu. Listen to me, Barrington, now is your opportunity to gain true greatness. To gain immortality.'

'What do you seek of me?'

'You must use your new powers to overthrow the Manchu. You must seize control of Canton, of the entire viceroyalty of Kwangtung. From here, you and I will begin the revolution that will destroy the Ch'ing.' He paused, staring at Martin, eyes blazing, mouth open, panting for breath.

Martin felt pretty breathless himself. Of Hung's genuine fervour there could be no doubt. Equally there could be no doubt that he hovered on the brink of madness. And Martin was reluctant to be the one who pushed him over that brink. But he was required to deal with the real world, with the fact that his father and Jane and her children were still in Nanking, and that the prosperity of the House of Barrington depended entirely upon the favour of the House of Ch'ing.

'Hung,' he said. 'I have been given a task: to protect the Pearl River and Canton against the British fleet – and to defeat that fleet. That is the task I must carry out.'

Hung stood up. 'You are saying you will not help me.'

'I am saying that it would be wiser for you to forget your dreams, and concentrate upon passing that examination. Or it will go hard with you.'

Hung's face convulsed in a snarl. 'One day I will sweep the Manchu away like dust before the broom. When that day comes, it will go hard with the House of Barrington!' He ran from the cabin.

*

'China is full of such fanatics,' Kang-ju observed, when Martin recounted the interview. 'You should have placed him under arrest, and taken his head.'

'A man can be forgiven his dreams,' Martin pointed out.

'When dreams become visions,' Kang-ju argued, 'men try to make them come true.'

'Then no doubt his head *will* wind up on a wall.'

'And you like the fellow,' Adrian suggested, when the brothers were alone.

'No, but I respect him. Though I am also sure he is as mad as a March hare, and will finish in the gutter.'

*

They dropped anchor off the Bogue, where Martin was delighted to find that General Teng had accumulated another half dozen ships. He had the makings of a fleet, but he knew he would need a lot more, so he took the *Yangtse Queen* further down the coast, both to round up more ships and to call in at

Macao. There, accompanied by Adrian, he visited the Barnes residence, while the people on shore gaped at the dragon and phoenix banners flying from his masthead, proclaiming him to be Admiral of the Manchu fleet.

'I could not believe my eyes,' Donald declared. 'But what does it mean?'

Martin explained the situation.

'You had best come home and see Mother ... and Catherine,' Donald said unhappily.

*

Martin was greeted warmly enough.

'Have you news?' Catherine asked anxiously. 'We heard reports that the *Yangtse Queen* was in the river some weeks ago.'

'I have been up to Canton,' Martin told her. He had no better course than sheer honesty.

'Have you spoken with Father?'

'Is he well?' Alice Barnes cut in.

'He is better than he was,' Martin said carefully. 'All of the prisoners are suffering from fever and various stomach complaints. But I have seen that they are properly housed and fed, and hopefully they will soon be on the mend.'

'Thank God for your influence with Commissioner Lin.'

Martin paused a moment. 'Commissioner Lin no longer commands in Canton.'

'Well, that is a step in the right direction. And the new commissioner is a more sensible man.'

'There is no new commissioner. Owing to the British declaration of war, the entire province of Kwantung has been placed under naval rule.'

'You mean the Manchu mean to fight? Where have they found an admiral?' Alice was scornful.

'You are looking at him, Mrs Barnes.'

For a moment both women were struck dumb. Then Catherine clapped her hands. 'But that is marvellous.'

'Then why did you not bring my husband here with you?' Alice inquired.

'Because I have no authority to release the prisoners. At least until after the British have been defeated.'

'You mean you intend to fight the Royal Navy?'

'Those are my orders.'

'You would command a Manchu fleet against your own people?' Alice looked aghast at her son and daughter.

Adrian broke in, 'The prosperity of the House of Barrington depends upon the goodwill of the Ch'ing.'

'Prosperity?' Alice cried. 'What can prosperity have to do with fighting against your own kith and kin?'

'I have no kith and kin in England, madam.'

Catherine licked her lips nervously, 'What did my father have to say?'

'He did not accept my offer. Therefore I must make it to you, again, here and now. Will you marry me?'

'I . . .' She looked at her mother.

'I'm afraid that is no longer possible, Mr Barrington.'

Martin looked at Donald. 'It would be difficult,' the young man said. 'Believe me, I am sorry, Barrington.'

'But I would hear the words from Catherine's mouth.'

Catherine licked her lips again. 'I . . . I cannot go against the wishes of my mother and father, Mr Barrington.'

'Then I can only wish you good fortune in another direction.' He left the room, and Adrian followed him.

'I'm sorry,' Adrian said.

'Some things were not meant to be,' Martin growled.

But what things were meant to be? Adrian did not know even a fraction of what had been at stake.

*

They regained the *Yangtse Queen*, and put to sea. Next morning they sighted a junk running north before a south-easterly breeze, and made towards her. The captain came on board in tremendous excitement, to tell them that a British squadron had put into Singapore harbour, on its way north.

9

THE GUNS OF WRATH

'How many ships did you see?' Martin demanded.

'Many ships. More than twenty.' The captain was obviously in a state of considerable alarm.

'Big ships?'

'Some of them were very big, Barrington.'

'Ships-of-the-line,' Adrian suggested. 'What is your plan?'

'I think we must leave them to make the first overt act of war, by attempting to enter the river', Martin decided. 'We can only hope to defeat them with the support of the forts.'

*

Meanwhile, he went on accumulating such ships as he could, while also despatching several small fishing boats down the coast to bring him early warning of the British approach. By the beginning of the summer he had mustered some twenty vessels, but he still had no precise information as to the whereabouts of the British squadron, until late in June his scouts came back to the Bogue to say that they had spotted sails on the southern horizon.

Martin himself put to sea in a fishing boat equipped with his father's telescope, and inspected the British squadron as it approached, feeling his heart slow as he counted sixteen ships which he estimated to be men-of-war, including six monsters – ships-of-the-line of hardly less than seventy guns each. The others were frigates and sloops, but accompanying them were a large number of merchantmen, clearly transports. In all he counted some forty vessels standing proudly on into the freshening wind. He returned to the Bogue to acquaint Teng and the others with just what they were up against.

'Our only real chance is that it is already summer,' he told them. 'If we can hold them for a couple of months until the autumnal gales start, they will find this a difficult shore.'

177

*

To their surprise, however, the British squadron made no immediate assault upon the Pearl, but sailed past, to the north.

'My God, if they mean to attack Peking . . .' Adrian said.

'Their force is not sufficient for that,' Martin argued.

In fact, the British entered the deep Gulf of Chusan, south of the mouth of the Yangtse, and there made a base on one of the islands, after bombarding the port of Ningpo and taking it by assault. This brought frantic letters from Viceroy Shung, demanding that Martin take his ships north and attack the enemy.

'There are an estimated four thousand barbarian troops, including many of dark faces, ashore on Chinese soil. This is intolerable. You must destroy them at once, Admiral Barrington.'

'He means sepoys,' Adrian observed.

'They have come to wage a regular campaign, then,' Martin said. 'And we must not be deflected from our plans.'

He wrote to Shung to explain the situation, and his strategy, and to his father to the same effect. He was very tempted to enclose a letter for Jane, but dared not, and had to content himself with a formal remembrance.

*

Shung was neither reassured nor convinced, and neither was Peking. Martin was bombarded with letters throughout the summer and autumn, all urging action, and to all of which he replied that he had not yet accumulated sufficient ships to take on a squadron of British ships-of-the-line, unless they first placed themselves at a disadvantage, as he was confident they would do when they sought to force their way up the river.

In fact he was informed by Robert Barrington that the British were still attempting to negotiate, and that messages were being exchanged between Ningpo and Peking. He was therefore content to wait, all the while training his men and keeping Teng and his garrison ready for action. He maintained a squadron of junks at sea, watching the gulf, but the British were apparently concentrating on returning their men to full health after their long sea voyage, and were also waiting to see if Peking could be brought to the negotiating table. Nor did they in any way interfere with the normal seaborne trade up and down the Chinese coast, although their frigates were apparently often to be found at sea, reconnoitring the bays and islands.

Martin worked his men as hard as he could, and was gratified by the aggressive intentions of Teng and his Bannermen, but far less so by the attitude of the junk captains, all of whom were praying fervently that the British would go away again.

Well, was he not doing the same? He also had his personal problems to brood on, whenever he was not actively engaged. If his brother Adrian were aware of the almost impossible task they had been set, he never revealed it, but seemed invariably confident and positive, his so often acerbic attitude to life well subdued. But he was also a constant reminder to Martin of what a mess he had made of his personal life. He did not know for certain whether he had actually loved Catherine Barnes, but he had seen in her a panacea for his wayward emotions. Now she had rejected him, and he would return – if he returned – to Jane's arms. And to all the imponderables that lay ahead of that.

*

A month after the arrival of the British fleet, a subsidiary squadron sailed past Macao. These were mainly additional transports, but they were escorted by a vessel such as none of the Chinese or Manchu captains had ever seen before, nor Martin himself.

Conventional enough from a distance, in that she carried two masts, the warship appeared rather low in the water, and belched smoke as she proceeded. When examined by telescope, she could be seen to possess two huge paddle-wheels, one on either side, which churned the sea as they drove her along her course, regardless of wind direction. The brothers had at least heard of steam-driven ships, whereas the Chinese had not. Morale suffered, even as Martin tried to reassure his people that the newcomer was, after all, just another ship.

*

The summer drifted into autumn, and the gales began. 'Well, that means we shall not see them before next spring, at the earliest,'

Adrian declared. 'Do you think it might be possible to go
home for Christmas?' The festival had always been faithfully
celebrated in the Barrington household.

'Possible – for you certainly. It is not practical for me,'
Martin said. 'Should anything happen in my absence, the
Emperor would have my head.'

'Nothing can happen in the winter,' Adrian argued. But he
decided that if Martin was staying, he would also, and in the
event they were both surprised when their junks came back
down the coast in January to report that the British had put to
sea. 'All we need is a real winter storm, and they'll be scattered,' Adrian said, snapping his fingers.

'They'll be looking for a sheltered harbour closer to the
Pearl,' Martin said thoughtfully.

'Macao?'

'The Portuguese would not dare allow it, unless the British
guaranteed them protection till the end of time.'

The weather remained settled, however, and the British
reconnoitring voyages had borne fruit; they had discovered a
group of islands which provided a natural breakwater against
the elements, close to the mouth of the Pearl. The main island,
known as Hong Kong, was uninhabited, used only by fishermen
from time to time, but that did not prevent the British from
setting up camp there and building a fort. This news was
brought to the Bogue – only a matter of a few miles – by
Martin's scouts.

'The effrontery of these people!' Adrian commented. 'They
seem to feel that they can appropriate Chinese territory as they
choose, and no one will do anything about it.'

Martin gave a wry grin. 'Well, isn't that the truth?'

*

He expected to be given a further respite, at least until the
spring, and was therefore taken entirely by surprise when, only
a week later, the alarm was sounded in the forts. Martin went
ashore, and accompanied Teng to the highest battlements, from
where he could look out at the sea. He gulped at the acres of
white canvas he saw, standing majestically down the coast.

'My guns are loaded,' Teng told him. 'Just let them come
close enough.'

'It is almost as if they were on review,' Adrian commented.

The suggestion was apt as, keeping carefully out of range of either gunshot or unsuspected shoal or rock, the men-of-war sailed past the mouth of the Pearl before a gentle north-westerly breeze, and then came about to repeat the manoeuvre. The return journey was much slower, as the ships now had to tack into the wind, but the way they were handled left both Martin and Adrian, experienced sailors themselves, filled with admiration. They were still studying the enemy through their glasses when a messenger arrived from the north, breathless and in a state of terrified excitement.

'They are landing their soldiers, your excellency,' he told Martin. 'Their transports have sailed across from Hong Kong island, and they are putting their people ashore in small boats.'

'While we admire their regatta,' Adrian commented.

'I shall send a Banner detachment to deal with these bar-barians,' Teng declared.

'You may well need them here,' Adrian told him, and pointed – for the squadron had gained its required position, and was coming about again, this time closing the shore.

'Prepare to open fire,' Martin said. 'It will take some time for their soldiers to march down the coast – they cannot have any cavalry to speak of. If, before they get here, we have matched their ships for gunfire, it will make them think again. Adrian, come with me. We will attack their flank while they are concentrating on the fort.'

Teng looked down at the courtyard, where another messenger was dismounting from a foam-flecked horse. 'Perhaps the barbarian soldiers are closer than you think.'

But the messenger was from Peking, having crossed the mountain trail from Hang-chau. 'A proclamation from the Son of Heaven, excellency,' he said.

Martin read the proclamation with a sense of horror. 'His Majesty announces that we are to offer ten taels for the head of every white-skinned soldier or sailor, and five for the dark-skinned ones.'

'This will make our people fight the harder,' Teng said.

'It is barbaric.' Adrian looked at his brother. 'What will you do?'

'I will obey orders. This proclamation is to be read to your men, General Teng.'

'And the fleet?'
'When it returns from this battle. I do not think we are going
to come to close enough quarters to secure any heads.'

*

Martin and Adrian hurried down the ladders, but before they
reached the courtyard the entire fort trembled as Teng opened
fire. The brothers hurried out of the main gateway and on to
the bluff above the river to see what damage had been done.
None of the ships appeared to have been hit, and such water as
was still seething indicated that the Chinese shooting had been
too short. But that was simply a matter of adjustment.

Martin turned away for the dock, and was enveloped in a
very hot wind. He fell to his knees, and was only then reached
by the sound of the six broadsides, rumbling across the morning
like thunder. He raised his head, and saw chunks of masonry
rising into the air, and heard the screams of the alarmed
Chinese.

'Some shooting,' Adrian yelled, helping him to his feet.

Martin made no reply as they ran down the sloping pathway
to the dock, where the boat's crew was waiting for them,
pointing and chattering amongst themselves. 'What are you
afraid of?' he bellowed at them. 'This is the battle we have been
waiting for.' Above their heads the fort's guns were firing again,
even if there was still no evidence of any damage to the English
ships.

Kang-ju was pacing the poopdeck of the *Yangtse Queen*.
'What is happening, Barrington?' he yelled.

'Signal all ships that we are going to put to sea and engage
the enemy.'

Kang-ju gave the orders, and men hurried to obey. The crew
of the *Yangtse Queen* had total confidence in their captain and
admiral. But the same could not be said for the rest of the fleet,
whose people were staring up at the forts, wreathed in smoke as
they fired again and again; but also wreathed in dust and rubble
from where the British shot had struck.

Yet Teng was at least fighting. Martin called for a sampan,
and had himself rowed through the fleet, as he recalled his
father telling him Cheng Yi Sao had done before the decisive
battle with the Manchu navy. 'Follow me,' he told his captains.

'To victory.' He regained the *Yangtse Queen* and gave orders to make sail. The anchor came up, and the huge junk slowly gathered way, slipping through the well-known channels between the sandbanks – additional defences against the British – and making more sail as she reached the open sea.

Martin looked up. Above his head the dragon flag flew proudly, and just beneath it the phoenix. He levelled his glass; he wanted the British flagship. The warships continued to be surrounded by smoke as they pounded the forts, but it did not take him long to identify the rear-admiral's pennant. 'There's our target,' he told Kang-ju. 'Steer straight for him.'

Adrian touched him on the arm, and he looked over his shoulder. Only three junks could be seen clear of the sandbanks.

'The others are coming,' Martin assured him.

'Do you really think so?'

'Would you have me call off the attack, now?' Martin asked. 'Would you commit suicide?'

Martin bit his lip, and went to the rail. Their approach had been observed, but instead of the British squadron turning away from the assault on the fort to face this new foe, a single ship had been detached ... Through his glass he could make out that she was the paddle-steamer, although at the moment under full sail.

She was still several miles away. That meant there was time for him to go about and regain the safety of the Pearl. But to do that would ruin what morale remained in his fleet. And how would the news that he had refused a fight be received in Peking, much less in Nanking? Especially as he did not yet know for certain that no more ships were coming to his support. Whereas, if he engaged, and inflicted some damage upon the British, and then broke off the action for lack of support, no one could blame him. And the British might well have to withdraw to effect repairs. 'We stand on,' he said.

*

Martin gazed at the approaching ship as she emerged from the smoke clouds drifting lazily upwards, her sharp bow slicing the shallow waves in bursts of white foam, her sails, pulled hard in to port, billowing in the breeze, her paddle-wheels for the moment still. No doubt the junks made a similarly impressive sight, he hoped, for the south-westerly breeze was free for the Manchu squadron, and their sails were full. If only there were more of them.

'All guns loaded and ready,' Adrian reported.

'You'll hold your fire until we are close enough to be effective.'

Adrian nodded, and went down to the main deck. As he did so, the wind dropped, and the slatted sails thudded against the masts.

'Damnation,' Martin muttered. But at least it would affect the British also. Save that that was why they had sent the steamship against him. For as he watched, the sails came down on the enemy vessel, and puffs of smoke emerged from the funnel, at the same time as the paddle-wheels began to turn. The Chinese could only stare at the apparition in consternation.

Kang-ju stood by the helm. 'When will they shoot, Barrington?'

'When they are certain of the range.'

But the moment was approaching very rapidly. He estimated the British ship to be hardly more than two sea miles distant, and she was making at least six knots, judging by her wake. Twenty minutes! He walked to the break of the poop and looked down; his men remained eager enough as they crouched over their guns, and Adrian was walking up and down behind them, speaking to each gun crew in turn, quietly and reassuringly. At least the drifting junks were starting to lose their forward momentum, and to fall away to right and left; they would be able to fire their broadsides.

'She is turning, Barrington,' Kang-ju said.

Martin watched the steamer altering course to present her broadside, gunports flopping open as she did so. 'Prepare to fire,' he called down to his brother. But he knew, left helpless by the absence of wind, that he was not going to be able to bring all his guns to bear.

Still looking at the British ship, Martin saw her disappear behind a veil of white smoke. A moment later the *Yangtse Queen* shuddered as if seized by a giant hand. Martin watched plumes of water rising to either side of the junk – but not enough had missed. Even half bows on, the *Yangtse Queen* had presented too much of a target to the Navy gunners, and forward was a mess of shattered wood and cut cordage, and dying men. The foremast came down with a crash.

There were shouts of dismay from the Chinese, while across the water there came the distant sound of cheering. Martin ran to the break of the poop. 'Adrian!' he bellowed. 'Adrian!'

'I am here.'

None of the shots had reached amidships, but Martin knew he had to see the damage forward for himself. 'Fire as you bear!' he shouted, and ran down the ladder into the waist. He had just reached the deck, however, when the *Yangtse Queen* was again shaken from stem to stern, and this time the hail of shot crashed into the entire ship. Martin, staggering against the starboard bulwarks, listened to the crackle of sheering timbers as the other two masts came down. He had supposed he would have several minutes while the British reloaded; instead they had simply used their steam power to go about and deliver their starboard broadside while the port guns were re-charged.

He gazed at a shambles. The fallen masts were strewn across the deck; the deck itself was a mass of cordage and blood and pieces of men; several guns had been dismounted and thrown on their sides by the flying shot.

The noise was tremendous, but it was mainly caused by screaming men; only two of the junk's guns had managed to respond, and there was so much smoke that it was impossible to tell if any of the shots had struck home. While the junk itself, apart from being dismasted and helpless, was also mortally stricken. Martin knew this, from the slight tilt of the deck below his feet as he regained his balance.

Miraculously, he was unhurt. 'Adrian!' he shouted, stumbling forward through a morass of blood and severed limbs, scattered brains and exposed bones. Adrian had been only a few feet away when last he had seen him. Now . . . He gazed at the crumpled heap beneath the fallen mainmast, dropped to his knees to tug at the body, even as he knew he was wasting his time.

'Barrington!' Kang-ju was beside him, blood dripping from a gash in the head. 'We are sinking.'

Martin continued to stare at the brother he had so betrayed, who had volunteered to fight at his side. And had died for it.

'Barrington!' Kang-ju wailed. There was another tremendous gust of hot wind, and the *Yangtse Queen* shuddered again. But not as violently as before; she had no life in her – was nothing more than a hulk settling into the sea.

In a cacophony of sound the remaining crew poured up from
below, shrieking their terror, not waiting for the command to
abandon ship. All the boats had been smashed by the British
fire, and the seamen started throwing themselves into the water.

'Barrington!' Kang-ju begged. 'If we do not leave now we
will drown. Your brother is dead. There is nothing you can do
for him now.' He dragged Martin to his feet, pushed him to the
gunwale, which was now almost at water level as the *Yangtse
Queen* listed even further, while from below came all the
unhappy groans and crashes of a ship about to sink. Instinctively Martin dived into the water, striking out vigorously, Kang-
ju at his side. They swam for several minutes before pausing for
breath and turning on their backs to look around them.

A catastrophe! Close at hand, the *Yangtse Queen* had not yet
disappeared, but her main deck was now awash, and it could
only be a matter of seconds. Further off, the British steamer
continued to be concealed behind the white smokescreen as it
delivered broadside after broadside at the remaining junks.
There was no evidence of any return fire.

Indeed, as he looked back, beyond the *Yangtse Queen*, he
saw two more of his junks dismasted and sinking, their crews
throwing themselves into the sea. Only one remained afloat,
and her crew were hastily abandoning her, taking to the boats
to escape the terrible fire of the steamer, and making for the
presumed safety of the Pearl as fast as they could.

'Here, Barrington,' Kang-ju panted. He had secured a
broken spar, and was pushing this towards his Admiral. 'You
must hold on to this.'

'Why?' Martin asked, sagging in the water, his mind a blank
of despair.

'It is a man's duty to his ancestors to preserve his life as long
as is possible,' Kang-ju said.

Martin wrapped his arms round the wood. Kang-ju's words
had reminded him that there was a great deal for him to live
for. But could he ever look his father in the face again? He had
led his fleet to utter destruction. Easy to say he might have
done better had he been supported. He knew that was not true.
If he had brought fifty junks into battle they would have been
shot to pieces by the accuracy and, above all, the speed of the
British gunnery, combined with the ability of the steamer to
move when the junks could not.

But his responsibilities were not over. They had hardly begun. All around him the sea was filled with men, his men, calling for help, shouting at each other, asking what to do. And he could do nothing for them.

The firing had stopped, and the steamer was standing away to rejoin the British squadron; while there were shouts in the distance, and several rockets could be seen flaring through the sky from the forts. 'Sampans,' Kang-ju said. 'They are coming from the estuary.'

Thank God for Teng, Martin thought. But would they be in time? Already some of the seamen were drowning, for the water was very cold; he supposed they were lucky it was so cold that at least there were not likely to be any sharks in the vicinity.

'You must keep moving, Barrington,' Kang-ju admonished. He himself was kicking his legs. Martin followed his example, but his limbs felt heavy, deadened by the weight of despair in his brain. He was only half-conscious, supported by Kang-ju, when the lead sampan came up to them and he was dragged on board, to be wrapped in warm blankets, and given heated sake to drink.

The British watched the proceedings from afar, making no attempt to interfere. Presumably, Martin thought drowsily, *they* had not been offered a bounty for each Chinese head.

*

'They have gained a victory, but they are still barred from the river,' General Teng said. 'I am sorry about your brother, Barrington. It is a sad thing to be lost at sea, with not even a prayer said over your grave, but he will be avenged. And we will make sure they cannot pass through the sandbanks – even if they knew the way.' He entertained the Admiral to dinner, Martin wearing borrowed clothes; all he possessed had gone down with the *Yangtse Queen*. Nor had his spirits risen in any way; those captains who had refused to support him had retreated upriver, beyond his immediate wrath, while his own principal duty still remained repulsing the British.

But other duties were crowding in on him, such as informing Peking of the disaster, and his father and Jane of Adrian's death. He remained chilled and shocked by the events of the

day but, with an effort, he made himself think. 'What news of
the men they landed up the coast?'

'They have pitched their camp, some ten miles away,' Teng
said. 'It is my belief that they do not mean to attack until they
see how their ships get on with forcing the river mouth. Well,
they can stay there and rot.'

*

Teng remained full of fight, although his forts had suffered
considerable damage in that morning's bombardment. But few
men had been killed, and slowly Martin's confidence began to
return, even if he was now an admiral without a fleet – save for
a cluster of sampans which had accumulated below the forts.
But it was still possible to bar the river.

Or was it? Next morning he was awakened early by the alarm
bugles, and hurrying to the battlements, saw the British squadron very close in, but hove to, while their boats pulled into the
entrance of the gulf. Teng joined him, and together they
watched while the boats began poling and using leadlines, as
calmly as if it was an exercise in the Solent. 'They have the
bravery of arrogance,' Kang-ju growled.

'You had better send them off,' Martin said, as he watched
the sailors dropping little orange buoys to mark the deep water
passage. Teng gave the orders, and the guns opened up. This
brought an immediate response from the fleet, and more
masonry began to fly. It was impressive, and reassuring, how
seldom any of the gunners were hit; even when a lucky shot
struck one of the embrasures and overturned the carriage, all
the crew but one escaped unharmed save for the odd cut from
flying splinters. Forts, Martin reflected ruefully, had one great
advantage over ships – they could not sink.

But the British were winning another battle, that of morale.
Distracted as it was by the fire from the ships, the Chinese
shooting was not accurate enough to disrupt the buoy-laying
detail. One of the boats was struck, scattering oars and bodies,
but the survivors were picked up and the rest continued their
tasks until, apparently satisfied, they pulled back to the waiting
frigates, close inshore.

'We must remove those buoys, Kang,' Martin said. 'We shall
need a dozen sampans.'

'And some brave men of our own,' Kang-ju suggested.

'I will signal the southern fort,' Teng said. Up till now the fort on the south bank of the gulf had hardly been engaged.

Martin and Kang-ju hurried for the dock, but had not yet reached it when there came a fresh flurry of alarm from the fort. They gazed at the British squadron which, without any hesitation, was now standing into the midst of the sandbanks; the commanding admiral was wasting no time in capitalising upon the courage of his boats' crews.

'We will not get there in time, Barrington,' Kang-ju said.

Martin chewed his lip in indecision. But now a messenger arrived from Teng, urgently calling him back to the battlements. He hastened up the ladders, in time to see the redcoats emerging from amongst the paddy-fields north of the fort, following the steady beat of their drummers.

His glass had gone down with the *Yangtse Queen*, so he borrowed Teng's. There were indeed Indian sepoys as well as British soldiers advancing on the fort. And now they could hear the squeal of the fifes.

'They have no artillery,' Teng said. 'We will blast them.'

'They have artillery,' Martin reminded him, as the fort trembled to a broadside from the fleet, now very close at hand. And a moment later there was a gigantic *whoosh*, and a plume of flame hurtled out of the ranks of the approaching barbarians, to zoom into the fort and start a fire.

Men screamed in horror, and ran away from their guns. 'By the great Lord Buddha, what was that?' Teng cried.

'A rocket,' Kang-ju muttered. 'We use them for sport, the barbarians for war,' he added bitterly, as several more rockets whizzed above the battlements, and more men scattered.

'You must defend this wall, at least.' Martin strode to the river battlements, and watched the British squadron majestically gliding into the calm water, bringing up and anchoring, their guns constantly blazing. They met with no resistance, since the Chinese gunners had all fled. Martin found himself on his hands and knees, sheltering from the hail of shot flying into the fortress. He drew a deep breath, and forced himself to stand upright again.

With the same ponderous, arrogant calm that characterised all their actions, the British were now putting down boats filled with red-jacketed marines, and these were then rowed across to the southern shore, to assault the fort there. This has also been blasted as the squadron had entered the estuary, and now there was hardly an answering shot from its garrison.

Behind him such defenders as Teng had been able to rally were screaming their defiance as the British troops advanced behind fixed bayonets. The Chinese were also loosing off rockets – aimed at the sky – and firing their guns, but the British never deigned to reply. The line of glittering steel, coming ever closer with such a measured tread, was at once mesmerising and terrifying. Martin knew the day was lost. Worse, the war was lost. There was something irresistible about this method of fighting, characterised most aptly by the way the marines sat in the boats, as they pulled shorewards, with backs rigidly straight and muskets between their knees, shoulder to shoulder, knowing full well that a single shot striking their boat would kill them all – yet not a man moved a muscle, or even spoke.

He could do nothing to help the defenders of the southern fort. But he could still die fighting for this one. He drew his borrowed sword and turned to hurry towards the sound of crackling fire. Then Kang-ju appeared out of the smoke and grasped his arm.

'This battle is lost, Barrington. We must leave.'

'This is the position we were ordered to defend.'

'We were told to defend Canton. We cannot do so from here. We must block the British higher up the river.'

Martin hesitated. It went against the grain to abandon Teng, who was fighting so gallantly and so hopelessly. But once again Kang had reminded him of his ultimate duty, which was to the Emperor. He allowed Kang-ju to lead him from the fort, to a place where horses were waiting on the river bank.

*

By riding hard they reached Canton the following evening. They were both exhausted, mentally and physically, but Martin immediately summoned a meeting of the various city officials, to report what had happened.

They had already learned of the destruction of the Chinese fleet by those captains who had earlier fled upriver, but the fall of the Bogue forts was most disagreeable news. 'How can that be?' someone asked. 'Did not General Teng command ten thousand men? Had the barbarians more than half this number?'

'There must have been treachery,' muttered someone else.

Martin glared at him. 'My own brother died in the battle. And you will soon have the opportunity to prove your own loyalty to the Son of Heaven, when the barbarians ascend the river.'

After the meeting had broken up, Sung Tang-chu took Martin aside. 'I do not know that these people will fight any better than your captains. If the barbarian fleet reaches Canton, then all is lost. You must stop them on the river.'

'How am I to do that, without ships?' Martin demanded. 'Anyway, an example must be made of those cowards who would not fight.'

'You wish their heads?'

Martin sighed. He had never ordered an execution in his life. 'Yes,' he said. 'I wish their heads.'

*

He slept heavily, to be wakened by Kang-ju with the news that the executions had been effected. 'Although I do not know what good it has done,' the mate said dolefully. 'All the crews have run away, and the people stand in the streets and mutter.'

'About me?'

'No, no, Barrington. They know you did what had to be done. They mutter about the British. They are very frightened.'

'Send men downriver to report back to us on the British movements,' Martin said, and he sat down to write the necessary letters to the Emperor, to Viceroy Shung, and, most difficult of all, to his father, telling them what had happened. He assured the Emperor and Shung that he would continue to defend Canton to the last, and his father and Jane that Adrian would be avenged, even if he as yet had no idea how either of those aims could be accomplished. As all sea communications were cut, he had to entrust his letters to despatch riders; and as formidable mountains lay between Canton and Nanking and the entrance to the Grand Canal, *and* it was dead of winter, he could not tell how soon his messages would be delivered.

Then the British again surprised him, by not ascending the

river with any great haste. His scouts reported that they were systematically destroying the forts, and tending to their wounded; they were also foraging the countryside for fresh supplies. The scouts also brought in tales of atrocities, including the robbing of graves by the invaders.

Martin had no means of knowing whether such rumours were true, but he had them circulated throughout the city none the less, in the hopes of stimulating an offensive spirit, of outrage.

'Our problem is,' Sung Tang-chu told him, 'that these people do not know whether being conquered by the British would be worse than being ruled by the Manchu.'

'You are Chinese,' Martin argued. 'And you have no doubts.'

'But I, like you, have a stake in the Manchu government, Barrington. The poor do not. And those whose habits you have overturned will reckon that the return of the British will mean also the return of the opium. I still say that your best course is to attempt to stop them on the river.'

*

Martin rode down the river to see if any sort of barrier could be constructed. The upper part of the gulf, before the Pearl proper was reached, was a mass of small islands, with various very narrow passages between, but Martin doubted he could block them all, and there remained the risk that, if checked, the British commander would simply land his troops and march round their defences.

How he wished his father could be at his side to advise him. Well, then, what *would* Father advise? Martin had no fighting ships worthy of the name, and he had little faith in the defences of Canton. So what *did* he have?

He gazed at the river flowing swiftly where it was compressed into various channels between the islands, and he watched a sampan, which had broken a sweep, trying desperately to bring up as the current caught it. He would have expected it to go around on one side or the other, fairly sharply, but it did not; it was whipped straight through the channel and into the deeper reaches beyond, its crew shouting for assistance.

Then suddenly he had an idea. He had been told often

enough about how Drake had put the Spanish Armada to flight in the Calais Roads. 'Kang-ju,' he said. 'I need as many sampans as you can find, and twelve brave crews.'

'The sampans will be easy, at least,' Kang-ju observed.

*

While Kang-ju was raising the necessary crews, Martin requisitioned the sampans. He chose the twelve most suitable, and moored them. The others he instructed their crews to rope together and anchor across the various channels between the islands, to make a barrier of boats. The widest and most navigable channel he left open; if the invitation was fairly obvious, he was relying on that British 'bravery of arrogance' to accept the bait.

He assembled his sampan flotilla above the islands, and placed them under guard; he did not wish news of what he was intending to spread downriver. As Kang-ju delivered the crews, Martin put them to work, filling the hold of each sampan with all the inflammable material he could find: fireworks, barrels of gunpowder, and tallow-impregnated ropes.

'Now, we wait,' he told his men.

'Will you lead us, Barrington?'

Martin nodded. 'I will lead you.'

*

He made them practise their drill every day, while the weather gradually improved; and the British sent an envoy up the river to demand the surrender of Canton. Sung Tang-chu, as defiant as ever, would have taken the lieutenant's head, but Martin forbade this, and sent him back downriver with a simple refusal. He had at least learned the name of the man against whom he was fighting: General Sir Hugh Gough was in overall command of the expeditionary force.

Martin also visited the British prisoners. He found them almost completely restored to health, if not to humour. They had heard of the disasters that had befallen the Manchu arms downriver, and confidently expected the arrival of the Royal Navy. 'Then you will be hanged, Barrington,' they declared.

*

At the end of April, news was received that the British squadron was at last coming up the river. Half of the frigates led the way, followed by the ships of the line. The transports brought up the rear, escorted by the remainder of the frigates and the steamer. Martin rode down the embankment with an escort of Bannermen. He presumed that the British admiral had impressed the services of Chinese boatmen as pilots, but the ascent was nonetheless appropriately cautious, the ships waiting for a fair wind, and then moving only after their immediate route had been reconnoitred by their boats.

Yet they again made an impressive sight – depressing for one who was committed to stopping them. He returned upriver to where Kang-ju and the sampan crews waited, leaving scouts to inform him further of the British progress. A week later the ships reached the islands, and surveyed the problem before them. They had a choice: either to smash through one of the subsidiary channels blocked by the sampan rafts, or to accept the challenge and take the main, open channel. Either way, Martin would soon know what they were doing.

The British anchored for the next couple of days, while their boats as usual reconnoitred. Martin's men were in a high state of excitement, and his main fear was that news of the fireships would reach the British commander. But three days later, when the wind was from the east, the anchors were raised and the fleet got underway, making for the open channel.

Immediately the sampans were cast off, and rowed to a position north of the channel into which the British were venturing. The torches were lit, the sweeps were brought on board, and at Martin's signal, the crews abandoned ship and climbed down into the small boats they were towing, to set off as rapidly as they could for the shore.

Martin and Kang-ju, in the same boat, waited to make sure all was well. From their position they looked at the tree-covered islands, and could only just see the mastheads and pennants of the lead ships. In front of them the sampans were drifting into the passage in a body, burning now, but not yet to any great extent. Martin had attempted to time their eruption for the best possible moment.

The British had by now spotted the flames and realised their situation. It was a considerable predicament, because the lead frigates had already entered the channel, in line ahead, and there was insufficient room to come about. Martin listened to the blaring of bugles, while Kang-ju snapped his fingers with delight.

But there was no sign of panic on the trapped ships. Martin saw the sails being brought down even as he heard the roar of the anchor chains. The entire squadron was anchoring where it was. But surely, then, the lead ships would be destroyed?

'We must get closer,' Martin decided, and the rowers took him to the mouth of the channel. There he gazed in dismay. With the utmost calm, the frigates, having anchored, had put down their boats, filled with seamen armed with long boathooks, and these were pulling straight for the fireships, regardless that these were now commencing to explode, their gunpowder barrels hurling smoke and flame skywards, while rockets seethed in every direction.

The boats rowed right up to the sampans, the boathooks were attached, and the flaming hulks were almost casually towed to either side of the channel, to beach themselves in the shallows. There they continued to burn and explode. Kang-ju gave the order to row for shore. Martin himself was incapable of speech. His last throw had failed as badly as the first.

*

Canton was in a ferment of excitement. Rumour crowded upon rumour, and people thronged the streets to gaze down the river while they chattered excitedly. 'As I feared,' Martin told Sung Tang-chu, 'it has come down to defending the city.'

'And, as I told you from the beginning, Barrington, I do not think this city can be defended.'

*

The British ships lay off the mouth of the Pearl a week later, and once again General Gough sent an envoy demanding surrender and full compliance with Britain's terms, otherwise, he announced, he would be forced to bombard the city. 'Be sure the city will fire back,' Martin told the lieutenant.

But the councillors were visibly terrified; nor were the

Bannermen manning the guns and the waterfront much better, and thousands of people were already fleeing the city and streaming into the hills, carrying their belongings in carts or on their backs. Meanwhile the British came inexorably closer, entering the river itself, the great ships towed by their boats. The Bannermen galloped up and down the banks with simulated courage, but by now tales of the ghastly wounds inflicted by bayonets had been spread wide by those who had escaped the capture of the Bogue forts, as equally tales of the terrible rapidity of British gunfire.

'What would you have me do, Barrington?' Sung asked, as they stood together on the waterfront to watch the ships-of-the-line dropping their anchors not four hundred yards away.

Martin knew he must accept the inevitable. 'There is nothing you can do save ask for terms.'

*

Sung duly sent an envoy of his own to the British squadron, and was told that the British general would speak only with the commander of the city garrison. By the time the envoy had returned, the British ships had delivered a preliminary broadside which had the Bannermen fleeing behind their families.

Sung promptly hoisted the white flag and went out to the ships, to return with a very long face.

'Well?' Martin demanded.

'The British have demanded a preliminary indemnity of fifteen million taels, or they say they will reduce the city to ashes.'

'You had better summon your council and inform them. I would say the British mean what they say. What else?'

'They also demand the surrender of the renegade traitor, Martin Barrington.'

10

THE TREATIES

Sir Hugh Gough was an Irishman in his sixty-second year, who had had a most distinguished career, his campaigning having included the West Indies and the Cape of Good Hope, although his principal claim to fame had been earned as lieutenant-colonel of the 87th Prince of Wales' Irish – later to be known as the Royal Irish Fusiliers – who had covered themselves in glory during the Peninsular War, where they earned the nickname of their own battlecry, *Faugh a Ballaghs*, or Clear the Ways.

He was a man of remarkable presence, standing as straight as a ramrod, with aquiline features, and spoke with a strong Irish brogue. 'Martin Barrington,' he remarked, as Martin boarded the flagship, HMS *Wellesley*, 74-guns.

Martin had determined not in any way to be subservient to these people, and had had a new suit of clothes made for his surrender. They were Chinese clothes, to be sure, a dark blue tunic over deep red trousers and boots, and a red hat, but then, he was a Chinese admiral. And there was no way he could match the brilliance around him, the blue frock-coats laced with gold thread of the naval officers, worn over spotless white breeches and stockings, the crisp blue uniforms and squarely set straw hats of the seamen, the brilliant red jackets with white facings and tall shakos of the marines, while Gough was a blaze of colour in his scarlet tunic with all his stars and medals on its breast, and his own cocked hat. But then, *Wellesley* herself was a magnificent sight. Her ports were open and her guns run out, but there was no indication that she had ever fired a shot in anger; her decks were holystoned to a perfection of white wood, her sails neatly furled on their yards.

Martin also wore a sword, but this he now drew and reversed, as he advanced towards the general between the double row of marines.

'General!' He saluted, and held out his weapon.

'Keep your sword, man,' Gough said. 'We'll take it when ye're to be hanged.' He gestured to the man at his side, also cocked-hatted, but wearing a naval uniform. 'My fleet commander, Rear-Admiral George Elliott.'

'Admiral!' Martin saluted again. 'Your gunnery was too good for my people.'

Elliott frowned. 'Were you in that skirmish?'

'I commanded the lead Chinese vessel, sir.'

'Then you are either a very brave man or a madman, sir. Four junks opposed to my squadron?'

'I was obeying orders, sir.'

The two men gazed at each other, and Martin thought he might have made a friend. 'Oh, ye're a brave man, no doubt,' Gough agreed. 'But still a renegade traitor, eh?'

'Sir, I was born here and am a Chinese citizen.'

Gough considered for some seconds, then said, 'Ye'd best come below.' He led the way, past saluting sentries, and past, too, the British merchants, who had been released from imprisonment, and were gathered on the quarterdeck to glare at their late captor. Josiah Barnes looked as severe as any of them. 'Those gentlemen,' Gough remarked, as they descended the ladder to the Admiral's day cabin, 'wish to see ye hang, Barrington.'

'If they are honest men, they will admit that I did all I could to improve the conditions of their captivity.'

'Sit down.' Gough sat himself, on one side of the table which occupied the centre of the large and comfortable cabin; the stern windows were open to allow a fresh breeze to enter, and a good deal of the smells of Canton as well, for the city continued to lie beneath the guns of the fleet while the ransom was collected ' 'Tis the fact of their captivity at all that angers them. Will ye deny it was your doing?'

'I cannot deny that it was I who brought the shameful consequences of the opium trade to the attention of the Emperor. I will admit that he reacted more strongly than I had anticipated.'

'Through the offices of this man ...' Gough looked at the various papers his secretary had placed before him. 'Lin. He at the least must be punished. Why has he not been surrendered?'

'Because he is not here, sir. Commissioner Lin was dismissed from his position by the Son of Heaven. It was my privilege to carry out that command.'

'And having done that, to fight against your own people?'

'And having done that, to carry out my instructions to defend Canton to the best of my ability.'

The two men stared at each other for several seconds.

'By God, ye're a bold rascal,' the General cried finally. 'But your courage is empty, Barrington. Ye've been beaten, man. Ye've nothing left to fight with.'

'Can you honestly support a cause that inflicts the curse of opium upon these people?'

Gough's cheeks were red with embarrassment as well as anger. 'Like yourself, Mr Barrington, I obey my orders,' he snapped. 'Your Emperor has challenged Her Majesty, God bless her, and he must pay for it. Ye seem to have the ear of this yellow devil. And I can talk to ye in a language we both understand. I've a mind to let ye carry me terms to Peking.'

'The Emperor already knows the British demands, sir.'

'He does, does he? Well, ye can tell him from me that we've upped the ante. Oh, there'll be an indemnity. Ye'll pay five million pounds sterling in silver. But now we want more. Her Majesty's Government has determined to maintain a presence in these waters. For that purpose, we shall need a permanent base. Your Son of Heaven will grant to Her Majesty's Government the island of Hong Kong, forever and a day, for the sole use of Her Majesty's forces.'

The effrontery of this man, or of the government he represented, seemed almost unbelievable.

'Her Majesty's Government also intends to trade with this Son of Heaven, or least his people. We need ports where our ships can come and go in peace, untroubled by your rascally Bannermen. I have a list here of the ports we require. I'll read them to ye. Canton, of course. Then we require Amoy, Foochow, Ningpo, and Shanghai. Ye'll make a note of them.'

'You expect me to put these proposals before the Son of Heaven?'

'They're not proposals, man. They're demands. There is a fourth demand ye'll note. We wish this Commissioner Lin surrendered to answer for his crimes against British subjects.'

'And when the Emperor refuses such conditions? Do you know how many men he can summon to arms? Perhaps ten million.'

Gough gave a brief smile. 'On the evidence of what we have

seen these last few months, Mr Barrington, ten million Chinese are worth maybe a hundred thousand British.'

'And you have six thousand. And a squadron.'

'It is the squadron that matters, Barrington. Ye tell the Son of Heaven that if he does not agree to our demands, we'll lay every seaport in this country flat.'

'Am I allowed to comment, sir?'

'Ye are.'

'Your government is pursuing a course of the most naked aggression.'

'It's our way,' Gough agreed, without rancour. 'When the merchants of the City of London see a possibility of profit, they'll batter down the Gates of Heaven itself to reach it. It's the way of the world, Mr Barrington.'

'The European world, sir. Not the Chinese.'

'The real world, Mr Barrington. Your Son of Heaven will have to understand that. Now, how long will it take ye to reach Peking and return?'

'Overland, four months. By sea and the Canal, four weeks.'

'Ye can take one of your junks. I'll expect ye to bring an answer within a month.'

'You'll not expect me at all, sir.'

'Ye refuse to take my ultimatum to the Emperor?'

'I will take your ultimatum, sir. But I do not expect to return with an answer. The Emperor will undoubtedly order my execution.'

'For being defeated, or for acting as our envoy?' Admiral Elliott inquired.

'I should think for both.'

'Then we shall have to send someone else, Sir Hugh,' Elliott said. 'We cannot ask a man to go to his death.'

'And why not?' Gough demanded. 'D'ye not suppose that if we were to convene a court-martial here and now on *Wellesley*, they'd have this fellow adorning your yardarm by sunset? He's a condemned felon. Let him face his Emperor.'

*

'But you are going, anyway?' Sung Tang-chu asked.

'I must report what has happened, at least.'

'And, as you told the British, lose your head. My advice to

you, Barrington, would be to take your junk and sail far away.'

'And leave my father and my sister-in-law and her children to the wrath of the Emperor?'

'If you are executed,' Sung pointed out, 'they will undoubtedly be also despatched.'

'Thus I can only prevent that by presenting the facts squarely to the Son of Heaven. Sir Hugh Gough told the truth when he said this war was undertaken at the behest of the City of London. It is not being fought over opium or over the arrest of a few British subjects. It is being fought because the money-grabbers in England seek new markets for their goods, and China is the biggest untouched market in the world.'

'What will you then advise the Emperor?'

'To reject the British commands, and gird himself for war with all the strength he can muster. Because, unless they are defeated decisively, the British will not go away, but rather will demand more and more, until China is theirs, as India became theirs because of the weakness of the Moghul emperors.'

Brave words. Did he not, in his heart, most fervently wish he had never penned that fateful memorandum? If he was condemned, his family would be also. It was the Chinese way – all members of a family were collectively responsible for the misdeeds of any member of it.

Kang-ju as ever at his side, he sailed from the mouth of the Pearl north, to the Yangtse, thence up to Nanking. He could afford only a day in his home city, before resuming his journey up the Grand Canal by sampan, to gain the Pei-ho. But there was time to report to his father. Robert Barrington listened, shoulders hunched. 'You have failed us,' he said when Martin was finished. 'You have failed China, you have failed this House, you have failed your brother. And you have failed me.'

That is unfair, Martin wanted to protest. But he merely bowed his head.

'Thank God I have another son,' Robert Barrington said, ruffling John's hair; the boy was now eight years old. 'If only I could live to see him a man.'

*

Jane listened in silence to what he had to say, having sent her children away.

'He died instantly,' Martin told her somewhat lamely.

'You expect me to weep?'

'No. But what of the children?'

Her mouth twisted. 'I will tell them that their father died a hero, so that they may always honour his memory. How did your father take the news?'

'He virtually disowned me.'

'What will you do now?'

'I must go to Peking and report to the Emperor.'

'And afterwards?'

'I will return here. If I can – and you wish me to.'

She was in his arms, and he was kissing her mouth and her nose, her eyes and her chin.

*

There was no further need for concealment. Martin ate alone with Jane that evening, in her apartment, having kissed the children good night. Then he accompanied her to her bedroom. But it was also necessary to visit his own apartment early in the morning. 'You have been with her,' Chun-wu accused.

'Yes. Now, I am in great haste. Pack me a box of clothes.'

'You have no more time for Chun-wu,' she said in a mixture of sorrow and anger.

He gave her a hug. 'Believe me, Chun-wu, there will always be a place for you in my household. When I return from Peking ...'

She clutched his arm. 'You go to Peking? You are taking her?'

'No. She will stay here with her children.'

'Then take me. How can you travel to Peking without a woman?'

He was ready to point out that he habitually sailed for months on end without a woman, then reflected that if he was going to his death he might as well be comfortable in his final moments. 'It will be very dangerous,' he warned her.

'I do not care about danger if I am with you.'

*

'What's this?' Sir Hugh Gough demanded. 'Not another damned delegation?'

HMS *Wellesley* had been visited by almost every merchant of any standing in Canton, seeking this or that concession.

'Well, I suppose it is a delegation,' Elliott conceded. 'Two young men who say they must speak with you most urgently.'

'Assassins, perhaps? Ye'll have them searched, George.'

A few minutes later the two young men were shown in. They were young and scruffy, and not Cantonese; Gough could tell that from a glance at their features.

'State your business,' the General commanded, speaking Cantonese, a language he had mastered with his usual efficiency during the year he had so far been forced to spend in China.

'My name is Hung Hsiu-ch'uan, sir,' said the first young man. 'This is my associate, Feng Yun-shan. We are from the Hakka people in the mountains. We wish first to congratulate you on your great victory.'

'There's a change,' Gough remarked to Elliott in English. 'And secondly?' He addressed Hung.

'We wish to offer your excellency the support and assistance of the Hakka people in your destruction of the Manchu scoundrels.'

Gough raised his eyebrows. 'Who are these Hakka?'

'We are a nation conquered by the Chinese. That we can accept – but conquest by the Manchu, never!'

'Ye've lived beneath them for two hundred years, man.'

'Two hundred years of shame. Two hundred years in which we have seen our people debauched. What do you see when you look around you? Fornication, adultery, usury, drunkenness and, worst of all, opium smoking. It is your duty to put an end to these iniquities.'

Gough smiled at the young man's vehemence. 'My duty is to Her Majesty the Queen. And her orders are to reinstate the opium trade.'

Hung was aghast. 'You will not help us in our fight against the Manchu?'

'I'm not here to become involved in local politics, man. If the Manchu government falls, who will replace them but anarchy? Or do ye see yourself as emperor?'

'You, sir, are as big a villain as any Manchu!' Hung shouted. Feng held his arm to restrain him.

Gough's smile changed to a scowl. 'Admiral Elliott, ye'll have this lout thrown off your ship, before I lose my temper.'

*

Martin used one of the House sampans, as luxuriously fitted out as any on the water, and set off down the river the following morning at dawn. Jane came down to the dock to see him off, her red hair floating on the breeze. 'I shall be waiting for you,' she promised. 'Mind you take care of him,' she told Chun-wu.

Martin squeezed her hands, then said farewell to Kang-ju who was left in effective control of the House, and boarded the boat. If he came back, as he promised, the world would be theirs. He felt a growing optimism – but he was soon disillusioned. The descent to Chin-kiang took two days, and on arrival he found that city in a ferment of disorder and uncertainty.

'Have you not heard, Barrington?' demanded the Governor, Hu Jen-wong. 'The barbarian ships are at the mouth of the river. They have bombarded Shanghai.'

Gough was not even waiting for his return before carrying out his threats; the British squadron must have followed the junk north, lying just beneath the horizon. Did this not make a nonsense of the whole business of negotiation? Save on British terms – at the end of a gun.

Yet Martin was still left with no choice, and he hurried north as fast as he could. But this was slow enough. The Grand Canal had over the centuries suffered from neglect and decay. In many places its banks had crumbled into the water, making the passage a feat of helming, and in other places weeds had clustered to such an extent that the sampan needed to be poled into deeper water.

But Martin kept his men at it, and after ten days they crossed the huge flow of the Huang-Ho, the Yellow River. Another week and they emerged into the Pei-ho just above the city of Tientsin. Here he abandoned the sampan, to await his return, and took horses for the last stage of his journey; crossing the flat North China plain was no hardship, since it was now high summer.

*

His father had told Martin of the glories of Peking, of the Imperial Park of white pines south of the city, of the high purple walls, of the hustle and bustle within – and he was not disappointed. But even Robert Barrington had never penetrated the Forbidden City. It was at this immense gate, the T'ien-an-men, dominated by turreted watch-towers which oversaw this inner walled domain, that he presented his credentials.

'No man save a member of the imperial family or the Grand Council of Government may enter the Forbidden City,' the captain advised. 'I will send your name in to the Chief Eunuch.'

Martin stood in the gateway and stared at the avenues within the walls, so uncrowded – only occasionally women or eunuchs could be seen – and in the distance, the pristine columns and edifices of various palaces; while, beyond, he could make out the gleaming White Dagoba, the Buddhist temple which looked for all the world like a huge bottle rising out of the trees.

He had not very long to wait, as soon a eunuch arrived at the gate. 'Great Barrington,' he said. 'Your presence here is pleasing to our lords. But His Majesty is at the Yuan Ming Yuan, the Summer Palace, and it is there that you must repair. Horses have been arranged.'

*

Chun-wu grumbled; she was weary of travelling. But the horses were mounted, and away they rode to the north-west. Not very far, indeed, before the sixty thousand acres of the Yuan Ming Yuan came into view, a dream world created by the great Ch'ien-lung Emperor, of marble palaces, trees and shrubs of every description, most of them unknown in Europe, quiet pools and miniature lakes filled with multi-coloured goldfish, arched bridges, gleaming white in the sunlight.

Even Chun-wu was impressed. 'I had not supposed such a paradise could exist upon earth,' she muttered.

'The Yuan Ming Yuan is the ultimate creation of the Ch'ing Dynasty,' their guiding eunuch, Ho Sen-fu, told her.

*

They were shown to quarters outside the palace complex, and Martin was given an audience with Prince Hui, the younger brother of the Son of Heaven, the man whose seal was on his original commission. He was taken into a very bare chamber; the floor was carpeted, the walls covered in drapes, but there was only one seat, an upright armchair in the very centre of the room, occupied by the Prince. Martin stood hatted just inside the door, next to the eunuchs escorting him, until one of their number gave a signal; then he was instructed to go forward and prostrate himself, crawling to the line where the carpet changed colours.

'Barrington,' the Prince said, 'I fear you bring ill news.'

This indicated that the Ch'ing royal family had a very thorough intelligence service; for Martin had travelled as fast as he could.

Kneeling, and facing the Prince – a thin-faced man in his forties – Martin explained what had happened, as clearly and succinctly as he could. When he was finished, the Prince commented, 'Do you suppose you would have gained the day, had you been supported by your entire fleet?'

'No, Your Highness. The British ships are too powerful, their guns too well served. And their use of steam power gave them a manoeuvrability we entirely lacked.'

'Then what of General Teng?'

'There, too, Your Highness. The British soldiers were too well disciplined, their fire power too great.'

'Are you telling me that these barbarians are invincible?'

'I do not believe so, Highness. But it will take a great effort, great determination, to defeat them. The task cannot be left to provincial viceroys with inadequate resources.'

'You were given ample powers to requisition ships and men.'

'There were not sufficient ships or men of quality to be requisitioned.'

'You admit to being a failure. You realise the fate of those who fail the Son of Heaven?'

'I do, Highness.'

'And thus you have come to beg for your head.'

'I have come to beg that, whatever fate I may be condemned to suffer, His Majesty place himself at the head of the eight Banners, as did Nurhachi in times of old, and lead his people against these barbarians. For if that is not done now, it will soon become too late.'

'You dare to advise the Son of Heaven?'

'It is the privilege of a condemned man, Highness.'

Prince Hui glared at him, and the councillors and eunuchs gathered beyond the open doorway shuffled their feet anxiously.

Then a quiet voice said, 'Close the door.'

There was the momentary hesitation of consternation, then the eunuchs closed the door. 'Draw the curtain,' the voice continued.

'Down with you, rascal,' Prince Hui muttered, himself dropping to his knees.

Martin immediately understood what was happening, and hastily prostrated himself again, banging his forehead nine times upon the carpet, as protocol demanded in the presence of the Son of Heaven. Prince Hui did the same beside him. Above his head he heard the curtain being drawn.

'Sit up, Barrington,' the quiet voice said. Martin sat back on his heels and gazed at the Tao-kuang Emperor. The Son of Heaven was now fifty-nine years old, a small, thin man, richly dressed in an imperial yellow surcoat blazoned with the red dragon design. But his face was that of an ascetic, his moustaches thin, his eyes tired. 'Your memorandum has seemingly brought calamity upon my people,' the Emperor said.

'A man must do as he sees right, Your Majesty.'

'That is true. And I wish there were more men who practised such a precept in my empire. Now you say that perhaps ten thousand barbarians could conquer my lands?'

'No, Majesty. But I am saying that they could be as disruptive to the trade of your empire as were the pirates led by Cheng Yi Sao a generation ago.'

'Cheng Yi Sao,' the Emperor mused. 'I received her, when I was but a boy. Your father was her admiral. Barrington, tell me what is it that these barbarians wish, to cease making war upon us.'

Martin took a deep breath. 'They demand an indemnity, Your Majesty, of fifteen million taels.'

'Is that so great a sum?' the Emperor asked. 'That is surely not all they wish?'

Martin licked his lips. 'They also demand the cession of an island called Hong Kong, situated off the coast, in perpetuity, upon which they mean to build a naval base.'

The Emperor half turned his head, and one of the eunuchs

bowed. 'It is a barren island, Majesty, a few miles north of the Gulf of Canton.'

'How many such islands are there off the coast of China, and in the gulfs along my coast?'

'More than a thousand, sire.'

'Is one barren island of importance to me, Barrington? Surely they wish more.'

Martin could hardly believe his ears. 'They demand also the right of unimpeded trade through five ports that they have named. These are Canton, Foochow, Amoy, Ningpo and Shanghai. Through these ports they mean to import many goods. It will have a profound affect upon the lives of your people.'

'This land of these barbarians, is it not many li away?'

'Indeed, Majesty, it is on the other side of the world. But the barbarians have many men and ships in India.'

'Even India is many li away,' the Emperor pointed out. 'It does not seem possible for people living so many li away to bring sufficient goods to China to disrupt my empire.'

'With respect, these barbarians are the most grasping, avaricious people on the face of the earth. If you give them one li of your territory, they will seek two, and when they have two, they will seek four.'

Prince Hui, kneeling at his side, hissed disapproval at anyone who would argue with the Emperor. But the Tao-kuang's voice remained quite. 'Is that all they wish?'

'There is a final demand, Majesty. They wish the head of Commissioner Lin.'

'He greatly exceeded his prerogatives.'

Martin did not like Lin, but still the man had been merely carrying out his orders as he interpreted them. 'Commissioner Lin, like myself, did what he thought was right.'

There was another hiss of disapproval from Prince Hui. But the Emperor smiled. 'We will consider the matter. But tell me again what you would have me do.'

'Majesty, these men must be fought, and driven away so decisively that it will be many years before they return.'

'Yet, as you have discovered, Barrington, this will be no easy task. It will cost many lives, and many taels.'

'It will save many lives, in the end.'

The Emperor studied him for some moments. Then he said,

'I believe you. I believe you are an honest man, and a courageous one. I believe you fought against the barbarians to the best of your ability. I will reward courage, and loyalty.' He raised his hand, and one of the eunuchs hurried forward with a cushion on which lay several glittering brooches. 'Come forward, Barrington,' the Emperor said.

Martin glanced at Prince Hui in consternation, and received a quick nod. He advanced on his knees, until he was close enough to the Emperor to be touched.

The Tao-kuang pinned a brooch to his breast. 'I award you this, the sapphire button of a mandarin of the third rank, and adorn you with the military badge of this rank, the leopard. But, in addition, for your services to the Dynasty . . .' He raised his hand again, and another eunuch hurried forward with a yellow silk garment. 'I award you the Ch'ing Hunting Jacket, to denote to all that you have found favour with the Son of Heaven.'

'I . . . I thank your Majesty,' Martin stammered.

'Go now. I will inform you of my decision, when I have considered the matter.'

Martin crawled backwards out of the room.

*

'You had an audience with the Son of Heaven!' Chun Wu was awed. 'And now you are a mandarin of the third class.' She hugged and kissed him. 'Tell me of him, Barrington. Tell me of his majesty, his power.'

'He revealed very little of either to me,' Martin protested. 'We shall have to wait and see.'

*

It was dusk before Martin was again summoned to the audience chamber, to face Prince Hui and Ho Sen-fu, and someone he had not met before. Obviously he was a Manchu, from his heavy build and thick moustache. Martin gave a quick glance towards the curtain, but there was no means of knowing if the Son of Heaven was again seated there, listening to their conversation.

'His Majesty has reached a decision,' the Prince said. 'You

will return at once to Nanking, Barrington. Ho Sen-fu will accompany you, as will the Imperial Commissioner, Ting-cheng.' He glanced at the man on his right. 'There you will meet with the barbarian general and agree to his terms, with but one exception; Commissioner Lin Tse-hu will not be surrendered. If he is to be punished for his excessive zeal, it will be at the behest of the Son of Heaven. Now go. Haste is essential.'

Martin swallowed, and glanced at the curtain again. 'If I may be allowed to speak with His Majesty ...'

'Do you suppose His Majesty has nothing better to do than listen endlessly to such as you? I have given you his instructions. Carry them out. Do this successfully, end these barbarian affronts, and the House of Barrington will be confirmed in its trading privileges until the end of time.'

*

Ting-cheng and Ho Sen-fu accompanied Martin outside. 'We leave immediately,' Ting-cheng said.

'Are we in such haste to surrender?' Martin demanded. 'I fear His Majesty has been given incorrect advice. The British should be fought and defeated.'

'It is too late for that,' Ting told him. 'News arrived this morning that their ships have entered the Yangtse and forced their way up the river.'

Martin stared at him in consternation. 'How far up the river?'

'They engaged the batteries at Kian-cyin and destroyed them, then sailed past Chin-kiang. A messenger this morning brought news that the barbarians are bombarding Nanking itself.'

*

Martin drove his men day and night in their descent of the Canal. Nanking, bombarded! His family under fire! Well, for Father it would be no new experience. But for his beloved Jane ...

'If she is dead, you will have no one left to marry,' Chun-wu remarked carelessly.

*

When they reached the river eight days after leaving Peking, they found the exit of the Canal guarded by two British frigates, which effectively prevented any traffic either on the Yangtse or on the Canal itself. Martin had been warned of this both by the Bannermen on the banks and by various sampan skippers who had already been turned back. Gough was proving that he could do what he had threatened, and bring China's water-borne trade to a standstill – even more effectively than Robert Barrington and Cheng Yi Sao had done thirty years before.

Martin hoisted a white flag. Once he had identified himself and stated his business, he was allowed to proceed.

*

Lying off Nanking were three ships-of-the-line and three more frigates, as well as the transports. The troops had been put ashore on the north bank, opposite the city, where a town of tents had arisen. Martin later learned that the remaining three ships-of-the-line had been sent down to the river mouth to prevent any risk of a Chinese fleet blockading the squadron.

He studied the city itself as the sampan was rowed up the stream. It looked undamaged, although he could see that the boat suburb, which usually extended along the bank for at least half a mile, had greatly diminished. As he drew closer yet, he could make out that the great godown belonging to the House also appeared undamaged, but there was no flag flying above it, which was strange. He made for the flagship.

'Well, Barrington!' Gough demanded. 'Is it to be peace, or war?'

'The Son of Heaven has chosen peace, Sir Hugh. For, as he said to me, how can the ravages of outer barbarians be more than pinpricks to the Manchu Empire?'

Gough glared at him, while Elliott could hardly suppress a smile. 'Come below, Mr Barrington,' the Admiral invited.

*

Martin introduced Ting-cheng and Ho Sen-fu, who had accompanied him on board, but Gough paid them little attention. 'So, ye say your Emperor agrees to our demands?' the General remarked, when they were all seated around the table.

'With one exception,' Martin said. 'His Majesty will not surrender Commissioner Lin. If the Commissioner is to be punished for excessive zeal, it will be a Manchu matter.'

'I warned ye there can be no negotiation,' Gough said. 'My demands are there as a whole to be taken or left.'

'The decision is yours, of course,' Martin told him.

Ho Sen-fu was looking anxious. Ting-cheng merely confused.

Elliott cleared his throat. 'With respect, Sir Hugh, we have surely obtained what we really came for. If Barrington can assure us that this fellow Lin will be suitably dealt with, then I would recommend we sign the treaty.'

'Harumph,' Gough commented. 'Very well, Barrington. Can ye give us such an assurance?'

Martin promised it. He knew that Lin would be punished, even if only by a fine.

*

Martin was in a hurry to get ashore and visit the House. The absence of that flag bothered him. And his apprehension was confirmed as he entered the gate to be met by bowing servants, their faces rigid with grief.

Yet the building was undamaged; there was no evidence of any damage caused by the bombardment in the town.

'How did it happen?' he asked Kang-ju.

'Perhaps it was his anger at what was happening. Great Barrington uttered a great shout, and died.'

Martin looked beyond him, at Jane. Unlike the Chinese, who were all wearing white, she was dressed in black. 'Or perhaps it was from learning about us two,' she said quietly in English.

*

Robert Barrington had been embalmed because, even if officially Christian, a man could not be buried save in the presence of his oldest surviving son. Tsen-tsing knelt by the bier. Her eyes were red, and Martin saw no reason to suppose her grief was not genuine. John Barrington knelt by her side. Both rose when Martin entered. 'He meant much more to me than he did to you,' Tsen-tsing hissed. 'It was the shock of learning of your adultery with Jane that killed him.'

'He was eighty-one years old,' Martin murmured sadly, and looked down on those features, so often harsh, now relaxed in death. His father had lived the sort of life many men would envy. He had seen it all as a struggle, at times against the entire world. But it had been a successful struggle, and he had been triumphant in the end ... until the waywardness of his younger son seemed to threaten to bring the entire House down in ruin.

Now that had been avoided, and the House would be more secure than ever. Martin was sorry his father had not lived to learn of the honour bestowed by the Son of Heaven.

'What will happen to us?' Tsen-tsing asked.

'You are my father's widow,' Martin assured her. 'And little John is my own brother.'

For a moment she was too surprised to speak. Then she bowed her head, grasped the boy by the hand, and led him from the room.

'She hates you,' Jane commented.

'But she cannot harm me now.' He put his arm round her shoulders. 'Nothing can harm us now.'

She gave a little shiver. 'Despite our guilt?'

'I intend to marry you,' he told her, 'and we are going to be happy. There is nothing can harm us now.'

*

Hung Hsiu-chu'an stood on a Canton street and watched the outer barbarians swagger by. How arrogant they were – the arrogance of power! He wished he could understand where such arrogance came from. It had to be more than merely the creation of huge ships and great guns, bristling bayonets and unswerving discipline. These things were important, he knew, but they could not be the whole. For physical power was merely an outer aspect of mental power. That was the outer barbarian secret; it was a secret he had to understand if he was ever going to find the men able to raise the Middle Kingdom from the supine sloth into which it had sunk, to expel the Manchu and create the Heavenly Kingdom of Great Peace – the T'ai-P'ing of which he dreamed.

His reverie was disturbed by a commotion on the next corner. One of the outer barbarians, a civilian rather than a soldier, was addressing a small crowd. He spoke Mandarin, which accounted for the meagre size of his audience. But Hung, working with Sung Tang-chu for so many years, had learned that dialect, and could even understand the man's strange nasal twang. Hung went closer, the better to listen.

'Come and be saved,' the man was saying. 'Forswear your false gods, your false philosophy, Our Father is the only true faith. Believe in Him. Believe in Our Lord, Jesus Christ, and you will be saved through all eternity. Fear not, to turn your back upon the past. For who can withstand the Might of the Lord?'

Hung moved closer yet.

BOOK THE THIRD
The Little Orchid

'Your face is as a book where men
May read strange matters. To beguile the time,
Look like the time; bear welcome in your eye,
Your hand, your tongue: look like the innocent flower,
But be the serpent under't.'
                    William Shakespeare, *Macbeth*.

11
THE COURTSHIP

A crowd was assembling on the beaten-earth central square of the city of Wuhu. They came from the shanty houses and the bazaars; they came from the boat city which formed a part of every Chinese community, especially on the Yangtse-Kiang – living, breeding, trading, and dying on the bobbing sampans which were the only homes they had ever known. They came, too, from the palaces of the wealthy, from the garrison fortress. Haughty Manchu Bannermen rubbed shoulders with pigtailed Chinese, men with women, adults with children. Their dogs snarled about their feet. They laughed and shouted at each other in high, raucous voices. They were happy. They were here to witness an execution.

They had followed the doleful procession which marched from the city gaol behind the slow beating of the drum and the wail of the pipe. The guard of soldiers surrounded four people, each of whom, on their shirts, wore a placard announcing the crime for which he or she was about to be punished. It involved only one crime. A lady had murdered her husband, and she had been assisted by three of her servants.

Chang Tsin cleared the way for Lan Kuei. Chang Tsin was fifteen years old, a man of Han, his inferiority indicated by his shaven forehead and long pigtail, as was worn by most of the men around him. Yet he moved through the crowds proudly. He was a servant of Hui-cheng, the *Taotai*, or Intendant, of South Anhwei Province, and as such was often deputed to accompany Lan Kuei on her excursions into the city. He was, indeed, intended by her parents as a chaperon, but this he found difficult. Once Lan Keui had made up her mind what she wanted to do, she did it, regardless of any objections her servant might make. And he preferred not to make any; he worshipped everything about her.

Lan Kuei was seventeen years old. The name meant Little

Orchid in English, and could not have been better chosen. She was just five feet tall, but possessed an almost virile athleticism of movement never to be found amongst upper-class Chinese women. Lan Kuei was a Manchu, a member of the ruling élite of this cosmopolitan nation – a fact of which she was well aware. Her head of sleek black hair, so long it brushed the seat of her loose pantaloons, tossed whenever anyone stepped in front of her and she hissed them commands to get out of her way. But now she stopped and smiled. She had seen the man she was looking for.

*

As the procession reached the square, the crowd filtered to left and right on the beaten earth. They called out to the unhappy culprits, jeering at them, reminding them just what was about to happen to them.

The four victims stood together, their wrists bound behind them, with heads bowed. The three servants stood firmly, stolidly. The gentlewoman could not keep still, but was constantly changing her position. Lan Kuei knew this was because she possessed the lily feet – not intended for standing on for any length of time. This practice was not countenanced by the Manchu for their own women, and to Lan Kuei it made the torment this woman was undergoing all the more horrific.

She went and stood next to James Barrington in order to watch. They had known each other for several years, as the tall young Englishman often called at her father's house. Hui-cheng was an old friend of Martin Barrington, James's step-father, head of the House of Barrington, and James, although only twenty-two, had been in nominal charge of the Wuhu office for three years. He stood out in the crowd not only because of his fair skin and hair, but because he was so much bigger in every way than even a Manchu Bannerman. Lan Kuei thought he was the handsomest man in the world. Now she turned up her face to return his smile.

The serving maid was dragged forward, fortunate in that she was sentenced to the bastinado rather than the sword; she had apparently only helped conceal her mistress's crime, not actually participated in it. While the crowd's jeers grew louder, she was stripped of her pantaloons and stretched in the dust, her black hair settling about her shoulders, which shook to her sobs. The crowd roared their approval. James Barrington looked at Lan Kuei to see her reaction. The Manchu girl's eyes were wide, and she licked her lips in anticipation. Clearly she felt no pity, not even a pang of shame for the woman so exposed to the eyes of the multitude.

The woman was pinned to the ground by four men, holding each wrist and each ankle. Two more men stood beside her, one to each side of her thighs. They were armed with long, thin bamboo canes, and with these they now commenced lashing the woman's exposed buttocks, not hard but with a steady rhythm. While one cane was descending, the other was rising.

The first blows hardly seemed to harm the woman, then the buttocks began to quiver and redden, and soon her whole body was heaving against its restraining bonds.

The spectators clapped their hands and shouted their advice to the torturers. 'Make her arse bleed,' they bellowed. Soon little red flecks spattered across the dust with every blow, while the woman howled her agony, and the men never altered their strokes. Lan Kuei twined her fingers in her hair as she watched.

*

The woman finally lay still, her whole body and the ground to either side of her a mess of blood and sweat and urine. The men poked her with their rods, and someone emptied a bucket of water over her.

Her head jerked, and she immediately began screaming again, but as she possessed no saliva, only a thin high-pitched moan escaped her dust-caked lips. The executioners abandoned her and seized the first of the two menservants. The mistress, unable any longer to stand upon her lily feet, sank to her knees, and was pulled roughly upright by the man holding her hair.

The first man was dragged forward. He had been stripped to the waist, and while two men held his arms, hauling them behind him as if to check him, a third had his fingers twined in the man's black hair, and was dragging him towards where the executioner stood, leaning on his great sword.

As always with Chinese executions, it was very quick. Still being tugged both ways, it seemed, the man was forced to his knees before the sword. The executioner, a big strong fellow also stripped to the waist and gleaming sweat in the afternoon sunlight, did not even give the man's neck a preliminary tap. He merely seized the haft of his huge weapon in both hands, and swung it in a perfect arc. Dragged both ways at once, the man's body seemed to disintegrate. The men holding his arms threw the blood-spouting trunk away from them. He clutching the hair raised the bleeding head to show the crowd, who clapped their approbation. Then he threw the head away as well. Instantly the dogs ran forward to lick it, only to be shooed away by a gang of small boys who commenced to kick the head to and fro. The dogs tore at the corpse instead.

James felt Lan Kuei's fingers very tight on his arm. The woman servant slowly rose from the dust, and limped into the crowd. Blood trickled down her legs and filled her footprints; she carried her pantaloons in one hand. The crowd made little effort to let her through, jeering and laughing at her, slapping her lacerated buttocks to make her hiss with pain, and pulling at her hair.

The second manservant was now dead, his head also used as a plaything by the shrieking boys. Only the gentlewoman remained.

She stumbled on her deformed feet, weeping now, huge tears rolling down her cheeks and small breasts as her blouse was stripped away. James wondered what she had suffered at the hands of her husband to kill him, knowing full well that this would likely be her fate. A woman born to dignity and prosperity, as her feet indicated, about to die in the most public and humiliating manner. The crowd cheered, and a moment later her head too was thrown to the boys' eager feet.

*

Lan Kuei led them in rushing away from the dispersing crowd, eager to be free of it before any busybody identified the Intendant's daughter. She headed up a sloping street, past the bamboo stalls of street vendors, empty now since everyone had gone to watch the executions, and thence on to a bluff overlooking the river. There she threw herself on the grass, panting with exertion.

Chang Tsin ran behind her. James Barrington followed more slowly. It was beneath the dignity of the manager of the House of Barrington's Wuhu office to run and, besides, it was simply too hot. In Wuhu, more than two hundred miles from the sea, it either blew a storm or was absolutely still, like today. The temperature either plummeted to below freezing in the winter, or soared to a scorching heat in summer, relieved only by regular, heavy downpours of rain accompanied by thunder and lightning. It was now summer, so would not begin to cool off until late that evening.

Lan Kuei stood up again and dusted herself off. Her clothes consisted of the loose blouse and pantaloons which were traditional Chinese garb, but over them she wore a tabard of pale blue, decorated with dragons and birds in brilliant red. This was to show her rank, as did her shoes: ordinary Chinese clogs, but decorated with seed pearls set into the wood. It was customary for Manchu women to reveal the wealth of their family in their clothes, and more especially their shoes. Hui-cheng wanted his daughters to stand apart from the common herd.

As if there could be any risk of confusing this sturdy, handsome, athletic young woman with the thick, shiny black hair and enormous, deep black eyes, with any lily-footed Chinese girl. He stood beside her. 'How do you feel?'

'I feel ... excited. I wish I had a husband, so that I could go to him now and be fulfilled.'

She gazed at him, mouth open with embarrassment. James glanced at Chang Tsin, standing quietly to one side. He knew the boy's devotion to his wayward mistress. But Chang Tsin would know that Lan Kuei was an impossible dream for him. For a slave boy.

But not for a Barrington. 'Then marry me,' James said quietly. 'And be fulfilled.'

Lan Kuei looked away. Then again those marvellous eyes glanced at him. But the embarrassment had faded. He had asked her once before, and she had treated it as a joke. This afternoon was not a time for joking. 'Would you make me very rich?'

'Very rich,' he promised her.

Lan Kuei showed her tongue, for just a moment. 'I wish to be very, *very* rich,' she said.

'I will speak with your father tomorrow,' he said.

'But we couldn't marry for so long,' she said dolefully.

That was because the Tao-kuang Emperor had recently died,

and the twenty-seven-month mourning period was only half completed.

'But we can be betrothed,' James reminded her. And he lowered his head to kiss her mouth. Lan Kuei was taken by surprise; it was not a gesture she had ever known of. But when his tongue touched hers it sent a thrill down the length of her spine. Then she jerked her head away – and she ran off down the street, trembling with excited embarrassment. What would Papa say? Of course, there was the *prophecy*. And in addition there was her birthday. To have been born on the tenth day of the tenth moon of the year clearly destined her for greatness. As yet she could not imagine anything greater than to be the wife of James Barrington!

*

James whistled happily as he strode beside the river. According to the Chinese, the Yangtse rose in mountains so far to the west that it was possible to believe they were speaking of Europe itself. Which was of course nonsense. But it was a dream of James Barrington to explore this river to its source, if only to see for himself the huge gorges and spectacular rapids of which the Chinese also told. By the time the river reached Wuhu, it was broad and slow-moving and majestic, except in flood, when it grew turbulent and angry, and still more majestic. But it was here also brown-yellow and, in its apparent disinterest in its surroundings, very Chinese. James's step-father said there was another river to the north that was even more yellow in colour than the Yangtse, which indeed called the Huang-Ho, the Yellow River.

Whatever the truth of the river, there could be no arguing that here was the greatest natural waterway of which James had ever heard. The traffic was constant up and down, from sampans to ocean-going junks. Several of those junks belonged to the House of Barrington; two of them were tied up at the dock below the bluff now, loading rice. But, as yet, there were no foreign vessels to be seen. If in the ten years since the signing of the Treaty of Nanking had opened up the China Coast to British trade, the numbers of ships flying the Union Jack had multiplied in the China Sea, no one had yet dared to contravene the treaty by venturing up the Yangtse – although undoubtedly many dreamed of doing so. James Barrington's grandfather remained the only Englishman to have taken an English ship above Nanking.

He paused for a moment to look down on the many hundreds of boats that were going nowhere, but spent their entire existences tied up to the bank. Here there was a life within the greater life that was China, people who lived their allotted span on pieces of wood perhaps twenty feet long and four wide, save for their occasional forays ashore to seek vegetables – or to watch an execution. They caught fish, and the river provided them with sanitation, as it did for the entire city, just as it also provided the irrigation for the rice paddies to either side.

As he approached the house his step-father had bought from a local mandarin, and which was perched on a hill, looking down on the river some forty feet below – and therefore safe from flooding when the river burst its banks – James realised that he loved the Yangtse-Kiang. And, through the river, that he loved all China ... rolling heads and snarling dogs not withstanding. There was an immense inert strength in this huge country, a strength he felt all around him, even if so many of its people looked poor and downtrodden. They were still capable of laughter, even if often cruel laughter. And besides, poverty and degradation was not something that involved the House of Barrington.

*

'I intend to marry Lan Kuei,' James announced at dinner.

His sister and step-uncle gazed at him in consternation.

They made an odd gathering, because 22-year-old James was actually the eldest. If it had been Martin Barrington's idea, three years before, that his youthful step-son should have the earliest possible introduction into managing one of the House's branches, he had equally raised no objection when the previous year Joanna had wanted to join her brother, to keep house, as she put it. James and Joanna had always been very close. Indeed, Martin regarded James as his heir, and the boy had always revealed himself to be sober-minded and with a deep sense of propriety. Martin had no doubt that he would look after his sister well.

And Joanna at twenty needed looking after, with the flaming red hair she had inherited from her mother, and the strong face and stature of a Barrington. Martin was in no hurry to see her carried off by one of the British merchants who from time to time visited Nanking, all of whom cast interested glances at the blossoming young woman – and none of whom he relished. Luckily Wuhu was safely beyond their reach.

It had also seemed natural to send young John along as well, to learn the trade. Apart from being half-Chinese, John was that anomaly, an uncle who was actually younger than his nephew and niece. Both factors suggested that he was doomed never to rule the House of Barrington, if Martin had anything to do with it. John did not seem to resent this, but his mother most certainly did; and it was Martin's intention now to separate the boy as much as possible from Tsen-tsing. Tsen-tsing had wept and wailed, and begged to be allowed to accompany her son, but Martin had refused. 'Let the young people find their own feet together,' he had told her. 'In them lies the future of the House.'

*

So Joanna and John now stared at James with their mouths open.

'Hui-cheng's daughter?' Joanna asked.

'Well, you know I have admired her for years.'

'But she is Chinese,' John pointed out.

'Manchu,' James corrected.

'Father will never agree,' Joanna remarked.

'Father and Hui-cheng have been friends all their lives,' James protested.

'It is Hui-cheng who will never agree,' John said.

*

Lan Kuei faced her mother. She actually feared her mother more than her father. Sho-an was of the Niuhuru clan of the Plain Yellow Banner – there was no superior Banner in all China: it was the Banner of Nurhachi himself. Of course she had turned her back upon her family when she had married. But she had married beneath her, and she had never forgotten that.

'Mr Wang was there,' Sho-an said. 'He saw you at the execution.' She glared at Chang Tsin, standing in the doorway. Chang Tsin was very nervous; he was sweating. 'You know your father does not like you to attend these events,' Sho-an went on. 'It is unseemly. Now you will kneel – on the bare boards.'

The most humiliating of punishments. But today was different. Lan Kuei thrust out her determined little chin. 'I wish to be married.'

There was a moment of stunned silence. Then Te Shou, her elder sister, snapped, 'That cannot be so. How can you get betrothed before me? Who is this man?'

'James Barrington.'

'A barbarian?' Te Shou was aghast.

Sho-an always went straight to the heart of the matter. 'Has he spoken with your father? Of course not. He is a barbarian. So you are not betrothed. You will kneel.'

Lan Kuei hesitated, but she knew her impatience had made her speak out of turn. She could not be betrothed until her father had given his consent. Until then, her mother must be obeyed.

She took off her tabard, folded it neatly, then knelt on the wooden floor. 'Keep your back straight,' Sho-an told her, and placed the clock before her. 'An hour you will kneel. And you ...' Sho-an turned to Chang Tsin. 'Fu lo,' she called. 'Take this creature outside and flog him till he bleeds.'

Chang Tsin started to tremble. Lan Kuei bit her lip. It had been on her insistence that they attended the execution. But she would not beg her mother, even for Chang Tsin.

The butler hurried the boy away, and a few moments later the sounds of the cane could be heard. It was a day for floggings, Lan Kuei thought; no doubt she was the lucky one. But her knees were already beginning to ache, and she had only been kneeling a few minutes. Perhaps a flogging would have been preferable.

Sho-an left the room, and was replaced by Te Shou and Kai Tu. The sisters sat on the floor, one on each side of Lan Kuei. Kai Tu, who was two years younger than Lan Kuei, gazed at her with a mixture of fear and admiration; she would never have had the courage to go to an execution. As for telling their mother that she was betrothed – and to a barbarian ...

Te Shou regarded her sister with sorrowful contempt. Te Shou was two years the elder, and she never got into trouble. 'Our father will be very angry,' she said. 'He is already upset. There is an uprising in the south, have you not heard?'

Lan Kuei shook her head. Her knees were now definitely painful. She did not know why an uprising should have upset Hui-cheng. There were uprisings against the Manchu rule almost every day of the year, in one place or another.

Te Shou could tell what she was thinking. 'This is a big uprising,' she asserted. 'It is called T'ai-P'ing T'ienkuo. That means Heavenly Kingdom of Great Peace,' she added unnecessarily: Lan Kuei knew what T'ai-P'ing T'ienkuo meant. 'The rebels have overrun all of Kwantung Province, and have advanced into Kiangsi,' Te Shou went on. 'Now they are marching on Anhwei. It is their declared intention to take Nanking.'

Lan Kuei at last turned her head. Before any force marching from the south or west through Anhwei could reach Nanking, it must first of all take Wuhu.

Te Shou smiled at having gained her sister's attention. 'The Viceroy is determined to stop them, and has called out a levy of the Anhwei Bannermen. Father is going too. The summons arrived this afternoon, while you were out.'

'Father?' Lan Kuei was aghast.

'In his military capacity, he has been told to do so. But he does not like it.'

Lan Kuei could believe that. Her father had always preferred the pleasures of his home to the perils of a campaign.

Te Shou looked at the clock; Lan Kuei had been kneeling just over half an hour. 'You should not anger Father when he is upset,' she warned again.

Lan Kuei sighed. Kneeling here was bad enough. To be lectured in addition was impossible. But poor Father, off to war against rebels. She raised her head suddenly – because there he was.

Hui-cheng was not a great deal taller than his daughters, but considerably heavier. His thin moustaches drooped to either side of his mouth, and gave him a permanent look of pessimism. But this was no deception either, Lan Kuei knew; he was a pessimist by nature.

The sounds of whipping and howling from outside had

ceased, and Sho-an had returned as well, to stand at her husband's shoulder. 'Wretched girl,' Hui-cheng remarked. 'You bring disgrace upon our name. And at such a time. You have been meeting Young Barrington clandestinely.'

'Only by chance, Papa.'

'And it is by chance that he has claimed your hand? What else has he claimed?'

Lan Kuei's head jerked up, her eyes flashing anger that anyone, much less her own father, should suspect such a thing of her. But Barrington had touched her tongue with his! Had that changed her? Hui-cheng coughed. He was rather in awe of his middle daughter. 'He should have spoken with me first,' he grumbled.

'He will come to see you tomorrow.'

'Tomorrow I shall be gone with the army.'

Lan Kuei began to panic. 'Then send for him now, Papa.'

'I will do no such thing. A daughter of mine will not marry a barbarian – even a Barrington. Anyway, he should have asked for the hand of Te Shou first.'

'It is all the fault of that Chinese lout,' Sho-an declared. 'Why do we employ him? Simply to keep Lan Kuei from mischief, is why. And he leads her into more mischief than ever.'

'Yes,' Hui-cheng growled. 'Yes, you are right, Sho-an. He is useless. I will sell him tomorrow, before I leave. Let us see if Weng-feng can make anything of him.'

Lan Kuei simply had to speak. She was aware of what would be Chang Tsin's fate were he sent to Weng-feng. 'It was not his fault, Papa,' she pleaded.

Hui-cheng frowned at her. Children were not supposed to talk back while they were being punished.

'I *made* him take me to the execution,' Lan Kuei declared. 'And I arranged the meeting with Barrington.'

'She is a wanton,' Sho-an wailed.

'It was my doing, and mine alone,' Lan Kuei insisted, gazing at her father. 'Chang Tsin tried to prevent me, but I told him I would be angry. He had no choice but to follow.'

Hui-cheng gazed at her for several seconds. Then he said, 'It is still his fault. He will go to Weng-feng tomorrow.'

Lan Kuei scrambled to her feet, and Te Shou gave a startled exclamation of terror. Such insubordination was unheard of.

Kai Tu hid her face. 'You cannot, Papa!' Lan Kuei shouted.
'Chang Tsin is a good boy. You cannot have him made into a
eunuch.'

Hui-cheng had raised his eyebrows and taken a step back,
almost as if he had expected to be attacked. Now he recovered
his aplomb. 'He should have been shorn years ago. It is
unseemly to have a grown woman escorted by a male who is
not her brother or her husband. There has been talk. Now the
talk will cease. He will go to Weng-feng,' he repeated.

'You are a brute,' Lan Kuei told him.

Hui-cheng looked at his wife.

'She is a wanton,' Sho-an repeated. 'And with your father
about to go to war, as well.'

Te Shou shook her head. Obviously she would side with her
parents against a rebellious sibling. Kai Tu shivered with fear.

Hui-cheng looked at the clock. 'How long has she knelt?'

'Nearly the full hour, Father,' Te Shou said.

'Let the punishment start again, now,' Hui-cheng said, and
left the room. Lan Kuei sighed, and resumed kneeling.

Sho-an stiffly followed her husband.

Lan Kuei had been so concerned about Chang Tsin she had
hardly given a thought to Young Barrington. But he had only
been a dream, anyway. Lan Kuei did not think he was in her
stars, although he would undoubtedly have made a fine
husband. But she ... the ache in her knees made her feel
inspired. There was no real ache in her heart. What was a little
discomfort, a few disappointments? Was she not a child of the
tenth day of the tenth moon? Was it not prophesied that she
would marry greatness? She was sorry about James Barrington,
but perhaps he was simply not great enough. She wished he had
not kissed her.

But no one knew of that, save Chang Tsin, and he would
never betray her. While for her there were virtually no bounds
to the heights she could scale. She would marry a clan captain
... no, a general. Maybe a viceroy. She would marry a viceroy,
and live in a palace with hundreds of servants and eunuchs, and
have people bowing low as she was carried past in her chair.
And when she was in such a position of power, she would smile
upon Young Barrington, and on the ugly barbarian woman he
would have married.

She would also be able to find poor Chang Tsin and take him

back into her employ. She would be very pleased to do that.

What were a pair of sore knees compared with that glittering prospect?

*

When Chang Tsin was told of his fate, he wept. He had been weeping anyway, from the sting of the cane. Now he wept some more. Then he begged to be allowed a few days to compose himself before he was sent to the slave-dealer. But this Hui-cheng refused, being in a fine fettle of anxiety and excitement as the Anhwei army prepared to move out and give battle to the T'ai-P'ing.

Chang Tsin was locked in his room overnight, his wrists and ankles bound to make sure he did not try to escape or to harm himself. Hui-cheng was well aware of what the boy's feelings would be. It was possible for a eunuch to make a reasonably successful life for himself; although he might be either slave or underpaid employee, a eunuch who used his brains could easily become an essential aid to master or mistress, useful because of his ability to go anywhere, valuable because most of his master's business acquaintances would also employ eunuchs, who would rather deal with one of their own kind. It would be a foolish fellow who could let a large amount of money trickle through his fingers without having a little of it stick. There were cases of eunuchs who had made themselves so much money they could afford to buy themselves lavish houses. These fellows often married, and even adopted children.

But the emasculation carried with it that terrible concomitant of being unable to enter the Celestial Heaven unless someone could be found to sew the member back on after death. These reflections did not soften Hui-cheng's heart. He had always been suspicious of Chang Tsin, had resented the way Sho-an had allowed the boy and his younger daughters to become play-mates. The fellow deserved to be punished. Besides, he was Chinese. The fewer Chinese who made their way into heaven the better.

Hui-cheng wasted no time; he sent word to Weng-feng that very night, and the slave-dealer came at dawn the next morning. A price was quickly agreed, once Weng-feng had seen the boy. Chang Tsin was big and strong for his age, and good-looking as well – but Hui-cheng was in a hurry to be rid of him and to get away; he feared if he did not sell the boy himself before leaving, his womenfolk would never sell him at all.

'He is a poor specimen,' Weng-feng commented. 'He is not worth more than ten taels, excellency.'

To Weng-feng's amazement, Hui-cheng agreed without the slightest attempt at bargaining. Weng-feng wondered why he had not begun at five taels – simply for fear of insulting the foolish Intendant. But he knew he would sell Chang Tsin for at least double what he was paying for him – and he knew where, too.

'Get him out of here,' Hui-cheng commanded.

Weng-feng signalled to the three men he had brought with him. The bonds securing Chang Tsin's ankles were cut and he was dragged to his feet; his wrists were left secured. Weng-feng paid over the fee, and his men hustled Chang Tsin from the house.

Lan Kuei watched from the window of her bedroom. Her knees still ached from her ordeal of last night, but now her heart was aching as well. Chang Tsin had been such a pleasant companion. But one day, she reminded herself, when she was rich and famous, she was going to find him, and buy him back.

*

Hui-cheng stood before his womenfolk. His sons were Bannermen, naturally, and were already with the army. 'Keep safe until I return,' he said, and embraced Sho-an.

'Until you return,' Sho-an promised.

'Until you return,' Te Shou said, and embraced her father.

'Until you return,' Kai Tu said, and also stepped forward for an embrace.

'Until you return,' Lan Kuei said, following the example of her sisters. Her body was stiff, and this Hui-cheng could feel. He held her away from himself to study her. 'You will be dutiful to your mother,' he said. Lan Kuei bowed her head. 'And you will not see Young Barrington again,' Hui-Cheng warned her. He stepped outside to where his servants waited, and swung into the saddle of his horse. All the women were bowing, now.

Hui-cheng rode out of the yard.

'He will never come back,' Sho-an said sorrowfully.

'He will come back, Mother,' Te Shou said reassuringly. 'Of course he will come back.'

Lan Kuei wanted her father to come back, so that one day she could punish him somehow for what he was doing to Chang Tsin.

*

Chang Tsin himself was marched along the street to the warehouse belonging to Weng-feng. As his wrists remained bound, and as Weng-feng was well known in the city, everyone knew what would happen to him. People sneered at him, and made obscene remarks. 'There's a dog will soon have no tail,' they shouted. Others called, 'The kettle is about to have its spout broken off,' accompanied by gales of laughter. Small boys ran up to him and pulled at the crotch of his pants.

When they reached the warehouse, Chang Tsin's nostrils were afflicted by the stench. One of the men laughed. 'You will soon stink like that,' he said. 'I can smell a eunuch downwind at a hundred yards.' Chang Tsin's knees shook against each other.

Weng-feng came in. 'Prepare him,' he commanded. Chang Tsin's wrists were released, and then he was stripped. Weng-feng's personal surgeon had been summoned, and he tested Chang Tsin's heart and circulation, to make sure they were sound. He pronounced himself satisfied. 'It is customary to ask you if you truly wish this to happen.' Weng-feng smiled. 'But, as a slave, you have no choice. I will leave you with these men.'

Chang Tsin began to weep again. He had been taught from birth that one must accept whatever misfortunes fate hurled at one, with a stoical understanding that sometimes there would be good fortune as well. He had had no such fortune in his brief life ... and now he did not see how he would ever have any. 'Now we are going to make you very happy,' the first man said.

Chang Tsin gaped at him.

'All happiness is but a transient state,' the man explained. 'So if you are happy for even a few minutes, be grateful.'

His two companions led Chang Tsin to the far end of the room, where there were stakes set in the floor in the shape of a triangle. They made Chang Tsin lie down, carried his arms above his head, and secured his wrists together to the apex stake. Then they pulled his legs apart, and secured one ankle to each of the other stakes. The ropes were drawn very tight, so that his spreadeagled body was unable to do more than tremble. 'Now you will be happy,' the first man said.

Chang Tsin's head jerked sideways, and he saw that they had been joined by a woman – not old, but certainly old enough to know what she was about. She was also quite good-looking – and naked. Chang Tsin reacted immediately, despite his fear. The men clapped their hands. 'You have a willing one here, Lu So,' one said.

'And he is so big,' Lu So said, kneeling beside him and taking him in her hands. 'It is a great shame.'

'It becomes a memory to all of us, sooner or later,' the first man said. He was apparently a homespun philosopher.

'I am Lu So,' the woman said. 'Have you heard of me?'

'I have heard of you,' Chang Tsin muttered. Lu So was one of the best known prostitutes in Wuhu.

'Then you know that I am descended from the great Lu Shan, of Nanking?' Lu So asked.

'I did not know that,' Chang Tsin said, keeping from screaming only with an effort.

'The immortal Chang Yi Sao was my aunt,' Lu So told him.

'I am pleased for you,' Chang Tsin muttered.

Lu So smiled, and played with Chang Tsin. The delightful sensations she induced brought him to orgasm within seconds. Lu So delicately wiped her hands on a towel, and then resumed. Chang Tsin panted, and hardened, and came again, very quickly.

'We will be here all day,' growled one of the men.

'Not too long now,' Lu So said. Because this time Chang Tsin took a little longer to harden, and even though the sensations were as pleasant as before, he took longer to spurt as well.

'He is ready,' the first man declared.

'Once more,' Lu So demurred. Clearly she was enjoying her work. Now she was sweating with her exertions, and she lay down on Chang Tsin and worked her body up and down his. Chang Tsin did not want to harden again. As long as he did not, he was safe, but there was no way he could resist this woman's sinuous movements. He tried desperately to think of other things, and instead found himself thinking of Lan Kuei, working her body over his, like this. He felt himself coming up, and Lu So felt him too. This time she sucked him as well as played with him, until he came again. Lu So stood up. 'That is enough happiness for any man,' she said. 'You will be able to look back on this morning, and remember how Lu So made you very happy.'

Tears dribbled from Chang Tsin's eyes. He felt utterly exhausted, utterly flaccid, incapable of any resource ... but no doubt that was how the men wanted him. While Lu So had been working on him, one of the men had brought in a tray containing a hideous assortment of tools, all of gleaming steel. Chang Tsin shuddered, and again he wanted to scream.

'Will you stay?' they asked Lu So.

The prostitute shook her head. 'I like only intact men. The others offend me.' She picked up her clothes and went to the door, looked back at Chang Tsin. 'Remember me,' she said.

Come back, Chang Tsin wanted to shout. *Oh, please come back!* The men gathered round him. One thrust a gag into Chang Tsin's mouth. Another tied a blindfold round his eyes. Chang Tsin commenced to scream, knowing that he could not be heard, but the high-pitched sound inside this head somehow relieved the unbearable tension of what was happening to him.

It did not relieve the pain, however, even if it was very quick. There was a gush of searing agony, and he thought his writhing body would even break the bonds, but it did not, and the pain continued to surge up and down his body. Even through this he felt a new sensation, a great weakness.

The men removed his blindfold, but not the gag. Chang Tsin could look down at himself. He saw nothing but blood ... and a steel tube which had been stuck into him, deep into the wound. 'It takes three days,' said the first man, not unkindly. 'If you can pass water through the tube, and do not fester, in three days you will begin to heal.' He ruffled Chang Tsin's hair. 'You will make a good eunuch.'

*

James Barrington presented himself at the house of Hui-cheng a little later than intended, for the streets were crowded with Bannermen. 'They are on their way to war, with the T'ai-P'ing,' the onlookers told him.

When finally he reached his destination, and asked to see the
Intendant, Fu Lo said, 'His excellency has already left the city.
He goes with the army, to fight the T'ai-P'ing.'

'Then may I speak with Sho-an?'

'That will not be possible.'

'Then, with Lan Kuei?'

'Certainly not. I am to say this to you, Young Barrington:
you are not welcome here.'

James chewed his lip in indecision. Clearly Lan Kuei had
been indiscreet. 'At least let me speak with Chang Tsin.'

'Chang Tsin is no longer in the employ of his excellency,' Fu
Lo said. 'He has been sent to Weng-feng.'

'Weng-feng!' James was tempted to visit Weng-feng himself,
but decided against it. Instead he wrote a letter to Sho-an,
formally requesting Lan Kuei's hand in marriage ... and
received no reply from her.

'I told you they'd never agree,' Joanna reminded him. 'For
you to aspire after the hand of a Manchu noblewoman would
be like some coolie asking to marry me.'

'I don't follow the relationship at all. Step-father always said
that the father of Hui-cheng, and indeed Hui-cheng himself,
regarded our family as on a par with any in the land. I shall just
have to wait until this T'ai-P'ing rebellion ends, and Hui-cheng
returns to Wuhu. I *am* going to marry Lan Kuei.'

*

A fortnight later Lan Kuei accompanied her mother and sisters
to the market. On their way they passed a line of slaves
shambling down to the dock to be placed on a sampan for
Nanking. Sho-an immediately herded the girls in the other
direction; she had recognised that these unfortunates were
eunuchs. Lan Kuei had recognised it, too, and wanted to look
at their faces, in case Chang Tsin was amongst them – to give
him some sign that she had not forgotten him. And he had been
there!

But Sho-an hurried her away before she could make any
contact with the miserable-looking youth. Then, only half an
hour later, they spotted James Barrington and his sister
standing on the other side of a meat stall. James and Lan Kuei
gazed at each other, but Sho-an had also noticed him, and once

again she hurried the sisters away. Lan Kuei's mood of confidence had passed, and she was utterly despondent. Her life had been ruined – and Chang Tsin's life as well. She had hoped against hope that Weng-feng might decide not to castrate Chang Tsin, that a hundred and one things might happen to prevent it ... but now she could hope no longer. Father had made it happen, robbed her childhood playmate of his every hope of joy and pleasure. And herself of the prospect of marrying a man both handsome and rich. She hated Father!

That was a terrible thought to have. If her wild Manchu ancestors had believed only in the gods of the wind and the thunder, the rain and the earth, since they had conquered the Middle Kingdom they had thoroughly absorbed the doctrines of Confucius, at least as revised by his later disciple, Mencius. In many ways, Lan Kuei felt this was a bad thing. Where the nomadic Manchu, who had ridden behind the banners of Nurhachi, had taken as their heroes men like Nurhachi himself, bold warriors who lived spear and bow in hand, ready to challenge the world, the Chinese chose their heroes from men who wrote exquisite poetry or spent blameless lives – as recommended by Confucius.

This had made them relatively easy to defeat, of course, but after their victory it had also confused the Bannermen. As decreed by Nurhachi, and confirmed by the great Ch'ien-lung Emperor, they were fighting men. They could undertake no other professions than that of a warrior or of a civil servant administering the conquered land. If unemployed, they received an imperial stipend, barely enough to live on, and those who could not get admittance to the civil service spent their time swaggering about or grouped on street corners, bragging about the deeds they had done or the deeds they would do.

When they beat the T'ai-P'ing, they would actually have something to boast about. But perhaps too many of them now believed in the teachings of Confucius. Certainly Father did.

Most important of the Confucian doctrines was respect for the family. One worshipped one's ancestors because without them one would not have life oneself; for that reason one honoured and obeyed one's parents more than any other living creatures ... and one honoured them even more after they were dead. Oddly, Confucius had never said one had to *love* one's parents. But one certainly could not criticise them. As for *hating* one of them ...

But she had other reasons than Chang Tsin and James Barrington for regarding her father with contempt. Hui-cheng belonged to the Yehe Nara clan of the Bordered Blue Banner. The Bordered Blue was least of all the Banners in the Manchu hierarchy.

No man could choose his ancestors. Every man, indeed, must worship them. And if for a man of such an inferior clan the highest echelons of government were closed, Hui-cheng had still done very well: as Intendant of South Anhwei he wielded a great deal of power. Yet he had not used his power to grow rich. The previous Intendant of South Anhwei had retired with enough money to buy himself a palace in Peking, and to live like an imperial prince. Father was too honest! And so his daughters must sew their own clothes instead of buying new, and wear virtually no jewellery on their shoes.

And have no very great expectations, either. In the cold light of day her dreams of marrying a provincial viceroy could be seen to be just dreams. Now Father's stiff-necked pride had prevented her marrying Young Barrington. Father was a wretch! And since he had ruined her childhood playmate, she was now left without a friend at all. She had little in common with Te Shou, while Kai Tu was just a child.

She felt herself to be very much alone.

12

THE KINGDOM OF HEAVENLY PEACE

'I'm afraid I find all of this very disappointing,' Martin Barrington remarked, surveying his step-children. 'I had supposed you had a sense of responsibility, James.'

'It is lacking in responsibility to fall in love, Uncle?'

'Certainly, where it is likely to cause a good deal of discord.' Martin coughed as he remembered his own indiscretion. 'But perhaps it is sometimes unavoidable. The pity of it is that the rift is with Hui-cheng. He has been a friend of the family for more years than I care to remember. We must hope that he comes back from this war in a better frame of mind.'

'Then I intend to approach him again.'

Martin pointed. 'You'll do no such thing, young man. I absolutely forbid it.' He waved the letter which James had shown him. 'This is a definite refusal, and there is an end to it. I require your most solemn assurance that you will not raise the matter again, or I will take you away from here. Now, tell me about this T'ai-P'ing movement. From what we hear down in Nanking, it seems more serious than the usual tax revolt.'

'It is indeed,' John said. 'A great deal more serious. It seems to have originated among the Hakka people, in the interior of Kwantung Province. You know the Hakka have always felt themselves to be victimised, by both the Chinese and the Manchu. Now they have found a leader, a man called Hung Hsiu-ch'uan ...'

'Who did you say?' Martin almost shouted.

'Hung Hsiu-ch'uan.'

'My God! I know the fellow. He it was who first stirred up all that trouble in Canton. He seemed to believe he has some mission to rid China of the Manchu.'

'More than that,' John said. 'Now apparently he is claiming to be the son of God.'

237

Martin frowned. 'God? What God?'

'Our God, Martin. The Christian God. He is telling his followers that he has been sent by his "father" to drive the Manchu out of China, and restore the Chinese themselves to their ancient purity. Actually, there seems to be a good deal of primitive Christianity in what he preaches. You know the sort of thing: sharing all goods, no adultery or concubinage ... It is appealing to the people of the interior, who are supporting him in great numbers.'

'Well, well,' Martin said thoughtfully. 'And the Bannermen aren't doing very well against him, from what I hear.'

'They are trying to restrict him south of Hankow,' James said. 'I suppose they reckon if they can stop him long enough, his support will dwindle away.'

'Hmm,' Martin commented, even more thoughtfully. 'Hung Hsiu-ch'uan. Taking on the world. He always wanted to do that. He wanted me to go along with him back in 1840. I'd give a lot to be able to get in touch with him now.'

'With a bandit, Uncle?' Joanna was horrified.

'Well, if he isn't stopped by the Bannermen, and from what I've been hearing I'm not sure they can do it, he'll suddenly cease to be a bandit, won't he? That's the unwritten law of this country. If he gets control of Kwantung and Southern Anhwei, he could be someone to reckon with. Someone we may have to deal with. And we have the advantage of knowing the chap.'

'I will visit this man.' John Barrington glanced at his stepbrother. 'I do nothing here save enter invoices. And because of my Chinese blood, as well as my name, I will be able to travel freely.'

'Your mother would throw a fit.'

John gave a sly smile. 'Then do not tell her. At least until after I have left.'

Martin stroked his chin. 'Let me think about that one.' He rose, stood at the verandah rail to look down at the river.

*

Li Chung-hu gazed at the eunuch. 'Another ugly brute,' he remarked. An opening gambit. Chang Tsin knew he was the best-looking of the six eunuchs presented for sale.

Weng-feng knew that too. 'Young,' he pointed out. 'Strong.

Uncontaminated,' he added importantly.

Li Chung-hu walked right round Chang Tsin. He was Chinese. From the appearance of his house, his clothes, and his servants, he was also a very wealthy man. Yet the front of his head was shaved and he wore the pigtail like any other beggar in the street. Like Chang Tsin himself.

Chang Tsin had never actually met a wealthy Chinese before. But, according to his fellows, Nanking was full of wealthy men, both Chinese and Manchu. It was certainly the greatest city Chang Tsin had ever seen. He had imbibed enough history at Lan Kuei's elbow to know that it had been made the capital of the Middle Kingdom by Hung Wu, founder of the Ming dynasty, in 1368. Hung Wu had built the great imperial palace, and the city wall, sixty miles in length, and sixty feet high, with eighteen gates.

It had been Hung Wu's son, Yung Lo, who had moved the capital to Peking in the north, and the Manchu had adhered to that location when they had conquered the Ming. Nanking had been neglected for two hundred years by the emperors. Yet it remained enormously wealthy. It lay in the centre of a vast, fertile plain watered by the Yangtse-Kiang, and drew its revenues from an abundance of rice, tea and silk. It had developed its industries, weaving, pottery, printing and brocade, to be the best in China. And it lay just upriver from Chin-kiang, where the Grand Canal crossed the Yangtse on its way south to Hang-Chau. In every way it was well-suited to be the hub of China.

But at the moment Chang Tsin was not really interested in Nanking's greatness. His only awareness was of being uprooted. This would have dominated his feelings even had there been no castration involved. He really could not remember life outside of Hui-cheng's household; he had been sold when a small boy. He could not imagine an existence not dominated by Lan Kuei, with her moods and her vanities, her arrogance and her wilfulness. He had been her slave in everything, dominated, when they had both been children, by her quickness of wit, her superior knowledge, her total confidence that she knew best.

He had been even more her slave as they had both entered adolescence, and she had wanted to explore life. He, being nearest at hand, had been the obvious object of her explorations, at least until the barbarian man had appeared on the scene.

It was odd, he reflected, how the Chinese, and the Manchu, always referred to the pale-skinned foreigners as long-nosed hairy barbarians. James Barrington's nose was actually rather short, although not as short as a Chinese one. But he was definitely hairy. Lan Kuei had often speculated about that, wondered aloud what it would be like to have sex with such a creature. While Chang Tsin had only ever wondered what it might be like to have sex with Lan Kuei.

Thus he often wept. Because although he had been shorn, although the incipient beard he had been sprouting only a few months ago had all but disappeared, although he knew his voice had risen an octave, although he now squatted to piss and had no sensation other than misery when he washed himself ... there were yet urgings inside him, urgings which could not now ever be relieved. He would never see her again. He wept every night at that thought. Instead he was to be the slave of this pot-bellied merchant, whose moustache drooped so far it descended past his shoulders, and whose eyes were dull with opium. And who was mean. 'I will give you ten taels,' he said.

Weng-feng bowed his head. 'Then we are engaged in useless conversation, good sir. This boy is worth far more than that. He has spent most of his life in the service of a Manchu nobleman.'

'What do you think him worth, then?'

Weng-feng appeared to consider. 'Fifty taels.'

'You are mad. For a fifteen-year-old who is undoubtedly a criminal? Fifteen taels, and that is my last offer.'

Weng-feng bowed again. 'If I let this boy go for less than forty taels, noble sir, my wife would never speak to me again.'

'Twenty, and there's an end to it.'

Weng-feng had barely had the time to straighten. Now he bowed again. 'The boy is yours, great gentleman.'

*

There could be no doubt as to Li Chung-hu's wealth, Chang Tsin reckoned. The mansion was not so very much smaller than the old Imperial palace a couple of blocks away, and in a much better state of repair. In the drapes, the flowers, the polished floors, the *cloisonné* work, in both enamel and silver, which filled the tables, it far outshone Hui-cheng's residence. Here there was luxury in every direction, even in the several bowing eunuchs who met their master on his return from the slave market.

'His name is Chang Tsin,' Li Chung-hu said. 'He is a present for the lady Sung-shu. Take him to her.'

The eunuchs bowed again, and beckoned Chang Tsin. He was escorted by three of them. 'Where are you from?' one asked, as they made their way along no less luxurious corridors.

'I am from Wuhu,' Chang Tsin told them.

'And how long have you been one of us?' asked another.

'Six weeks,' Chang Tsin said.

They made a curious hissing noise. 'Our mistress will teach you your position,' they said.

'This mistress ... is she young or old?' Chang Tsin asked.

'Oh, she is young. She is our master's latest wife.'

Another young woman, Chang Tsin thought, who would doubtless be as attractive as Lan Kuei. He had after all been lucky, perhaps.

'Be careful,' warned the eunuch beside him, as they entered an antechamber, opened the doors beyond, and stepped through.

'The new slave, my lady,' he announced. 'Chang Tsin.'

Chang Tsin received a nod from the second eunuch, and also stepped through the doorway, to bow, as his mentor was doing. He was in a large room, high-ceilinged and airy, with doors opening on to an inner garden. It was a place of divans and a huge bed, and women. Several of these clustered around him, peering at him. They were of all ages, some quite pretty. But he knew that he should have eyes only for the one who remained lounging on the bed. She wore a deep red undressing robe, slit to above the knee on its left side to allow her legs freedom to move, and they moved languorously as she rolled on the pillows. Her midnight hair was loose, and scattered past her waist. Jewelled rings adorned her fingers, and her feet were bare.

As she was *en déshabille*, her make-up had not been renewed in several hours, but traces of the heavy lead-based cream still clung to her eyelids and beneath her ears. Her small face might have been pretty but for its arrogance. Now she sat up, a long rustle of silk.

'Chang Tsin,' she remarked, her voice high and shrill. 'It is an amusing name. Will you amuse me, Chang Tsin?'

'I ... I will try, my lady,' Chang Tsin said.

'Try?' she shouted. 'Try?' She glared at his three companions. 'He has angered me. I will teach him a lesson. I will strip the skin from his arse.'

Before Chang Tsin could react he was seized by the two eunuchs and spreadeagled across a divan, while a third yanked down his pantaloons. The girls screamed their pleasure and gathered round to watch. To be exposed to these gibbering hoydens was far worse than the actual caning ... which he assumed was being administered by Sung-shu herself.

Yet the caning was painful enough, and he started to weep. They were more tears of despair and humiliation than agony. This was what fate had ordained for him, for ever and ever. Until the day he died and plunged into the fiery chaos.

*

'Uncle Martin is quite right,' Joanna told James, as they watched the sampan carrying Martin Barrington slip away from the dock and begin its journey downriver. 'For you to continue pursuing Lan Kuei will only cause trouble.'

She could speak as freely as she liked to him, because they were so close. Their intimacy had been born during the harsh days of their childhood, when their real father had done nothing more than bark at them and occasionally take a strap to them.

'You just do not know what it is like to be in love,' James argued, equably enough.

'Do you? Lan Kuei is a pretty girl, but really, James ... love? You come from entirely different backgrounds, customs, manners ...'

'I am as Chinese in outlook as the next man.'

'But Lan Kuei is Manchu. Her ideas are entirely different from yours. What did she say when you proposed?'

'Well ...' James could not prevent a flush. 'She asked if I would make her very rich.'

'And when you said you would, she said yes. Oh, James!'

'I have work to do,' he said.

'John is waiting to say goodbye.'

'He's going upriver by boat. I'll be here when he's ready to leave.'

*

Joanna made her way up the hill to the house, where John Barrington was standing on the veranda. He had abandoned western dress for Chinese, which made him look as Chinese as she had ever known him. He held her hands. 'Will you miss me?'

'Of course I shall, Uncle John. Mind you take care. These T'ai-P'ing may *sound* like old-fashioned Christians, but apparently they don't object to killing people.'

'I am protected by my name,' John said. 'No sensible man is going to make war upon the House of Barrington. But I understand that it is a dangerous mission I undertake.' He continued to hold her hands. 'I shall carry your image with me.'

Joanna frowned at him. He was not usually this serious. 'That is kind of you, Uncle John.'

'I would not have you think of me as an uncle, my dear Joanna. Your image is engraved on my heart.' Joanna gave a nervous tug at her hands. 'I felt it necessary for you to know this before I departed; it may be some months before I return.'

Joanna licked her lips. 'I shall pray for that happy day.'

'And wait for it?'

Joanna tugged her hands free. 'Really, Uncle John, of course I shall wait for it. Where do you think I am intending to go?'

'You are deliberately misunderstanding me,' he said sadly. 'What you are suggesting is impossible. And indecent.'

He seized her hands again and kissed them. 'We will speak of it when I return. Until then, I should like it kept secret.'

'I would be ashamed to mention it to anyone.'

'Not even James?'

'Most especially not James.' There were pink spots in her cheeks, and she was breathing heavily.

'I will speak with him myself,' John Barrington said. 'When I return.'

*

Joanna stared after her youthful uncle as he marched down the hill behind the servants who were carrying his boxes. He had proposed marriage. A funny little boy who was a year younger than herself! And her uncle into the bargain.

At least, she presumed he had proposed marriage. It would be laughable, were it not insulting. And also a little sinister. Growing up in China had left Joanna far removed from the sheltered prejudices of her English forebears. She had learned merely to look the other way when she came across a convict in a cage, or wearing the cangue, the great wooden collar to which his hands were secured, leaving him helpless and subjected to whatever torments the passersby might choose to inflict. Men and women urinating, or worse, on the street caused her only a momentary feeling of distaste.

These were everyday events, and to pretend that they were not happening was senseless. But equally she had been educated by her mother to feel that, as an Englishwoman, she was superior to any Chinese or even Manchu, and certainly to their womenfolk, who were subjected to the most abject slavery by their husbands and the other male members of their married family – not to mention the various matriarchs who ruled the domestic establishment. As for their sexual habits – Mama had always given her to understand that those were beyond discussion.

But the mere fact of being forced to submit to the rule of Tsen-tsing would be unthinkable enough. Of course neither Mama nor Uncle Martin would ever consider it for a moment. But if Uncle John was foolish enough to propose the matter ... she could not imagine what would happen then. She almost hoped that he would not return from his visit to the T'ai-P'ing leader.

*

John Barrington should have reached Hankow within a month of leaving Wuhu. Instead his sampan was forced to put in to one of the villages which lined the upper reaches of the Yangtse because of the flood of water-borne traffic coming down. Hankow had fallen to the T'ai-P'ing! He stood on the river bank and watched not only the civilians but the Bannermen streaming by on the land. Some had even lost their weapons; all were totally demoralised. 'They are like a flood,' one captain told John. 'There are hundreds of thousands of them. My arm has grown weary with killing them. But they still keep on coming.'

'And the people are with them,' said another. 'They believe in them. They say the T'ai-P'ing is the only true way. They are unstoppable.'

John's crew refused to go any further, so he bought a horse from one of the fugitives – paying several times its real value – and rode up the south bank of the river. He was not in the least afraid. From what he had learned, it seemed that the T'ai-P'ing were against the Manchu and the rich. He was certainly not a Manchu, and he was not rich either, no matter how wealthy the House of Barrington might be, or how well provided he was with ready cash. He was a side-shoot. He had resented this all of his brief life, ever since had been old enough to understand what his mother was telling him. Sometimes he had even hated his pure-bred relations with their stiff-necked arrogance, their certainty that they belonged to the greatest nation on earth. But he had never revealed those feelings, had been prepared to wait, despite the anger of his mother. And a triumph here would force his half-brother to accord him proper notice, a proper place in the business.

And who could tell what might follow from that? John knew what he wanted to follow: he wanted his niece as a wife. Ever since reaching puberty he had watched that blossoming figure, that rich Titian hair, with an increasing desire. That, too, was a secret he had never confided to anyone, not even his mother. He had felt she would disapprove, and there was the question of consanguinity, which seemed to matter so much to the barbarians. Undoubtedly he had been careless in confiding his dream to Joanna herself; she had been both surprised and dismayed. But could he succeed with this fellow Hung ... And clearly it was more than just a matter of establishing relations now. He did not see the Banner army recovering in time to stop the T'ai-P'ing, even if it was still several hundred miles from Nanking.

*

He did not halt for the night until he was clear of the refugees. He was not afraid of a confrontation, as in his pocket he carried one of the new Colt revolvers, capable of firing six shots before reloading. But when he did stop, he made sure he was in a defensible position, with the river at his back and a hummock of ground concealing him from the road. Then he hobbled his horse over a patch of good grass, had his quick meal of rice and water, and lay down. On the road, only a few hundred yards away, he could hear the chatter of voices and the rumble of wheels as a new contingent of those not prepared to conform to the T'ai-P'ing ideals hurried on their way. They had no time to turn aside and look for someone to rob.

John Barrington slept with utter confidence. He was a confident man. When he awoke, it was to a great silence, save for the whisper of the river. He washed himself in the flowing water, led his horse down to drink as well, and then walked him up the slope to where he could overlook the road.

This was now empty save for various discarded pieces of household goods, and one cart which had lost a wheel and been unceremoniously pushed into the ditch. The country beyond the road was flat, a mass of rice paddies which stretched as far as the eye could see, with no sign of human habitation. But in the far distance there was a plume of smoke.

John mounted, and proceeded along the road, the river on his right. He had travelled perhaps five miles when he saw people in the distance, one or two at first, and then a great number. The morning sunlight picked out the blades of their swords and pikes, but he saw no firearms. He went towards them, heart pounding, but still relying on his name, the obvious fact that he was only partly Chinese ... and his plan of action. He kept his Colt concealed; it would be of no use here.

The advancing people paused when about half a mile away, staring at the lone horseman, unable to believe that someone was actually coming towards them instead of running way from them; while he could identify them as rebels against Manchu law from the simple fact that they had cut off their pigtails.

They continued to stare at him as he approached to within fifty feet of them, and then drew rein. 'I represent the House of Barrington,' he shouted. 'I seek Hung Hsiu-ch'uan.'

A ripple spread through the T'ai-P'ing, and John, looking from face to face, observed that there were women as well as men in the mob; since they all wore the invariable Chinese garb of loose pantaloons and looser blouse, and were all armed, this had been difficult to tell at a distance. But it was a man who stepped forward. 'The House of Barrington serves the Manchu.'

'The House of Barrington serves whoever rules this country,' John corrected him. 'It is also Christian – and for these reasons I have been sent to speak with Hung Hsiu-ch'uan, for our mutual benefit. My brother and Hung are old friends.'

The man and his fellows stared at him. Then they held a brief discussion between themselves, before their spokesman turned back to John. 'The T'ien Wang' – the words meant Heavenly King – 'is in Hankow,' he said. 'I will send you to him.'

*

A squad of three men and three women were detached to escort John further up the river. The journey took four days, and was of considerable interest, not least for the behaviour of his new companions. They were all young, and full of boisterous vigour. They laughed and joked, and spoke of when they would take Nanking – they did not seem to have any doubt of that. They slept together on the ground, often touching. Come dawn, they stripped off and bathed together in the river, splashing water over each other. Yet, so far as John could see, they never attempted to touch each other sexually. He found this intriguing and, as the girls were extremely pretty, disturbing, and ventured to ask one of them, on the second night, if she would care to share his blanket.

'Fornication is a sin punishable by death,' she told him. 'That is the word of the T'ien Wang.'

*

To John's astonishment, he learned that Hung Hsiu-ch'uan had not only forbidden fornication, but even sexual intercourse between married couples! Yet everyone seemed happy enough. Well, the revolution had only been in process for a few years, he supposed, and for the moment they were all carried forward in a fervour of battle and victory – and ferocity. Those who adhered to the T'ai-P'ing philosophy of total equality, between men and men, women and women, and women and men, were welcomed and well-treated. Those who resisted the rebels in any way, or belonged to the landlord class, were ruthlessly butchered. Fornication between members of the T'ai-P'ing might be forbidden, but rape of a Manchu or Chinese woman from the gentry class was positively encouraged – before the victim was executed. Before he came to Hankow, he passed many a burned and looted manor house, its erstwhile inhabitants now mutilated corpses rotting in the sun.

*

In Hankow he was again surprised. Christian, indeed communistic, simplicity and sharing were the hallmarks of the T'ai-P'ing, and for obvious reasons the philosophy appealed enormously to the hordes of Chinese peasants who from time immemorial had lived beneath the heel of both imperial taxes and the landowners to whom tax-collecting had been farmed. Little was being done to repair the infrastructure of the provinces which the civil war had destroyed, but that, he supposed, could be attributed to the fact that this rebellion was still very much in progress. Surviving by looting and pillaging the rich rice merchants of the fertile Yangtse plain, the T'ai-P'ing adherents had not yet encountered shortage of food any greater than they had always known – and it seemed to trouble nobody that there would be no crops the following year unless someone planted them now, or unless the entire rebellion moved on into a new province.

There had been no attempt to restore Hankow to being the great city of which he had been told by his step-brother. Fires smouldered in many places, ruined buildings abounded, and the skeletons of murdered men and women still lay in the streets. Yet the city teemed with eager men and women clad in looted finery, parading with their weapons, and eager to resume their march downriver. John Barrington was escorted through them to the viceregal palace. This had been damaged in the conflict, but he trod on still gleaming marble floors before being instructed to remain in an antechamber while his name was taken in to the Heavenly King.

Once admitted, he was forced to crawl forward, and perform the kowtow at the foot of the viceregal throne. He was aware of this being the supreme moment of his mission; there could be no turning back now – only total confidence would see him through.

'You say your name is Barrington,' remarked a quiet voice. 'Let me look upon your face.'

Still kneeling, John sat upright, and blinked towards the throne. Before him was a dazzling array of colours, in the clothes of the men clustered around the Heavenly King, in the jewel-encrusted hilts of their swords, and their rich brooches and necklaces. But none could equal the T'ien Wang. Hung Hsiu-ch'uan wore an imperial yellow gown embroidered with red dragons, as if he were the Son of Heaven himself. He was unarmed, and displayed no jewellery save for several rings – but the most striking thing about him was his extreme youth. John knew he could hardly be much more than thirty but, in contrast to his commanders, he seemed anxious to accentuate his youth by remaining clean-shaven. Yet the thin lips and hard eyes indicated the strength as well as the ruthlessness in his character. He subjected John to an appraising stare, then nodded.

'Yes,' he said. 'You are a Barrington. Why have you come here?'

'I have been sent by my brother, Martin Barrington, to congratulate an old friend on the success of his arms.'

'Old friend!' Hung's lip curled. 'He could have shared in my success. He could have made it happen twelve years ago.'

'My brother recognises his error, your Majesty,' John protested.

'Has he sent me gifts? Tribute?'

'He has sent his only living brother to assist you.'

Hung gazed at him for several seconds. 'How can you assist me?' he asked at last.

John had already worked out a plan of campaign; its success depended upon gaining this man's confidence. 'Do I not know the river, and the lands to either side of it, as well as I know my own hand? Equally I know the Manchu generals, and the forces of which they dispose.'

'You wish to aid me in defeating the Manchu?'

'I would show you the way to Nanking, your Majesty.'

'You are but a boy,' sneered one of the men at Hung's shoulder.

'I am a Barrington,' John declared.

Hung nodded. 'I would speak with you, Barrington.'

*

John was escorted by eunuchs into the domestic apartments of the palace, observing all around him with great interest. The

common herd who followed the T'ai-P'ing hierarchy might
revel in sharing everything they, and everyone else, possessed,
but obviously the leadership did not practise what it preached.
John found himself surrounded by greater wealth than he had
ever seen, and by more than that. On passing an open doorway
he heard female giggles, and spotted several scantily clad,
nubile young women peering at him. They rushed off with
shrieks of laughter when they realised they had been seen. He
looked in question at his escorting eunuchs, who grinned.

'They are members of the Heavenly King's harem.'

This entirely restored John's faith in human nature, and also
started him thinking. If he had never doubted that the T'ai-
P'ing would be the force of the future, and that the House of
Barrington must ally itself to them in order to survive, he had
not immediately reckoned how he and Martin would cope with
this insensate determination to share everything, or with the
outlawry of all of the acts and comforts which made life worth
living. But if Hung so clearly practised a double standard
between his immediate confidants, and the people he led – then
it was necessary to make sure he, John, became one of those
confidants.

His confidence in his own future increased as he found
himself lying on soft scented cushions, being served plum wine
by yet more scantily clad young women. They wore a single
robe, cut to the thighs, which swayed entrancingly as they
moved.

'You have achieved much, much,' he told Hung Hsiu-ch'uan,
who sat opposite.

Hung subjected him to a long stare. 'I will not be criticised,'
he said.

'I had no such thought in mind, your Majesty.'

'It is my appointed task to cleanse the Middle Kingdom of
the filth which has adhered to it for so many centuries.'

'A mighty responsibility, your Majesty.'

'But I who have struggled so long, and fought so long, am I
to be denied the fruits of my triumph?'

'Of course not, sire.'

'My people wallow like pigs – or they did before I raised
them up and gave them a star to follow. I and my generals lead,
and they come behind. It is necessary that our people look up
to us, and understand that we are greater than they. I am the

Son of God ... to me all things are possible. Your brother did not understand that when we met. Well, perhaps I did not then understand it myself. There were many mysteries in my life which I did not understand.'

John realised he must discern whether this man was mad, or if he genuinely believed what he was saying. 'Tell me how you became aware of your true calling, Majesty,' he begged.

Hung Hsiu-ch'uan leaned back on his couch and looked up at the ceiling. 'It is amazing how, when one's life seems to be at its lowest ebb, true understanding lies just beyond our reach. Yet it is there, Barrington. I once appealed to your brother for help in ridding the Middle Kingdom of the Manchu, when he was placed in command of Kwantung Province, but he refused me. I then appealed to the commander of the British forces which took Canton. He refused me also. I felt crushed. In my despair, I wandered the streets aimlessly, unable to decide what I could do next.

'It was then that I encountered a missionary, a man named Roberts. He was the first missionary to preach in Canton, and he introduced me to the Christian Word. I did not believe all of it, but yet there was enough evident truth in it to encourage me. I went home to my people, with my friend Feng Yun-shan, and we spoke of Mr Roberts and his word. We found what he had to say uplifting: a moral way, perhaps, to a rebirth of the Men of Han. We formed a society. We called ourselves the God-Worshippers. Our parents did not approve, but we did not care.

'I personally was inspired to sit the civil service examination a fourth time. I knew I could not fail. But those Manchu diehards and their Chinese toadies *did* fail me. Again I was crushed, Barrington. I sought only death. I returned to my Hakka people, and I collapsed. They say my brain gave way before the strain and the disappointment. But while I lay in my bed, hardly aware of what was going on around me, I was visited in my dreams by a man, not Chinese, but a man of lofty stature, high forehead, big nose and flowing beard. With him was a younger man, also bearded, with acute features. They spoke to me. They called me son and brother. They told me that it was my fate – more, my duty – to lead the Men of Han out of the slough of despond into which the Manchu had reduced them.

'I did not then understand. It was only afterwards that I

realised that the man with the long white beard was God the
Father, and the younger man was God the Son. They had
hailed me as their son and brother. Since then, I know who I
really am. I am the Son of God! The brother of Jesus Christ!
And my appointed task is to rid China of the Manchu and
create in their place my own Kingdom of Heavenly Peace. This
I have set out to do, and God the Father has blessed my efforts
with success. Can you understand this, young Barrington?'

'Indeed, my lord,' John said. Clearly the man *was* mad – but
the people believed in him. And, equally clearly, for those
closely associated with the Heavenly King the rewards could
prove enormous. Far more than anything he himself might
hope to achieve as a Barrington out-child. The vague ideas of
earlier began to crystallise. He owed Martin Barrington
nothing, yet he wanted a great deal from his step-brother. 'I
understand perfectly.'

'So, let me put this to you, young Barrington. Your information will be of great assistance to me, I know. But can you also
persuade your brother to place the support of the House of
Barrington, its wealth and its ability to control the river and
supply us with weapons, behind the T'ai-P'ing movement? In
open defiance of the Manchu?'

'I wish I could say yes, sire.'

Hung frowned. 'You will not assist the cause?'

'*I* will assist the cause,' John said, 'with all my heart and all
my power. But my brother ... is a stiff-necked fellow who
follows the eight Banners in all things.'

'Then he must be destroyed.'

'Absolutely. Yet, as you have pointed out, the House of
Barrington is very powerful on the Yangtse-Kiang. It could
prove difficult to defeat. But I will show you how.'

'You would do this – against your own family?' Hung asked.

'My brother and I do not agree on many things. Were I ruler
of the House, now ...'

'Deliver the House of Barrington into my hands, and it shall
be yours.'

John bowed his head. 'Your Majesty is most gracious, and
wise. Only a Barrington may successfully rule the House of
Barrington. Be sure that under my rule the House shall always
operate for the benefit of the Heavenly King.'

'Do this, and you may ask what you wish of me.'

*

Lan Kuei awoke with a start to the sound of hooves in the yard. She scrambled out of bed, wrapping herself in the blanket, and hurried outside. Te Shou was already there, half dressed, as were Sho-an and Kai Tu. The servants crowded the far end of the corridor, staring at the front door as if seeing a ghost. Hui-cheng stood there.

'Husband! Husband!' Sho-an hurried forward to bow before him, and then straightened, expecting an embrace. She frowned.

Lan Kuei had already observed that her father's clothes were filthy: freshly stained with dust and flecked mud, to suggest that he had been riding hard. Behind him stood an officer, very young but clearly a Bannerman, and the tallest Manchu that Lan Kuei had ever seen. His face was as strong as his body, and handsome too, even if he presently wore an expression of undisguised contempt. 'Quickly, woman,' Hui-cheng said. 'Pack your things. Everything of value.' He looked at his daughters. 'You, too. Help your mother.' He stamped into the room, summoning Fu Lo. 'Have the maids draw me a bath. And prepare food.' He glared at Sho-an. 'Why are you standing there, woman? I have instructed you what to do.'

'You have told me nothing,' Sho-an retorted. 'Are we to leave Wuhu?'

Hui-cheng nodded.

Sho-an stared at him, and Lan Kuei felt her knees knocking. Something terrible must have happened. Her mother persisted. 'How can we leave Wuhu? Are you not Intendant here?'

'I have resigned my position.'

Sho-an clapped her hands together in despair.

'We will go to Peking,' Hui-cheng said, 'and I will obtain a new position there. Now will you pack your things, woman?'

Still Sho-an stood her ground, her daughters following her example. 'Tell me what has happened,' she insisted.

Fu Lo was now placing food on the table, and Hui-cheng stood before it, holding the bowl to his lips, greedily shovelling rice into his mouth with his sticks. He seemed not to have eaten in several days. The young officer ate more decorously, but was also clearly half starved. 'The army has been defeated,' Hui-cheng said at last between mouthfuls.

'Our army? By the T'ai-P'ing? But how?'

'Because there are too many of them: they're like a horde of ants. Because they are not afraid to die: they *threw* themselves at our swords. Because they are savage beasts; they slaughter every Manchu they can find, and every Chinese, too, who does not immediately surrender to them. They rape the women, and then slaughter them. I cannot permit that to happen to you – or to the girls.'

Sho-an looked at her daughters, and then back at her husband. 'Where are my sons?'

Hui-cheng made a gesture of despair. 'They are dead.'

'My sons are dead?' Sho-an was now screaming, 'You let my sons die? Where is the army?'

'Somewhere out there.' He waved his hand in a westerly direction.

'You deserted the army?' asked Sho-an in consternation.

'I told you: I have resigned my position. Now will you make haste? I wish us to be out of Wuhu this morning.'

Sho-an's shoulders were bowed as she left the room in tears, after beckoning the girls to follow her. None of them spoke. None of them dared. Then Lan Kuei darted back towards the handsome young captain at the table. 'What is your name?' she asked.

'I am Jung-lu.' His eyes were hungry as he gazed at her.

'Why are you here? Has the army really been defeated?'

'The army has lost a great battle, lady. And I am here because I was commanded to escort your father.' His contempt was evident, but Lan Kuei hardly noticed it as she turned to follow her mother and sisters. *The Manchu army has been defeated,* she thought, *and my brothers are dead.* They had both been much older than her, so she hardly knew them. But they were dead – and Father had run away. A Manchu army running away?

She could not imagine this Jung-lu running. She believed him: that he was here simply because Father had ordered him. And now the T'ai-P'ing were coming, like a river which had burst its banks, sweeping everything before them, intent on killing every man who opposed them, and every woman too. She felt quite sick.

But her fear was not for herself; it was fear for the Manchu – for the Dynasty. If an élite army of Bannermen could be swept aside by this horde of rebels, what was going to halt them?

Aided by the bemused servants, she worked as her mother directed, packing clothes into the huge chests which had stood waiting throughout the years they had spent in Wuhu. It began to grow light as they worked, and by then more than one of the servants had sneaked off to spread rumour of the disaster that had happened. Wuhu awoke with a great rustle of fear. People hurried to and fro, shouting. The army had been defeated! The T'ai-P'ing were coming!

The weary women had sat down to a meal, while Hui-cheng paced the floor impatiently, when Cho-chung arrived. He was governor of the city, a self-important man with a large belly; it was not usual practice for him to call on his inferiors.

'What is this I am hearing, Hui-cheng?' he demanded. He handed his staff to a waiting servant, together with his leather wallet. Outside, Lan Kuei could hear the jingling harnesses of his mounted escort. Sho-an stood up and bowed, her food bowl still in her hands; the girls followed her example.

'And what are you doing here, when you should be with the army?' Cho-chung continued.

Hui-cheng glowered at him. 'I have resigned my position with the army.'

'Resigned?' Cho-chung was just as scandalised as Sho-an had been. 'How can you resign your position?'

'I have sent my resignation to the Viceroy,' Hui-cheng said with as much dignity as he could muster.

Cho-chung had been looking around at the scurrying servants, the growing pile of boxes. 'You are leaving Wuhu?'

'Yes,' Hui-cheng told him. 'As I have resigned my position, I am going to seek another in Peking.' He added, as an afterthought, 'My brothers live in Peking.'

'You have abandoned our army,' Cho-chung reproached him.

'I have resigned my position and am now going to Peking,' Hui-cheng repeated with infinite patience.

'It was your duty to see me first,' Cho-chung declared, 'to inform me of what has happened.' He considered for a moment. 'So what *has* happened?'

'The army has been routed, and the T'ai-P'ing are approaching.'

'How can our army have been routed?'

Lan Kuei sighed, and resumed eating. She was still hungry, and, once on their journey, she had no idea when they would see their next meal. Besides, she did not want to listen to the Governor telling Father he was a coward.

Clearly Jung-lu also thought he was a coward.

But was he not a coward? He had run away. No one could argue that. And now he was running away again. But he was going to Peking. She was going to Peking. She had always wanted to go to Peking. But not as the daughter of a coward.

When Cho-chung had finished questioning Hui-cheng, he asked him to stay and help put Wuhu into a state of defence.

'I am going to Peking,' Hui-cheng insisted.

'Ha!' Cho-chung snorted. He suddenly turned and left the room without saying goodbye.

'The rudeness of the man,' Sho-an commented.

They soon heard Cho-chung shouting for his staff.

'Let us get back to work,' Hui-cheng said. 'We must make haste.' The women obeyed.

Lan Kuei was inspecting her room for the final time, putting last-minute trinkets into her big cloth satchel, making sure she had packed everything of the least value, when one of the servants appeared.

'What is it, Ting?' she demanded.

'Mistress, the Governor forgot to call for his wallet. What shall I do with it? Your father and mother are so agitated that I hesitate to trouble them.'

It was a large leather bag, and looked heavy. A Governor's wallet! 'Give it to me,' Lan Kuei decided.

As Ting handed it over, it made a gentle clinking sound.

'Don't you think we should return it to the Governor's palace?' Ting asked.

'I will see that he gets it,' Lan Kuei said firmly. 'Thank you. You did right in bringing this to me.'

The servant bowed and withdrew.

Lan Kuei sat down on her bed. The satchel was sealed, but it took her only a moment's hesitation to make up her mind. She was leaving Wuhu forever, and she would never see Cho-chung again. She locked her door, forced the bag open, and peered inside. It was filled with silver coins, more money than she had ever seen in her life. She emptied them all on to the bed, and counted them rapidly. Three hundred silver coins: a small fortune. Hastily she scooped up the coins and crammed them into her own satchel.

The Governor's wallet she placed in there as well – that could easily be dumped along the way.

While she had three hundred silver coins, no matter what might happen, she at least was not going to starve.

*

'It is true?' Joanna asked.

'It's true that Hui-cheng has fled Wuhu with his entire family,' James said bitterly. That meant that Lan Kuei was gone forever.

'I meant that the Banner army has been defeated.'

'God knows. I must send down to Uncle Martin, to let him know.' He frowned at her. 'You had better go, too.'

'Why on earth ...?'

'If the T'ai-P'ing are really coming ...'

'They're still hundreds of miles away, surely? And, they won't trouble us. We're Christians.'

'Mother will want you in Nanking.'

'While you stay here alone? No. I *won't* go. I think we should at least wait for John to return.'

'If he ever is coming back,' James said gloomily. Nothing further had been heard from John Barrington since he had gone up the river several months ago. Apparently Tsen-tsing was having daily hysterics at the thought that her son might have got himself killed. James had never been very good at bullying his sister, but reflected that once Uncle Martin heard the news, he would take control – and of Joanna as well. Instead of arguing with her, he hurried down to the dock to despatch a sampan.

*

It was on the following day that the first fleeing Bannermen came into Wuhu, setting off rumours all over again: that the T'ai-P'ing were actually only a few miles away, and spreading over the countryside.

'Well, that is absolutely it,' James said. 'We have no time to wait for instructions from Uncle Martin. I'm putting you on a sampan for Nanking, right now.'

'But will you stay here?'

'It is my business to stay here, Joanna. I cannot just walk away from the warehouses and leave them unsupervised. Now you must go, even if I have to tie you up and carry you on board.'

They glared at each other; but Joanna could tell he was serious. And besides, she was now rather frightened, although she would never admit it to her brother.

'Very well,' she agreed, 'I will go. And I will get Uncle Martin to send up instructions for you come as well.'

She packed her boxes and was ready by lunchtime. All around her Wuhu was a huge bustle, as Cho-chung attempted to put his city into a state of defence, marshalling all such Bannermen as were available.

'At least he seems full of energy,' James confided to Joanna, as he saw her on board.

'You will come the moment Uncle Martin sends for you,' she interrupted anxiously.

'I have said I will do whatever our uncle wishes.'

*

It was difficult for Joanna to believe there was a civil war raging close by as she sat in the stern of the sampan beneath a huge umbrella, served with cooling drinks by the captain while the coolies walked back and forth, heaving on the great sweeps which sent the craft slipping along with the current. Indeed, she had just about nodded off, when some ten miles downriver from Wuhu she was startled by a flurry of excitement amongst the crew. Several of them released the sweeps and threw themselves down on the deck.

Immediately the sampan turned broadside on to the current, and began drifting closer to one bank.

Joanna sat with a start. 'What is going on, Chi?' she asked the captain.

'There are people shooting at us from the bank, mistress.'

Joanna stood up. There was quite a crowd at the river's edge, and she could see puffs of smoke as they fired their muskets. 'Are they bandits?' she asked.

'I think they are T'ai-P'ing, mistress.'

'T'ai-P'ing, south of Wuhu?' Joanna strained her eyes. As the sampan was quite close to the land now, she could discern that the men with muskets were not wearing pigtails.

'What are we to do, mistress?' Chi wailed.

'Get your men back to the sweeps. And then . . .' she chewed her lip. But the river narrowed on the next bend, and if the T'ai-P'ing were in sufficient force they might be able to block the sampan's progress. 'We must get back to Wuhu,' she decided.

*

James stared at her in consternation. 'You were fired upon? My God!' He hurried off to report the news to Cho-chung, who was equally concerned that the city might be already cut off.

'I have sent for reinforcements from Nanking. They will clear those scum away.'

James could only hope he was right.

*

Nothing happened for a full week. But the city was effectively sealed off, except for the need to admit groups of terrified farmers who clamoured for refuge. They told all the usual horrific tales of murder and robbery and rape.

Nobody could concentrate on any work, and even the bazaars seemed subdued. James armed all of his own people, warning them they must be prepared to fight. Like Cho-chung and the other Manchu officials, he spent much time up on the walls looking downriver for sight of the relief column from Nanking.

*

Joanna awoke to a mighty din. It was hardly dawn, yet Wuhu seethed. Bugles blew, guns exploded, people screamed.

'James!' she yelled, scrambling out of her bed and pulling on her dressing-gown. Running on to the veranda, she looked down the hill towards the river. There some people were putting out in boats, apparently prepared to risk the T'ai-P'ing on the river banks rather than face those at the walls. Sheng the butler joined her.

'Where is Mr James?' she demanded.

'At the first alarm he went to the walls, mistress.'

'Then I must go, too.'

'We are to stay here. Your brother has said so.'

Joanna hesitated. But of course she would probably just get in the way on the walls.

'Then we must secure the house, Sheng. Close the shutters and put the bars in place.'

Sheng began shouting orders to the servants. Within ten minutes all the windows and doors were barricaded. By then the noise of the fighting on the walls was so loud that they could hardly hear themselves speak. Above the city rolled huge black clouds from fires which had been started. Sheng looked at Joanna.

'Yes,' she said. 'If you and the servants wish to go to your families, you have my permission to do so.'

'I cannot leave you, mistress,' Sheng protested. 'But these others ...' A few minutes later all the other servants had left.

Joanna stood at a window where the shutter did not fit precisely, admitting a crack of light. She stared out at the street, praying for a sight of James coming to stand between her and the T'ai-P'ing. But the street was empty.

Then suddenly it was filled with running men. Bannermen, she realised. They were fleeing down to the harbour in an attempt to escape.

The street emptied once again, and she took her eyes away from the crack. Looking out again, about five minutes later, she saw several men gathered in front of the house, staring and pointing at the flag. Naked from the waist up, they were covered in blood, though not their own blood. They carried an assortment of weapons, muskets and pistols, pikes and swords; the pikes and swords were also stained with blood, and none wore the pigtail.

'T'ai-P'ing,' she whispered. Inside the city!

She could hear snatches of what they were saying. They knew the flag belonged to the long-nosed hairy barbarians.

'Death to all opium dealers!' they shrieked, and ran up the front steps to pound on the door.

'What must we do, mistress?' Sheng was shaking.

As the door began to splinter, Joanna stood quivering against the shutter, sucking in deep breaths. She knew nothing of the animal lusts of men. Now she was about to learn.

Another panel splintered, and the voices grew louder. Then a sword slashed across the shutter, beside her ear. It could not penetrate the wood, but it drove from her mind the last concept of meeting her approaching end with dignity. She left the window and ran blindly up the stairs to her room. Closing and locking the door, she leaned against it for a moment, panting, then threw herself to the floor and crawled beneath the bed. There she lay still, her hands pressed to her face.

When she heard footsteps on the stairs, then in the corridor outside, she had to hold her mouth closed to prevent herself from screaming. A hand tried the doorknob. A shoulder was hurled against the wood, then again. The door burst open, and the room was filled with men. The bed was surrounded by naked feet, mud-stained and blood-stained. For the moment they were preoccupied with tearing open her wardrobe and scattering her clothes around, amidst gales of laughter.

If she lay absolutely still, they might go away ... The bed was shifted violently. She had to jerk her head aside to avoid being struck by one of its legs. But now she was exposed.

The men shrieked their delight, and flung themselves at her like a pack of dogs. She was dragged to her feet while they tugged at her red-gold hair, exclaiming in wonder at it. Then they began to tear off her clothes. Her arms were gripped by fingers like claws, while they pulled at her bodice and ripped her dress down the front. Joanna realised she was screaming continuously.

Having ripped her dress open, the clutching fingers sought to do the same with her petticoat and stays. But here they encountered stronger material. Knives were drawn and flashed in front of her face. *Why don't I faint?* she wondered. *Oh, why don't I faint?*

She felt a knife-blade skim her flesh as it sliced through bone stays and their straps. The corset fell away, and she was left with only her shift. That was torn away in a moment, and she was naked in their grasp. They gazed at her, lust mingled with amazement. They had never seen a woman so big-breasted. They they surged at her. Hands reached her nipples, while those still holding her hair yanked at it. Her knees gave way and she sagged, no longer capable of screaming and hardly capable of feeling, knowing only one long explosion of pain and misery ... and was released to tumble to the floor.

When nothing further happened to her, she opened her eyes. She gazed at boots ... and looked up, at a man. He was better dressed than the others, yet his face was no less cruel. And he looked at her with equal lust in his eyes.

But he stopped the other men from raping her – and was now shouting orders at them, so that they began reluctantly to leave the room, staring over their shoulders at her. Stooping, he grasped her wrist and jerked her to her feet. Her knees could not support her, and she fell against him. He put an arm round her waist to steady her and, leaning forward, pulled the blanket from the bed.

'Wear this,' he said, wrapping it round her.

'What is going to happen to me?' she sobbed.

The man grinned at her. 'There is one who wishes you, Barrington lady,' he said.

*

The captain pushed Joanna in front of him down the stairway into the hall. She saw a scene of total devastation: doors torn from their hinges, furniture hacked, upholstery ripped ... and the body of Sheng, decapitated, lying in the middle of the floor. She gave a little gasp, half a retch, and her knees gave way. The captain caught her and jerked her upright again.

'You walk now, or I will beat you,' he threatened, then pushed her through the front door into the open air. For a moment this seemed blessed relief, but then she smelt the odours, wafting across the city on the morning breeze. The heavy stench of smoke was everywhere, but interlaced with other smells, some of them sickly sweet and repulsive.

There followed a nightmare progress through the devastated city. Joanna wore no shoes, and within minutes her feet were as mud-stained as everyone else's. Corpses lay everywhere, men, women, children – even cats and dogs. They lay in scattered profusion while the flies hummed in clouds from one feast to the next. High in a cloudless sky, the noon sun played down on the holocaust that was Wuhu.

The fires were sporadic; there were parts of the town which were intact, others which were still burning. Everywhere, amidst the corpses, was the evidence of looting. And every-where, too, were the T'ai-P'ing: men and women, armed and bloody, clutching bales of cloth or strings of jewellery, strutting and shouting, or driving prisoners before them. The prisoners were nearly all young men and boys, young women and girls. Most were naked; all were terrified. Some looked at Joanna in wonderment. Many recognised her, but none had ever expected to see her out on the street wearing only a blanket.

The T'ai-P'ing stared at her too, calling out obscene suggestions. Some of them even snatched at her blanket, but were driven off by the captain. 'She is for the Heavenly King,' he yelled.

At last they reached the Governor's palace. Surrounded by its extensive gardens, this had not been touched by fire, but there had been the usual carnage. Here, at least, men and women were dragging the corpses into tidy heaps, while stripping them of their clothing in the search for valuables; their high-pitched chatter filled the air. Where the smoke did not reach, the stench of death was heavy in the air.

Joanna had never seen a dead body before, and today she must have seen thousands. Amongst them might be her own brother. She had been so concerned with her own fate that she had not considered that. But James had been up on the walls; so would have been killed in the first assault. Tears streamed down her face, caused as much by pain as grief. Her feet were cut and bleeding, and her whole body ached from the manhandling she had received. And she could not doubt there was much yet to come.

After her captor exchanged greetings with the captain of the palace guard, they were permitted to enter. She was hustled up the familiar wide staircase – she had attended official receptions at Cho-chung's palace before – and on to the gallery which gave access to a large assembly room.

Here were a great many people standing around, heavily armed, but in the centre of the hall was a group, kneeling and wailing. Joanna recognised them as Cho-chung's family. The Governor himself stood at the far end of the room, restrained by two men. He had been stripped of his robes, and even from a distance could be seen to be shaking.

Joanna could hear nothing that was being said, but she could see clearly the man before whom the Governor was standing. He looked surprisingly young, with regular, not unhandsome features. He was sumptuously dressed in a floor-sweeping yellow tunic decorated with imperial dragons, while his yellow hat bore a strong resemblance to a bishop's mitre.

The captain saw her staring, and muttered, 'The Heavenly King.' Joanna was surprised. The face was not that of a brutal, cruel man; rather was it that of a dreamer. Yet this was the one who had been responsible for all this slaughter. Even as she watched, Cho-chung's appeal for mercy was refused, and his head was rapidly struck from his shoulders. His women screamed their despair as they were dragged away. 'The pretty ones are for his bed,' the captain snickered. 'The Heavenly King has more concubines than there are stars in the sky.'

Joanna felt her stomach lurch. Was she herself to be given to this man? This bloodstained ogre? She did not dare think of it. But perhaps he would take one look at such a dirty, dishevelled creature and order her head off.

Now the captain led Joanna forward through the throng, till they stood some ten feet away from the Heavenly King. Before them stood three other people; two T'ai-P'ing soldiers and a woman. The woman had once been elegantly dressed, but her clothes were now in rags, and her elaborate *coiffure* had collapsed on either side of her face in black strings. She was not unattractive, although by no means young, and she carried herself with a definite air.

'What is her crime?' the Heavenly King asked in a clear, penetrating voice.

'She is a prostitute, Majesty.'

'I am Lu So,' the woman declared. 'You will not find more comfort in all Wuhu, your excellency.' She smiled. 'Why do you not try me for yourself?'

'Strike off her head,' the Heavenly King commanded.

Lu So opened her mouth to protest, but she was decapitated so quickly there was not time to utter a sound. One of the soldiers tossed her open-mouthed head into a corner with the others.

Joanna's knees gave way again, and again the captain had to hold her up. 'What have you there, Teng?' the King asked.

'The barbarian woman I was told to seek, Majesty.'

'Joanna!' John Barrington said. His back had been turned as he faced the rebel leader.

Now he stepped forward, glacing sideways at Hung.

'Uncle!' Joanna cried, holding out her arms. She could hardly believe that she had, after all, been saved.

13

THE CONCUBINE

'You ran away and left your sister to the mercy of those savages?' Jane Barrington stared at her son in disbelief.

James slumped in his chair. His clothes were torn and still damp in places, his hair an untidy matted mess. He trembled. 'The house was burning,' he muttered. 'Please believe me, Mother. To have gone back was to die. And Joanna was already dead ...' He burst into tears.

Jane gazed past him at her husband. Martin sighed, and rested a hand on his nephew's shoulder. 'Tell us how it happened.'

James raised his head. 'They were everywhere. We could not stop them. They got over the walls in several places, moving behind us, cutting us off. We fought, Uncle. I swear we fought. Your people fought harder than any, which is why some of us are still alive. But when we saw that the city had fallen, we determined to escape. We hid in a cellar until it was dark, then I led them back towards our house. But before we got there I saw it had been fired. I knew then that Joanna must be dead. And I felt I was responsible for the lives of the men who had fought at my side. I could not betray them. So we made our way down to the river and managed to secure a sampan ...' His voice faded.

'And then your sampan was sunk,' Martin observed.

James nodded. 'It capsized in the strong current. But some of us made the north bank, and set off down the river.'

'You had better go change your clothes,' his uncle said at last.

Jane watched her son leave the room, his shoulders bowed.

'He will carry this burden for the rest of his life,' she said. 'But what will you do?'

'I will go now to see the Viceroy.'

*

265

'Your daughter will be avenged, Barrington,' Shung-wong said. 'Come.' He led Martin through bowing secretaries to an inner chamber. 'I would have you meet some gentlemen.'

Martin was introduced to an elderly, dignified man, who bowed to him. 'I am Tseng Kuo-fan. I have been appointed commander-in-chief of the army of the Yangtse.'

A Chinese? Martin thought.

But Shung-wong looked contented enough. 'I would also have you meet my aide, Li Hung-chang.'

This was a much younger man, hardly more than thirty years of age, but with a most determined face, and a strong physique. 'We have heard of your personal tragedy, Barrington,' he said. 'Be sure that your daughter will be avenged.'

'First, we must recruit a new army, from the remains of the old,' Shung-wong explained.

*

The journey from Wuhu to Peking was the most exciting experience Lan Kuei had ever known. She had never comprehended that China was so huge. Of course, one was brought up to the tradition of its vastness, but that had been an abstract concept, and more a matter of pride than anything else. For all that really mattered was the Middle Kingdom, set amidst an outer world of barbarians. Not all of these were long-nosed and hairy, and came in ships. And it was salutary to remember that only two hundred years ago the Manchu had themselves been regarded as barbarians.

As to where the Middle Kingdom ended and the barbarians began, no one knew for certain. Many centuries ago a Chinese emperor had begun the Great Wall to keep out the barbarians from the north – for until the coming of the British these had been considered the most dangerous. The Ming had extended the wall as a hopefully impregnable barrier. Yet no wall had ever succeeded in keeping out the barbarians. In the old days, these had collectively been termed as the Hsiung-nu: people who emerged at varying intervals, hordes of horse-riding archers destroying all that lay before them. For two thousand years Chinese history was littered with the stories of barbarian invasions; and according to James Barrington the Hsiung-nu had also ridden west, into the world of the Christians and the

Muslims. He called them by various names: Huns, Mongols, Tatars. Europe still remembered the name of the Great King, Genghis Khan, and his grandson, Kublai Khan, who had founded the Yuan Dynasty in China.

But all of these different invaders had eventually been absorbed by the Chinese, through their sheer numbers, and by the peaceful simplicity of Chinese philosophy. Nurhachi had determined this should never happen to his Manchu, and that the Chinese would always remain a subject people. Hence his laws regarding dress and marriage.

And thus the T'ai-P'ing would also succumb, she knew. Invaders and rebels had always been crushed or absorbed. The Empire would remain inviolate, as it had always done. The people on its fringes – the Vietnamese and the Thais, the Japanese, the Mongols who still roamed the great deserts to the west, and now these long-nosed hairy barbarians everywhere strutting the streets as arrogantly as any Bannermen – they could do nothing more than tug at those fringes.

*

It took three weeks to travel from Wuhu to Peking, and Hui-cheng used the simplest and quickest route – he went by water. From Wuhu the chartered sampan took the gradually-slowing flow of the Yangtse down to Nanking and then to Chin-kiang. The river made its way with majestic power through a vast plain, of which the people inside the boat saw little, partly because of the huge reedbeds which clustered the banks, and partly because the banks themselves had been built up to form levees, in the hope of containing the water when the river chose to flood.

On the water they made about fifty miles each day, and then would stop for the night, either in a port if one was close by, or simply tied up to the bank. Eventually they spent a night outside Nanking itself. Lan Kuei would have loved to explore, but Hui-cheng forbade anyone to go ashore. He wanted no one, least of all the Viceroy, to know he was here.

Thus Lan Kuei could only stare at Nanking from the deck of their craft, which was moored just beyond several other sampans forming a raft of boats which swayed back and forth on the current. But at least she could see the immensity of the walls, and the pagoda roofs of the old Imperial palace rising beyond.

'Peking is far greater,' Sho-an assured her.

*

From Nanking the river bent towards the east, bringing them to Chin-kiang. This city's importance lay in the fact that the Grand Canal debouched from the north into the Yangtse on the bank opposite, and from there resumed its course towards the south, and eventually to Hang-chau. Lan Kuei had never seen so many sampans and ocean-going ships accumulated together, some moored and others painfully crossing the river like crabs moving upstream to combat the current.

Next day they entered the Canal itself.

*

For all her innate Manchu chauvinism, Lan Kuei had to accept the fact that the Canal, like the Great Wall, had been built by Chinese emperors. In fact the Canal had been constructed so long ago, and over so great a period of time, that no one knew who was really responsible for it. The honour of conceiving it was accorded to Shi Huang-ti, the first Emperor, some two thousand years in the past, and it had taken over a thousand years to complete. Most of what was known about Shi Huang-ti was legendary, but he was regarded as the greatest man in Chinese history, far greater than Confucius – so much so that his name, Huang-ti, had become synonymous with the word 'emperor' when used in the past tense.

But whether Shi Huang-ti had begun the Grand Canal or not, it remained an amazing construction for any man to have envisaged, much less carried out. More than a thousand miles long, it overcame all natural obstacles in its way. In the Canal itself there was less of a current, and they did not make such fast time, but the journey was constantly interesting. For the first few days the country to either side was flat and featureless, yet teeming with life – as was the Canal itself. The channel was not very deep, and in places the edges had begun to crumble, while often their progress was impeded by huge banks of water lilies, some several feet across, which had to be nudged to either side by the crew.

After a week they entered a series of lakes, some surprisingly large, so that for several days they remained almost out of sight of land, although occasionally the Canal resumed its normal confines between the reed banks. This proved the most trying part of their journey, for the sampan was besieged by constant hordes of mosquitoes. The sequence of lakes finally ended in the great Huang-Ho, the Yellow River, so called from the huge quantities of yellow silt washed down from the mountains. They crossed the wide river with difficulty – the Yellow River was smaller than only the Yangtse itself, and proceeded faster – and then knew they were at last in north China, for they were surrounded now by hills, and the cultivated land to either side was under wheat and barley rather than rice.

And so, finally, more than a fortnight after leaving Wuhu, they came to Tientsin on the Pei-ho. Here they spent a night before setting off again, crossing the Pei-ho and resuming the Canal, which roughly parallelled the river as far as Tung-chow, a town only a few miles from Peking. Then the Canal turned away from the river and made for the high purple walls of the city itself – since the waterway flowed right round Peking.

They entered the city through the Yun-ting-men, or Imperial park. Lan Kuei gazed at the groves of white pines, but had no eyes for nature as she craned her neck for the first sight of the wonders wrought by man. In fact their entry, over a raised causeway, was disappointing, for the sky was overcast and the water everywhere was muddy. Rooks cawed dismally overhead. Having arrived by boat, Hui-cheng and his party had no horses, and their footwear soon became soggy and dirty.

Once inside the gate, Lan Kuei could look in awe at the T'ien-tan and the Sheng-neng-tan. Between these two altars stretched the Grand Avenue, which crossed the Grand Bridge into the Chinese City. Now the travellers found themselves amidst a huddle of houses and pagodas, of dogs and people, the populace gradually increasing in number as they approached the Tsien-Men, or gate into the Tatar City. *Wuhu had had nothing to match this*, Lan Kuei thought. To either side were pavement shops which sold everything from sweets to aphrodisiacs – each denoted by a different flag fluttering in the breeze. Gangs of beggars constantly surrounded them, shouting for aid.

Everywhere were dogs which snarled at each other and at passersby. Fortune-tellers offered them almanacs to decide their futures. Barbers cut hair and shaped pigtails. Lily-footed Chinese ladies hobbled by, followed by their servants. Jugglers thew balls and sticks into the air. And everywhere was a powerful stench ranging from roasting meat to human excreta.

Hui-cheng, as a mandarin, even if of the Ninth or lowest class – he wore a worked silver button and the civil badge of the jay – had his way cleared for him by his servants, who brandished their bamboo rods from side to side, careless of who they struck so long as their master and his family were not hindered.

And, only a short way inside the Tatar City, Lan Kuei could look up at the massive, castellated T'ien-an-men, the Gateway of Heavenly Peace, which led to the Imperial, or Forbidden, City itself, and from either side of which stretched the high purple walls which surrounded the Manchu sanctuary. But common folk like herself were barred from the T'ien-an-men.

Hui-cheng turned to the right and made for the Hai-la-hu-tung, or Pewter Lane, in the Tatar City close by the walls. There his kinsmen lived.

*

Here they said goodbye to their escort of Bannermen. and Lan Kuei said goodbye to Jung-lu. The handsome captain had been partly responsible for her continuing enjoyment of the journey. Whatever his contempt for Hui-cheng, he had been unable to conceal his admiration for the ex-Intendant's three daughters, and especially for Lan Kuei. It was Jung-lu who had pointed out the sights they passed, and explained them. Hui-cheng himself had passed the entire time in a deep gloom.

Lan Kuei felt herself strongly attracted to Jung-lu more, even, than to James Barrington. What a pity he was only a Banner captain, with nothing to his name but his stipend. She sighed as she watched his stalwart frame recede, followed by his men. For all the prophecy and her auspicious birthday, her life was undoubtedly star-crossed in that every man she encountered whom she thought she could love was placed by circumstances beyond her reach.

*

Hui-teng was the general of the Bordered Blue Banner, as well as being patriarch of the Yehe Nara clan. He gazed at his cousin with dismay as Hui-cheng unfolded his tale

'To run away,' he muttered.

Lan Kuei felt herself squirming. Indeed, she had done so ever since she arrived here. Hui-teng's house was nowhere as grand even as theirs in Wuhu. And if this city itself was grand beyond her wildest dreams, it did not appear as if she was going to benefit from that personally.

Hui-cheng protested. 'I saw our troops being scattered. I saw the captives being executed, and I knew there was nothing left for me there. So I left to give warning of what is happening. In my opinion there is no one in all Anhwei who can stop the T'ai-P'ing.'

'You mean they will take control of the whole river? And Nanking? You had best escort me to the Grand Council, and tell them all about it.'

'And you must ask the princes for a new position,' Sho-an interrupted. She had not enjoyed the journey north, pre-occupied as she was with their predicament.

'That will be difficult at the moment,' Hui-teng murmured. 'A man who has abandoned his post . . .'

'Do you wish us to starve?' Sho-an demanded.

'You will not starve,' Hui-teng reassured her.

'So we will exist on your charity,' Sho-an said bitterly. 'I have lost my sons. These girls are all I have left. It is time they were married. How am I to find them husbands if their father is disgraced and we have no money?'

Hui-teng appeared to notice Te Shou and Lan Kuei for the first time; he paid no attention to Kai Tu, as she was obviously still a child. 'They are pretty girls,' he remarked.

'And talented,' Hui-cheng said eagerly. 'They paint well, and compose poetry. They are well read.'

An exaggeration, Lan Kuei thought; *I am well read, but Te Shou hardly opens a book unless she has to.*

'The most beautiful and talented girls still need a dowry.' Sho-an, as usual, concentrated on essentials.

'Hm,' Hui-tent commented. 'Yes, they are pretty girls. And if they are also talented – and their blood is good . . .'

'Their blood is the best,' Sho-an declared. 'The blood of the Niuhuru clan flows through their veins!' That did not go down too well with the Yehe Nara elders gathered in the room.

Hui-cheng frowned. 'What are you suggesting?'

'I am considering,' Hui-teng said. 'There may be a solution both to the problem of establishing your daughters, without a dowry, and to restoring your own fortunes. It has been announced that since the mourning period for the late Emperor will be completed in the New Year, the Hsien-feng Emperor wishes to bring his harem up to the correct number of sixty. I believe he has only nine concubines at the moment. It has been announced that next spring there will be a great presentation to the Empress Dowager, for all the girls thought suitable for His Majesty's bed. The general of every Banner has the right to put forward a certain number of names. Should I put forward the names of your daughters?'

Sho-an gave a little clap of her hands. Te Shou and Lan Kuei sat like statues.

'It is something to be thought about,' Hui-cheng conceded.

'It is something to be thought about right now,' Hui-teng told him. 'The time for nominations is very nearly up. I know it is a gamble, but *you* are a man who needs to gamble.'

Hui-cheng stroked his chin. His cousin was right in describing this as a gamble: not in the sense that the girls might be rejected; that would involve nothing more than the necessary outlay in clothes and jewellery for their presentation. The gamble lay in what might happen if they were accepted!

Custom and protocol demanded that an Emperor maintain a harem of sixty concubines, just as an imperial prince must have one of thirty, and the Heir to the Throne one of ten. And, of course, were a concubine to gain the ear of her lord and master through pleasing him, she would have enormous opportunities for suggesting the names of her male relatives, especially her father, for advancement whenever a position fell vacant.

But only a small fraction of these sixty concubines maintained by the Emperor ever got into his bed, much less pleased him when they did so. Indeed, only a fraction ever even saw his face. The girls would be selected by the Empress Dowager, and then be given apartments within the palace – where they would spend the rest of their lives. If favoured by the Emperor, those lives could be full of influence. If not favoured, they would be forgotten, living as nothing more than ladies-in-waiting upon the Empress, and useless to their families. Far better for these girls to marry some rich and powerful mandarin. But if they *could* please the Emperor . . .

Hui-cheng glanced at Sho-an, who was watching him intently. There was no doubt about *her* choice. When he looked at the girls, he did not have much doubt about their choice, either. Of course, women were incapable of seeing ahead – but, as Hui-teng had said, if there was ever a time in his life to gamble . . .

'I think you are right, Hui-teng,' he decided. 'I would like you to put forward the names of my daughters as concubines for the Emperor.'

Lan Kuei gave a great sigh of relief.

*

'I have resolved to move the headquarters of the House down-river to Shanghai,' Martin Barrington announced.

Both Jane and James looked up in surprise. Tsen-tsing merely gave a snort.

'Surely you don't suppose the T'ai-P'ing can take Nanking?' Jane asked.

'I sincerely hope not. But they are moving closer, and they are already dominating the river traffic.' The week before, a Barrington junk had been fired upon just east of Wuhu; and in any event, such was the devastation spread by the rebels, there was nothing with which to trade west of Nanking. 'As almost all of our business is now conducted by the sea routes, Shanghai is the obvious place for our headquarters – at least until the T'ai-P'ing have been defeated. James, I will put you in charge of this move.'

*

The move itself began the next day. The House of Barrington already had several warehouses and a large office in Shanghai, and outside the city Martin had built a family house, so it was mainly a matter of removing records, logbooks, clothes and furniture.

The removal was at least absorbing work. James kept engaged at it throughout the daylight hours, and he had the sampans moving up and down the river in a constant stream. Naturally, the removal of the House of Barrington from Nanking to Shanghai did not go unnoticed by the English merchants who were arriving in great numbers to take advantage of the trading freedom allowed them by the Treaty of Nanking.

'Getting out while there's still time, eh?' asked one of them as James supervised the unloading of yet another sampan. The man's name was Mayhew, and he had been in Shanghai about a year. 'Don't want to have another Wuhu on our hands, do we?' Mayhew persisted.

James raised his hat to the young woman standing beside her father; she was small and softly blonde, attractive and yet irritating by her very presence, and the fact that she knew all about him.

'Why, no, Mr Mayhew, we don't.'

He went up the sloping road from the dock.

'Mr Barrington!'

He checked, and Lucy Mayhew caught up with him. 'I will apologise for my father, Mr Barrington,' she said. 'I am sure he really meant to convey his condolences on the death of your sister.'

James looked down at her, and bit back the angry retort on his lips. She was trying to be nice.

'I am sure he was, Miss Mayhew,' he said, and went on his way. But he could not get her out of his mind. In the oddest fashion she reminded him of a yellow-haired version of Lan Kuei.

*

'The chairs are ready,' Hui-teng announced.

A rustle of excitement went through the room, while Sho-an and Kai Tu fluttered like birds. The past several months had been spent in frantic needlework by the female members of the clan, and Te Shou and Lan Kuei were each dressed in the finest clothes they had ever possessed. Their blouses and pantaloons were of silk: red for Te Shou and blue for Lan Kuei. Their tabards were matching, in reverse, red for Lan Kuei and blue for Te Shou, and were heavily embroidered with green dragons. They wore no hats but their hair had been elaborately coiffed on the tops of their heads, and secured with ivory brooches. Their shoes glittered with pearls and semiprecious stones.

Lan Kuei had contributed her three hundred pieces of silver to the family finances for this outfitting, and if her mother and father had been surprised at so young a girl possessing so much money, no questions had been asked – the family needed every tael it could raise to give the two girls a chance at the presentation.

But the moment had come. Both were now escorted outside, where the sedan chairs waited, surrounded by a guard of eunuchs hired for the occasion – all dressed as brilliantly as the clan had been able to afford.

The girls sat cross-legged in their separate chairs, which were then raised up and carried off. The streets were packed with crowds eager for a glimpse of the sixty hopefuls converging on the Forbidden City. Naturally the curtains of each chair were closed, but occasionally an exquisitely manicured hand drooped through for a moment, before being withdrawn.

The curtains in front of each chair, however, were semi-transparent, so Lan Kuei could see where they were going. They were taken first of all to the T'ien-an-men – but through a smaller doorway, to the side of the huge arch. Now in front of them rose the Wu-men, the Gate of the Zenith, dominated by its four huge towers, which could be seen from outside the city walls. Beyond the Wu-men lay the Forbidden City.

*

Lan Kuei was conscious of a slight sweat on her forehead and back, a clamminess at her thighs. When the suggestion had first been made, last autumn, she had been almost overcome with excitement. The thought that she might become an Imperial concubine ... That meant, she knew, that she would never see her parents again – or Kai Tu, or even Te Shou, unless she too was selected. It meant that she would never see James Barrington again. She had hardly expected to see him again in any event, but now she was to fly high above anything the barbarian could possibly hope to aspire to.

The several months between had hardly diminished her

confidence. Te Shou on the other hand had grown ever more nervous, and ever more ill-tempered, as the day approached. They were going to meet the Emperor! Lan Kuei's tongue stole out and circled her lips, then was hastily withdrawn; she did not wish to spoil her lip rouge.

*

The first thing Lan Kuei noticed, on entering the Forbidden City, was its beauty. Behind her, Peking might seethe with life and excitement, squalor and stench, cramped and disorganised. Within the Wu-men one entered a world of dignified calm, in which each building – and they were numerous – was set well apart from every other, separated by green lawns and flowering bushes. Each was constructed from carved white marble, and stood on stilts so that it could never be flooded, and each was fronted by verandas on lower and upper floors.

Those verandas were filled with women and with white-clad eunuchs, servants of the imperial household – for the only whole man allowed to live within the Forbidden City was the Emperor himself. All the sedan chairs came together and halted just within the gate.

The servants from the city outside the walls were now dismissed, to be replaced by eunuchs of the imperial household. The girls were then requested to leave their chairs. They looked at each other curiously as they stepped down, sizing them up, wondering who would become a friend, and who a rival, or even an enemy. But there was no time to speak, for they were immediately ushered away by their attendants.

In front of them lay the Dragon Pavement Terrace. The centre stairs leading up to it were decorated with the Imperial five-clawed dragon, so skilfully painted as to make it seem that the great mythical beast was actually moving down towards them – it was called the Floating Staircase. Only the Emperor could ascend the Floating Staircase over the dragon itself; the girls were guided up side steps, then directed round the Throne Hall of Supreme Harmony, and the various other Throne Halls. Now they approached the temple area of the Forbidden City; vermilion walls and pagodas rose to every side, decorated with dragons, horses, snakes, tortoises, lion dogs – and, the Chinese symbol of happiness, the bat.

Beyond the Throne Halls, they were led to the left: towards
the Nei Wu Fu, the office of the Imperial Household Department. Here, totally awe-struck, they were assembled in a vast
hall, surrounded by their eunuchs. There was no furniture
save for two long bench seats extending along opposite walls.
The walls themselves were decorated with paintings of flowers
and birds in exquisite colours. No sound could be heard except
the shuffling of feet and the rustle of silk; none of the girls
dared speak.

Then as one, the silent eunuchs bowed, the girls following
their example. Into the hall swept the Empress Dowager, the
Hsien-feng's mother; she was accompanied by another eunuch,
obviously very important, for his robes almost matched those of
the Empress herself.

She wore yellow silk – the imperial colour – emblazoned with
red dragons. The last two fingernails on each hand were several
inches long, and covered in silver paint. Her hair was concealed
beneath a huge head-dress, its wings pointing upwards to either
side. Her face was all but lost beneath the make-up and lacquer
applied to her eyelids and cheeks, lips and ears.

The Empress paused for just a moment, surveying the girls
grouped before her with a proud, almost disdainful expression.
Then she swept on, still accompanied by her attendant, through
an inner doorway.

Lan Kuei's knees knocked. Surely now would come the
Emperor himself.

But no one else entered the great hall. Instead, one of the
eunuchs went to stand by the same doorway, and called out a
name. After a moment's hesitation, one of the girls hurried
forward and disappeared inside. Other girls craned their
necks.

'You will all have your turn,' someone reassured them. 'Now
you may sit.'

Slowly, almost reluctantly, the girls sank on to the bench set
along the left-hand wall. When two of them moved to the other
side, they were sent back by the eunuchs; they must all sit on
one side. Intently they watched the door.

After about five minutes the first girl came out. Her cheeks
were flushed and she trembled, glancing to right and left as if
contemplating flight ... but one of the servants escorted her to
the other long bench against the far wall, where she could sit

and look at the rest of the candidates but could not communicate with them.

For the first time Lan Kuei felt really nervous. What had they done to that girl to make her react so? And if it took five minutes for each, and there were sixty of them present, that meant they would be here for five hours. She glanced at the girl on her right, who sat very quietly gazing in front of her. She was quite pretty, although from the blankness of her features she had closed her mind to what was happening.

Lan Kuei introduced herself. 'I am Lan Kuei.'

The girl started, as if she had not expected to be addressed. 'I am Niuhuru,' she replied.

'That is the name of a clan, not a woman,' Lan Kuei almost snapped.

The girl did not take offence. 'I was named after my clan.'

How ridiculous, Lan Kuei thought. On the other hand ... 'My mother is of the Niuhuru clan,' she said.

'How nice,' the girl Niuhuru said. 'Then we are related.'

'I myself am of the Yehe Nara clan – of the Bordered Blue Banner,' Lan Kuei said importantly.

'The Niuhuru are of the Plain Yellow Banner,' Niuhuru said. Lan Kuei realised that, of course, with some irritation; the Plain Yellow was the superior of all the Banners. 'The Empress Dowager is of my clan, and my Banner,' Niuhuru added.

Lan Kuei gazed away from her towards the doorway, from which the second girl was now emerging. She looked even more distressed than the first, and although they sat down beside each other on the opposite bench, they did not speak.

'I am sixteen years old,' Niuhuru continued.

'I am eighteen,' Lan Kuei said grandly.

Niuhuru considered for several moments, then asked, 'Are you afraid?'

Obviously she was referring to the looming interview.

'Certainly not,' Lan Kuei lied, though she was becoming more nervous with every minute.

'I wish I were brave like you,' Niuhuru said. She seemed to wish to be friends.

'We will gain courage from each other,' Lan Kuei said, comfortingly.

'I am so glad to have met you, Lan Kuei. If I am chosen, I hope you are, too.' Lan Kuei didn't know what to make of her.

Of course such a girl, so well connected, would be chosen. But, then, she herself was destined to be chosen, she reminded herself.

The minutes drifted by, as girl after girl was summoned into the inner room ... then returned to sit on the far bench. Now some of them were talking to each other in anxious whispers. It was impossible to hear what they were saying.

Lan Kuei watched Te Shou's fingers curl into fists as a girl on her other side was summoned. 'There is nothing to be afraid of,' she said suddenly. Te Shou gave her a startled sideways glance, as if not recognising her, then stared straight in front.

Another girl came and went, then Te Shou's name was called. She nearly fell over as she stood up, and one of the eunuchs – who paraded ceaselessly up and down before them – had to clutch her arm. *I am going to be next*, Lan Kuei felt convinced. *What will they want of me?* But she was not going to reveal her fear. Deliberately she rested her hands on her lap, fingers extended, forcing herself to keep them still.

'You are so brave,' Niuhuru murmured.

But as she watched Te Shou emerge from the doorway, she felt almost sick; she had never seen her sister, normally so arrogant and superior, look quite so much like a little girl who has just been thrashed.

'The Lady Lan Kuei,' called out the eunuch at the door.

Lan Kuei drew a long breath, and stood up. She hesitated, to regain her balance, then started towards the doorway, forcing herself to move slowly and elegantly, trying to make her features seem relaxed yet intelligent. As she reached the doorway, she smiled at the waiting eunuch, but he gave not a twitch in reply. Still smiling, she stepped through into a surprisingly large room – and heard the door close behind her.

The Empress Dowager sat in a high-backed chair, her hands drooping to either side of its arms. Though presumably she had been sitting there for the past three hours, she held herself absolutely upright. Her eunuch stood a little distance away, beside a large table on which lay several piles of paper. The only other furniture in the room was another table, quite wide but not as large, which stood only three feet high from the floor.

The eunuch began reading from one of the sheets of paper in his high sing-song voice. 'The Lady Lan Kuei, second daughter of Hui-cheng, of the Yehe Nara clan of the Bordered Blue

Banner,' he said coldly. 'The Lady Te Shou is her elder sister.'

'Your father is a disgraced man,' the Empress said. 'How dare he present *two* daughters for our consideration?'

Lan Kuei would not lower her gaze. 'Because my father's daughters are beautiful and accomplished, Your Majesty.'

The Empress's head jerked back a little. 'You will speak only when spoken to, girl, or I will have you caned for impertinence.'

Lan Kuei bowed her head to show contrition. 'With humble respect, Your Majesty, but you did ask me a question.'

'The Lady Lan Kuei is high-spirited,' the eunuch remarked maliciously.

'Yes,' the Empress snapped, and Lan Kuei's despair grew. But she was determined not to let these people crush her, as they had apparently done so with all the other candidates, including Te Shou.

'As for my father's disgrace, Your Majesty, he was sent to fight the T'ai-P'ing with inadequate resources.'

'What is T'ai-P'ing?' inquired the Empress.

Lan Kuei could scarcely believe that no one in this secluded court knew what was happening in the country they ruled. 'They are rebels, Your Majesty, who seek the downfall of the Ta Ch'ing.'

The Empress half-turned her head towards the eunuch.

'I believe there are some rebels south of the Yangtse who call themselves T'ai-P'ing, Majesty. They will soon be rooted out.'

The Empress intoned, ' "Respectfully we receive the blessings of Heaven. Oh, how they shine with magnificence ..." Continue, girl!'

Lan Kuei gasped. The Empress was quoting a sacrificial hymn – if only she could remember it. Desperately she began, ' "... now the country has been at peace for a long time. The people within the four seas are united. We offer a grand and sincere sacrifice. In Obedience ..." '

'Enough,' the Empress said. Now she was frowning, and Lan Kuei felt a strange surge of confidence. 'Tell me what Confucius says of honour,' the Empress commanded.

Another long pause. But this one was simple. 'The man of honour makes demands upon himself. The man without a sense of honour makes demands upon others.'

The Empress's right hand moved almost in a gesture of approbation. 'Tell me,' she said. 'Who was the greatest man living in the reign of the Hsuan Tsung Emperor?'

Lan Kuei's confidence sagged. The Hsuan Tsung Emperor had been the greatest ruler of the Tang Dynasty, and the Tang – who had ruled China from 618 to 907 A.D., as James Barrington might have computed it – were still revered as the greatest of all the dynasties of the Middle Kingdom. Therefore, the greatest man of the Hsuan Tsung reign had to be the Emperor himself ...

But she could not believe that was the answer the Empress wanted. For one thing, it made the question too simple. For another, the reign had abounded in men of extraordinary talent, both artistic and mechanical. The Hsuan Tsung Emperor had attracted greatness, and rewarded it lavishly. Men like the figure painter, Wu Tao-hsuan, or the landscapists, Li Ssu-hsun and Wang Wei, were still regarded as the greatest masters of their art in Chinese history. I-hsing had invented the clock, and that reign had also seen the invention of printing on paper. Then there had been the great poets ...

She gazed at the Empress, and the Empress stared back, her face expressionless.

'Well?' she demanded. 'Do you not know of the Hsuan Tsung Emperor?'

'I know of the Hsuan Tsung Emperor, Majesty,' Lan Kuei said – and made a decision; she could only follow her instincts. 'The greatest man of the reign was the poet, Li Po.'

'A drunken rascal,' the Empress declared, 'who drowned while trying to embrace the reflection of the moon. How could *he* have been the greatest man of that reign?'

'Because he wrote the most beautiful poetry ever known,' Lan Kuei said, 'and will live forever in his verse.'

The Empress continued to gaze at her for several seconds, then she spoke. 'As Ching has said, you have a sharp mind, daughter of Hui-cheng. Provided you learn how to use it, it may serve you well. Undress.'

Lan Kuei stared at her. 'The lady will undress,' repeated Ching the eunuch.

Lan Kuei reflected that there were only the Empress and her eunuch present ... though until now she had only ever undressed before her mother and sisters. Carefully she removed her shoes, lifted her tabard over her head, and laid it on the floor – there was nowhere else. Then she paused.

'Everything,' Ching urged.

Lan Kuei could not but wonder if he really was a eunuch: he seemed so eager. So this was what had disturbed all the other girls. Well, it was not going to distress her, she resolved, and swiftly removed her blouse and pantaloons.

'Stand on the low table yonder,' Ching commanded. When Lan Kuei had stepped up, he came close to her. She was repelled by his stale breath and body odour as he peered into her face and eyes, made her open her mouth and inspected her teeth. She shuddered when he fingered her small breasts, and raised her arms to look into the pits. And then shuddered again as she realised where his painstaking investigations must next lead him. 'Lady will kneel with legs apart.'

Lan Kuei wanted to glance over at the Empress, but dared not. How all those other girls must have been horrified at this enforced ritual. As she knelt on hands and knees, she felt his breath warm on her buttocks, felt his fingers sliding between. It was a very gentle probing: he dared not risk damaging her hymen. But, as he examined her minutely, she again could not escape the feeling that he enjoyed his task.

'The lady will stand.'

Lan Kuei scrambled to her feet in undignified haste. Her entire body felt aglow with outraged heat as she turned to face the Empress, seeking some sign.

'Dress yourself, girl,' the Empress commanded.

Lan Kuei pulled on her clothes, careless now of her elaborate *coiffure*.

'You may go, daughter of Hui-cheng,'

Lan Kuei hesitated, desperate to know whether or not she had been successful, but the door was held open for her, and she had to leave.

Lan Kuei stepped outside and gazed at the other girls. Those now to her left hand had already undergone her ordeal, and they now stared at her, wanting to know how she had reacted to it. Those few remaining on her right still had it to come.

And by chance the next one was Niuhuru. She was already on her feet and moving toward the doorway. How would this naive youngster react to being probed by a smelly eunuch?

Lan Kuei glided across the room and sat down beside her sister. Te Shou gave her a quick glance and then looked straight ahead. 'I want to vomit.' she said.

'You must not concern yourself,' Lan Kuei said urgently. 'They are but seeking blemishes.' Te Shou shuddered. 'Can you believe they know nothing of the T'ai-P'ing,' Lan Kuei said, still incredulous. 'Can you believe it?'

'They know only what their viceroys choose to tell them,' Te Shou replied.

But Lan Kuei could tell that her sister was no longer interested in the T'ai-P'ing. And indeed, Lan Kuei realised, here in the Forbidden City, surrounded only by fawning eunuchs and the symbols of the majesty that went with being the Son of Heaven or one of his immediate entourage, it was very difficult to be interested in what might be happening south of the Yangtse. Yet the T'ai-P'ing were still there.

Niuhuru came out. She looked well composed, although with pink spots on her cheeks. She did not sit by Lan Kuei, but moved further along the bench. Other girls went in – and came out. Lan Kuei began to grow tired, and only with difficulty stopped herself from yawning. Suddenly she realised that the last girl was returning: the opposite bench was now empty.

'The ladies will rise,' one of the eunuchs announced.

They had been sitting for so long that several of them staggered noticeably as they stood up. The Empress Dowager emerged. Behind her came Ching carrying a large sheet of paper in his hand. The Empress stood perfectly still while he began to speak.

'As senior concubine, with the rank of Pin, the Lady Niuhuru.'

Heads turned as Niuhuru slowly made her way down the room. She did not even look at Lan Kuei as she passed. Neither did she appear particularly pleased – or even relieved. But of course, Lan Kuei thought bitterly, *she* had always known she would be chosen.

Niuhuru reached the Empress Dowager, and bowed. The Empress touched her on the shoulder, saying something in a low voice which could not be overheard by the other girls. There were two eunuchs waiting at the far end of the great hall. Niuhuru's life as a mere girl had ended.

Lan Kuei realised she was having difficulty in controlling her breathing. Ching was now calling out more names, and giving them ranks – although all inferior to Pin. He had not yet called either Te Shou or Lan Kuei. Each girl, as she was summoned,

went forward to be congratulated by the Empress, and then was
escorted out of the room by attendant eunuchs. Some seemed
clearly terrified at having been chosen; others were obviously
elated. One girl tried to escape and had to be checked by the
eunuchs.

Ching marked off each name as he called it. It was impossible to see his paper, to discover how many names were
included on it, but Lan Kuei began to feel weak with despair as
the pencil went lower and lower. Twenty girls were called.
Twenty-five ... Twenty-six ... Twenty-seven. Ching's pencil
was now at the very bottom of the page. Perhaps he had
another page to read out.

But Lan Kuei knew this was not the case. She turned her
head to gaze at Te Shou in consternation. *Neither of them.*
What a catastrophe! And after she had spent her three hundred
silver coins. She might as well have given them to a beggar – or
returned them to Cho-chung. 'The Lady Lan Kuei,' Ching
called. For a moment Lan Kuei could not move. Then she
sucked in an enormous breath, and went forward. She did not
dare look at Te Shou. Ching had now definitely reached the
end of his list ... he was folding his sheet of paper ... she was
the very last to be chosen.

She stood before the Dowager Empress with head bowed.

'My congratulations,' the woman said, and tapped her lightly
on the shoulder. 'You have been chosen as a Yi concubine.' It
was the lowest possible order. 'As of this moment, you are a
Kuei Jen, an Honourable Person, and your sole duty is to make
my son happy. Your father will be rewarded for presenting you.
Now go.'

Lan Kuei turned to face the waiting eunuchs. She felt she
wanted to explode – with joy, and relief. She wanted to scream
and shout. She had been the last chosen, and she was only a Yi,
the lowest of her order. But she had been chosen! With bowed
head she walked away, between the eunuchs and out of the
room.

*

The news of the presentation, and the names of the girls
chosen, was then disseminated throughout the Empire. It
reached Nanking in June.

'Now perhaps the Emperor will turn his attention to the T'ai-P'ing,' Sung-shu remarked, throwing the broadsheet on the floor.

Chang Tsin retrieved it before his mistress could lose her very short temper. He was not interested in the Emperor's concubines, but his natural curiosity led him to look at the names, and his heart nearly stopped beating. Lan Kuei! His old playmate was now the bed-mate of the Emperor!

Chang Tsin wondered at the injustice of life, that he himself should have sunk so low, and that she had risen so high.

*

'Well, of all the remarkable things,' Martin Barrington said. 'Despite his cowardly behaviour, one of Hui-Cheng's daughters has been chosen as an imperial concubine.'

'Which of them?' Tsen-tsing asked.

'Ah ...' Martin glanced at James. The whole family had now evacuated from Nanking down to Shanghai, and James had done a splendid job. 'It is Lan Kuei.'

James raised his head. *Will you make me very, very rich?* she had asked. In that quest, she had soared to the top. While he ... It was time to go and take tea with Lucy Mayhew. She was the only solace he had.

*

As Martin had reckoned would be the case, Tseng Kuo-fan's army was defeated, early in 1853, and Nanking fell to the Heavenly King.

14
THE MOTHER

'This is what you seek: *The Thirteen Classics with Commentary*, by Juan Yuan.' Lin Fu laid the volume on the table before Lan Kuei. 'This is only the first volume, you understand, Honourable Person. There are three hundred and sixty in all.'

He beamed at the girl as he spoke. Well, hardly a girl any longer; Lan Kuei was now twenty-two years old. But of all the imperial concubines she alone was interested in the history and literature of China. As chief librarian, the old eunuch spent most of his time alone with the huge collection of books gathering dust along their myriad shelves – but since the coming of Lan Kuei he had been sure of company most afternoons of the week.

'I shall read them all,' Lan Kuei said. Lin Fu did not doubt that she would. He sometimes thought that she should have been born a man; then her brain and her retentive memory could be put to some use. He watched her open the book, almost reverently, and he shuffled away to his desk at the far side of the huge room.

Lan Kuei looked at the first page, the elaborate characters, and felt a thrill of excitement. Three hundred and sixty volumes. All as large as this one. Even if she could read one a month, it would still take her thirty years.

Thirty years! She would be past fifty. And still a virgin. She leaned back in her chair. She had never considered her new position in such terms before. For the fate that she had most feared had overtaken her. She had never even seen the Hsienfeng Emperor. She belonged to him, but she doubted he was aware of it. She was too lowly-bred. The Emperor had eyes only for Niuhuru, and the other Pin concubines. A Yi counted for nothing.

Thus she had failed her family. She knew that her father had received the customary presents after his daughter had been

286

chosen as an imperial concubine: bolts of silk, a portion of gold and silver, two horses with expensive bridles and saddles, and an inlaid tea-set. There had been nothing more, and now the poor man was dead ... no doubt from disappointment. She knew that Te Shou had married a Manchu mandarin, and that Kai Tu still sought a husband. But where would she find one, with no father and no dowry? How Sho-an must be grinding her teeth with rage.

Lan Kuei had, of course, seen nothing of them since the day she had been brought to the Forbidden City; she had not even been allowed to attend her father's funeral. Once one entered the inner sanctum, one was there forever – until one in turn received the blessing of death. She remembered how hopeful she had felt in those early days, four years ago. Every morning the Emperor wrote on a jade tablet the name of the concubine with whom he would spend the night. The tablet was read by the Chief Eunuch, whose responsibility it was to fetch the girl and take her to the imperial bedchamber. Thus every time the Chief Eunuch was seen, especially in the evening, there was an anticipatory rustle among the girls.

He had never come for her.

At first Lan Kuei had railed against her fate, silently at least. She was young, she considered herself at least as attractive as any other inmate of the harem, she was bursting to reveal the arts of love as she had been taught them by her mother, she knew she was the most intelligent of all the girls ... and she was utterly neglected. All because her family was not good enough. Then why had they chosen her at all?

It was not a question to which she dared seek answers – except from her personal eunuchs. The head of these was Lien Chung. 'One's life is governed by the stars, Honourable Person,' Lien Chung had once said. 'To wonder at what may or may not be is futile. To feel anger because one's ambitions cannot be fulfilled is criminal.' Lan Kuei had thrown a teapot at him.

But she was forced to accept that he was right. Her days were filled with a bright nothingness. She took her bath in the morning, then was required to join the Empress Dowager and the other girls in one of the many cloistered gardens, to play at cards. The Empress's sole recreation was gambling. It was not done to win against her, so the concubines' main concern was merely not to lose too much, for she insisted upon collecting every tael. As if that mattered. They were given quite considerable sums of money regularly, but there was nothing to spend it on; most of it was stolen by their eunuchs.

Often in the evenings there were amateur theatricals. These could be fun, depending upon the role allotted. Lan Kuei was usually required to play a boy, which suited her, but because she was so small it was always the brother of the hero, never the hero himself.

Then came supper – and bed, alone.

This was only half a life. Most galling to her was being so totally cut off from the outside world. For the other girls, bred to the inward-looking life that was Peking society, this was no hardship. But Lan Kuei had been bred to the physical freedom of the provinces, and had listened eagerly as her father and mother had discussed local political problems.

No problem had loomed so large as the T'ai-P'ing, who in a ghastly fashion were responsible for her being here at all. Yet, as she had observed on her first day, the Dynasty seemed totally unaware that such a force existed, or certainly that it could ever pose a threat to the Throne of Heaven. But the T'ai-P'ing were still there, and coming closer. Lien Chung informed her how they had overrun both Wuhu and Nanking. Lan Kuei shuddered to think what must have happened to her old home.

And, then, what of Chang Tsin – and the Barringtons? Presumably the Barringtons would have boarded their ships and sailed further down the river. And no doubt Chang Tsin had survived; eunuchs always did. Then Lien Chung told her that the T'ai-P'ing armies had crossed the Yangtse and were marching north, their aim Peking itself. Lan Kuei had been unable to sleep, had gazed in wonderment at the Empress Dowager as that great lady had pursued her futile amusements, apparently either unknowing or uncaring. Lan Kuei longed to raise the subject with her, to sound a clarion call to arms – even for the concubines and the eunuchs – to defend the Emperor. Yet perhaps she had been wrong in her assessment. Perhaps it was secret worry that killed off the old woman – for only a few months earlier the Empress Dowager had died.

And the T'ai-P'ing *had* been halted. It was Lien Chung again who had told her of the rebels' repulse by the Banner army only seventy miles from the capital. That army had been commanded by the greatest living Manchu soldier, Marshal Seng-ko-lin-ch'in, leader of the same Tatar cavalry who had for so long been the terror of the world. The T'ai-P'ing had been sent reeling back to Nanking – while life in the Forbidden City had remained unchanged. But why had Marshal Seng not been sent on against the rebels in Nanking? For, despite their repulse, the T'ai-P'ing were still there, masters of the Yangtse and all south China.

To these frustrations Lan Kuei had found compensation only in the library. She had spent every afternoon there for the past three years. Once she had naively thought her education was complete; now she understood that she had been totally ignorant.

Her reading included histories and commentaries several hundred years old. Two thousand years before she had been born, the first and mightiest of the emperors, Shi Huang-ti, had decreed that every book in the Empire should be burned, save for those on religion, medicine or husbandry, so that all philosophy should start afresh from his reign. Of course the old madman had been defied: many texts had been hidden, and the moment he died, a huge literature of recollection was created.

Prepared by scholars working together, these very early books had, however, a quality of sameness which made for boredom. Even the precepts of Confucius and Lao-tzu were really rather boring to read, although Confucius remained the proper guide by which every right-thinking man or woman was required to live his or her life. But Lan Kuei had never cared too much for Confucius, while she found books like Pan Chao's *Lessons for Women* positively offensive in its harping on all the traditional feminine virtues – especially submissiveness.

Lan Kuei instead preferred later works such as the *T'ung Tien*, the encyclopaedia of history compiled in the eighth Christian century by Tu Yu; or the *New History of the Tang* by Ou-Yang Hsiu. But even more did she enjoy the somewhat risqué novels of the Mongol 'Yuan' Dynasty, and the huge number of histories of the Ming. And now she was to enjoy the *Thirteen Classics*. It was all she had to look forward to. She gave another heavy sigh and bent over the book – then heard a sound. Someone had entered the library. She could not see the door from where she sat, because of the intervening bookcases, but she heard Lin Fu get up.

'What brings you to the library, Te An-wah?'

Te An-wah, she knew, was the Chief Eunuch.

'I am seeking the Honourable Person, Lan Kuei. I have been told that she spends much of her time in here.'

'On, indeed,' Lin Fu said. 'She is here now. Come.'

Lan Kuei realised that her heart was pounding. She watched as the two men came round the corner of the nearest bookcase and walked towards her. The Chief Eunuch was carrying a jade tablet.

Lan Kuei rose from her chair, the first volume of the *Thirteen Classics* left open and forgotten on the table.

Te An-wah said nothing. He knew she would understand why he was here. So did Lin Fu, who bowed in respect to her sudden importance.

*

Te An-wah himself escorted her to the bath chamber, and supervised the washing and drying of her hair, the perfuming of her body. Never had she been so carefully attended. Te An-wah, however, would not let her get above herself.

'You are the twelfth different woman our lord has chosen during these past twelve days,' he commented.

'How interesting,' Lan Kuei agreed, refusing to be put out.

'Our lord is disappointed in the selection made for him by his mother,' Te An-wah continued, implying of course his predecessor Ching in his criticism. 'They are unable to bear our lord a son. As our lord already has a daughter, this fault clearly lies with the women.'

'Even the Empress?' Lan Kuei asked innocently. For, after the death of his mother, the Hsien-feng Emperor had raised Niuhuru to be his consort rather than merely his chief concubine; and she was now the most powerful woman in the Empire. Not that she ever, in any way, sought to use that power. Lan Kuei found her ever the same uncomplicated, placid, slightly apprehensive girl she remembered from their first meeting.

'Not even the Empress has been blessed,' Te An-wah agreed.

If such a thing were only possible ... Lan Kuei thought. Suddenly she was nervous. She was a virgin, yet he had slept with many different women for the past four years.

'Enough,' Te An-wah announced, indicating that he did not see how she could be improved further. The eunuchs stepped away from her, and Lan Kuei stood up. Lien Chung held a looking-glass for her.

She had not grown upwards at all since she was fifteen, and remained no more than five feet tall. But her figure had filled out disconcertingly; her hips and buttocks were more pronounced than she felt they should be, her breasts were large enough to fill a man's hand. In contrast, her features had tightened; she had not smiled enough these past four years. But they were still undeniably handsome. And no one could deny the splendour of her hair, long and thick, and black as a raven's wing. This same hair was presently gathered on the top of her head, secured by a single pin which could easily be removed, with one tress hanging past her shoulder. It was now her eunuchs' ambition, as much as her own, to please the Emperor, for where she prospered, so would they.

'Come,' Te An-wah ordered. 'Our lord retires early.'

She was apparently not even to have her supper, lest she repel her lord by an unseemly belch, or grow sleepy.

Te An-wah led her into her bedchamber. There another eunuch had spread out a blanket of imperial yellow, over-stitched with the invariable red dragons. Lan Kuei lay down on the blanket, and was rolled up in it. Then Te An-Wah lifted her on to his shoulder, and carried her to the imperial bedchamber. It was a long walk down secret corridors, so that no one could possibly know for whom the Emperor had sent this night. Apart from the eunuchs – which meant that everyone would know tomorrow. But Lan Kuei *wanted* everyone to know. She had been chosen at last.

*

As they entered the Emperor's chamber, Te An-wah muttered, 'Remember, you must crawl up the bed to our lord. Do not perform the kowtow, but crawl.'

Wrapped up as she was, she could not immediately see the bed, and was thus surprised, when the blanket was unrolled, to find herself sprawled in a most undignified fashion upon a soft mattress.

'The Honourable Person, Lan Kuei, Your Majesty,' Te An-wah said, and backed from the room, still carrying the blanket.

Hastily Lan Kuei gathered her scattered legs and arms, and rose to her knees, glancing right and left. The room was vast, and as only four candles burned, close to the bed, it was mostly lost in shadow. But she gained an impression of great splendour, of walls decorated in vermilion and gold. The candles themselves gave off a heady fragrance. And there were four eunuchs inside the room, one in each corner, standing motionless, and facing inwards. They showed no signs of moving. Was she to perform before an audience? Well, she could hardly see them ... so they just had to be forgotten.

The sheets on which she knelt were imperial yellow silk, and slippery. The bed was some ten feet long, and at the top end of it, reclining against several yellow silk cushions, was the Emperor himself.

Lan Kuei was taken aback by his youth; he was clearly only a few years older than she was. He was also somewhat small, with narrow shoulders and chest, and he did not look very healthy. His hair seemed lank and unbrushed. Like herself he was naked, and was half aroused – to her consternation she realised that he was sustaining an erection with his fingers. She wondered what he saw, looking down the bed. He gave no sign of whether he liked or disliked what he was looking at.

Crawl up the bed, Te An-wah had said. But she had been given no other advice. She must rely upon her own instincts. Her hair was her greatest beauty; so she released the pin and flicked it across the floor. The heavy black tresses fell across her ears as she crawled forward slowly, letting him gaze his fill.

Lan Kuei arrived between his legs, spread wide. She had stared into his eyes the whole way up the bed. Now she lowered her gaze to his penis, which was still held loosely in his left hand. She had only ever seen one erect penis close up, and that had belonged to Chang Tsin. Yet she knew what she wanted to do, if she dared. The Chinese called it Jade Girl Playing on a Flute. Gently she moved his hand and grasped the member in her own, then lowered her head to take it into her mouth. The entire body before her stiffened. Was he offended? Should she release him now, and be sent from his room in disgrace?

But she was determined to succeed entirely, or fail entirely. She closed her lips around it, flicking its tip with her tongue. A moment later she felt a hand on her hair, then slipping over her neck and shoulder.

'Come closer,' he said, his voice hardly more than a whisper.

She raised her head, replaced her lips with one hand, and moved up the bed. The Hsien-feng's fingers slid from her breasts to her belly, then between her legs; he knew what to seek as well as any eunuch. *Well*, she thought, *he had sixty women to choose from each night.*

Now as she leant against his chest, his other hand moved round behind her back to caress her buttocks. So far she had done well, she felt, even if her mind was too preoccupied to feel any passion herself. Yet must she feign passion, even though she must also control events. Clearly the Emperor had difficulty in maintaining an erection – but at this moment he was as hard as a rock. She spread her legs, and made to envelop him between.

'No,' he said.

She looked up in alarm. 'Is it too soon?'

He made a little moue of despair. 'It will not succeed. The Fish Interlocking the Scales is beyond me.'

'It will succeed, lord. I will make it succeed.'

They stared at each other, faces only inches apart, and Lan Kuei remembered what James Barrington had done to her. If it had been beyond her comprehension, surely it would also be beyond the comprehension of the Emperor. It was certainly obscene. But it had been so enjoyable. If the Hsien-feng were also to find it enjoyable ... She leaned forward, and brushed her lips against the Emperor's. He gave a little start, jerked his head away, staring at her. But Lan Kuei would not be rejected. She stuck out her tongue and licked his lips. He gave another jerk. Lan Kuei licked his lips again, and while she was doing so, swiftly inserted him into her with one hand, then gently lowered herself on to him.

The sharp pain made her gasp, but she hastily suppressed it, because he had put out his tongue now as well. Their tongues touched, and then she was holding him close, him sitting upright, she kneeling astride his thighs. She moved her body up and down, feeling as if nails were being driven into her vagina, yet refusing to stop – or to stop kissing him – until she felt the explosion within her.

Even then she continued working her body for several seconds, the pain now beginning to fade, while she felt him dwindle. They stopped kissing only to gaze at each other.

'I should have sent for you before,' he said.

'I am here now, lord.'

He subsided down the bed, and she lay still within the embrace of his legs, feeling his damp member against her stomach. She made herself lie still for perhaps an hour, praying that he would not go to sleep. And indeed he did not, but played with her hair, her nipples, her buttocks, and then raised her head to look at him. He wanted to be kissed again. Lan Kuei squirmed her way up his body to oblige, and felt a twitch against her thigh. She put her hand down to clasp him.

'It will soon be time again.'

'Again? In one night? *That* can never be,' the Hsien-feng said, his voice bitter.

'It will be tonight,' Lan Kuei told him.

*

At dawn Te An-wah came for Lan Kuei. He wrapped her sweat-moist body in the blanket once more, and carried her from the room. But they did not go directly to the bath-chamber. Instead he took her to his office, and laid her on a settee while he opened the records book and entered the date and her name. That done, he carried her to her bath, and left her with her own eunuchs. He made no comment.

Lan Kuei did not know whether she was on her head or her heels. She was no longer a virgin, and she was sure she had proved she could bring great happiness to her lord. But how many of the others had proved that? And when would she know?

The whole day was spent in an agony of hope and despair. The other girls soon learned from their eunuchs that she had been summoned the previous night, and they poked fun at her.

'Another four years, and then he will send for you again,' they teased.

But Lan Kuei recalled that none of them had seemed particularly agitated after *their* night with the Hsien-feng. They dared not discuss their experience with each other, of course ... but she was sure she must have done better than they.

That afternoon Niuhuru approached her as she walked in the garden. 'You have pleased our lord,' the Empress said.

Lan Kuei looked up anxiously, but there was no trace of

jealousy in Niuhuru's features. She seemed genuinely pleased.

And that night Lan Kuei was once more sought by Te An-wah. 'Our lords sends for you again,' he told her. Lan Kuei's consternation must have shown on her face, for he added, 'It is most unusual.' Clearly he could not believe it himself. 'As of this moment you are named Pin concubine.'

Two months later, Lan Kuei was confirmed as pregnant.

*

A soft sound awakened Joanna Barrington, had her sitting up in the bed, the coverlet clasped to her throat. Even after four years, the thought that John Barrington was coming to her made her feel sick. When she recalled her feelings of that first day ... disbelief that her uncle should be standing at the Heavenly King's shoulder, followed by a flood of immense relief that he *was* there, and would therefore rescue her from that fate worse than death so alarming to Christian morality. She had not understood his intention even when he had handed her over to his eunuchs to be bathed and dressed for the Heavenly King's pleasure. When realisation had dawned, she had fought them with a desperate strength she had not known she possessed.

But it had not been sufficient – and then the King had come to her, in all his splendour. In her worst nightmares she had never suspected she could undergo such an experience; her near rape at the hands of the T'ai-P'ing soldiers seemed no more than horseplay in retrospect. As she had still been inclined to resist, Hung Hsiu-ch'uan had ordered his eunuchs to hold her down, in the most obscene of postures, while he explored her body, before raping her. She assumed he had never enjoyed a barbarian woman before, so was excited at once by the size of her breasts, the whiteness of her skin, the glory of her hair, as compared with the native women in his harem.

That had been bad, but then he had been followed by John Barrington. Afterwards she had lain exhausted and debauched, hating herself as much as she hated the man who had made her so. And John, the boy with whom she had grown up, had often teased ... to be in his power had been the worst of all. John had also needed the aid of his eunuchs for the first month, alternating sexual pleasure with sexual mistreatment, until she was too exhausted, emotionally and physically, to resist him further. Thereupon he had become kindness itself, but his ambitions had still seemed equally loathsome. 'You will bear me fine sons,' he told her. 'Fine Barringtons to rule the House.'

'Don't you think my step-father and my brother will have something to say about that?' she snapped.

'Your brother is undoubtedly dead,' he pointed out cruelly. 'And your step-father will die when we take Nanking.'

*

To defend his capital, the Viceroy had attempted to meet the T'ai-P'ing in the field, but was routed. By now Joanna had realised that these T'ai-P'ing victories were not gained merely by their fanatacism and overwhelming numbers – as the Manchu claimed. Supporting Hung Hsiu-ch'uan were some very capable military leaders, men such as Li Hsiu-ch'eng, his immediate deputy – he was known as the Loyal Prince – and Yang Hsiu-ch'ing, the general commanding the army. While, for all his youth, John Barrington had also revealed an unsuspected military talent.

They were all too energetic for the Manchu. Equally they seemed totally dedicated to the cause of the Heavenly Kingdom of Peace, although they mostly followed the example of their master, and maintained vast harems of captured women and boys and eunuchs, in defiance of their movement's precepts. John Barrington was no exception, even if his principal delight was in playing with the big breasts and long legs of his beautiful yellow-haired niece.

He seemed also to have adopted the bloodthirsty characteristics of his new companions, and Joanna was forced to watch in horror as Nanking's leading merchants – men like Li Chung-hu, with his wives and children – had been dragged before the conquerors to be humiliated and executed, while their eunuchs were divided up amongst the T'ai-P'ing generals. She could only thank God that her parents had escaped downriver to Shanghai. John Barrington had been furious about that; he had dreamed of executing them all except for his mother. He was even more angry when he learned that James had after all survived the fall of Wuhu, and was now also in Shanghai.

Joanna had wept with relief at that news, and John had beaten her.

*

But that had been a long time ago. Since then the T'ai-P'ing armies, led by Yang, had ranged north of the Yangtse almost to the gates of Peking. They had failed to take the city, and had come tumbling back to face the Heavenly King. Joanna had been present when Hung had confronted his only slightly crest-fallen general in utter disbelief.

'You have been defeated?' he gasped. 'You,' he shouted, 'have been *defeated*! Have you lost your senses? Or have you' – he pointed – 'broken the word of my father?'

'Rather must we ask ourselves if there ever was any word from *your father*,' Yang had retorted. '*His* only value was as a rallying cry to the peasants, who understood nothing. And as an inspiration to yourself, Great Hung. But *you* would not come north with your armies. You preferred to wallow in luxury here in Nanking.' Hung's face became contorted with anger, but Yang would not be checked. 'So I was left to receive messages of my own, from above. Why, the old man with the golden beard appeared to me but a few days ago, and he told me that any man who kicks his concubines should be whipped and degraded.'

Hung sprang to his feet. 'Blasphemer,' he shouted. 'Foul thing from the pit of hell. Take off his head, Barrington. Take off his head.'

John Barrington, standing at his master's shoulder, had not hesitated. For only Yang stood between him and command of the T'ai-P'ing army. 'Guards,' he snapped.

Taken by surprise, Yang had no time even to draw his sword before his arms were seized, and he was forced to his knees. 'You cannot kill me,' he yelled. 'I am general of the army. My men will avenge me.'

'Your men know only that you led them to defeat,' said John contemptuously, and grasped Yang's hair, signalling to one of his men.

'You cannot ...' Yang was still screaming, when the sword blade sliced through his neck. John threw the bleeding head across the floor, to come to rest at Hung's feet.

'Blasphemer,' Hung growled. 'Now my kingdom will rest easier.'

Thus Joanna came to understood the true nature of the blood relative to whom she was now tied.

*

John Barrington duly received the command he sought, but for the meantime Hung forbade any further attempt to campaign north of the Yangtse, or to move downriver towards Shanghai. Even if they were opposed only by a hastily mobilised and ill-equipped Chinese army, he yet feared the consequences of another defeat. The fact was that his great movement had run out of steam. Hung Hsiu-ch'uan had achieved his dream of ruling in Nanking. Now he spent his time in issuing decrees, executing his opponents, and enjoying his harem.

Hung remained a magnetic speaker, and his people continued to worship him. But his ignorance of the requirements of government were apparent. He was the Son of God; nothing else was necessary to the masses who prostrated themselves before him. He proclaimed that Confucius and Buddha and the Mandate of Heaven were alike spurious, but gave nothing of substance in their place – his knowledge of Christianity was limited to a few precepts, and he had no real understanding of the meaning of Christ's word.

Commanding that every farmer and merchant must contribute his every last possession to the common cause, Hung made no allowance for the fact that these were the very men who supplied the food and the services on which the country subsisted. Driven from their holdings, their crops and cattle consumed, their houses looted, they became landless brigands – or they joined the T'ai-P'ing in the hopes of getting some plunder for themselves. Their godowns became tumbled ruins, their farms were overgrown with weeds, and their untilled fields turned to dust. If anyone pointed out to Hung that his people were starving, he replied, 'My Father will provide.'

Where people starved to death, or were butchered by the T'ai-P'ing, there naturally followed disease. Reports came in from the lands invaded by the rebels of thousands of people dying every day. Hung was not interested. He and his intimates never wanted for their slightest desire. Joanna was forced to accept that she was fortunate to be a member of this privileged group, if it was indeed a privilege to live at all amidst so much death and despair. But she was still young enough to dream of surviving even the T'ai-P'ing, and one day regaining her true family. Even if that entailed suffering the obscene maulings of her uncle every night.

*

Now she sat up and stared into the darkness, bracing herself for the coming ordeal – and realising with a shock that it was not John Barrington standing by her bed, but a eunuch she had never before seen.

'Hush, mistress,' the man whispered. 'I am Chang Tsin. I was a friend of Mr James before misfortune overtook me. I wish to serve you, mistress.'

'Why do you wish to do so?'

'You are the sister of my friend.'

'Then I thank you, Chang Tsin. We will be companions, in misery at least.'

'In misery, mistress?'

'You must know of the misery which surrounds the Heavenly King, and all those who serve him.'

He was silent for some seconds, then said, 'Do you speak from your heart, mistress?'

'Why, would you betray me to him? Barrington will only beat me.'

'It is I who fear betrayal by you, mistress. Do you suppose I honour this man, this living falsehood, this usurper of the prerogatives of the mighty Ch'ing?' His voice was low but intense. 'Listen to me, mistress. It was my intention to escape Nanking, and flee down to Shanghai, and thence north to Peking. And then I heard of you, held captive by your uncle. So I changed my plans until I could gain access to you. But I would still escape. Will you come with me, mistress?'

'To Shanghai? Oh, if it were possible!'

'If you are brave, it is possible, mistress. But you must also be patient. I will tell you when.'

*

For a eunuch to plot escape was simple. The T'ai-P'ing regarded them as hardly better than yard dogs, to be suffered and otherwise ignored. It was much less easy for Joanna, who must remain her normal submissive self whenever John Barrington chose to visit her. And it became even more difficult as Chang Tsin, recently a member of John's household, now served her as a personal eunuch, attended her bath ... for she had become as sensuously dependent on her attendants for true pleasure as any Chinese lady did.

What made it more difficult yet was her uncertainty as to why he should wish to help her and risk so much. She suspected it could not simply be through loyalty to James, but she had to chance whatever purpose he truly had in mind, because he was her only hope.

She was taken by surprise when, massaging her after her bath only a week later, he remarked, 'Mistress is happy today.'

'Oh, Chang Tsin,' she whispered, unable to keep still beneath the soft touch of his fingers. 'What must you think of me? Am I not a depraved creature?'

'You are a woman,' Chang Tsin said seriously, and dropped his voice. 'Tonight.'

Since there were other eunuchs in the room, it was half an hour before they found another opportunity to speak.

'Suppose Barrington comes tonight?' she whispered.

'Then I will wait until he leaves again. Be brave and strong, or you will betray us both.'

*

Be brave and strong, she thought. In the event, she almost overdid it, received John with enthusiasm, and pleased him.

'Now I feel you are truly mine,' he whispered in her ear. 'I will spend the night with you.'

Joanna's brain raced. 'But, Uncle,' she protested, 'you need your sleep. And I will still be here tomorrow.'

He gazed at her for several seconds, and her heart sank as she supposed he suspected something ... then he stood up. 'You are right. I would not sleep well if I shared this bed with you. I will come to you again tomorrow.'

She watched the door close, and collapsed in a turmoil of apprehension. She lay there, it seemed, for an eternity before she opened her eyes to see Chang Tsin standing by her bed.

He held a finger to his lips. 'I have some clothes for you.' A Chinese blouse and pantaloons, no shoes, but a large bandanna. 'We must hide your hair,' he explained.

He had clearly given the matter thought. She swiftly pulled on the clothes, and tied up her hair inside the kerchief. Then they left the room and entered the central corridor of the harem. Joanna had presumed that somehow Chang Tsin would negotiate their way past the guards on the doors and into the main palace – but these guards were also eunuchs, and Chang Tsin knew that would be impossible. Instead he led her into the bathing chamber. Here the water had been emptied, as was done every night; in the far corner was an inspection hatch.

'When you slip through there,' he told her, 'you must hang by your hands, and then drop. You will fall only a few feet, into water which is only two or three feet deep.' He squeezed her hand. 'Have courage, Joanna.' It was the first time he had ever used her name.

She nodded, and he raised the lid. The aperture was not very large; a square black hole out of which emanated an offensive smell.

'You go first,' he explained. 'I must close the trap behind us.'

She sat down and thrust her legs into the hole. Then she turned on her stomach and eased her hips through, resting on her elbows.

'There is a sill a few inches down,' Chang Tsin told her. 'Hold on to that with your fingers.'

She obeyed, extending her right hand down and lodging her fingers on the ledge, then sliding her shoulders through the opening and grasping with her left hand as well. There she hung in the darkness, panting with a mixture of apprehension and discomfort.

'Let go, and drop,' Chang Tsin commanded.

Joanna took a deep breath, and let go. She went straight down into shallow water, as he had promised, but the floor beneath it was slimy, and she slipped in over her head. She came up immediately, spluttering, suffocated by the stench, which was much greater down here. She realised she was in a sewer.

Chang Tsin was now hanging above her by one hand, while he reached for the lid with the other. It came down with a clang, and he dropped beside her. The darkness was so intense she could not make out his face. He fumbled for her and found her hand.

'You are not afraid of rats?'

Rats! she thought. *I am terrified of rats.* 'No,' she said.

*

Chang Tsin guided her along innumerable channels, some of them so low she had to bend double. Mostly they were half filled with water, and from time to time there came a rush of water from behind them, sweeping round their thighs and pushing them on – Joanna dared not allow herself to consider what it might contain. She was grateful for the darkness, and not only because it concealed whatever she was wading through; it also concealed the rats. She heard them often enough, shrill squeaks and sinister rustlings to either side of her, but her fear of having one leap on her never happened. They waded for perhaps forty-five minutes. Joanna was becoming exhausted and wondering if they were lost and doomed to die in this ghastly place, when she saw a faint glimmer of light ahead of them, and heard a strange swishing sound.

'The river,' Chang Tsin told her.

'Oh, thank God,' Joanna said. But as they approached the exit she realised it was blocked by a series of upright iron bars.

'We are about six feet above the river level,' Chang Tsin explained. 'We will slip down and into the water. We must be very quiet, because we are under the walls, and there will be guards above us. Once we are in the river we will swim to a sampan which is waiting for us. Joanna, I have paid this man well, but I have promised him more when we reach Shanghai.'

'When we reach Shanghai.' She nodded. 'But, Chang Tsin, I cannot swim.'

'I will tow you. Do not be afraid.'

She only just squeezed through the bars, but Chang Tsin passed through with much less trouble, sliding down the little bank into the water. She followed, dislodging a stone which seemed to make a huge splash. She could hear the tramp of guards on the wall some thirty feet above her head, and their voices as they spoke. But none of them seemed to hear the sound. A moment later she was beside Chang Tsin.

'Turn on your back,' he whispered.

Joanna obeyed, trusting him absolutely. He seized her armpits and drew her backwards. Her head sank into the water and her ears were submerged, leaving only her mouth, nose and eyes exposed. She realised that Chang Tsin must be swimming only with his legs, because his arms never left her shoulders.

She stared up at the walls, and saw the vague shadows of the soldiers. There was no moon, which was obviously why Chang Tsin had chosen this night above all others, and the river was very dark. The constant turmoil of the water deadened all other sounds. The wall retreated and she gazed at stars.

She had no idea how long they had been in the water when suddenly a shadowy figure loomed above her, and hands were reaching down for her.

'You are safe now, Mistress Joanna,' Chang Tsin said.

*

'Chang Tsin,' said James Barrington, 'we owe you more than we can possibly express.'

'You must settle my debt with the sampan captain,' Chang Tsin reminded him.

'That will be done, certainly. But what of you? How can I reward you?'

'Write for me a letter explaining what I have accomplished.'

'Willingly. Then we will speak of money – and employment, if you wish.'

'I do not wish money, Barrington. Nor employment here in Shanghai. Only write me the letter.'

'But what can you do with a mere letter? To whom shall I address it?'

'To the Honourable Person, Lan Kuei.'

James frowned at him. 'Was it not her father who had you cropped?'

'Hui-cheng is nothing now. It is his daughter who is the road to my prosperity.' He gazed at James. 'And for you, Barrington? Do you think she has forgotten her old love?'

'Good Lord! I understand your ambition, Chang Tsin.' He frowned. 'Did you take such a risk, to rescue my sister, simply for a letter to Lan Kuei?'

'She is the road to true prosperity,' Chang Tsin repeated.

'I hope you are right. Well, I will write your letter, and wish you good fortune.'

*

Joanna wished only to be left alone to think about what had happened. To understand, perhaps.

'Would you like to leave China?' her mother asked.

Leave China? She could never leave China now, to become an object of comment wherever she went. 'No, Mother,' she said. 'I wish to see my uncle hang.'

Tsen-tsing left the room.

'Horrible woman,' Jane remarked. 'I wonder that Martin does not throw her out.'

Next day Tsen-tsing had disappeared; and no one knew where she had gone.

'Unless it is to join the T'ai-P'ing,' Martin suggested. He was not the least inclined to look for her.

*

Whatever her own feelings, there were several people eager to speak with Joanna. Tseng Kuo-fan was one, together with his youthful assistant Li Hung-chang, anxious to learn about the T'ai-P'ing military dispositions. Joanna could tell them little.

Then there was Harry Parkes, the British Minister. He was the sort of man she most disliked. Tall and spare, red-faced and balding, his prominent chin escorted by enormous sidewhiskers, he was supremely confident and utterly certain that he knew best. He was the accepted British expert on China and the Chinese, for he had lived in the Far East since boyhood, and the true expert, Martin Barrington, was still regarded as a renegade.

'My dear Miss Barrington,' Parkes said, 'how my heart bleeds for you. How I wish your step-father had abandoned Wuhu before the T'ai-P'ing reached it.'

'My uncle had no idea what would happen then, Mr Parkes. What I cannot understand is why the British' – she gestured from the veranda to several warships anchored in the river – 'are not helping the Manchu put down this rebellion.'

'Aid the Manchu? Heaven forbid! It is Manchu misrule

which has sparked this revolt. God knows, any right-thinking person must deplore the cruelty and violence which seem to go hand in hand with Chinese politics, but that is the way of these heathen people. If we can see past the blood, we must understand that the T'ai-P'ing represent a genuine grievance felt by the vast majority of the Chinese population: a repugnance for the Manchu. The T'ai-P'ing movement will only end when the Manchu have been driven back across the Great Wall, where they belong.'

Joanna stared: 'You cannot be serious.'

'Of course I am serious. And it is a point of view I am persuading my superiors to accept.'

'That way lies anarchy – a total destruction of Chinese civilisation,' Joanna cried. 'Mr Parkes, I have lived with the Chinese, and the Manchu – and the T'ai-P'ing. The Manchu rule is harsh, but the Chinese at least prospered until the coming of the T'ai-P'ing. The ordinary Chinese hate and fear the T'ai-P'ing. They regard it as a curse spreading across their country. What, would you make Hung Hsiu-ch'uan Emperor of China? It would be like inviting Attila the Hun to rule Europe.'

Parkes' smile was indulgent. 'I understand how you must feel about the T'ai-P'ing, Miss Barrington. It is very natural. But, you see, people in my position – diplomats, experts, if you like – can never allow personal feelings to interfere with our reasoned judgements.' He patted her hand. 'That is why women have no place in diplomacy, my dear.'

Joanna was tempted to spit at him.

*

The baby prince was named Tsai-ch'un. His birth caused a great sensation throughout the Empire; there was a spate of rumours, including that Lan Kuei had been mated with another man to provide an heir, or that the babe was a changeling ... These whispers, reported by Te An-wah, made Lan Kuei furious.

She was even more furious when she was given her new title, that of Kuei Fei, or Concubine of the Second Rank. She had not aspired to be co-Empress with Niuhuru, but the mother of Hsien-feng's daughter Jung-an was a Huang Kuei Fei, Concubine of the First Rank. *She* had given the Emperor an heir, yet she remained only in the Second rank. It was her inferior birth keeping her down, she knew. She would never forgive her father, even though dead, for that. Nor would she ever forgive the Emperor's uncles, Prince Hui and his half-brother Su-shun, for she knew they were the ones really responsible.

Yet the babe was a delight, and Lan Kuei adored him. For six months she fed him herself, before giving him to a wet nurse, and she had him sleep in her own apartment, knowing full well that soon enough he would be taken away for his education – as if she could not give him a better education than any mandarin.

Despite her frustrations, her life took on a new dimension of happiness and security, for there could be no doubt, Second rank or no, that she *was* the Emperor's favourite, and not just because she had produced an heir to the throne. It was *her* body he desired more than any other, and, even more, her lusty unabashed love-making. Since he had not been able to touch her during the long months of pregnancy, he sent for her every night for a month when she was again fit for intercourse.

This was reassuring, but also exhausting – the more so as she was horrified to observe the deterioration which had taken place in the Emperor during the long period she had been absent from his bed. His left leg had swollen up, and apparently he was having difficulty in relieving himself. Also he was having still more problems with his erections, and if Lan Kuei found that she could again have more effect than any other concubine, she was disturbed to discover that he now sought strange, and to her absurd, diversions.

More than once he made her share him with another of the concubines – in a diversion known as 'The Phoenixes Dance in Pairs' – and although on these occasions she took care to remain the dominant partner, there was not much she could do about his sudden desire to take her from behind – 'The White Tiger Leaps' – all but an impossibility in his impotent condition, yet a long series of exhausting clinches and manipulations.

'In your absence, Honourable Person,' Te An-wah explained, 'His Majesty, feeling lonely, has sent out into the city for prostitutes and transvestites. He likes the transvestites best.'

Lan Kuei was outraged, less by the thought of the transvestites, who were of course unobtainable within the Forbidden City, where the Emperor was the only intact male resident amongst the entire six thousand inhabitants, than by the idea of his summoning prostitutes of either sex when he had so much willing female flesh available.

*

Most irritating of all, however, was the familiar inertia which gripped the imperial regime. Feeling more secure in her own position than ever before, Lan Kuei was prepared to approach the Emperor about the fears which haunted her. If the T'ai-P'ing rebels had not again tried to invade the north, they yet lay along the Yangtse, and over the country to the south and west of the great river, like a horde of locusts.

'They are a cankerous sore eating away at your kingdom, lord,' she told the Hsien-feng as they lay together. 'They must be destroyed.'

'They are destroying themselves, Little Orchid,' he said. 'My viceroys tell me they are dying like flies from disease and internal squabblings.'

'Then surely now is the time to launch your armies against them, to defeat them utterly and drive them into the dust.'

He ran his fingers through her hair. 'You are nothing but a child, Little Orchid. You do not understand affairs of state. Our real enemies are the long-nosed hairy barbarians, with their big ships and their opium and their insidious ways.'

Lan Kuei raised her head in alarm. 'We are at war with the barbarians?' As well as the T'ai-P'ing? – she wanted to scream.

'It is my intention to go to war with them, yes,' the Hsien-feng said, 'as soon as the time is right. They must be expelled, for they are the true canker in our Empire.'

Lan Kuei was appalled. It was not that she had any special interest in the barbarians, save perhaps for James Barrington, but she had caught glimpses of their power in Wuhu. Though few in numbers, they seemed to show more energy than any Bannerman, while their ships and artillery were far superior to anything commanded by the Emperor. She did not doubt that they could be beaten, but to go to war with them while the T-ai-P'ing were still undefeated seemed to her the height of madness.

She could not say this to the Emperor, of course, and there was no way a concubine could ever gain admission to the Great Council where the Emperor sat in consultation with his uncles and court officials. But she thought Niuhuru might have some influence, and so she approached the Empress. Now that she was at least a Kuei Fei, she could do this of her own volition. Niuhuru merely stared at her uncomprehendingly.

'Have you not heard of the T'ai-P'ing?' Lan Kuei asked in despair.

'Of course I have heard of the T'ai-Ping,' Niuhuru said. 'You told me of them when first we met.'

'They hold the whole south of the Empire, save for Canton. Have you not a map of China, that I may show you?'

'A map of China?' Niuhuru was astonished. 'How may a country as vast as China be represented on a map?'

Lan Kuei felt like tearing her hair.

*

And then one day Te An-wah brought her a letter. Lan Kuei had never received one before. Slowly she unfolded the paper.

Honourable Person, it is with shivering hand that I write these words, only praying to your ancestors and mine that you will look kindly upon them. Honourable Person, throughout the early years of my life I sought only to serve your family and yourself with loyalty and to the best of my ability.

Honourable Person, if my fate is my misfortune, it was my good fortune to rescue Miss Barrington from the hands of the T'ai-P'ing and restore her to her own people. I did this because I felt it was what you would wish me to do. Appended here is a certificate signed by James Barrington to this effect. Honourable Person, James Barrington would have rewarded me, but I knew it was my destiny to serve one greater than he.

Honourable Person, it is my earnest desire to serve your illustrious self. If it can be found in your heart to accept one whose whole reason for living has been to do your bidding, then I shall be the happiest man in the world. Honourable Person, I have the acquaintance of one of your people, Lien-chung, and will beg him to convey this to you. He will know where to find me should your answer be favourable.

Honourable Person, I am your always-obedient servant.

Chang Tsin.

'Chang Tsin,' Lan Kuei said happily.

'Do you know this fellow?' Te An-wah demanded. 'I have ordered Lien-chung to be caned for accepting such a missive. Shall I have this other vermin sought out and strangled?'

'You will do no such thing,' Lan Kuei snapped. 'You will order Lien-chung's punishment to be stopped immediately. Instead, you will bring him to me so that I may reward him for having acted so wisely.'

'And you will give this Chang Tsin employment?'

'Oh, yes,' Lan Kuei said. Chang Tsin! A voice from the past come to make her happy.

*

James Barrington and Lucy Mayhew were married in Shanghai just before Christmas 1856. By then the entire European community was in an uproar because of an incident at Canton a couple of months previously, when Manchu officials had boarded a ship, *Arrow*, flying the British flag but with a Chinese crew, to arrest some sailors accused of piracy.

'Depend upon it, they will pay for this,' Harry Parkes growled. And, indeed, in the New Year word reached Shanghai that, the Crimean War having been brought to an end, an expeditionary force was on its way, escorting Lord Elgin to demand reparations at the point of a gun.

'More trouble,' Martin grumbled.

*

John Barrington took the news to the Heavenly King. This was always a disturbing business, for though Hung Hsiu-ch'uan was still a young man, his excesses and debaucheries had ruined his health, and his temper was more uncertain than ever. He ruled now more through fear than any magnetism of personality; yet to the masses who never got close to him he remained their T'ien Wang, and they would willingly die for him.

'The British will make war upon the Manchu,' John said. 'Now is the time to crown our movement with ultimate success.'

'You would take my people north of the river again?'

'No, Your Majesty. I would take them to the mouth of the river.'

'That is where Tseng Kuo-fan has his army. And where the British have their ships.'

'Tseng Kuo-fan's army is a rabble, Majesty, and the British intend to fight the Manchu. Now is the time for us.' He unfolded his map before Hung. 'There. Let me assault Tzeki and take it. Tzeki is not fifty miles from Shanghai.' Hung chewed his lip in indecision. 'My lord, you promised me the House of Barrington,' John continued urgently. 'That was several years ago. Now we need the House, and the ships, to supply our people.'

'Tzeki,' Hung muttered. 'Very well, take Tzeki, Great Barrington. But do not attack until the British are actually engaged in fighting the Manchu. And do not fail.'

*

'He has given me permission,' John reported to his mother. 'Now, at last, we can finish this business.'

Tsen-tsing's eyes gleamed. Since rejoining her son, she had allowed herself to blossom. She was still a beautiful woman; now she wore gaudy silks and all the jewellery she could load upon her person. She maintained an army of eunuchs, and even, it was said, interviewed privately the most handsome male captives before they were sent for execution. But her true love remained her son, and her true hatred was reserved for the remainder of the Barrington family. 'You will give those women, Jane and Joanna, to me,' she said, 'when we take Shanghai.'

*

The naval squadron based on Hong Kong undertook various reprisals immediately, but they were regarded merely as pirates by the Chinese, and in fact Elgin did not appear as expected. The outbreak of the Indian Mutiny caused his escorting regiment to be diverted to Calcutta, and his lordship, proceeding only with his staff, was then shipwrecked, so that it was the end of 1857 before he even reached Hong Kong.

To the great relief of the British community, on his arrival, the Manchu government seemed willing to negotiate, and a new Treaty of Tientsin was signed in the summer of 1858. This conceded everything the British – and the French, who now also sought concessions from the Chinese, and, since the Crimea, were Britain's allies – demanded, even the right to send ambassadors to Peking and establish them there, and to have them received by the Emperor without the kowtow.

This was too good to be true. Soon the Manchu announced that their negotiators had exceeded their prerogatives, and there could be no question of any foreign ambassadors taking up residence in Peking. Immediately the British prepared again for war, Elgin's regiment having finally arrived from India.

*

But things were not quite so easy as in 1840. On 25 June 1859, Sir James Hope, commanding the British squadron in the Gulf of Chih-li, bombarded the Taku forts at the mouth of the Pei-ho river, and than landed soldiers and marines to storm them. But the Chinese, again commanded by Seng-ko-lin-ch'in, were prepared to fight, and the British were shot to pieces. Hope had to call off the attack, and indeed only got his men re-embarked through the help of covering fire from a hitherto neutral American squadron whose commander, Commodore Josiah Tattnall, made the immortal remark that 'blood is thicker than water'.

The British were not prepared to take such a drubbing lying down. Throughout the rest of the year and into 1860, men and ships were moved steadily east, the assembly point being Hong Kong as – still in conjunction with France – Great Britain prepared for all-out war with the Manchu empire.

Martin and James Barrington watched the situation with considerable alarm. Shanghai and its environs were now virtually an independent state, as the Royal Navy patrolled the seaways, while the river from Chin-kiang west was controlled by the T'ai-P'ing. Peking and the Mandate of Heaven might have been a million miles away. And now the T'ai-P'ing army moved further east, and assaulted and took the town of Tzeki, only fifty miles from Shanghai. Tseng Kuo-fan marched his army against them, and was defeated, but the battle at least seemed to give a check to the rebels, for the time being.

What was most galling was the news that the T'ai-P'ing were now commanded in the field by John Barrington.

'What happens when he arrives before Shanghai?' James asked.

'We defend the city,' Martin told him. 'We have nowhere else to go. And I want to see that bastard hang for what he did to Joanna.'

'And while we're fighting for Shanghai, the British are trying to bring down the Dynasty,' James remarked bitterly.

'I do not believe they really want that,' Martin said optimistically. Meanwhile, he went on supporting Tseng Kuo-fan with money and guns and ammunition, as much as he could afford.

*

Jane spent more time watching Joanna, and worrying about her. The girl had never been one to share secrets, and now she refused to speak of her experiences. Jane could not suppress an unholy curiosity.

More important was what they were to do with this girl, who was fast ceasing to be a girl; for in 1858, Joanna was twenty-six. True she was an extremely beautiful woman, and caused a stir amongst the British bachelor population of Shanghai whenever she went abroad. The stream of callers at the Barrington mansion just outside the city was continuous. To them all Joanna smiled politely, but she revealed not the slightest interest in them. Jane sometimes felt like giving her a shaking; surely having been raped was no reason to remain a spinster all one's life. Clearly Joanna needed an older man, kindly but firm, who would restore her ability to become a complete woman. Jane pinned her faith on a Welsh missionary, Arthur Jenkins, ten years older than Joanna, and a regular caller. He was clearly a sober, ultra-respectable man. He would make a woman of her yet.

Joanna was well aware of her mother's anxiety, and that it affected her brother and her sister-in-law. James maintained his own establishment, but Lucy, now the mother of a baby boy, often came to call, and would sit with Joanna and extol the happiness of marriage. Joanna could stomach this while Lucy was praising her brother, but whenever the conversation shifted in her own direction, she simply retired to the room and locked the door.

It was not that she in any way wished to reject her family, or the society in which she lived. But that society would reject her if they knew the swirling emotions which too often confused her thoughts. She had lived for four years in an environment none of them could even imagine, a society devoted to death, destruction, disease and decadence. She could never explain how much her experiences had bitten deep into her personality. What would James and her Uncle Martin say if they knew that she still yearned for John's obscene caresses ... even though she dreamed of being present when he was hanged?

What would Mama or Lucy – so concerned with the humdrum aspects of their lives, the necessity of being proper English ladies – say if they knew that she still dreamed of the searching fingers of her eunuchs as she lay naked on her back to be massaged after her bath?

Intimacy with any other human being was a terrifying thought. The intimacy of marriage with a man who would know none of these things, but who would very soon have to suspect they existed in his wife's mind, was a concept abhorrent to her.

Thus she would sit on the front veranda of Barrington House, in her rocking-chair, and watch the world go by. And one morning she found herself looking at a man who was standing at the gate. He was young, about her own age, slightly built, and he wore sea-going clothes.

He raised his cap. 'Miss Barrington?' His voice had a curious nasal accent.

'I am she.'

'May I come in, ma'am?'

'Pray do.'

He closed the gate behind himself, and ascended the steps.

'The name is Ward, ma'am. Frederick Ward.'

'You're an American,' Joanna said, identifying the accent.

There were an increasing number of American traders and missionaries in China.

'Correct, ma'am. I wonder if I might have a word with you?'

'Won't you please sit down? Would you like some tea?'

Ward seated himself in one of the bamboo chairs. 'That would be very nice, ma'am.'

'Wan Chung,' Joanna called, knowing that the butler would be hovering just inside the jalousie door in order to dispose of the visitor should he prove offensive. 'Tea for two, if you please.' She spoke, of course, in Mandarin.

'You speak the language like a native,' Ward remarked – also in Mandarin.

'I am a native, Mr Ward. But you also speak it well.'

'I'm learning. I hope you won't take offence, but I would like to discuss a subject which you might find a little touchy.' Joanna sighed with disappointment. She had liked this young man on sight. 'I've just made a voyage up the Yangtse,' he explained.

That was at least unusual. 'How far did you go?'

'Nanking, and beyond a little way. As far as Wuhu.'

'The T'ai-P'ing let you use the river without hindrance?'

'I was flying the Stars and Stripes. Seems it was an American missionary taught the Heavenly King.' Joanna shuddered. 'I've heard it said that you have first-hand knowledge of the T'ai-P'ing, Miss Barrington.'

'I am sure you know that I was their prisoner for several years, Mr Ward.'

'Sorry, ma'am, I didn't mean to bring that up. What puzzles me is why nothing has ever been done about them?'

'I'm afraid the government hasn't been very successful against the T'ai-P'ing. It has too many other problems.'

Ward nodded. 'Meanwhile, that country out there is turning into a desert. And I can tell you they're starting to think of coming on down the river. Well, I guess they'll have to, soon enough, just to find food and plunder for their army.'

Joanna felt a stab of real alarm. 'Have you told that to the authorities?'

'I've told it to Marshal Tseng, sure. Trouble is, most of his men are so scared they're beat before they ever see a T'ai-P'ing. I've also spoken with the British. They don't want to know. And then I heard about you. Your father carries a lot of weight around here, and he, and you, I reckon, have a reason for wanting the T'ai-P'ing beaten.' He leaned forward, 'Miss Barrington ... I can beat those people.'

'You, Mr Ward? Are you a soldier?'

'No. I'm a sailor. But I've studied soldiering. Kind of a hobby of mine. I guess you've heard of Alexander the Great?'

Joanna gave a faint smile. 'Yes, I have heard of Alexander the Great, Mr Ward.'

'Well, as I understand history, he beat a Persian army of maybe a hundred thousand with no more than ten thousand or so of his own. He did it by better strategy, better tactics and, above all, better discipline. And, above even those, by making his people believe not only that they *could* win, but they were *going* to win. The T'ai-P'ing have no discipline, no strategy save the creation of terror, no tactics save for an overwhelming onslaught. Let them receive one check, and they'll start to fall apart. Trouble is, Tseng's people don't have any discipline either, and, as I said, no confidence.'

'And you believe you can give them that? Why should you wish to fight for the Manchu?'

'I want to fight to stop the T'ai-P'ing laying waste this entire country. I've nothing going for the Manchu, but I can't believe any of them is half as bad as this fellow Hung and his people. Would you say I'm wrong?'

'No, Mr Ward, I would not say you are wrong.' She found him fascinating, if slightly absurd. How could an itinerant sailor, with no experience of warfare, hope to beat the T'ai-P'ing?

'Then will you help me? Persuade your father to see me. I don't reckon I can do Tseng's Green Flags, or even his Bannermen, much good. I mean to recruit my own force. But I need muskets and ammunition. A battery of artillery would be a treat. And some cloth to make up some kind of uniform. That's important. I also want your father to persuade Tseng Kuo-fan that I'm not setting up to be some kind of a bandit, but that I'm really on his side.'

He was so vehement he was almost convincing. Joanna rested her hand on his. 'I will speak with my step-father, Mr Ward.'

*

During tea Ward told her something about himself. Born in Salem, Massachusetts, he was twenty-seven, a year older than herself. He had been a sailor from boyhood, and had been sailing to China for some ten years, rising to the rank of mate. But he had now abandoned that profession. He had no wife, and no family in which he was particularly interested. His every spare moment was spent in reading military history. Her fascination grew.

*

Martin did not share her enthusiasm. 'Frederick Ward?' he remarked. 'The fellow is an adventurer. He is already trying to recruit a force amongst the riff-raff of the Shanghai waterfront. I can tell you, Joanna, that if he wasn't an American citizen, Marshal Tseng would have had his head by now.'

'Then you won't help him?'

'I think the situation right now is sufficiently fraught without the House of Barrington attempting to equip an army of bandits.'

Joanna went off to find James, but he was hardly more helpful, and obviously had no intention of going against his step-father's decision.

*

Ward called again three days later, in the middle of a steamy afternoon. 'How did it go?'

'It didn't go, Mr Ward. My step-father regards you as a would-be incendiary.' He looked so downcast she felt quite upset. 'Shall we take a walk in the garden?' she invited, and led him down the steps, wondering just what she was doing. But he was the first man to arouse the slightest spark of interest in her since her escape from Nanking. And he wanted to avenge her.

He walked beside her. 'If you spoke with your brother ...'

'I have spoken with James.'

'And the same reaction?'

'I'm afraid so.' She stopped walking and turned towards him. 'I'm sorry.'

He gazed at her for some seconds, then said. 'Sure. Well, I guess I'll have to see what I can do without British assistance. Or Chinese either, for that matter.'

Joanna held his arm. 'I may be able to help you.'

'How?'

'Have you heard of a woman named Lan Kuei?'

'Can't say that I have. No, wait a moment. Isn't that the name of the concubine who's just given the Emperor an heir?'

'That's the one. She and my brother James were once friends in Wuhu. And she now has to be one of the most powerful women in the country, as the mother of a future emperor. I could give you a letter to her, and if you could enlist her help, all doors would be opened to you.'

'You mean you could arrange for me to meet an imperial concubine?'

'No.' Joanna smiled. 'Not even I could do that without having your head chopped off.'

'Or something else first,' he muttered.

'But it so happens that I have another friend in the Forbidden City. He is a eunuch named Chang Tsin. He rescued me from the T'ai-P'ing, and he has written us to say that he is one of Lan Kuei's eunuchs now. I will give you a separate letter to him. I know he will help you.'

'You'd trust a eunuch?'

'I would trust him with my life. I have already done so.'

Ward considered for a few moments. 'Sounds like the answer to a prayer,' he said at last.

*

After her bath, it was Lan Kuei's custom to dismiss her other eunuchs and remain only with Chang Tsin for her evening massage. This put her in a sufficiently sensual mood for her summons to the Emperor's bed. And if the summons did not come ... then Chang Tsin's soft fingers could still give her pleasant dreams.

When Chang Tsin thought about how he had resolved that if the Kuei Fei, his old playmate, would not employ him, then he had no alternative than suicide ... and compared it with his present position, only two years later, he almost believed in miracles. Now he had all the money he could spend, all the fine clothes he could wear. Even mandarins paid him respect.

And he had this wonderful, strong, supple, and so-smooth body to play with. If he could no longer know desire for it, as he once had, he could still enjoy feeling it beneath his fingers, and even more, he could enjoy watching the visible manifestations of the pleasure he was giving – not to mention the knowledge that the woman yielding to him now was the mother of a future emperor. He had come a long way from that hateful shed in Wuhu.

His position, however, was not one of unalloyed satisfaction. If Lan Kuei had been delighted to see him again, and to take him into her employ, and indeed to make him her favourite, she was no longer the girl of eighteen he remembered. It was not that she had actually changed in any way. It was merely that her true characteristics had become more pronounced. Her temper

was more easily aroused and more vehement. Her wilfulness
was more stubborn than ever. The streak of avariciousness he
recalled had deepened, while at the same time the humiliations
of poverty she had suffered as Hui-cheng's daughter – or
what she considered to be poverty – had led her into the greatest extravagances in the clothes she had him buy for her, the
jewelled shoes ... It was also disturbing to note the appearance
of vanity, which was something he did not recall: now her shoes
had special platforms, several inches high, to raise her above
her normal five feet in height. But it was her temper which was
the most formidable drawback to pure contentment. And this
evening she was clearly in a very bad humour, which was irritating in view of what he wanted to say to her.

'Honourable Person is upset,' Chang Tsin murmured, as he
worked.

'Ha!' Lan Kuei turned on to her back so abruptly she took
him by surprise. 'You are an oaf, Chang Tsin. Have you not
heard the news?'

Chang Tsin poured a little of the sweet-scented oil into the
palm of his hand, and then gently caressed the swelling mounds
of her breasts. 'Tell me this news which has upset you.'

'The British and the French have stormed the Taku forts.'

'But that is impossible. The last time ...'

'The last time they failed. This time they succeeded.
Someone's head will have to come off. But looking over our
shoulders is no use. They have seized Taku. They control the
river. Now they are threatening to march on Peking. And
Prince Hui would treat with them. He is encouraged by Prince
Su-shun, of course. The man is a coward – or he is in the pay of
the British. He is the one should lose his head.'

'How would you deal with the situation, Honourable
Person?'

Lan Kuei spread her legs as an indication of where she would
have him go next. 'They want war,' she said dreamily. 'I would
give them war. Do we not have an army of Bannermen many
times stronger than that of the British and the French? We
should destroy them without trace.'

'What is the opinion of the Emperor, Honourable Person?'

'The Emperor is confused. He would fight, I am sure, were
he not swayed by his pernicious uncles. So would Prince Kung
his brother, but they keep muttering that we cannot fight the

barbarians and the T'ai-P'ing at the same time. Ha! Why did
they not destroy the T'ai-P'ing long ago? Why do they not
replace Tseng Kuo-fan and cut off his head? He is useless!'

At last he had been given his cue. 'I have learned of a way in
which the T'ai-P'ing might be defeated, Honourable Person.'

'You?' Lan Kuei sat up, swinging her legs over the side of the
table. Chang Tsin gave her both letters to read.

'Joanna Barrington,' Lan Kuei said. 'She is English.'

'She wishes to help the Dynasty, Honourable Person. And
this man Ward is an American. The Americans have never
sought to make war upon us.'

'But to persuade the Emperor to give him authority to raise
an army ... a man we have never even seen? What if this army
is turned against the Dynasty?'

'I have met this man, Honourable Person. I believe him to be
trustworthy.'

'You have met him? He is here in Peking?'

'He brought the letters, Honourable Person.'

Lan Kuei's eyes gleamed. 'Then I must meet him also.'

'You?' Chang Tsin was so alarmed he forgot his manners.
But for an imperial concubine to meet with a whole man other
than the Emperor or his relatives – and *they* could only be met
on ceremonial occasions – and be discovered would mean
instant decapitation. And for the eunuch who arranged it.

'I must judge him for myself. You will bring him to me.
Tonight. His Majesty is so perturbed by the news from Taku
that he has announced he will sleep alone this evening. Do not
fail me in this, Chang Tsin, or I will have your head.'

If I succeed in this, Chang Tsin thought dolefully, *I am even
more likely to lose my head*. But he bowed. 'It shall be as you
wish, Honourable Person.'

*

He went to the inn in the Chinese quarter where Ward was
lodging. That a long-nosed hairy barbarian was in Peking was
of course widely known, for all Ward's adoption of Chinese
dress. But the fact that he was an American rather than British,
and that he claimed to travel on behalf of the House of
Barrington, spoke Mandarin fluently, and was well equipped
with silver coin, had protected him. He looked up eagerly as

Chang Tsin stood above the table at which he sat. 'You are to come with me,' Chang Tsin told him.

'To see the lady?'

'Be quiet, man. If this is discovered, we will lose our heads. Can you swim under water?'

Ward nodded. Having come so far, and waited so long, he was not going to be put off by a whiff of danger.

*

Chang Tsin led Ward through the streets of the Tatar City up virtually to the north wall. This served the purpose of ensuring they were not being followed; and, just to make sure, Chang Tsin doubled back several times. Just inside the north wall, they came to the reservoirs which fed the Ornamental Water, the series of large artificial lakes which lay to the west of the Forbidden City. There was no moon, and here, in the shadow of a tall building, Chang commanded Ward to strip. 'I am to appear before the lady naked?' Ward demanded.

'There will be clothes waiting for you when we leave the water. As these will be waiting for your return.'

Chang himself stripped to his loincloth, and Ward followed his example, retaining only his drawers, into which he tucked his revolver. 'You must leave that here also,' Chang told him. 'It is not possible to see this person when armed.'

Ward hesitated, but this was clearly a case of in for a penny, in for a pound. He wrapped the revolver in his jacket, then he and Chang carefully lowered themselves into the water.

To gain access to the Ornamental Water the reservoirs dipped under the purple walls of the Forbidden City, and it was into this utterly dark cavern that Chang Tsin led the way. Ward took a huge breath and followed. It was the most uncanny feeling, for he had no idea where he was going – he felt his way along the wall beside him, occasionally reaching up to touch the roof above his head, against which the water brushed – or for how long he was required to hold his breath. It actually was not far, but the uncertainty had his lungs on the point of bursting, when the darkness faded and he went up, to break the surface and gulp air. Chang Tsin was only a few feet away.

'We must remain in the water until we gain the moat,' Chang told him. 'But there are no more tunnels.'

They alternately swam or went on foot, depending as the water shallowed or deepened again, until they reached the moat, where they could walk the whole way; it was only five feet deep. Yet it was necessary to proceed with the utmost caution, and to freeze against the wall whenever they heard voices above them. Their journey seemed to take forever, but it was not much more than an hour before they reached the place where Chang Tsin had placed towels and clothes for them to wear. When they were dressed, Chang Tsin led Ward through a large and very lush garden, in which was a well with a high wall.

'Stand against this wall, with your face to it, Mr Ward,' Chang Tsin instructed. 'And as you value your life, do not turn round.'

This provided another uncanny feeling, especially as Ward immediately heard footsteps behind him, soft on the grass. But he reflected that had the Manchu decided to murder him, they had no need to bring him on this elaborate journey.

'You are sent to me by Joanna Barrington,' a woman's voice said.

'Yes, Honourable Person.'

'In her letter she says that you can defeat the T'ai-P'ing. How is that possible, where the imperial generals have failed?'

Ward told her exactly what he had told Joanna.

'Where will you find the men to follow you?'

'I have already found some, Honourable Person.'

'But you will need a great number.'

'I do not think so, Honourable Person. I believe five thousand will suffice.'

'You will lead five thousand men against a hundred thousand T'ai-P'ing? That is madness.'

'Victories have been won against greater odds than that.'

'Who will captain these men?'

'I will, Honourable Person. As I will train them.'

There was silence, and Ward hoped he could estimate what was going through Lan Kuei's mind. An army of five thousand men could hardly pose a threat to the Empire, while if he could defeat the T'ai-P'ing ... And if he failed, and his force was massacred, the general situation would not have altered for the worse.

'Close your eyes,' Lan Kuei commanded. 'And do not open them. Then turn round.' Ward obeyed, and inhaled her perfume as she came closer to peer at his features in the gloom. The temptation to open his eyes was enormous, but he kept his eyelids firmly shut. Then he felt fingers touch his face, stroking down the side of his jaw. He forced himself to relax, and wait.

'I will have a commission prepared for you,' Lan Kuei said. 'This will give you the power you require. Chang Tsin will bring it to you at your lodging. Now go, and prosper.'

15

THE BARBARIANS

Lan Kuei approached the Emperor at the first opportunity, to obtain Ward's commission. She was exhilarated. She was at last doing something that befitted her position. Even if the American went off and got himself killed, as seemed most likely, it was yet a positive action ... and his death might inspire the barbarians to help the Manchu instead of fighting them.

Which was of course woolly thinking, as the Hsien-feng pointed out. 'They are forming a huge military camp outside Tientsin,' he moaned. 'They are threatening to march on Peking.'

'Bah,' she declared. 'Will not Marshal Seng defeat them, as he defeated the T'ai-P'ing? Sign this paper.'

The Hsien-feng signed without even looking at it. 'No one can stop the barbarians,' he said. 'We must negotiate.'

The Son of Heaven does not negotiate, Lan Kuei wanted to remind him. But she had obtained what she wanted, and sent Chang Tsin to deliver it to Ward.

*

James Barrington stood before his step-father. 'An urgent message from Lord Elgin. I am to travel at once to Tientsin, to join a party designated to undertake negotiations with the Emperor. As assistant interpreter.'

'Good God! Well, I suppose you will have to go. Anything that contributes to ending this sad war is worthwhile.'

James then had to reassure both Lucy and Joanna. 'I am being chosen because of my old friendship with Lan Kuei,' he suggested. 'Who knows, I may even see her again.'

Joanna made no reply to that. She had not told her brother, or anyone else, about having written to the Honourable Person. As Ward had not returned, it lay heavily on her conscience; she had undoubtedly sent that pleasant young dreamer to his death.

*

The southern reaches of the Grand Canal still being in T'ai-P'ing hands, James had to take a junk round to the Gulf of Chih-li, but he made the journey in a week, and was greeted by Sir James Hope Grant, commanding the British forces, and by Harry Parkes, who was to be principal interpreter.

'You are here only because you speak Manchu, Barrington,' Parkes said. 'I personally would not have chosen you, but his lordship would have it so. I wish you only to remember one thing: these Manchu are presently our enemies, and must be treated as such. Is that understood?'

'I understood that my business was to interpret, Mr Parkes.'

Parkes glared at him, then turned away in disgust.

*

The meeting between the European allies and the Manchu was to take place at Tung-Chow, a town some forty miles from Peking. The allied party numbered twenty-four. It was headed by Harry Brougham Lock, Elgin's personal representative, and a French officer, and included Parkes and James Barrington, two French and two English secretaries, and an escort of fifteen Indian dragoons commanded by an English subaltern. They rode out of the British encampment at dawn – it was the middle of September – under a white flag, and covered the forty-odd miles to Tung-Chow by nightfall. Their journey was overseen, from a distance, by a body of Bannermen, but these never approached.

A hotel had been prepared for them. 'I had not known these people were at all civilised,' Lock remarked, as the waiting girl delicately picked the roast duckling clean, before spreading the sauce and wrapping the meat in tasty small pancakes.

'Even if they have some pretty uncivilised habits,' Parkes commented. James snorted into his sake.

'Any people who can make crêpes as good as these must be civilised,' said Captain Lemarche, the Frenchman.

*

Next morning the Manchu delegation arrived, smiling politely, thrusting their hands into the sleeves of their silk tunics, and bowing whenever they spoke. Their leader, who arrived separately an hour after the others, in a palanquin carried by six men and draped with yellow silk, was introduced as I Huan Prince Ch'un, one of the Emperor's younger brothers, a sleepy-looking young man who waved them to their seats and then closed his eyes.

'My master wishes to know what justification you have for invading our country,' said a man seated beside the Prince.

Parkes translated for the benefit of Lock and Lemarche, then replied, 'The justification of the treaty signed by you with Lord Elgin in 1858, and which you have now broken.'

'That was not a good treaty.'

'Nevertheless, it was signed by you,' Parkes reminded him. 'But we are here to negotiate a new treaty.'

The Manchu brightened. 'Perhaps this one will be more acceptable.'

'I wouldn't count on it,' Parkes muttered in English, and then proceeded to outline the proposed terms. James studied the Manchu faces as Parkes listed the usual indemnity – far greater than before; the demand of the British government for an increase in the number of treaty ports, including Wuhu and Hankow up the Yangtse – which was either ignoring the presence of the T'ai-P'ing or a threat to negotiate with the Heavenly King if the Manchu refused to co-operate; the punishment of various offending viceroys and commissioners; the cession of the territory of Kowloon on the mainland opposite Hong Kong; the free movement of British and French nationals within China; and of course, the ultimate requirement, the establishment of British and French embassies within Peking itself.

The Manchu faces grew longer and longer as this list was itemised, although Prince Ch'un did not appear to react at all; he could well have been asleep. He was not sleeping, however, for when Parkes had finished speaking, and the Manchu spokesman was gazing at him in dismay, unable to reply, the Prince suddenly opened his eyes.

'These are many and varied requests,' he remarked. 'They will have to be studied. My brother the Emperor will inform you of his decision when this has been done. Until then, it is my brother's assumption that the invasion of your army into his territories will cease.'

'Providing the Emperor's reply is not too long delayed,' Parkes told him. 'Our armies will remain in their present position for a space of thirty days. On the thirty-first day from today our advance will be resumed.'

'Thirty days,' the Prince said reflectively. He signalled his guards, who assisted him to his feet and into his palanquin, which was then carried out of the courtyard. The rest of the entourage remained, while jasmine tea was served.

'I think that went off very well,' Lock observed.

'But *you* don't look content, Barrington,' Parkes remarked.

'I was wondering what would be the reaction of Lord Palmerston were a Chinese delegation to arrive in London demanding the cession of the Isle of Wight, an indemnity, and the right of free trade in our major ports.'

'That would depend, would it not, Mr Barrington, on whether the Chinese had recently defeated the British Army and the Royal Navy,' Lock said.

*

The allied delegation left in high spirits the next morning, on its journey back to the encampment.

'Depend upon it,' Lock remarked. 'Those fellows have no desire to hear British guns battering at the walls of Peking.'

Again they were accompanied, at a distance, by a body of horsemen, who today were Green Flags, and who seemed greater in numbers than the Bannermen of two days earlier.

'I think the sooner we regain the army, the better,' James muttered to Parkes.

Parkes glanced at the distant horsemen. 'They look peaceable enough to me.'

'They are irregulars.'

'Is that important?'

'Were anything to happen now, the Ch'ing could either take advantage of it, or disown the action and punish the offenders, depending on which circumstances might appear more favourable.'

'Oh, come now. They will hardly restart the war, having asked for a truce, until our ultimatum has at least been considered by the Emperor.'

'I think Prince Ch'un had plenipotentiary powers,' James

told him. 'And whatever decision we are going to receive has already been made.'

'Well, we shall have to find that out. I am certainly not going to flee from a bunch of bandits.'

James sighed. For all his lifetime in China, Parkes still could not grasp the fact that the Chinese also believed in the use of naked force – when they were in a position to apply it. So the party proceeded at hardly more than a walk, and halted for lunch as usual. To James's dismay, not even a picquet was mounted, the Indian troopers being left to eat their curries and chapatis some distance away from the white men.

'Those are curious fellows,' remarked Captain Lemarche, gesturing at the Green Flags, who had moved perceptibly closer.

'They are clearly interested in our habits,' Lock explained.

But the Chinese soldiers were now forming ranks. James leapt to his feet, his meal half eaten. Parkes also rose, while the others looked around them in surprise.

It was too late. At a signal, the Green Flags moved forward to block the roadway, while others had moved up behind. That left only the river on the right, and open country on the left – but other horsemen were already waiting out there.

'Lieutenant Brown,' James snapped, 'form your men into a perimeter and prepare to fire.'

'Captain Lemarche is the ranking officer present,' Lock protested. 'You are not even a soldier, Barrington.'

'For God's sake,' James yelled. But the Green Flags were already charging. The troopers, not yet alerted by their officer, had no time to form any kind of rank before they were surrounded. James drew his revolver and fired once, bringing down his man, but then he was struck by a charging horse, and bowled over – then kicked and beaten, dragged to his feet and tied by his wrists to a horse's saddle. The same treatment was meted to the others. Dimly James heard Lock protesting, but soon there was no breath for that, as the clouds of dust from the horses' hooves clogged their nostrils while they returned to Tung-Chow.

In Tung-Chow waited a crowd of hooting, jeering, stick-wielding populace, men, women and children. Here they were at least given a cup of water, but allowed no rest before their captors moved on again, dragging the prisoners behind them in a half-conscious daze.

Full awareness returned in a cell, half underground and very small, with but a single barred window looking out on to a patch of bare ground. Here they were again given water, and fed some rice – and then abandoned. Twenty-four men packed shoulder to shoulder in a space intended for half that number.

'The scoundrels,' Lock gasped. 'When General Grant hears about this ...'

'But will he ever hear about it?' Lemarche asked. He had cut his face and had bled heavily; the blood had been stanched but he was clearly weak, and he would be scarred for life. 'What is your opinion, Mr Parkes?'

'The General can hardly fail to understand what has happened to us when we do not return. Besides, I imagine the Manchu will make some kind of ransom demand. As to whether General Grant will feel empowered to agree ...' He shrugged.

'In which case we could be kept in this hell-hole for a very long time,' Lock pointed out.

'Well, sir, we must meet our situation like true-born Englishmen. And Frenchmen, of course,' he added hastily. He made no mention of true-born Indians, James realised, gazing at the troopers, who were clearly mystified by the mess their officers had got them into through lack of clear orders.

*

They had been several hours in the cell before the door was thrown open and an official peered in at them. He was backed by a file of soldiers. 'Parkes,' he said.

Parkes hesitated, then got up.

'By God!' Lock exclaimed. 'Can they mean to execute you?'

'I must hope not,' Parkes said, and went through the door.

There could be no doubting the fellow's courage, James thought.

Parkes was gone for some two hours, and then was thrown back into the cell. They knelt round him.

'My dear fellow,' Lock said. 'What have they done to you?'

James held the last of the water to Parkes's lips. After a moment or two he was able to sit up, and even smile. 'Nothing irreparable,' he said. 'A few kicks. A few needles ...' he looked down at his swollen hands, and shuddered.

'The swine,' Lock said.

'What did they actually want?' James asked.

'They wanted me to sign, on behalf of us all, a document to the effect that the treaty agreed with Lord Elgin is invalid, and to indicate that the British and French governments agree to a new treaty with China.' Parkes looked from face to face. 'Remember this! We must refuse to treat with them except on the terms demanded by our governments. No matter what pressures are brought to bear. No matter what!'

'They will get nothing out of me,' Lock asserted.

An hour later the door of the cell opened again.

'Parkes,' the gaoler said. 'Are you ready to see Prince Ch'un again?'

'I will see the Prince again,' Parkes said, 'when he has given orders for all of my companions to be released, and when he has indicated that he is willing to agree to the terms put forward by my colleagues and myself.'

The Manchu grinned at him for several seconds, then he gazed at each of the prisoners in turn. He pointed at the lieutenant. 'That one.'

Brown gave a strangled exclamation as the guards forced their way into the cell and grasped his arms. In the crowded and confined area it might have been possible to overwhelm them, but the corridor had suddenly filled with armed men and there were others out in the courtyard. Neither Parkes nor Lock gave any signal for resistance, although Brown called for help as he was taken away.

'For God's sake,' he shouted. 'Help me!'

'Act the man, sir,' Lock shouted back. 'Act the man.'

The subaltern was hustled into the courtyard and there stripped, while the others peered through the bars. 'My God,' Lock muttered. 'They're not going to castrate the poor boy?'

'They are going to bastinado him,' Parkes said. 'I wouldn't say that is an easier fate.'

James's memory took him back to that day in Wuhu ... but the victims had been Chinese, steeped in stoic fatalism. Brown was a white-skinned Englishman, with an Englishman's belief in hope and destiny. And he was very young. He was screaming in terror even before he was stretched naked in the dust and the first blows began to fall. Then his cries took on an almost animal-like shrill of pain and humiliation.

His comrades watched in furious horror as the beating went

on. Soon there was blood dribbling from his buttocks, then
flying into the air with every stroke of the canes. And the
strokes went on and on ... The white body writhed and heaved,
and piteous sounds issued from the boy's mouth. Until
suddenly he lay still.

'They've murdered him,' Lock whispered in disbelief.

Water was thrown on Brown's head. After a moment he
stirred again. Instantly the beating recommenced.

'No,' he screamed. 'No!'

The secretaries, also young men, could look no longer, and
slumped to the bottom of the cell. It was not until Brown had
received some four hundred strokes, and had fainted at least
four times, that he was thrown back into the cell, without his
clothes. James took off his shirt to spread over the lacerated
flesh. The others stared in horror.

*

Chang Tsin informed Lan Kuei of what had happened to the
barbarians. All Peking was agog with the news, and with the
triumph it was felt had been achieved over these arrogant and
vicious intruders. The Emperor and his court were still out at
the Yuan Ming Yuan, where they had spent all summer
enjoying the rural quiet and the cooling breeze which came
down from the mountains to the north. But it was the business
of the eunuchs to keep their respective mistresses up to date
with all the gossip.

Lan Kuei listened to Chang Tsin with a gleam in her eye.
'They deserve everything that can be inflicted on them, for
invading our realm,' she declared.

'Even young Barrington?'

'Young Barrington is with the invaders?'

'He came with them as an interpreter, and has been arrested
with them. Now it is said they are all going to die.' Lan Kuei
pinched her lip. 'He is our friend,' Chang Tsin reminded her.
'Did he not once brush your lips with his?'

'Be quiet,' Lan Kuei snapped angrily. 'No one must ever
know of that.' The secret of her power over the Emperor!

'We cannot let him die, Honourable Person. Will you not
approach His Majesty's brothers and ask for a paper authorising his release?'

Lan Kuei was in a quandary. She might be the mother of the future Emperor, but she was well aware how hated she was, certainly by the Hsien-feng's uncles, and probably by his brothers as well, both because of her inferior birth and because, through her child, she was a threat to their dominance over the increasingly unhealthy and indecisive Son of Heaven. She dared not take the slightest risky step which might enable them to turn the Emperor against her. At the same time, she could not let Young Barrington die.

'You will return to Peking, Chang Tsin,' she said. 'To where these barbarians are being held, and you will tell those in charge that under no circumstances must Young Barrington be harmed, whatever may happen to the others.'

Chang Tsin looked uncertain. 'Whose authority am I to give for such a command?'

'They know the name of your mistress, Chang Tsin. You will tell them that the Kuei Fei speaks with the tongue of the Son of Heaven, but that the matter is otherwise to be kept secret. Young Barrington is the son of a mandarin who has given long and faithful service to the Throne of Heaven. That is sufficient.'

*

A few days later news reached the Summer Palace that the British and the French, having learned of the arrest and mistreatment of their envoys, had resumed their advance on Peking. The concubines were thrown into wild despair, even Niuhuru. 'What will become of the Mandate of Heaven?' she wailed.

Lan Kuei alone was filled with spirit. 'How could a small army of barbarians conquer Peking?' she demanded.

'Then why is everyone fleeing?' Niuhuru cried. News had reached them that every resident who owned or could hire a cart or a mule or a horse was leaving the city.

'Because they are fools and cowards,' Lan Kuei snapped. 'The barbarians will be ground into the dust. If this Elgin wants war, then he shall have war! Is not Marshal Seng-ko-lin-ch'in in command of our armies before the city? The foreign devils will be taught the error of their ways.'

She proceeded to her private apartment, to the nursery, to kiss Tsai-ch'un good night. The warm love she had once felt for the boy had long passed. Giving birth to Tsai-ch'un had been a painful and demeaning business, and one she was not anxious to repeat. Fortunately, in the Hsien-feng's present state of health, that was unlikely. She did not care for the company of small children; Tsai-ch'un was now four years old, yet he still burst into tears at the slightest excuse. The reason, she realised, was his health, and this was a source of great concern to her. The little boy was the source of her present prosperity – and her every hope of future power. Yet nothing she could do seemed to stop the constant dribbling from his nose or cure his unceasing cough. The fault was his father's of course; for she herself was as healthy as she had ever been. It was the Emperor who had passed on these physical defects to his son. Yet she dutifully kissed the little boy before returning him to the maids who would put him to bed. Then she went to her own bedchamber.

There she found Chang Tsin, who had just returned from Peking, and assured her that her orders had been delivered. Whether they would be carried out was another matter.

'Do you suppose the armies have yet met, Tsin?'

'I expect they have, Honourable Person.'

'Oh, to be there, overseeing the battle.' Lan Kuei's eyes shone. 'How I wish I was born a man.'

'Then would the world have been a poorer place for beauty.'

Lan Kuei smiled. 'You say the sweetest things, Tsin. Now, is there no news of that man Ward?'

'No, Honourable Person.'

'I wonder if he was a charlatan. We shall have to find out the truth of him once this Elgin has been driven into the sea.' She stared out of the window at the night sky. 'You may undress me, Tsin. The Emperor will not send for me this night. There are too many great affairs for him to discuss with his ministers.'

Chang Tsin obeyed, and soon Lan Kuei nestled on the pillows. 'Does the Honourable Person need attention?' he asked archly.

Lan Kuei considered. 'Not tonight, Tsin,' she said. 'I am too excited. I seem able to hear the roar of the guns, the shouts of the Bannermen as they charge to victory. I shall go to sleep and dream of them in their hour of triumph.'

Chang Tsin turned down the lanterns and left her. He would sleep outside her door, as he always did. And Lan Kuei did indeed dream of battles, and squadrons of horsemen charging to victory beneath the eight Banners ... She was annoyed to be suddenly awakened, and find Chang Tsin standing by her bedside, his face contorted with alarm.

'Honourable Person,' he said, 'a messenger has just arrived. Marshal Seng has been utterly defeated, and his army is no more.'

Lan Kuei leapt from the bed. It was still dark outside. 'What time is it?'

'It is two hours to daybreak.'

'Has His Majesty been told?'

'I believe there is to be a meeting of the Grand Council within the hour.'

'Dress me,' Lan Kuei snapped. 'I must be there.'

'You, Honourable Person?' Chang Tsin was aghast at such a potential breach of protocol.

'Dress me, you fool!' Lan Kuei screamed. Perhaps she was still asleep – her happy dream turned into a nightmare. But if it was all true ... She knew that the Hsien-feng had been per-suaded only with the greatest reluctance to send Marshal Seng against the barbarians. He had previously talked of retreating beyond the Great Wall, to Jehol, where the barbarians would not dare to follow him. Of course, there must have been treachery! Probably by Seng himself – even if he had previously beaten the T'ai-P'ing. What was needed was a young and vigor-ous leader. Then she thought suddenly of Jung-lu. She had not seen him since the day he had escorted her into Peking with her family in 1852; in the past nine years she had seen no men at all save for her lord and his immediate relatives – except for that one strange, dangerous encounter with Ward. But now Manchu China needed a man of action.

*

Chang Tsin escorted Lan Kuei along private corridors to the little room which was separated from the council chamber by a curtain. Through this curtain she could peep at the Hsien-feng, seated in his high-backed chair, and the men standing before him. Several of them she did not recognise, but Prince Hui, Prince Kung, and Prince Su-shun were there.

Prince Hui was not tall, but seemed even smaller than he was because his shoulders hunched. He was the oldest living male member of the House of Ch'ing, and as such was highly regarded by the mandarins and scholars, the men who guarded the law and who maintained a very real check on even the imperial power.

His half-brother, Prince Su-shun, was several years younger, being the son of their father's second wife. He was a big, burly man, and one of undoubted talent, who had earned a great reputation as President of the Board of Revenue, although his tenure of office had left him unpopular with the masses. He had inherited a department riddled with corruption, and set out to clean it up with enormous vigour. Before he had finished his task, however, the entire offices of the Board had burned down.

The arsonist was undoubtedly a clerk who had feared his peculations would be discovered, but popular gossip had it that Su-shun had himself burned down the building to hide his own fraud; and since the incident had happened just as the conquests of the T'ai-P'ing caused a severe rice shortage, the people had even abused Su-shun in the streets. That he was a man of immense determination and energy could not be doubted, and he was the driving force behind his brother.

Their nephew, Prince Kung, on the other hand, was a true Ch'ing, small and compact, with a drooping lower lip and drooping eyelids as well. He equally was a man of talent and determination. Lan Kuei often thought that he should have become Emperor, rather than his sickly brother. He was her own age, twenty-seven, and hardly taller than she, but he possessed a toughness of body and mind which was lacking in the Hsien-feng. He obviously disliked Prince Hui and his half-brother, and envied their influence. Behind the throne stood Te An-wah; and in front of the Emperor knelt the messenger from Marshal Seng.

'Can this be true?' the Hsien-feng was asking. 'How could my armies be defeated by a mere handful of barbarians?'

'Speak, man,' Prince Hui rasped. 'And speak the truth.'

The man replied tremulously. 'The marshal engaged the barbarians before Chang-chiawan, Majesty. The barbarians are devils. Our artillery fired great volleys, but few of the barbarians fell. Their artillery was scanty, but every discharge of theirs knocked down our people. And then the barbarians advanced behind the short swords which they fix to the muzzles of their muskets.' Not a sound was heard in the chamber. Lan Kuei could feel her blood boil with outrage. 'Our men fired their muskets at the barbarians, Majesty, and some fell, but the rest advanced. They did not fire a shot in reply, but charged with their short swords. Majesty, despite all that Marshal Seng and his officers could do, our people fled.'

'The curs,' Prince Hui growled.

'The Marshal rode with them, and rallied them at the bridge of Palichao.'

'Palichao is only a few miles from Peking,' Su-shun snapped.

'It was the first place where the Marshal could rally his men, your excellency.'

'Then Chang-chiawan has fallen,' Prince Kung said.

'Chang-chiawan is no more, your excellency. The barbarians entered the town and looted everything they could remove. Then they fired it; the flames could be seen for miles.' Lan Kuei heard a soft snap, and looked down; one of her long fingernails had broken off, so tightly had she been clenching her little fists. 'The Marshal prepared to make a stand at the bridge, Majesty,' the messenger went on. 'He felt that the water would prevent the barbarians bringing their short swords into action. Our men fought well. The battle lasted for seven hours. But the barbarians brought up their artillery and began to blow great gaps in the ranks of our people.

'The commander at the bridge was General Sheng-pao. He was hit by a shell fragment, and had his jaw blown off. He was very angry, Majesty. In response he had two of the barbarian officers taken on to the bridge and beheaded in full view of the barbarians. Their bodies were thrown into the stream. Then he died himself.' The princes nodded their approval of such bold action. 'But the barbarians were not dismayed, Majesty. They only fought harder. And at last our men could stand the firing no longer, and began to withdraw. The barbarians took the bridge.'

'Then Peking is at their mercy,' Su-shun declared.

'Where is Marshal Seng?' Prince Kung asked quietly.

'He is in the city, preparing for its defence, your excellency.'

'And the barbarians?'

'They have halted – on this side of the bridge.'

'They are preparing for an assault,' Prince Hui declared. 'The city is lost. We must leave this place, Majesty, and retire beyond the Great Wall.'

'Then you would be abandoning the Empire,' Prince Kung snapped.

'What else can we do?' his brother asked.

'These barbarians are not invincible,' Kung insisted. 'They are dangerous to meet in the open field. But they are few, and their guns are light.'

'How can you say their guns are light?' Prince Hui demanded. 'Have they not outfired our own?'

'Because ours have been badly used,' Kung said. 'The barbarians are aware of their own weakness. If they were not so, would they not have marched on Peking without hesitation once they had crossed the bridge? They have halted now, hoping that we will resume negotiations. They know they have not the artillery to batter down our walls. And they lack the men to take so great a city, even if they could make a breach.'

'That is true,' the Hsien-feng said. 'Is that not true?' He looked at Prince Hui almost pitifully.

'That is not true, Majesty,' his uncle told him, casting a scornful glance at his other nephew. 'Prince Kung is inexperienced. He knows nothing about these things. If Marshal Seng fights for Peking, he will certainly be defeated again.'

'Yes,' the Emperor muttered. 'He has always been defeated.'

'He beat the T'ai-P'ing,' Prince Kung protested.

'The T'ai-P'ing are not so formidable as the barbarians,' Su-shun pointed out. 'Our principal duty is to preserve the safety of the Emperor. Prince Hui is right, Majesty. You must withdraw beyond the Great Wall, into Jehol.'

'And abandon your people,' Prince Kung said again, bitterly.

'By no means,' Su-shun said. 'We will issue a decree announcing that the Emperor wearies of the summer heat, and is visiting the imperial parks in Jehol to hunt.'

'Do you imagine the barbarians will believe that?'

'It matters naught whether they believe it or not. The people will believe it.'

'Do you think so?' the Hsien-feng asked eagerly.

'Of course, Your Majesty. Do you not hunt in Jehol every year?'

'Yes,' the Hsien-feng said. 'Yes, indeed.'

'And what will happen here?' Prince Kung inquired.

'Who can say?' So-shun replied. 'But autumn is now with us. The barbarians will withdraw with the first winter frosts.'

'After having burned Peking. This is what this Elgin has threatened if his envoys are harmed. Now we are told that apart from those who have already died of their injuries, two more have been beheaded in view of their companions.'

'Bah,' Prince Hui said. 'There is no possibility of the barbarians burning Peking. Su-shun is right. They will negotiate once they know the Emperor is beyond their grasp.'

'Yes,' the Hsien-feng agreed. 'They will negotiate.'

Lan Kuei could stand it no longer. She stepped through the curtain. Chang Tsin made an effort to stop her, but she evaded his hands. Every head turned as the men looked at her; even the still-kneeling messenger looked at her in consternation. The Hsien-feng was the most astonished of all. Lan Kuei realised she must look a remarkable sight, with her hair undressed and her face entirely lacking make-up. Hastily she pulled the midnight strands from around her cheeks and tossed them over her shoulder.

'The Honourable Person is unwell?' the Hsien-feng inquired.

'I am distressed, lord,' Lan Kuei said, 'by what has been said here this morning.'

'You have been listening?' the Hsien-feng asked.

'Could I do otherwise, lord? This is the Empire you are discussing. The Empire you would throw away. Is not the immortal Nurhachi at this moment turning in his grave?' The Hsien-feng frowned at her, and Lan Kuei realised that for the first time that she could remember, the Emperor was looking angry. Yet to stop now was impossible. 'Your Majesty,' she cried, and dropped to her knees before him. 'Can you not see that Prince Kung is right? It is not possible for eighteen thousand men to overrun an empire this size. It is not even possible for them to take Peking. Let us return there, all of us who would fight, and if necessary, die, and take our places on the walls beside our people. If these barbarians want war, let us give them war. If they wish their envoys back, let us throw them their heads!'

'The Honourable Person is demented,' Prince Hui remarked.

Lan Kuei rose from her knees and whirled to face him, pointing. 'And you are a coward,' she shouted. She turned back to the Emperor. 'Can you not understand his game, lord? He seeks to dominate you.'

'Your Majesty,' Prince Hui protested. Su-shun puffed with

outrage. But Prince Kung made no comment.

'It is unseemly to speak thus of my most valued counsellor,' the Hsien-feng remarked.

'Your least trustworthy counsellor,' Lan Kuei snapped.

'Majesty,' Prince Hui said, 'it is more unseemly that our councils should be interrupted by this . . . this girl. What, will you listen to her?'

'Who now offers treacherous advice,' Su-shun put in.

Lan Kuei gasped, suddenly realising the danger of the position in which she had placed herself. 'How can I be a traitor, lord?' she cried. 'Am I not the mother of your son?'

'Such a person is not a fit mother for the heir to the throne,' Su-shun said.

'You are right.' The Hsien-feng turned to Te An-wah. 'Prince Tsai-ch'un will be removed from the apartments of the Honourable Person and taken to the apartments of the Empress.'

Lan Kuei stared at him in consternation, then turned to Kung. But the Prince remained impassive. She had got herself into this impasse; she must also extricate herself. 'How may any mother be deprived of her child, lord?' she cried.

'When that mother has proved herself unfit,' Su-shun said.

'We need a decision, Majesty,' Prince Hui interrupted, less interested in Lan Kuei's fate than in getting away to the north. 'With every minute the barbarians approach.'

'It is my decision that the summer heat is too great to be endured even in the Yuan Ming Yuan,' the Hsien-feng said. 'I shall visit Jehol for the autumn, and there hunt. Have this made known to the people, and have my women and eunuchs ordered to make ready to move.'

'Within the hour,' Hui said. 'I will also arrange an escort of Bannermen.'

'You are a coward!' Lan Kuei screamed at him.

The Hsien-feng glared at her. 'Remove that woman,' he said. 'As of now she is no longer an Honourable Person. She is no longer my concubine. I shall not look upon her face again.'

Lan Kuei gasped at this second crushing blow.

'She will travel with the servants,' Prince Hui said. Even a discarded concubine could not be turned loose to spread gossip about the imperial bed. In his opinion, she should be strangled there and then.

Te An-wah moved round the high-backed chair. 'Come, lady,' he said.

Lan Kuei looked left and right, like a trapped animal, seeking support and finding none.

'Remove the woman,' Prince Hui commanded.

Te An-wah lifted Lan Kuei from the floor and carried her from the room. It was nearly dawn, and women and eunuchs emerged from their apartments to peer at the disgraced Kuei Fei. 'Prepare to leave this place,' Te An-wah told them. 'His Majesty is departing for Jehol within the hour.'

'Te An-wah,' Lan Kuei begged. 'Are we not friends?'

'I have no friends,' the eunuch reminded her.

'Well, set me down. I can walk. I will not run away.'

Te An-wah hesitated, then set her on her feet.

Lan Kuei straightened her robe, and took several deep breaths.

'You have been very foolish, lady,' Te An-wah said. 'To anger the Emperor is the worst thing one can do.'

'Even when he will no longer face his duty?'

'Lady speaks treason. The Emperor's duty is to sacrifice to Heaven. Nothing else is of importance.'

They had by now reached her apartment, where her ladies and eunuchs were gathered – but not Chang Tsin; the wretch had clearly run off the moment he had heard of her looming disgrace. 'You are dismissed,' Te An-wah told them. 'This lady is no longer an imperial concubine. You and you' – he pointed at two of the dismayed girls – 'fetch the Prince Tsai-ch'un and take him to the Empress's apartment.'

'Am I not allowed to bid my son goodbye?' Lan Kuei pleaded.

Te An-wah considered, then nodded. 'It is permitted.'

The little boy, only half awake, was brought out, swaddled in his blankets, and Lan Kuei kissed him on the forehead. *For you I risked so much*, she thought. *And now it has all been torn from my grasp.* At least he was going to the care of Niuhuru. He would be safe with that gentle person. While she ... 'Am I to be allowed no servants at all?' she asked.

'You may keep Chang Tsin,' Te An-wah said.

'Then find him and send him to me,' Lan Kuei begged.

'What is to become of us?' asked one of the ladies.

'Positions will no doubt be found for you. Haste now. We leave within the hour.'

They hurried to and fro, but collecting their own belongings, not Lan Kuei's. Te An-wah supervised the removal of Prince Tsai-ch'un's clothes and toys, and then took his leave.

There was no sign of Chang Tsin.

*

Lan Kuei sat on her bed in total desolation, but looked up at the sound of male footsteps. 'Prince Kung!' She bowed, while her brain raced. His presence in her apartment was indicative both of the utter confusion into which even protocol had descended – and of the utter collapse of her own position. 'Have you come to take me to execution?'

'You are impetuous, Lan Kuei,' Kung told her. 'That is no recipe for success. All moves should be planned carefully. Listen to me. I am remaining in Peking to see what can be done to halt the barbarians.'

'How I wish I could be with you, my lord.'

'You will be of more use to me in Jehol. I agree with your suggestions in the council chamber.'

'But you said not a word in my support,' Lan Kuei muttered.

'How could I? I am not the Emperor. My brother is at the moment very afraid, as he is also very sick. Thus he is entirely under the influence of my uncle and that pernicious fellow Su-shun. But I know these men. They will overreach themselves soon enough – and my brother will regain his health and strength of mind. You will go to Jehol with the imperial party ...'

'As a nothing,' Lan Kuei moaned. 'Not even a mother.'

'You *are* a mother. No one can take that from you. Remember that. Go to Jehol, and watch, and listen ... and say nothing. But write me letters, keep me informed.'

'Can I trust you, my lord?'

Prince Kung gave her a peculiarly grim smile. 'I had supposed you were prepared to die for the Dynasty, Lan Kuei. Besides, who else may you trust, if not me?'

*

'God,' muttered the officer who had opened the door. 'God! Is there anyone alive here?'

James Barrington turned round, still leaning against the wall. He had spent the entire night staring out through the bars – that was far preferable to looking back into the cell, and he was the only one who still retained the strength to stand. 'Most of us, I think,' he said.

They had sensed the British troops were coming. For the past forty-eight hours they had heard the rumble of gunfire, and the uproar of the population of Peking in flight. Their own guards had fled the previous morning, so they had been left alone without food or water.

But not quite alone. Last evening a face had appeared at the bars. 'Are you there, Young Barrington?'

'Chang Tsin!' James had stumbled through the prone bodies to reach the window.

'I have food,' Chang Tsin said, and handed him a bowl of rice.

'And water?'

'No water.'

'We need water. But, Chang Tsin, what is happening?'

'Your people are storming the city. I must leave before I am killed. But, Barrington, remember that I helped you.'

'Of course. But ... did Lan Kuei send you?'

'Lan Kuei is disgraced,' Chang Tsin said. 'I do not know what will become of her. But you will remember that I helped you, Young Barrington. Once you offered me employment.'

'You shall have it,' James promised. 'Can you not let us out of here?'

'I cannot. I have no keys, and they would cut off my head. You will soon be rescued, when your soldiers take the city. I will come to you when it is safe to, and you will remember that I brought you rice.'

He ran off into the darkness.

'Water!' James had shouted after him, but to no avail.

'You know the damndest people,' Parkes had commented.

'Yes,' James had said. 'Share out this rice.'

*

Now he helped the officer and his men to carry the weaker prisoners out of the cell and into the fresh air. Several of them had died – including Lieutenant Brown, whose open cuts from the flogging had filled with maggots – and two had been dragged away for execution. Several were totally incapable of movement; even Lock and Parkes could barely stumble along.

'By God, but these yellow devils will pay for this,' the officer growled. 'But you, sir, you seem to have managed to survive well.'

'He survived because no one laid a finger on him,' Parkes croaked.

The officer looked puzzled, then said. 'If you are fit enough, sir, would you come with me to report to Lord Elgin?'

'Willingly,' James agreed.

*

He was given no opportunity to bath or change his filthy clothing; instead he was given a drink of water laced with rum, a hasty breakfast, and then mounted on a horse, with an escort of three troopers. He was relieved to see that so little damage appeared to have been done to the city itself, although there were British soldiers everywhere, watched by passive crowds. But the main force had apparently by-passed Peking and were marching to the west. 'They're chasing this Son of Heaven fellow,' the accompanying corporal told him. 'We know he's out there somewhere.'

After a couple of hours' journey they heard distant drums and the squeal of fifes, and saw first the mule-drawn supply wagons, next the artillery caissons bouncing along in a swirl of dust, then rank upon rank of red-coated infantry, following an advance guard of Indian cavalry splendid in their turbans and blue tunics, pennons fluttering from their lances. Thicker dust rose and hovered in the still air, yet in the front centre of this mass of moving men James could discern a cluster of bright uniforms. A few minutes later he found himself face to face with Lord Elgin.

His lordship was wearing civilian clothes and a huge straw hat. He was a large, florid man with a not unintelligent face, but one currently marked with impatience and annoyance.

'James Barrington,' he grunted. 'I've heard of your father. What's this about our people being tortured?'

'I'm afraid it's true, my lord.'

'They'll pay. By God, I've a mind to stretch the neck of this

Hsien-feng fellow meself! I'm told he's at some place called the Yuan Ming Yuan. Do you know it, Barrington?'

'I have heard of it. My father visited it once. It is the summer palace, a place of unequalled beauty.'

'It is at present being looted by the French troops, my lord,' intervened an officer who had just ridden from the west. 'The Emperor and his court have fled north.'

'Looting? Damnation! I gave orders that there was to be no looting.'

'Well, my lord, I would say those French do not consider your orders to apply to them.'

'We had best make haste, my lord,' said Sir James Hope Grant, general in command of the British contingent. 'We can't leave everything to the Frogs, what?'

The British army seemed to quicken its pace as news spread through the ranks of what was happening only a few miles away.

'My lord,' James begged, riding beside the plenipotentiary, his exhaustion forgotten. 'You must not encourage this looting.'

Elgin glanced at the General. 'The fellow has a point. It'll look bad in the papers, eh?'

'You intend to stop the French?' Grant asked grimly.

'We must see what we can do about them. Yes, indeed. Will you send a message to General Cousin-Montauban asking him to attend me as soon as is practical.'

Grant turned to instruct one of his aides. But at that very moment they topped a low rise, and gazed at the Yuan Ming Yuan now bathed in the fullest splendour of the midday sun.

'I say,' Elgin remarked. 'What a splendid-looking place.'

'It is the work of eighty years' delight in beauty, my lord,' James reminded him. 'Which your allies seem eager to destroy in but eighty minutes.'

Elgin urged his horse down the slope. The drum beat had increased at the sight of the palace complex. The evidence of the French presence was a host of discarded knapsacks, even rifles, and the immense hubbub heard from inside the nearest of several huge buildings.

As Elgin rode off to confer with General Cousin-Montauban, Grant sent sentries to stand guard over the four palaces which had not yet been assaulted. The rest of the British army was commanded to bivouac, much to its displeasure.

Barrington used the time to wash himself in a pond, even if he could do nothing about his ragged clothing. Soon he saw Elgin returning from his discussion with the French commander, and he joined the throng of officers who now clustered about him.

'I have made my decision,' Elgin announced. 'Summon Gordon.'

A few minutes later a trim young man with a pencil moustache, wearing the dark-green uniform of the Royal Engineers and the insignia of a captain, appeared and saluted.

'Ah, Gordon,' Elgin said. 'I have a task for you. It will be at once a challenge to your people and a pleasure, I would suppose.' He pointed. 'I want that entire park destroyed.'

There was a moment of utter silence. Even Hope Grant was taken aback.

'The entire park, sir?' Gordon ventured.

'Yes. All the palaces burned. And the summerhouses. I wish the bridges pulled down and the gardens torn up. You may plant explosive charges to assist you.'

Gordon swallowed. 'Yes, my lord.'

'With respect, my lord,' James said. 'You are surely not serious.'

'I was never more serious in my life. We'll teach these heathens that they cannot mistreat civilised Englishmen!' Elgin pointed at him. 'I know you, James Barrington. These people are your friends. Do you suppose I am not aware that you alone of all my delegation was not ill-treated by these beasts? But this pernicious Dynasty will be punished. I am being generous, sir. I threatened to burn Peking if my envoys were harmed. Now we do know that they were harmed most grievously. Should I not then burn Peking? But I am aware of the difference between the Chinese and the Manchu. It is the Manchu against whom we are waging war, not the Chinese. To burn Peking would be to destroy the homes of many thousands of innocent Chinese. This place, this Yuan Ming Yuan, is the creation of the Ch'ing. It is their proudest creation. Therefore its destruction will strike at the Ch'ing, and the Ch'ing alone.'

'They will hate you for it, forever,' James said.

'They are welcome to do so if they choose. Captain Gordon, you have heard my orders. I wish all those palaces in flames by dawn.'

Gordon saluted and withdrew.

'Well, my lord,' Hope Grant said, 'if these palaces and their contents are to be consumed by tomorrow morning, might not the men be given a chance for an hour or two?'

'Indeed, General, I can think of no reason why your men should not be allowed a little freedom of action. But discipline must be maintained.'

James watched helplessly as the soldiers broke ranks to rush into the palace grounds. Amongst them, he was disgusted to see, were even men wearing the dog-collars of regimental padres.

He moved away from the men to seat himself on a hummock and look down at the buildings. It was difficult to understand the reasoning which could destroy such irreplaceable works of art out of sheer revenge. Great Britain prided itself on its civilisation. He had read of the Great Exhibition held at the Crystal Palace in London in 1851, which had represented the apogee of British achievement. But no British achievement had ever even approached the beauty and splendour of the Summer Palace ... Yet the whim of one man, who doubtless considered himself a civilised Englishman, was now going to destroy it forever.

It grew dark, but there was a moon. Lights flared everywhere in the palaces and it occurred to James that Captain Gordon might be saved his dismal task ... But his men were down there, tearing down drapes and soaking them in spirits so they would burn more easily, and planting mines ...

James dozed, and awoke to a series of sharp explosions. He realised that it was dawn. Gazing down the hill, he saw trees and shrubs everywhere rise into the air, then settle again in clouds of dust. Almost simultaneously the great palaces burst into flames.

He heard the crunch of boots nearby. It was Gordon himself, looking exhausted. 'Barrington, is it? Camp not to your liking?'

'I've never been inside the Yuan Ming Yuan, but my stepfather has told me of it. Are you pleased with what you have done?'

'If you mean, do I suppose my dispositions will be successful, yes.'

'But you do not look forward to the result.'

'I am a soldier, Barrington.' Gordon sat down. 'I carry out

orders. The results of those orders are the burdens borne by my superiors.'

'But you are surely allowed to express an opinion in private?'

Gordon smiled. 'If it will make you feel any better, I share your dismay.'

'It does make me feel better.'

'I have not been in China long,' Gordon said thoughtfully. 'But from what I read before ever coming here, and from what I have seen since my arrival, and the people I have met, I would say this is a nation from which we could learn a great deal. And as we are not prepared to do so, we have no business in this land. God knows I am a good Christian, and can think of nothing better than to have the whole world as myself. But to attempt to impose Christianity where it is not wanted, and to promote our version of civilisation at the point of a gun, is unworthy of our nation. Instead of waging war in pursuit of a few trading ports or absurd differences of protocol, we should surely be restoring the wealth of this land by helping the government put an end to the T'ai-P'ing. I often wonder if those who sit at Westminster, and whose greatest danger is of losing their seat in the next election, ever truly understand the problems ensuing from those actions they so carelessly decree.' He gave a charming smile. 'You must now forget I said those things, Mr Barrington.'

16

THE GIRL WHO WOULD BE QUEEN

Like a long, weary, frightened snake, the entourage of the Son of Heaven wound its way over the roadway towards the Great Wall, now clearly visible in the distance. No Chinese emperor had ever before abandoned his throne by way of the Great Wall, Lan Kuei thought bitterly. That had been their entrance gateway to power, not an exit to exile and disgrace. The weather was at least still dry and reasonably warm, although autumnal clouds were beginning to gather. On the other hand, the absence of rain meant that the caravan sent up huge clouds of dust, which hung on the still air and then settled everywhere, penetrating everything, affecting every mouthful of food.

A regiment of Tatar cavalry preceded the caravan, despatching patrols to either side as well as ahead, to make sure no enemies lurked in waiting for the Emperor. Behind them proceeded a regiment of Bannermen on foot, flags drooping, and heads, too. This was not a task they had ever expected.

Following the Bannermen marched the household eunuchs, carrying the imperial regalia and the sacred dishes and whatever items of furniture and jewellery the Hsien-feng regarded as indispensable. The library, Lan Kuei noted, had been abandoned to the barbarians. Then came the Emperor himself, carried in the imperial yellow palanquin, curtains drawn to conceal him from vulgar gaze. Beside the palanquin walked Prince Hui and his half-brother; they were not prepared to let the Hsien-feng out of their sight.

Behind the Emperor, in another palanquin, followed the Empress; and with her was young Prince Tsai-ch'un. In the next palanquin sat Princess Jung-an and her mother, and there were litters too for the other senior concubines. To each side of the palanquins marched lines of eunuchs. Behind the litters came several wagons carrying the necessary tents, linen, food and drink, cooking utensils, as well as golden eating utensils for

when the caravan camped for the night. And behind the mule-
drawn wagons followed the rest of the concubines and domestic
eunuchs. These women walked, the thick dust coating their
jewelled shoes and elaborate robes and head-dresses, forever
trying to avoid the dung which littered the road.

Lan Kuei walked to the very rear of them. She did not wish
to mix with the others. She had hoped to find Chang Tsin in the
procession, but after their first day on the march was forced to
accept that he had either remained behind in the Summer
Palace or simply run away.

Behind her came the remaining supply wagons, and then, at
a suitable distance, all the ordinary servants and eunuchs who
had tagged on to the caravan. And at the very rear came
another regiment of Bannermen, inclined to look fearfully over
their shoulders, as if expecting at any moment the crack of
British and French muskets.

*

On the first day the great caravan proceeded in a reasonably
orderly fashion, and at a good speed, for many were terrified.
On the second day discipline began to disintegrate, and
progress slowed. On the third day, as the Great Wall itself
become clearly visible, orderliness disappeared altogether. The
Tatar horsemen galloped off and came back, galloped off again
– and came back again. The Bannermen straggled and cursed
and swore. The Emperor proceeded placidly on his way as if
this was indeed just another expedition to go hunting in
Jehol. The Bannermen of the rearguard closed up on the
milling mob in front of them, and soon were marching alongside the throng of concubines, who stared at them in wonderment.

Lan Kuei ignored them all – wrapped up in her own dark
thoughts. She had been robbed of her child, and her position.
Why had she not made her escape during the confusion of
leaving the Yuan Ming Yuan? No one would have sent after
her. She could have made her way back to Peking, and perhaps
found that wretch Chang Tsin who had so shamelessly deserted
her. She might have died at the hands of the barbarians, but
would that not be preferable to this weary, humiliating march, a
rejected concubine? Yet she was still a mother and, as Prince

Kung had advised her, no one could take that away from her as long as her son still lived. And that son was only a short distance ahead ...

There commenced a great deal of noise in front of them. One of the imperial supply wagons had caught its wheels in a dip and had fallen on its side. Women screamed, dogs barked. Bannermen came hurrying up, their officers shouting orders as the wagon was slowly hauled erect and a new wheel fitted. The women sat down, glad of the rest. But Lan Kuei remained standing, watching the men work, and gazing, too, at the Great Wall looming before them. It was only a few miles away. And then she noticed one of the Banner officers staring at her. He was young, and strong, and handsome, and very tall for a Manchu.

Jung-lu!

Lan Kuei's heart pounded. He did not appear to have changed much since she had last seen him, except to bulk out with mature strength. But *she* had changed, she knew: eight years ago she had been only a girl.

They did not speak. Jung-lu soon went back to his duties; the supply wagon was repaired, and the procession resumed its progress. But he had seen her – and the story of her disgrace must have travelled the length of the caravan.

What would she do, if he came looking for her? Even if the strict discipline of the Forbidden City had clearly broken down, it would still be a capital offence for any man to approach an imperial concubine – or even for that concubine to speak with him. But suddenly she desired that more than anything else in the world.

*

Camp for that night was pitched in the very shadow of the Great Wall, after the entire caravan had passed through its gate. This was then closed, and a guard of Bannermen mounted over it. Everyone felt much safer to have the wall between them and the barbarians, even if there was still no sign of any pursuit. Tents were erected for the concubines; they were to sleep in groups of four, their eunuchs bivouacking outside. As they ate their evening meal, they watched the sun, huge and round and red, dipping into the mountains to the west. After eating they were escorted to the newly dug latrines by their eunuchs. It was quite dark now, and Lan Kuei found it easy to slip away; she no longer had a personal eunuch, and no one was keeping a close watch on her.

She moved away from the encampment perhaps a hundred yards, and sat down on a slight hummock, looking back towards the flickering lights of the campfires. Out here the air was clean instead of foetid, and the camp noises were muted. Out here Jung-lu, if he desired it, might find her. It grew chilly as the heat dissipated. Lan Kuei's clothes, which had clung so warmly during the day, were not adequate for sitting on a hillside by night. She had almost decided to abandon her vigil and return to the warmth of her tent, when she heard a male voice.

'Is the Honourable Person troubled?' Jung-lu asked.

'I am no longer an Honourable Person. Did you not know?'

'You will always be an Honourable Person to me.'

Lan Kuei's heart began to pound. 'I came out here to wait for you,' she said boldly. 'Will you not lend me your cloak? I am cold.' He stooped and wrapped his cloak round her shoulders. 'Now sit beside me,' she commanded. 'You have heard of my disgrace? I begged the Emperor to stand and fight, but he would not do so.'

'I have heard so.' They sat in silence for a minute, then Jung-lu said, 'Would you flee this caravan?'

'Where could a woman go alone?'

'I would accompany you, Honourable Person.'

Lan Kuei had never felt so excited. 'Where would we go?'

'To the ends of the earth, if need be.'

'Would you really become an outlaw for me?'

'I have never dreamed of any woman but you.'

If they left now, by dawn they would be far beyond the reach of any pursuers. They could ride west, to where the sun set, and she would be free ... But she would never be free. She was a mother. One day her son would be Emperor. And one day soon, in view of the Hsien-feng's health. 'I cannot leave my son.' Jung-lu bowed his head. 'Had I no son, I would come with you,' she continued.

Jung-lu raised his head again.

'You have already committed a crime,' Lan Kuei reminded him, 'by being here with me at all.'

*

She realised she had never known a proper man. The Hsien-feng had been an exhausted invalid when she had first gone to his bed, and had deteriorated ever since. Here was strength, and vigour, and experience. He took her on to his lap, wrapping his cloak round them both for warmth. They removed only their pantaloons, but his hands searched inside her blouse to massage the velvet of her breasts. She kissed him, and then taught him to do the same to her. She loved, with all the passion that was a part of her nature, but which had been suppressed and distorted for so long. And she felt certain he loved her back. He had to, since she had placed her life in his keeping.

'What would you do?' he asked, as the first fingers of dawn stole across the plain.

'Look for me again tomorrow night,' she told him.

Undoubtedly the eunuchs knew she had slept away from the encampment, but they did not know that she had met someone. And as there was no time for dalliance on the march, there was no way they could find out. They decided to ignore her: she was a nothing now.

But she was happy. The march was no longer a purgatory. Even the exhausting days were enjoyable, because they preceded even more exhausting nights. Lan Kuei soon realised she had fallen in love. But more than that, in her own way she was avenging herself upon the imperial court.

Three nights later they were a march away from Jehol. 'Will I see you again?' Jung-lu asked.

'I do not know when, but you *will* see me again.'

*

Once the imperial caravan was safely in the Jehol palace, the old routine was resumed, as well as the old segregation. In her new disgraced situation, Lan Kuei was given only a tiny two-room apartment, with a single eunuch named Lo Yu. He did not attract her in the least, nor did she dare risk suborning him, so her clandestine meetings with Jung-lu had to cease. But she felt sure she had gained a faithful ally, although how Jung-lu's services might eventually be used she had not yet determined. She continued to be ignored by the Emperor, whose health had

suffered further during the journey north. To Lan Kuei's pleasure, however, Niuhuru sent for her a few days after their
arrival. The Empress had certainly not been put out by the
rigours of the journey; she was as placid and pleasant as ever.

'It grieves me to learn of your misfortune, Lan Kuei,' she
said. 'You were the only one who seemed truly to make our
lord happy. It is a pity you angered him.'

'I spoke as I thought best for the Dynasty.'

'That is man's work,' Niuhuru reproved her. 'We women
have greater responsibilities. Would you like to see your son?'

Tsai-ch'un seemed pleased to see her; he appeared well
looked after, and his health had improved – but she suspected
he had not missed her in the least.

'I think the mountain air is good for him,' Niuhuru
remarked. 'Let us pray that it will also be good for our lord.'

*

Even more reassuring than the knowledge that Niuhuru
remained her friend was the arrival of a letter from Prince
Kung, brought to her by Te An-wah, who eyed her suspiciously
as she opened it. 'I am not going to read it to you, Te An-wah,'
she said. 'So you may as well take yourself off.'

He bowed and left, no doubt to report to his masters. Kung
wrote:

> You will not forget that I asked you to communicate with me
> in order that I can know what is happening. I am certain that
> only from your pen will I learn the true condition of my
> brother. The situation here is as grave as we feared it would
> be. The British have burned the Summer Palace. It is utterly
> destroyed. I was powerless to prevent this. Indeed, I feared
> for Peking itself, but we have been spared this ultimate
> disaster.
>
> Yet Elgin has brought disaster enough upon us. The
> indemnity he demands is eight million taels, as well as the
> cession of the mainland opposite their naval base of Hong
> Kong. He has reiterated the barbarian demands for an
> embassy in Peking, without due respect being paid to the
> Emperor. Sadly, I had no choice but to agree to these exac-
> tions, for I had no force with which to resist the barbarian

soldiers. I am writing separately to the Emperor conveying the sad news and begging him to confirm my actions. On a happier note, the barbarians are withdrawing to the coast. Elgin has announced his intention of leaving a fortified post outside Tientsin, and I understand he has already dismantled the forts at Taku. The barbarian fleet remains at anchor in the Gulf of Chih-li. May a mighty storm destroy it.

It is now my task to restore order in Peking. This will be less difficult than might be supposed. The barbarian exactions have angered the people, and they are filled with a determination to regain our strength and avenge our wrongs. Should the opportunity present itself, impress these facts upon my brother. And reply to me, telling me of the position of my uncles. I am aware of the difficulties you may encounter in doing so. Write as you must, and rely upon me to understand what you have said. Burn this letter before anyone can see it.

I Tsin.

Lan Kuei gazed at the letter for several seconds. The Yuan Ming Yuan destroyed? Who could be so uncaring of beauty as to commit such a crime? Barbarians! She would hate them forever. She would destroy them one day. She would watch *them* burn. Her entire small body was convulsed with fury and outrage. Then she remembered the Prince's instructions, and held the paper to a candle, watched it turn to ashes. For all her anger, she felt tremendously exhilarated. Now she had two friends, one powerful of arm and muscle, the other powerful in his position. As brother of the Emperor, I Tsin Prince Kung could never hope to aspire to the Throne of Heaven itself, but, as the most capable of his generation of princes, he would obviously be a great influence on that throne for years – once his uncle could be removed from power. And he had chosen her as his confidante!

She had burned the letter just in time. Te An-wah returned within a few moments.

'The Emperor commands your presence,' he said.

*

Lan Kuei was given no time to prepare herself before being

hurried along the corridors to the imperial apartment. Here she discovered not only the Hsien-feng, but Prince Hui and Su-shun as well. The Hsien-feng lay in a deep chair. His left leg was extended on a stool, and even through his robes it could be seen to be grotesquely swollen. His shoe was tied on to his foot as it could not contain his toes. His face was mottled, and he breathed noisily. Much of the time his eyes remained shut. A eunuch stood by his head, fanning him constantly. It was impossible to believe he was only twenty-nine years old.

'Your letter bore the seal of my brother.' His voice was hardly more than a whisper.

'What business has Prince Kung writing to one of His Majesty's concubines?' Prince Hui interjected.

'The Prince was in serious error,' Su-shun added. 'Now repeat to His Majesty what the Prince wrote to you.'

'The Prince said that he had written at the same time to His Majesty.' Lan Kuei spoke loudly, because she harboured new suspicions.

Correctly, it seemed. The Hsien-feng's eyes opened. 'My brother has written to me?'

Prince Hui and Su-shun exchanged glances. They might utterly dominate this sick young man – but he remained the Emperor, who could command their deaths with a wave of his hand.

'The letter contained ill news, Your Majesty,' Prince Hui said.

'What did he say?' The Hsien-feng sat up and stared at Lan Kuei. 'Tell me what he said.'

'He told me that the barbarians had burned the Summer Palace, my lord.'

The mottling of the Hsien-feng's face seemed to deepen as he turned to his uncle. 'Is this true?'

'It has been utterly destroyed,' Lan Kuei said.

'The Yuan Ming Yuan destroyed?' His voice rose an octave, and he began pounding his breast. Flecks of foam appeared on his lips as he shouted again and again, 'The Yuan Ming Yuan destroyed!'

The Emperor appeared to be having a fit. Lan Kuei glanced at the two princes.

'This is your doing,' they hissed.

'I spoke only the truth,' she retorted.

The Hsien-feng's anguish slowly subsided. He lay back in his chair, gasping for breath.

'Prince Kung also wrote that the barbarians are demanding an indemnity of eight million taels, and the opening of several more treaty ports, and the cession of the land opposite Hong Kong. Also the right to maintain an embassy in Peking, with access to Your Majesty without the kowtow. Prince Kung wrote that he felt forced to agree to these demands, for fear that Peking also would be destroyed. He begs Your Majesty to ratify his decision.'

The silence was broken only by the sound of the Emperor's breathing. At last he asked, 'Did you know of these things, Uncle?'

'Prince Kung is but a boy,' Prince Hui said. 'He should not have been left to handle such responsibilities.'

That was a mistake. The Hsien-feng sat up again, eyes wide, finger pointing.

'Yes. He should not have been left to such responsibilities. I should have been there.'

'Your Majesty's health ...' Su-shun began.

'It cannot be improved while such vital information is kept from me.' The Emperor turned to Lan Kuei. 'Where is my brother's letter?'

'It is destroyed, Your Majesty. That was Prince Kung's wish.'

The Hsien-feng gave a sigh, and fell back into his chair.

'What would you have done with her?' Prince Hui asked, trying to regain the advantage.

'We would send her the silken cord, Majesty,' Su-shun said. 'Although she richly deserves beheading.'

Lan Kuei stood straight, watching the Emperor. Had she again pressed too hard – and for the last time?

'The Honourable Person will not be punished,' the Emperor said. Lan Kuei could not control her gasp of relief. 'She has suffered enough unjustly. She was right; she advised me to remain with my people. You were wrong, Uncle.'

The hiss of anger through Hui's nostrils was audible.

'I restore you to your rank, Lan Kuei,' the Hsien-feng said. 'I thank you for telling me the truth.'

Lan Kuei hesitated. 'Am I allowed to reply to Prince Kung, Your Majesty?'

'This is unheard of, my lord,' Su-shun protested. 'An Honourable Person communicating with a man?'

'With my brother,' the Hsien-feng said sharply.

'Yes, Lan Kuei, you may reply to my brother. Bring me what you write. And also his reply.'

Lan Kuei bowed low, and backed from the room. The princes glared after her, tigers balked of their prey. *But one day*, she thought, as she met their eyes, *perhaps you will be the prey, and I the tigress.*

*

She wrote:

My lord Prince, I thank you for your letter. I related its contents to His Majesty, and he was sorely grieved, although grateful for your efforts on his behalf. His Majesty is sadly unwell. It is with great difficulty that we have restrained him from mounting his horse and returning to be at your side. This he will do as soon as he is restored to health.

His Majesty is greatly sustained by the constant presence of your uncle, Prince Hui, and of Prince Su-shun. The noble princes encourage him in every way, and relieve him of all possible burdens. His Majesty gives you gracious permission to write to me again, if it pleases you to do so.

Lan Kuei.

When she read this to the Emperor, in the presence of the princes, even Su-shun looked pleased. But Kung would know what she meant.

*

It was time to look to the future. Lan Kuei visited Niuhuru. 'I am very pleased that you have been restored in rank, Lan Kuei,' the Empress said. 'I had felt you suffered an injustice. Has he sent you the tablet?' Her voice was wistful.

Lan Kuei sat beside her, very close. 'I do not think His Majesty will ever use the jade tablet again,' she whispered. Niuhuru's head turned, sharply. 'Have you not visited the Emperor recently?' Lan Kuei asked.

'No,' Niuhuru said. 'He never sends for me, either.'

Lan Kuei drew a breath. 'I think His Majesty is dying.' Even to suggest such a thing was treason; and Niuhuru's eyes opened very wide. 'He cannot move one of his legs,' Lan Kuei told her. 'He breathes with difficulty. There is no physician attending to his needs. I am very afraid for him.'

Niuhuru had no guile in her nature. 'If His Majesty dies, your son will become Son of Heaven.'

'Only if he is named,' Lan Kuei pointed out. Primogeniture was not the law amongst the Manchu. It was the custom, certainly; few fathers would set aside their own eldest surviving son. But there were many precedents when a son had been replaced by an uncle, or the son of a dead uncle – it could not be the son of a living relative, as by Confucian law no father could kowtow to his own son; and by custom it was never one of the reigning monarch's own brothers. 'Prince Tsai-ch'un must be named, before our lord mounts the Heavenly Chariot.'

'But how is this to be done?' Niuhuru asked.

'You must insist upon visiting the Emperor, and discuss this important matter with him.'

Niuhuru looked apprehensive. She well understood that for anyone to approach the Emperor and tell him he was dying could involve the charge of treason ... but presumably it was permissable for a wife to inquire after her husband's health, and to suggest that one or two future plans be made.

'If you do not,' Lan Kuei went on, 'our own lives will be in jeopardy. Can you imagine our fate if Prince Hui should become Emperor? Or even if he be named regent for my son?'

'Yes,' Niuhuru said. 'You are right. I will speak with the Emperor.'

Lan Kuei gave a sigh of relief.

*

How she longed for the arms of Jung-lu. He had been appointed colonel of the palace guard, and from time to time, looking down from the window of the spacious apartment she had been allotted since the restoration of her rank, she even saw him. Clearly he knew she was there, for he often enough would glance up at the window, to her great re-assurance. Because of one thing she was certain: whatever arrangements Niuhuru managed to make with the Emperor on their behalf, his death was going to provoke a crisis which could only be resolved by force.

*

After her visit to the Emperor, Niuhuru was in tears. 'He is so ill,' she moaned. 'Oh, he is so ill.'

'Have you talked with him about the succession?'

'I cannot. Not while he is in such agony. Oh, it breaks my heart to see him so.'

Lan Kuei realised that, unlikely as it seemed, Niuhuru was genuinely fond of her husband. But the Empress was well on the way to making her lose her temper. 'His Majesty's health is not going to improve,' she insisted. 'You must speak with him now, or it will be too late.'

'I cannot,' Niuhuru moaned. 'Oh, I cannot.'

Lan Kuei left Niuhuru's apartment, grinding her teeth in frustration and anger. And fear. The Hsien-feng might die at any moment ... and Hui and Su-shun never left his chamber. Who could tell who they were putting forward as successor?

And there was nothing else she could do. Even as an Honourable Person, she had no access to the Emperor unless he sent for her. And he had not; since the onset of winter had meant there were no more letters from Prince Kung. Until spring came, Niuhuru was her only hope. But what a feeble hope.

*

Ward wrote:

My Dear Miss Joanna,

This is my first opportunity to thank you for your aid in securing me an interview with Lan Kuei. I had not envisaged being able to approach so near the Throne of Heaven, but in the event it turned out most successfully, as I have received my commission, and have now been accepted by General Li Hung-chang. Thus I am most busy recruiting and drilling. It is hard work, but I have no doubt will be rewarding in the end. I wish you could see my fellows presenting arms! I sometimes find it difficult to believe that I am here, only a few miles outside Shanghai, and you are there within the city, yet we are as separated as if I were on the moon.

I have heard that those envoys who survived the Manchu imprisonment have been released, and that your brother is amongst them. I know this must be a great relief to you. I cannot say what the future holds for me, but I wish you to know that meeting you has been one of the greatest pleasures in my life, and one I will always treasure.

Frederick Ward.

Joanna lowered the letter. Her whole body seemed to glow. After such a letter, perhaps when he returned . . .

*

Two weeks later, James Barrington came home. His family naturally gave him a rapturous welcome. They could tell that he was deeply affected by what he had experienced, although he would not speak of it. With him was Chang Tsin, now proud to be his old friend's servant.

'But what of your mistress, Lan Kuei?' Joanna asked.

'Lan Kuei is disgraced, Miss Joanna. We shall never again hear her name.'

'And you promptly deserted her, you wretch.'

Chang Tsin bowed. 'A servant must go where his destiny takes him. And am I not happy to be working for the House of Barrington?'

It was impossible to stay angry long with Chang Tsin.

*

Joanna showed James her letter from Ward. She felt she had to share it with someone, and what Chang Tsin had said now caused her worry.

'You don't think that, if Lan Kuei has really fallen from power, Mr Ward's commission will be revoked?' she asked anxiously.

'Do you have any idea of the risk you took in becoming involved with him?'

'He is the bravest man I have ever met,' Joanna declared. 'And I asked you a question.'

James raised his eyebrows; his sister was not usually so vehement. 'I doubt anyone at court, save Lan Kuei, even knows that he received a commission. So he's actually raising an army. I think I will just go out there.'

'What for?' Joanna was instantly suspicious.

'If he really is forming a volunteer army, I might just offer to give him a hand.'

'You?' Joanna could not believe her ears.

James gave a wry grin. 'So I once ran away. This time I want to fight.'

'And avenge me? With Mr Ward?'

'Yes. But I also want to serve the Manchu in any way I can.' He went off to see his step-father, not doubting that he would concur with the idea; Martin himself had fought for the Dynasty. Only Lucy wept.

*

Winter settled on Jehol with an icy grip. The city had long been regarded as a summer residence; no Emperor had wintered there since Nurhachi had led the eight Banners across the Great Wall. Now the imperial court was entirely cut off from the south by a plain of thick snow; and when the spring thaws finally arrived, the whole countryside was flooded. Communication with Peking was lost, and Jehol seemed the very centre of the universe. This was a normal state of affairs: for most of the court the Forbidden City had been similarly cloistered from the outside world. But for Lan Kuei it was purgatory, and she had no means of corresponding with Prince Kung.

She had, however, at last made an intimate of Lo Yu. He was in thrall to her beauty and personality, and mindful of his hope that she would one day be Dowager Empress. As her creature, he would do anything for her. And as weary day succeeded weary day, with the rain beating down on the palace's pagoda roofs, Lan Kuei felt that he could be entrusted with her most guilty secret.

'I fear that the Emperor has not long to live,' she told him. 'And when he dies there will be those who seek to suborn the Throne of Heaven. This must be prevented.' Lo Yu's eyes gleamed with ardour. 'Thus we must be certain of the loyalty of the garrison. I knew Colonel Jung-lu when I was a girl, so I must meet with him again, and make him understand where his duty lies. You will tell him I wish to see him secretly.'

'Here, Honourable Person?' Lo Yu was every bit as alarmed as Chang Tsin had been when ordered to escort Frederick Ward into the Forbidden City.

'That would be too dangerous. We will meet in the Court of the Nightingales, tomorrow morning, one hour after midnight.'

*

It was a wet and windy night, but ideal for Lan Kuei's purpose. She had hardly slept, and was ready long before the appointed hour.

Lo Yu was intensely nervous. 'Honourable Person, should you be found out ...'

'We will all be decapitated. So you must remain here and announce to anyone who comes by that I am asleep and am not to be disturbed.' She then wrapped herself in her cloak, and stole through the empty corridors. Although there were eunuchs on duty all through the night, she knew precisely where they were stationed, and also that most of them slept when they were supposed to be keeping watch.

She gained the garden without hindrance, and out in the teeming rain she knew she was safe. The wind plucked at her cloak as she hurried across the open spaces, hearing the branches of the trees swish back and forth above her head, till she reached the shelter of the Pavilion of the Nightingales. No birds were to be heard tonight above the rain. Inside the pavilion it was utterly dark. Lan Kuei stood in the doorway, accustoming her eyes to the gloom, and heard a movement.

'Jung-lu?' she whispered.

Then she was in his arms. Both of them were soaked to the skin, and water ran from their hair to mingle with their kisses.

'Your eunuch told me of some crisis,' Jung-lu said.

'Not yet. But I could not live another day without you.' There was no place in the pavilion to lie down, so they resorted to the Fragrant Bamboo – both standing.

Jung-lu slipped her pantaloons to the floor, and lifted her by her buttocks. She put her arms round his neck, and kicked off her pants altogether. She wrapped her legs round his thighs as he entered her. She yearned at the delicious sensation as he surged inside her.

'I adore you,' he murmured. 'I wish only to die for you.'

She waited for the last gasp of his climax, then slid down his legs to the ground.

'I would rather have you live for me,' she said.

*

After that night they met regularly, although, as the weather slowly improved, greater caution became necessary. Now Lan Kuei actually wanted the Hsien-feng to die – the very moment he had acknowledged Tsai-ch'un as his heir. But Niuhuru appeared to be making no progress. Indeed Prince Hui had forbidden the Empress to visit her husband, claiming it made him feel uncomfortable; and Niuhuru was not the woman to assert herself. Lan Kuei alternated between the ecstasy of Jung-lu's arms and dark despair for the future. Even when the roads at last opened, and a letter arrived from Prince Kung reassuring her of his support, she could feel no more confident. When she hurried with it to the Emperor, she was not allowed in to see him – instead the letter was taken by Su-shun. She was again totally isolated. If only she could regain Peking, Kung's support might count for something. But the Emperor was clearly too ill to travel.

*

In June came a crushing reminder of the insecurity of her position, when the Hsien-feng celebrated his thirtieth birthday. A great reception was held, the Emperor even managing to leave his bed for an hour to attend. Niuhuru was allowed to preside over the festivities – but Lan Kuei was not invited. She could only comfort herself by dashing off another letter to Kung, complaining of the way she, the mother of the heir to the Throne, was insulted and ignored.

'It is all Su-shun's doing,' she wrote. 'That man hates me. Well, I hate him, too. I hope I live to see his head roll in the dust.' But she knew it was equally possible that Su-shun would watch her own being kicked around the streets by small boys.

*

Cold in winter, Jehol was all but unbearable in the August heat, and, with the long hours of daylight, Lan Kuei's meetings with Jung-lu had to cease. She had never anticipated remaining in this remote place for a year. And now that year was nearly complete, she seemed as precariously placed as ever.

Even more so than she realised. One morning she lay in the

bath as usual, attended by Lo Yu, when one of Niuhuru's ladies rushed into her apartment. 'Honourable Person!' she gasped.

'Whatever is up?' Lan Kuei scrambled from the tub and Lo Yu hastily wrapped her in a towel. 'The Prince! Is he all right?'

'The Prince is well, Honourable Person. But the Empress has sent me to tell you that the Emperor is near death.'

Still wrapped only in the towel, Lan Kuei hurried from her apartment and along the corridors towards Niuhuru's. It was the middle of the morning, and the palace was busy. Women and eunuchs stopped to stare. Lan Kuei threw open Niuhuru's outer door, and ran into the bedchamber. The Empress was sitting in a chair, tears rolling down her face.

'Is it true?' Lan Kuei demanded.

Niuhuru nodded. 'They say he will not last the day.'

'Have you spoken with him?'

'How could I? He is so ill. He is in so much pain!'

Lan Kuei wanted to scream in sheer desperation. But now was no time for hysterics. Her head was already precarious upon her shoulders, so what did she have to lose? She sped for the nursery.

Tsai-ch'un sat on the floor playing with his toy soldiers, and attended only by two nursemaids. He was now four years old, but looked younger.

'Mama!' he cried, pleased to see her.

'Come with me,' Lan Kuei urged him. The nurses protested, but Lan Kuei gathered up the child in her arms.

'What are you doing?' Niuhuru cried, entering the room behind her.

'I am going to see the Emperor. Will you accompany me?'

Niuhuru stared at her in consternation, but Lan Kuei was already hastening from the apartment, on her way towards the imperial bedchamber, Tsai-ch'un clutched in her arms.

There were eunuchs at the door. 'You cannot enter, Honourable Person.'

'Would you try to prevent the Emperor from seeing his only son for the last time?' Lan Kuei demanded.

The eunuchs hesitated, then opened the doors. Lan Kuei went inside, pausing only to assess the situation. Prince Hui stood by the bed; Su-shun was on the far side of the room. There were several councillors and eunuchs in attendance.

All turned to stare at the intruder, and Su-shun said, 'Now

she has gone too far. Seize that woman.'

The eunuchs moved forward – and Lan Kuei held up the Prince. 'Would you dare lay hands upon your future emperor?'

They hesitated, and she was past them. When Prince Hui endeavoured to intercept her, she skipped round him and reached the bedside, kneeling to gaze up at the Emperor himself.

'What is that noise?' the Hsien-feng whispered.

'An intruder, Majesty . . .' Su-shun was at her shoulder.

'It is your son, lord,' Lan Kuei said.

The Hsien-feng's eyes opened; he looked at her, rather than the child. 'Little Orchid. It is good to see you.'

'She came here unbidden,' Prince Hui protested, and then was quiet as the Hsien-feng's hand moved to touch Lan Kuei's bare arm.

'I have brought your son,' Lan Kuei repeated. The Hsien-feng touched the boy in turn. 'He has never been named as your heir, lord. Will you not do so now?'

'Majesty,' Prince Hui intervened, 'now is not the time . . .'

'Of course he is my heir,' the Hsien-feng said weakly. 'My son shall be the next emperor. I name him so now.'

The room fell silent. Lan Kuei gazed up at Prince Hui, who stood glaring at her, on the other side of the bed. She knew Su-shun stood immediately behind her, but she did not dare turn her head. Prince Hui attempted to regain control.

'Of course Prince Tsai-ch'un shall be the next emperor, Majesty, but should dread misfortune overtake this land, and Your Majesty not fulfil his allotted span, the Prince would still be a babe. It would be necessary to name a regent.'

Lan Kuei caught her breath; she had not anticipated the old man retaliating so quickly.

The Hsien-feng almost smiled. 'You are too polite, Uncle, to pretend that we will see another dawn. Yes, I will name you regent. You may form your own council.'

Lan Kuei's jaw sagged – while Prince Hui smiled. To have gained so much, and have it all dashed away.

'And what is to become of us, my lord husband?' asked Niuhuru. No one had heard her enter the room. They gaped at her as she approached the bed.

'You will have to mourn me, Niuhuru,' the Hsien-feng said.

'You know I will do that, my lord. But I fear that I will also have to mourn the death of the Dynasty.' She knelt beside the bed. 'Can you truly leave the fate of this boy and his mother, even of myself, to the whims of Prince Hui?'

'Majesty,' Prince Hui protested, 'am I not the most loyal of your subjects?'

'You are indeed loyal, Uncle – but to what, I have never been certain. I think the Lady Niuhuru speaks some truth.'

Lan Kuei looked from face to face, scarce daring to breathe. If she wanted to hug Niuhuru for her intervention, she still did not know how it was going to save her. Prince Hui had been named regent.

'It is my decision,' the Hsien-feng, continued, 'that upon my death the Empress Niuhuru will be named Dowager Empress, with the title of Tz'u-an. I further decree that the Honourable Person Lan Kuei will be named second Dowager Empress, with the title Tz'u-hsi.'

Breath hissed through Lan Kuei's nostrils. She was to be Dowager Empress! Prince Hui remained Regent, with powers of life and death. He looked contented enough.

But the Hsien-feng was still speaking. 'It is my further decision that both Dowager Empresses will sit on the Council of Regency, and that all decrees from the Council, in order to be effective, must bear the signature of the Dowager Empress Tz'u-an at the top.'

Su-shun clenched his fists in anger.

'And,' the Hsien-feng went on, 'the signature of the Dowager Empress Tz'u-hsi must appear at the bottom. Let my words be recorded immediately.' Now at last he smiled, stroking Lan Kuei's bare shoulder again. 'I do not expect you to sign your own death warrant, Little Orchid.'

Lan Kuei wanted to burst into tears. It was a very long time since she had felt like doing so, except through frustrated anger. For all his apparent breakdown, the Hsien-feng had remained aware of what happened around him. More than that, he had retained his love for her.

'I shall not fail you, my lord,' she promised. Now she could look up at Prince Hui and smile.

That night, the Hsien-feng Emperor 'mounted the fairy chariot and returned to the nine sources'.

*

Niuhuru and Lan Kuei remained in prayer at the bedside of the dead Emperor for several hours, until the embalmers were ready to commence their work. Then they returned to their apartments.

'I will always be grateful to you, Niuhuru,' Lan Kuei sobbed.

'You had thought that I would never act,' came the gentle reply.

Lan Kuei smiled; they were of equal rank now. 'I had despaired, truly. But now ...' she knelt before her bewildered son, 'all is well, as long as we can keep an eye on Prince Hui and Su-shun. Where are those two now, do you suppose?'

Lo Yu supplied the answer. 'Prince Hui has convened a first meeting of the Council of Regency, Majesty.'

Lan Kuei had to reflect for a moment to realise that he was addressing her! 'Already? Why were we not informed? Come, Tz'u-an, we must attend this meeting.'

'Oh, Tz'u-hsi, I am in no mood for meetings. And it will make the old man very angry for us to appear.'

'That is what I intend,' Lan Kuei said firmly.

So she went to the meeting herself. The eunuchs on the door gave way to her imperious demand, and soon she stood at the foot of the long table, glaring at the eight men seated there. They looked back with apprehension.

'What is the meaning of this intrusion, Your Majesty?' inquired Prince Hui mildly.

'And what is the meaning of summoning a Regency Council without informing the Empress or myself?' Lan Kuei countered.

'Is it not unseemly,' Su-shun grumbled, 'for a young woman not yet thirty years of age to attend a Council?'

'You can do no formal business without me,' Lan Kuei retorted.

'We had supposed Your Majesty would be exhausted and overcome by grief,' Prince Hui said pointedly.

'I do indeed grieve,' Lan Kuei agreed. 'Yet I can never forget it is my duty to protect the interests of the new Emperor.' She looked around the table. 'You have selected the Council?'

'As I was instructed to do.'

'I am sure His Late Majesty did not mean you to exclude his own brothers. What of I Tsin, Prince Kung? Or I Huan, Prince Ch'un?'

'The princes are not here,' Prince Hui explained patiently. 'It was necessary to form the Council immediately; there is much to be done. The soothsayers must decide when it will be auspicious to remove the Late Emperor to Peking. We must also decide upon a Reign Name. These are urgent matters, Your Majesty.'

Lan Kuei nodded. 'Then let us attend to them.' She took her seat. 'I will convey our decision to Tz'u-an.'

*

The Council meetings in fact proceeded quite amicably. Though Niuhuru seldom appeared, Lan Kuei was always present. However, not even she could argue with the early decisions made, for soothsayers consulted their almanacs and announced it would be three months before the Late Emperor could be removed to Peking. This she found irritating, but no one could argue with the soothsayers. Lan Kuei had already written to Prince Kung, informing him of his brother's death and that she was now Dowager Empress. She could feel sure that at least the capital was in good hands.

Nor could she cavil at the Reign Name granted her son: he ascended the Throne of Heaven as T'ung-chih, with the additional title of Ch'i-hsiang – 'Well-Omened Happiness'. The Hsien-feng's posthumous title was Wen Tsung Hsien Huang-ti.

*

Then it was merely a matter of waiting for their departure date, which would not occur until November. She could only hope the weather did not break before then. Meanwhile, Lan Kuei could resume her liaison with Jung-lu. It had to remain clandestine, because she did not doubt Su-shun was having her watched, seeking any advantage. For all the apparent harmony of the Council meetings, she knew how much Hui and his brother hated her.

She wrote to Prince Kung regularly, more than ever seeking his support for when her showdown with his princely uncles came; and he replied with an equal regularity. Government business was virtually at a standstill, with the country in mourning and the Council of Regency many miles from the capital. Since not even the British and French could argue with age-old Chinese custom, the treaty Prince Kung had agreed with them thus remained unratified.

But it would have to be ratified sometime, and Lan Kuei recognised this. She would never forgive the foreign devils for looting and burning the Yuan Ming Yuan, but at the moment the Empire was helpless before the strength of the barbarians. Her mind was already ranging forward to the future. She even dreamed of creating a navy with which to defeat these greedy foreigners.

But first must come the defeat of the T'ai-P'ing. Nothing had been heard of Ward for a year, indeed since he had departed Peking with the Emperor's commission. He had either failed to raise this modern army of which he had boasted, or he had died or absconded. Clearly that venture had been a mistake.

Nothing was heard from Viceroy Tseng Kuo-fan or Marshal Li Hung-chang either. The Yangtse might as well have been a million miles away.

*

The Regent and his brother seemed to regard the T'ai-P'ing as an evil which would eventually go away of its own accord. But, then, they also held this attitude about the British. Feeling themselves safe in Manchuria, they were again full of martial ardour. The British and French had retreated; there were only a few ships in the Gulf of Chih-li, and a small garrison outside Tientsin. Perhaps the barbarians would grow tired and go home.

'And if they do not?' Lan Kuei demanded. 'What if they send another army against us? This time they may well burn Peking itself.'

'A mere girl seeking to tell men what to do,' Su-shun grumbled.

*

In the event the weather did not wait for them; the autumn rains began early.

'It will be a difficult journey to Peking,' Jung-lu commented, 'but I will be at your side, Tz'u-hsi.'

The thought of that made her feel more secure. But in fact her confidence grew with every day, as she increasingly dismissed her enemies as impotent old men. Obviously they must know of her relationship with Jung-lu, but obviously they were afraid to challenge it until their return to Peking, for Jung-lu commanded the only military force in Jehol. Indeed, they treated Jung-lu with exaggerated respect; when late in October news arrived that a caravan from the north had been attacked by bandits, Prince Hui himself approached Lan Kuei and asked if she would permit the colonel to lead the pursuit. Lan Kuei had no objections; the more military glory Jung-lu could attain before their return to Peking, the better.

'I shall return a week from now,' he promised her. 'In time to escort you to the south.'

She stood at her window to watch the Tatar cavalry ride out.

*

Three days later she attended another Council meeting. Niuhuru, as usual, was absent.

'The soothsayers have revised their opinion,' Prince Hui announced, smiling at her. 'They have declared it is best that the body of His Late Majesty leave for Peking tomorrow.'

'That is not possible,' Lan Kuei protested. 'It is not the date chosen.'

'No special date was chosen,' Su-shun pointed out. 'The soothsayers said we must wait three months.'

'And the three months have not elapsed.'

'It is very nearly three months,' Su-shun said. 'And the soothsayers have now named a date.'

'We cannot leave for Peking,' Lan Kuei insisted. 'More than half the imperial guard is absent with their commander.'

'What is there to fear?' Su-shun demanded. 'We needed a strong escort when we came from Peking, because of the barbarian threat. But the barbarians have now gone. The only bandits in the area are those being chastised by Colonel Jung-lu. It is only a week's journey to Peking. He can follow us on his return.'

Lan Kuei looked from face to face; did these men take her for a fool? 'I cannot agree to expose the Emperor to such a perilous journey until the return of the Guard.'

'The decision has been taken by the Council.'

'It lacks the signature of Tz'u-an and myself.'

'On the contrary, Tz'u-hsi. Your signatures are already appended.' He laid the document on the table. 'It was decided two months ago that the body of His Late Majesty would commence its journey to Peking on a date to be selected by the soothsayers. To this Tz'u-an and yourself agreed, and this paper contains both of your signatures. Now that the soothsayers have named that date, tomorrow, there is no need for any further decree.' He smiled. 'Or any further signatures.'

Lan Kuei hissed in anger as she realised that she had been outwitted by these 'impotent' old men. 'You have suborned the soothsayers,' she snapped.

'Accusations which imply dishonesty in a prince of the House of Ch'ing bring dishonour only upon the accuser,' Prince Hui said mildly. The other members of the Council nodded.

*

Lan Kuei hurried to Niuhuru's apartment. 'The Council claims that the soothsayers have decreed we must leave tomorrow.'

'Oh, that is good news,' Niuhuru said. 'This endless waiting has tried my nerves.'

'We must refuse to go.'

'How can we do that if the day has been named?'

'I do not believe a day has been named. I believe the soothsayers have been instructed what to say by Prince Hui.' Lan Kuei knelt beside Niuhuru's chair. 'Listen to me. The Regent intends our murder on the road. Without Jung-lu, without witnesses, anything can happen.'

'An imperial prince? I cannot believe that of him,' Niuhuru stated. 'You do not wish to leave without your lover, Jung-lu. I have heard rumours of that.'

'I am trying to save our lives,' Lan Kuei yelled. 'And the life of my son, the Emperor.'

'Now I know you are demented,' Niuhuru declared. 'Who would dare raise his hand against the Emperor? If the soothsayers have named a day, then that is the day we shall leave. The Emperor will accompany me.' She glared at Lan Kuei. 'You may remain here, if you wish, and await the return of your paramour.'

*

Lan Kuei faced perhaps the gravest crisis of her life. Like many placid people, Niuhuru could be enormously stubborn. And now she was angry as well, at the thought that her co-empress might be conducting a liaison. She was an utterly good woman, and for that reason a most dangerous one in their present situation. Yet Lan Kuei also understood that to allow the imperial entourage to return to Peking without her could dissipate all the credit she held at Court.

But she was surely going to her death – unless she acted very promptly. Hastily she returned to her own apartment, and summoned Lo Yu. 'I wish you to leave Jehol clandestinely, tonight, on horseback, and follow the imperial guard.' Lo Yu gulped. He was an old man. 'This is a matter of life and death,' Lan Kuei told him. 'For us all. When you catch up with Colonel Jung-lu, tell him I am forced to leave Jehol for Peking, without him. Tell him to abandon his pursuit of the bandits, and ride with all speed to my rescue. Tell him my life and the life of the Emperor are in danger.'

Lo Yu looked terrified. 'But suppose I encounter the bandits before I reach him?'

'Do your best. The future of the Dynasty is in your hands.'

*

With a blowing of bugles and clashing of cymbals, the funeral cortège of the Hsien-feng Emperor left Jehol. As all the cavalry had accompanied Jung-lu north, the advance guard was composed of Bannermen marching on foot – there were only a hundred of them. Then came the wagon which carried the coffin containing the embalmed body of the Emperor. It was surrounded by his personal eunuchs, headed by Te An-wah.

Next came the palanquin bearing the new Emperor, the T'ung-chih. And behind the Emperor came the Dowager Empresses. Out of respect for the dead monarch they marched on foot, despite the dreadful sludgy mess into which the road had been turned by the rain. Behind them, six-year-old Princess Jung-an was, like her brother, carried in a litter. Behind the two Empresses and the Prince and Princess followed their eunuchs, and then the late Emperor's concubines. Behind the concubines came the supply wagons, and then the Court, amongst them the Council of Regency led by Prince Hui and Su-shun. Behind them rolled the remainder of the supply wagons. And at the very rear marched another contingent of Bannermen, numbering less than half of those who had made the journey north. Lan Kuei found most sinister the fact that the princes did not march alongside their great-nephew.

It rained without ceasing, a continuous drizzle. The eunuchs held umbrellas over the heads of the Dowager Empresses and the Honourable Persons among the concubines, but these did not prevent the soaking of elaborate tunics and head-dresses while there was no way of saving pricelessly jewelled shoes from the mud. Whenever they stopped, Niuhuru, Lan Kuei and Jung-an changed their clothes, but within minutes they were soaking again. Only the T'ung-chih, in his palanquin, and his father, in his coffin, remained dry. The little boy seemed bewildered by the whole affair, and he wept throughout.

The procession had set off at daybreak, at eight in the morning; at noon the skies were no lighter, and the drizzle limited visibility to half a mile. Lan Kuei found herself peering into the mist, praying for a glimpse of Jung-lu, though Lo Yu had left only a few hours before.

*

Niuhuru had ceased speaking to her, and when they camped for the night they ate in silence. At least inside their tents they were dry, and the eunuchs had erected cots for them. But the T'ung-chih was not to be comforted; he alternately slept and wailed and sneezed. Lan Kuei could not have slept in any event. She lay awake and listened to the patter of rain on canvas. Oh, to have Jung-lu at her side now.

The second day was no better, and now things began to go really wrong. The advance guard kept disappearing into the mist, and having to be recalled by bugle blasts. The funeral wagon got bogged in a rut and had to be dug out, the body of the Late Emperor being jolted about in a most unseemly fashion. The T'ung-chih continued to wail.

Behind them the cortège travelled more and more slowly, and gaps began to appear between various segments of the procession. But Te An-wah kept urging the imperial eunuchs on, insisting they must keep up with the advance guard.

*

By the time the Empresses stopped for a midday meal, the remainder of the caravan was out of sight. Nor did anyone else appear during the break.

'It is my opinion that we should wait for them to catch up,' Lan Kuei broke the silence.

'We cannot delay in this weather, Tz'u-hsi,' Te An-wah said. 'We must get to Peking before the Son of Heaven takes ill. What are you afraid of?' He pointed at the Bannermen of the advance guard, who were grouped some fifty yards away.

Lan Kuei sighed, and they resumed their march. They now entered a series of valleys between low hills. Often they encountered streams rushing down the hillsides, which caused further delays. But Te An-wah's eunuchs, driving the mules which drew the wagon, continued to press on.

'We must slow down,' Lan Kuei begged again.

'What nonsense,' Niuhuru said. 'Do you intend to expose our dear son to this foul damp a moment longer than is necessary?'

'Her Majesty is right,' said Te An-wah. 'Tonight we will camp within the shadow of the Great Wall.'

Lan Kuei wanted to scream with frustration.

*

As the rain grew heavier than ever, all they could do was put one foot in front of the other, staring through the mist. Once again the advance guard disappeared. Then came a bifurcation in the road. Unhesitatingly, Te An-wah directed them to the left.

'It is to the right,' Lan Kuei protested.

'That is not so, Tz'u-hsi,' Te An-wah argued. 'I know this road.'

'I remember how we came up,' Lan Kuei insisted.

'We must follow the Bannermen,' Te An-wah said. 'They went to the left. You can see their tracks.'

There were certainly a great number of tracks, but they seemed to lead in both directions.

'I am sure Te An-wah knows the way,' Niuhuru said irritably. 'Let us get on.'

Once again Lan Kuei had to accept her decision. They had progressed for another hour, when she heard an unfamiliar noise. Looking left and right through the rain, she saw nothing. She then turned round and stared into the wall of mist behind them. They had recently entered a sodden defile between two hills, and there was nothing to be seen. The remainder of their entourage had simply vanished. Experiencing a sudden almost painful pang of alarm, she clutched Niuhuru's arm.

'We are lost!'

Niuhuru glared at her. 'Of course we are not lost.'

'Then where is the rest of our party?'

'They are hidden by the mist. They will be along any moment. Why, here they are now.' She pointed.

Through the mist Lan Kuei made out the shadowy shapes of horsemen. But there had been no horsemen travelling with the caravan.

*

For a glorious moment Lan Kuei thought these might be the men led by Jung-lu. But then she observed that they were not Bannermen. She swung round in the vain hope that she might see the advance guard nearby, but there could now be no doubt that they had taken the other road. She and Niuhuru were entirely alone save for the imperial corpse, the boy Emperor, the young Princess, and eleven eunuchs. As doubtless Prince Hui and Su-shun had planned.

'Who are these people?' Niuhuru demanded.

'Our executioners, as I warned you,' Lan Kuei said bitterly.

'You are demented ...' Niuhuru's voice faded as she watched some of the horsemen move to either side of the imperial party. The rest remained immediately behind. 'Where is our escort?'

The eunuchs leading the wagon mules stopped. Those carrying the young Emperor's palanquin set it on the ground. All looked inquiringly at Niuhuru, who seemed suddenly to realise their peril.

'What are we to do?' she wailed.

Lan Kuei went to stand immediately beside the T'ung-chih's

litter. She watched one of the bandits, clearly the leader, walk his horse away from the rest and dismount. He wore a heavy moustache, and was a well-built man, armed with sword and bow. His face was the hardest Lan Kuei had ever seen. When he looked at her, her knees felt weak.

He stood beside the wagon and gazed at the coffin of the dead Emperor. Then he came over to stare at Lan Kuei and Niuhuru, and smiled at the Princess Jung-an, who had stepped out of her litter. When he smiled, the feeling of weakness surged from Lan Kuei's legs to her stomach.

'Great ladies,' he said.

Niuhuru clutched fearfully at Lan Kuei's arm. But Lan Kuei determined that, if she were to die, she would remain defiant to the end.

'How dare you approach your Emperor thus?' she snapped. 'Down on your knees, and perform the kowtow.'

The man grinned again. 'Great ladies have much spirit.' By now several of his men had dismounted, and they hemmed in the two women. The T'ung-chih had been asleep, but now woke up, and drew aside the curtains of the palanquin. 'Who are these people?' he piped imperiously. 'Why do they not kneel?'

The chieftain gave a shout of laughter. 'He speaks well, indeed. Kneel before the Son of Heaven.'

The rest of the bandits now dismounted, and they all solemnly knelt. Niuhuru released Lan Kuei's arm.

The bandits stood up.

'Kill those creatures.' The chieftain pointed at the eunuchs.

'You cannot kill me,' Te An-wah protested. 'I serve Prince Hui. I am here by his instruction.'

Niuhuru gasped as she realised his treachery.

The chieftain continued to smile. 'Then it is best you die first,' he said. 'So that you can never also betray your Prince.'

The eunuchs screamed as they began to run. But the bandits were all around them. Swords flashed and blood spurted, as the bandits swiftly cut off their heads. Niuhuru made a strangled noise and collapsed against the boy Emperor's palanquin. The children gazed at the scene in bewilderment.

'Now great ladies,' said the chieftain, 'before we take your heads, we will have sport with you.' Coming right up to Lan Kuei, he stretched out his hand and knocked off her hat. Her hair started to uncoil. 'You will amuse us, great lady, or we will cut the boy's throat.'

Lan Kuei swallowed her panic and began to speak. 'If ... if we please you, will you spare his life? He is your Emperor.'

'We have no emperor,' the man replied. 'We are as free as the wind because we ride with the wind. But amuse me, and the boy may sit here and starve. Now, show yourself.'

Lan Kuei took a deep breath, then removed her sodden cloak.

'All of it,' the chieftain said. 'I wish to see your body.'

Niuhuru sobbed, knowing her turn would come next, while Lan Kuei threw her tabard on the ground.

'Mother, why are you undressing?' the young Emperor inquired, mystified.

Ignoring him, she began to pull at her blouse, to lift it over her head. Then she heard a distant bugle call. She leapt for the T'ung-chih, and pulled him from his seat. 'Run!' she screamed. 'Run, Niuhuru!'

The astonished men grabbled for her. But, unencumbered by cloak or tabard, Lan Kuei twisted past them, the boy clutched in her arms. Racing for the edge of the path, she leapt over it, careless of what might lie beneath. It was a shallow drop into a knee-deep, rushing stream. The impact of the water nearly knocked her over, but she staggered the few feet to the far side, and scrambled out. She was aware from the splashing that Niuhuru must be just behind her.

Gasping for breath, they stared at each other in consternation. Niuhuru's hat had fallen off, and her hair was also down, plastered to her shoulders by the rain, but she clasped Jung-an safely in her arms. Behind them came shouts, as the bandits concerned themselves with the threat presented by the steady drumming of approaching hooves.

'Hurry,' Lan Kuei said, still carrying the T'ung-chih over muddy, stony ground. Niuhuru stumbled behind her with the Princess. When they looked back, the road was already lost to sight, but now they could hear the din of horses neighing, men shouting, firearms exploding, swords clashing. Lan Kuei carried the boy towards a mound of boulders, then set him on his feet within their shelter.

Niuhuru crouched beside her, trembling. 'Who are fighting?'

'We shall soon find out,' Lan Kuei replied, as the shouting

turned to moans and cries for mercy. Lan Kuei's heart pounded. These could prove to be the last moments of her life – or the first moments of a new life.

'Majesty!' a voice shouted. 'Tz'u-hsi – where are you?'

'Jung-lu,' Lan Kuei breathed, and stood up.

*

Jung-lu himself carried the child Emperor back to the road. There waited eighteen of the bandits with their wrists bound. Most were wounded, amongst them their chieftain. Another dozen lay dead.

'Only a score escaped us,' Jung-lu said.

'They wished to isolate us,' Niuhuru said. 'They laid hands upon us, the Dowager Empresses.'

'Then they will die.'

'After they have been castrated,' Lan Kuei said firmly. 'Save their captain till last.'

Jung-lu gave the orders, and Lan Kuei steadfastly watched as one after another the prisoners were robbed first of their manhoods, then their heads. Most accepted their fate with stoicism; their chieftain even grinned. 'Another five minutes and I would have held an Empress naked in my arms,' he gasped, as the knife sliced through his flesh. Jung-lu's own sword cut off his head.

'Get rid of the bodies,' Lan Kuei instructed. 'Throw them down that ravine, so that no one may know what happened here. Leave the eunuchs where they lie.'

Jung-lu looked puzzled. 'But where is the rest of your cortege, Majesty?'

'You have passed no one else on the road behind us?' Niuhuru cried. She looked back into the mist.

Lan Kuei said, 'They must have taken the other road, as did the Bannermen.'

'Then we must follow them.'

'No,' said Lan Kuei. 'We will stay on this path. It is essential we do not encounter Prince Hui until we reach Peking. But it is also essential that we reach Peking before them.'

*

Jung-lu's horsemen constantly urged the wagon on. Lan Kuei
had appropriated two of the bandits' horses for herself and
Niuhuru. The T'ung-chih rode in front of his mother; Jung-an
was mounted before Niuhuru.

'It is not correct procedure for us to ride beside the body of
our husband,' Niuhuru protested. 'The Council of Regency will
criticise us.'

Lan Kuei sighed. The poor woman still did not understand.

*

They reached Peking two days later, and it was still raining. Lan
Kuei instructed Jung-lu to send no one ahead and warn of their
coming. The coffin of the Hsien-feng was covered up. Lan Kuei
and Niuhuru cloaked their faces and that of the boy Emperor.
But Jung-lu uncovered himself at the gate, and the small party
was let through.

An hour later, within the Forbidden City, Prince Kung
listened carefully to Lan Kuei's story. When she had finished,
he said, 'These are grave accusations you bring against a prince
of the House of Ch'ing, Tz'u-hsi.'

'Do as I ask, and the matter will be proved.'

'I will do as you ask. But if your charges turn out to be false,
then you will have me as your enemy.'

'And if I am proved right?'

'Then I remain your friend and supporter, now and always.'

*

They did not have long to wait. Only the next day, outriders
galloped into Peking with a tale of catastrophe. The rest of the
caravan struggled in during the afternoon, exhausted and terrified. Prince Hui and Su-shun went straight to the Grand
Council chamber, where Prince Kung awaited them, together
with his brother and several senior mandarins. The new arrivals
paid no attention to the curtain which concealed Lan Kuei and
Niuhuru, for Lan Kuei was determined to make sure of her future.

'Uncle,' Kung said, 'what is this I hear?'

Prince Hui was still bedraggled and mud-stained. 'We have
suffered a terrible blow.' He sank into a chair. Su-shun
remained standing at his shoulder.

'Where is my brother's body?' Kung demanded. 'Where is our Emperor? Where are the Dowager Empresses?'

'Taken and killed, I fear. We were separated in the rain and mist. Because of the bad weather, I issued instructions that we should take the longer road, instead of risking the passes through the ravines. I assumed everyone would obey my orders, but apparently the Dowager Empresses must have taken the original route, ignoring my wishes. We were unaware of this until late in the day, when the Bannermen of the advance guard came to tell us they could find no trace of the Emperor or the Empresses. You can imagine our concern. I despatched men to search for them immediately. We found the wagon, and traces of blood. Their eunuchs had been massacred. There were signs of many horses. But of the Empresses and the Emperor there was no sign. They must have been carried off by bandits.'

'You let them take the road without a proper escort?' Kung inquired softly.

'They did have an escort – but the escort was in front. And the Empresses chose the wrong road,' Prince Hui said impatiently. 'We were short of men. The bandits had been active around Jehol, and I was forced to send Colonel Jung-lu out to chastise them. He had not yet returned when we departed.'

'You left Jehol without an adequate escort?'

'We left Jehol when the soothsayers told us the day was auspicious,' Prince Hui argued. 'By what right do you criticise my decisions? I am the Regent, appointed by the late Emperor himself. We have suffered a grievous loss, but the work of government must go on. I will make an announcement to the people. I must assume executive power until a new emperor can be chosen.'

He glared at Prince Kung. The mandarins shuffled their feet. This was an unheard of situation.

'You need not go to that trouble, my uncle,' Kung said at last. 'I have good news for you.'

At a signal to the waiting eunuchs, they drew aside the curtain. Prince Hui stared wildly at the boy Emperor, who was flanked by Lan Kuei and Niuhuru. He gasped and fell back in his chair. The mandarins hastily performed the kowtow, kneeling and banging their foreheads on the floor. Su-shun followed their example.

'You will see that we have managed to survive the bandits,

my lord Prince,' Lan Kuei said. 'All of our eunuchs were killed – including your servant, Te An-wah. Although he managed to confess that he led us astray upon your orders.'

Prince Hui seemed incapable of coherent speech, but Su-shun recovered more quickly. He scrambled to his feet. 'No servant of ours was with you, Tz'u-hsi. You are lying.'

'I also heard what the eunuch said,' Niuhuru said softly.

Su-shun swallowed. 'I am sure you were mistaken, Tz'u-an.'

'And I too heard what the man said,' the T'ung-chih chipped in, to general consternation.

Lan Kuei did not know whether he had heard anything or not, but this was what she had coached him to say. Su-shun could only stare at the little boy, his mouth opening and shutting. Not even he could accuse the Emperor of lying.

'You are both charged with treachery, through seeking to procure the death of the Emperor,' Kung broke in. He turned to the mandarins, who nodded as one man.

Prince Hui sat up. 'It was my brother's plan,' he whined. 'I am an old man. I sought only to govern China as Regent.'

Su-shun stared at his half-brother in consternation.

Prince Kung signalled to Jung-lu's guards, quietly assembled in the ante-chamber. 'Confine these men in their homes until their sentences are determined.'

*

'I have discussed the matter with the mandarins,' Prince Kung said. 'They agree this crisis must be ended as rapidly and quietly as possible. I have commanded that the silken cord be sent to both men this very night.'

'No,' Lan Kuei said.

Kung was surprised. 'You do not wish their death, Tz'u-hsi?'

'I wish them to die. And your uncle may have the cord; he is an old man. But Su-shun must be decapitated.'

Kung gazed at her in surprise. 'He is not a prince,' Lan Kuei said. 'And he is a scoundrel who hates me. He has hated me ever since I can remember.'

'Su-shun cannot be sentenced to execution without being condemned by the Council of Regency,' Kung pointed out.

'Then convene the Council,' Lan Kuei snapped. 'You will replace Prince Hui as its head. And Prince Ch'un will replace Su-shun.'

Kung raised his eyebrows. Though Ch'un was his brother, he had always seemed uninterested in the serious business of government. 'It is necessary for every imperial prince to sit on the Council,' Lan Kuei told him. 'Convene the Council now to condemn Su-shun, and have the sentence carried out.'

Kung hesitated, then he bowed and left the room.

*

Lan Kuei could watch the execution from a window, as it took place in one of the inner courts of the Forbidden City. The Emperor stood beside her, but Niuhuru would not attend.

Su-shun did not die with dignity. He snarled defiance, and struggled with his executioners. Lan Kuei smiled, as Su-shun's head rolled in the dust. She gripped the T'ung-chih's hand.

'Now you are truly Emperor,' she said. 'And I am your mother.'

17
THE EVER-VICTORIOUS ARMY

James Barrington awoke to the sound of a bugle call. But, then, he had awoken to the sound of a bugle call every morning for the past several months. Around him the camp was already stirring. Chang Tsin hurried in with a bowl of warmed water for him to shave with. Soon it was time to join the other officers, and commence the morning's drill. Ward's second-in-command, Henry Burgevine, was waiting for him. A big, heavy-set man with a walrus moustache, he clearly disliked the wealthy young Anglo-Chinese who had apparently taken up soldiering as a hobby. But James had been accepted by the General, and even Burgevine stood in awe of Frederick Ward.

It was Ward's energy which dominated his subordinates; he regularly drilled his men from dawn until dusk, with only the shortest of breaks for meals. His toughness, both mental and physical, was astounding; he solved every problem so very quickly. Yet he showed immense patience not only with the new recruits, but in obtaining arms and ammunition from Li Hung-chang. He had even been able to secure two batteries of artillery, and these he had placed under James's command. Ward had only a single squadron of cavalry, but he admitted that he did not properly understand how to handle mounted troops, so therefore had no use for them except as scouts. He had even set about procuring uniforms for his mixed band; in addition to native Chinese he had also recruited Englishmen, Frenchmen and Americans from the waterfront of Shanghai. Now every man wore a blue tunic over white breeches, leggings and boots, with a blue cap.

His patient preparations had been criticised not only by Li's officers, but by the British observers. Yet Li had accepted Ward's imperial commission, and he retained his basic faith in the young American.

Now, at last, the brigade was ready to go to war as soon as the rain ceased; and it had been slackening for several days now.

*

Ward's mind was already ranging ahead to the consequences of the victories he planned. 'We won't smash the T'ai-P'ing until we can take their cities. I don't think these field guns are going to make too much difference to stone walls. We need a qualified military engineer.'

'The British have engineers,' said James. 'I met one, last year. A man called Gordon. At the Yuan Ming Yuan. If you approached him, he might agree to fight with you.'

'Only if the British army agree to his secondment,' Burgevine objected.

'Well, why don't we find out?' Ward said. 'James, why don't you write a letter and get Marshal Li to endorse it.'

This was effected, but nothing further had been heard, when the brigade got its first taste of war. The weather had now improved considerably, and Ward was making his plans for a reconnaissance in force towards the T'ai-P'ing, grouped around Tzeki, when he heard that they were coming against him. They had already occupied Chen-Kiang, and were probing up the Grand Canal in their continuing search for provisions as they ate the countryside bare. So far they had avoided coming further downriver than Tzeki, for fear of encountering the British, but now it was reported that a large body of rebels was on the march towards the neighbourhood of Shanghai.

'Well, glory be,' Ward said. 'Our baptism of fire, Colonel Burgevine. Prepare to move out.'

Li Hung-chang did not agree with him. The news of the T'ai-P'ing approaching had sent a panic through his army. 'We must prepare to defend Shanghai,' he declared. 'You will move your brigade into the city, General Ward.'

'My men are not garrison troops,' Ward protested. 'They are trained only to attack.'

'General, if Shanghai were to fall ...'

'The quickest way to have Shanghai fall, your excellency, is to man the walls and sit tight. That's how the T'ai-P'ing have won so many victories – simply because your people have always stood on the defensive.'

'But there are too many of them for us to attack,' Li complained.

'The more there are, the bigger the target for us,' Ward reassured him.

*

Li finally shrugged and gave way, and Ward made his dispositions. He despatched his small cavalry force under Captain
Feng-shan, the most reliable of his Manchu officers, to discover
the whereabouts of the enemy. The brigade was then set in
motion for a forced march behind the cavalry; that night it
pitched camp in the shadow of a low rise. Ward, Burgevine and
James Barrington then mounted horses – as always they had
marched on foot with their men – and rode to the top of the
rise, whence they could overlook an extensive plain. To
their right lay the river; to their left the land remained featureless: mainly rice paddies through which continued the same
road along which they had been marching all day.

James was suddenly reminded of the stories he had been told
at his grandfather's knee, of how Cheng Yi and the army of the
White Lotus had fought the eight Banners on just such a field,
only north of this same river – and had been routed.

But Ward seemed totally confident. 'This is the place to stop
them,' he declared.

That afternoon the cavalry returned in high excitement. They
had encountered the T'ai-P'ing, and exchanged shots with
them, before galloping off.

'How many were there?' Ward asked.

Feng-shan spread his arms. 'Difficult to say, sir. Not less than
thirty thousand.'

Burgevine gave a low whistle.

Still Ward was undisturbed. 'How far away?'

'They will not reach here until after midnight.'

'That will be ideal,' said Ward. 'Rest your men and water
your horses, Captain. But be ready to mount again at midnight.
Now, Barrington, I want you to move your guns up on this
ridge. Emplace them on the reverse slope, so they won't be
spotted by the T'ai-P'ing until they're in action. Once they're
emplaced, establish a mark one mile down the road, and train
your sights on that, so that they can fire even if the enemy come
at us in the dark. Got me?'

James fell to work immediately. It was dark by the time the
last gun was emplaced, but all were given the same elevation
and sighting, on the mile marker. Meanwhile Ward moved the
brigade forward to the reverse foot of the slope, so that their

presence was hidden from the west. The men were well rested, and now sat down to cook their dinners.

'Shall I keep the mules handy, in case we need to withdraw in a hurry?' Burgevine asked him.

'No,' Ward replied. 'There isn't going to be any withdrawal.'

*

James slept beside his guns, but was awakened by a huge stir in the distance. Instantly his men were alerted, and stood to their weapons. He levelled his glass. It was nearly dawn, and Feng-shan's cavalry were returning at the gallop.

Ward came up to him. 'Three miles,' he said. 'Prepare to open fire as soon as they reach the marker.'

James wiped sweat from his face. 'This is only my second action,' he confessed. 'And the first didn't go too well.'

Ward grinned. 'If it'll cheer you up, this is my *first* action.' James stared in surprise, but Ward continued. 'You'll aim at that marker until we are within four hundred yards of it. Then concentrate your fire at closer range on any of the enemy who continue to advance.'

James was not sure he had heard correctly. 'You intend to take the brigade out there?'

Ward slapped him on the shoulder. 'I told Marshal Li, remember? My men aren't trained to defend.'

*

As Ward went off to join his men, James once again turned to the west. Chang Tsin at his elbow was very nervous – with good reason. It seemed they had all just been commanded to commit suicide. James's every instinct was to defend the hillock. With Ward's discipline and fire power that might prove quite successful. But to take the brigade down into the plain, outnumbered ten to one.... He levelled his glasses. What he saw resembled the Yangtse in flood – pouring alongside the river, in the dawn's first light, was a tide of flashing sword blades.

The enemy mass had now reached the marker, and Ward was already leading his brigade down the western slope of the hill.

'Fire!' yelled Barrington, and the twelve guns roared. 'Load,' he bawled. 'Fire!'

The gunners were as highly trained as all the other components of this strange little army. The second salvo was already on its way before the rumble of the first had died away – to be followed by a third. White smoke rose into the air above the guns, as James peered through his binoculars. He had done considerable execution; the plain was dotted with multi-coloured heaps of dead and wounded. But these now lay behind the main body, which continued to advance.

The morning was now growing bright, and Barrington experienced a choking sensation. Feng-shan had estimated there might be thirty thousand rebels in the field; but James was sure he was looking at twice that number, an immense accumulation of men entirely lacking discipline but brandishing swords and muskets as they surged forward, spreading out to either side, and splashing through the paddy fields to form two huge arms seeking to encircle the small body of blue-and-white-uniformed men. These had now reached the foot of the hill and were marching along the road, bayonets gleaming in the sun, for all the world as if they were merely on parade. Ward was visible at their head, several paces in front. The only weapon he carried was a cane.

James caught his breath as the T'ai-P'ing horde now entirely surrounded the little brigade; he could no longer fire into them for fear of hitting his own side. But even as he watched, the brigade formed a square with perfect precision, extending from the road into the paddies, two ranks to each side, the first kneeling, the rear rank standing. Each man had his musket at the present, and on the end of each musket gleamed an eighteen-inch bayonet. Ward stepped into the centre of this square, to join Burgevine.

The T'ai-P'ing uttered a mighty roar and closed on their prey. There was a ripple of musketry as the first rank fired, at a range of scarcely fifty yards. The T'ai-P'ing recoiled as the bullets tore into them; the front ranks of the brigade rose to their feet and took a step backwards to reload, while their comrades stepped forward and knelt in turn. There was another explosion of fire, and then the drill was repeated again with perfect precision. The muskets might have only a single shot each, but by discharging their pieces in alternate ranks – and

thanks to the hours of practice at top speed which Ward had
imposed upon them – they made it appear as if the fire was
continuous. The T'ai-P'ing could not face this deadly hail of
lead; those who fought through it died on the even deadlier wall
of steel within.

This battle raged for perhaps ten minutes, till the T'ai-P'ing
began to retreat, leaving hundreds dead or dying on the ground.
But Ward had set out to destroy morale as well as men. Once
again carrying out their manoeuvres with perfect precision, the
square turned itself into a phalanx of bristling bayonets, and
while the T'ai-P'ing soldiers were still trying to recover their
breath, moved in a straight line for the enemy generals.

The T'ai-P'ing officers watched as the massed bayonets cut
their way through all who tried to oppose them. Meanwhile
Ward's flankers continued to fire on those who approached to
either side. The rebel leaders turned and fled, their men
following them.

'Now, Captain Feng-shan – now's your chance,' Barrington
shouted. He leapt into the saddle and drew his sword, to lead
the two hundred horsemen in a gallop down the hill, cutting
and slashing all around them.

One of the T'ai-P'ing generals did attempt to rally his men,
but already the horsemen were upon them, and they too were
scattered. But not before James and this rebel general had come
face to face, staring at each other in consternation. Then John
Barrington wheeled his horse and galloped off.

*

'A great triumph. You've shown these bastards what we can
do.' Burgevine drank his wine at a gulp.

Ward looked exhausted but pleased. The brigade had lost no
more than a handful of men. 'It's a start,' he agreed. 'But
remember, gentlemen, one battle never won a war. We still
have a lot to do. Say, Barrington, you reckon they're going to
let us have this Gordon?'

*

'Mr Barrington.' Charles Gordon saluted as he stood to attention in front of the command tent. The brigade had now moved

some thirty miles up river from Shanghai, but Ward always maintained contact with the water, and Gordon had arrived by sampan.

'Well, glory be!' James shouted. 'Am I pleased to see you, Captain. General Ward, allow me to present Captain Charles Gordon of the Royal Engineers.'

The two men gazed at each other for a moment, then they shook hands.

'You'll forgive me for not having a reception for you, Captain,' Ward said. 'But the fact is, you're the first intimation I've had you were coming.'

'Her Majesty's Government moves in a mysterious way,' Gordon agreed. 'But you ... the Ever-Victorious Army, that's what they're calling you.'

Ward grinned. 'On the strength of eleven battles?'

'Eleven defeats for the T'ai-P'ing.'

Ward was suddenly serious. 'Sure we have. We can lick them in the field every time. Even Li's people are starting to get aggressive. But smoking Hung and his people out of their cities is another matter. That's where you come in, Charlie. Our first business is to retake Tzeki.'

*

For Barrington it was like living a dream. Frederick Ward was unlike any man he had ever met; he could now understand why Joanna had been so attracted to him. The American seemed to bear a charmed life; he had taken his brigade into the midst of the T'ai-P'ing hordes on eleven occasions, and routed the enemy each time ... receiving not a scratch. Casualties on the whole had been light. Yet Ward, never armed with anything more lethal than his cane, and always recklessly exposing himself, seemed invulnerable.

His fame had grown, and had spread the length and breadth of China, giving him an importance out of all proportion to the number of men he actually led. Li Hung-chang now commanded some thirty thousand soldiers; Frederick Ward, however, maintained his brigade strength at only three thousand. Still, he was the essential spearhead of the Ch'ing forces. Where the Ever-Victorious Army marched, the rest followed.

*

The assault of Tzeki was set for 20 August 1862. They had already had the city under siege for a fortnight, while Gordon dug his mines and James bombarded the city with his artillery, supported now by the massed batteries of Li's force.

On the morning of the 20th the brigade assembled to carry out the main assault. Li's men waited in reserve. The day began with the usual bombardment, while James surveyed the walls through his glass, Chang Tsin as ever at his side, bobbing about nervously. The balls thumped through the air and smacked away chunks of masonry wherever they landed – but the defenders answered each shot with shouts of defiance and cannon-shot of their own. They were totally unaware of the catastrophe lurking beneath their feet; the entrance to the mine shaft had been so cunningly concealed that the T'ai-P'ing had no idea of its existence. If they ever heard odd sounds from under the earth, it had not seemed to alarm them, since they had no knowledge of siegecraft themselves.

James watched Gordon canter towards him, followed by the rest of his engineers. Though mudstained, they looked pleased enough; Gordon had earned their absolute loyalty within days of his arrival – he was as much a born leader of men as was Ward himself.

'The train has been lit,' Gordon said. 'It will explode in ten minutes.'

*

James's pulse rate slowly increased as the minutes ticked away. The artillery continued to growl on both sides, while the Manchu army waited motionless for the signal to advance.

Expectant as he was, the huge roar of the explosion took him by surprise. It seemed to swell out of the bowels of the earth. One of the towers on the outer wall soared into the air, and then fell apart, carrying its defenders with it. Where it had stood was now nothing but rubble.

There arose an enormous wail of terror from the T'ai-P'ing; their firing slackened. Barrington also called for a ceasefire as he saw Ward raise his cane and move forward, followed by his brigade in its usual compact mass.

To the left, Li's men advanced simultaneously, equipped with their scaling ladders. They would assault the unbreached wall while Ward's men forced their way through the breach, into the city itself.

The attack proceeded like clockwork – because Ward's assaults, so meticulously prepared and calculated, always went like clockwork. Peering through his glass, James saw the brigade easily disperse the few T'ai-P'ing gathered to defend the breach in the wall, and pour into the town. Within an hour the dragon flag of the Manchu was hoisted over the captured city.

'I think we could go down there now,' Gordon suggested.

They were only halfway to the now open main gate when they saw a horseman spurring towards them. It was Feng-shan, as much a veteran of victory now as any of them.

'Colonel Barrington,' he gasped. 'Captain Gordon ...' Tears streamed down his cheeks.

James sensed immediately what had happened. In every battle, however meticulous the planning, there was always risk of the unforeseen. He kicked his horse forward, followed by his officers. They rode for the breach. There James leapt from the saddle and scrambled over the rubble. He stopped dead when he saw Ward lying on the stones, surrounded by his stricken men.

Ward's grin was tired. 'A stray bullet,' he said, his breath coming in great heaves, frothy with blood. 'Of all the luck.'

'We'll get you back to Shanghai,' James said.

Ward looked at his soldiers, whose faces were masks of misery. 'These guys don't know how to lie, James. I'm done, God damn it. I wanted to see that flag flying over Nanking.'

'You will,' James promised.

'You settle with Hung,' Ward muttered. 'And that uncle of yours. And say, tell Joanna ... thanks. Without her, this wouldn't have happened.' His head fell back, and then he raised it again. 'Say, James, will I get into the history books?'

'You're already there,' James told him.

'That'll please Dad,' Ward said, and closed his eyes.

*

James returned to the encampment, where the flags hung at

half-mast. Tzeki had fallen, but there was no elation over this their greatest victory – because no man knew what would happen now.

Boots crunched on the earth. James gazed up at Feng-shan. 'Burgevine has gone,' the Manchu said.

'Gone where?'

'He was seen riding west. He has gone to Hung.'

James leapt into the saddle to take the news to Li Hung-Chang.

'Who will take over command of the brigade?'

'I have no idea, Barrington. Perhaps the brigade will have to be disbanded.'

'That cannot happen, Marshal Li. You know as well as I that the Ever-Victorious Army is our only hope of beating the T'ai-P'ing.'

'The Viceroy himself is on his way,' Li said. 'He will tell us what should be done.'

*

'Obviously we must keep General Ward's brigade in being until the T'ai-P'ing have been finally defeated,' Tseng Kuo-fan announced. 'I shall write to Prince Kung in Peking, explaining this. But who will command it, now that General Ward has died and Colonel Burgevine has absconded?' He looked at James. 'You had General Ward's confidence, Colonel Barrington – and you bear a famous name.'

James had anticipated this – but he was also haunted by the memory of the boy who had run away at Wuhu. 'I am a gunner, excellency,' he said. 'I know nothing of leading an army in the field.'

Tseng studied him for several seconds, then he looked at Feng-shan . . . but no Manchu could possibly have the impact of Ward. James found himself gazing at the dark green uniform of Charles Gordon, at the tight features above it. He stood to the rear of the others, but his face seemed to glow. Charles Gordon was as different a human being from Frederick Ward as could be imagined. He would fight a totally different kind of war from the flamboyant marches and assaults of the American.

Yet suddenly James knew the answer. 'You must appoint Captain Gordon, excellency.'

Tseng gave Gordon a hard look. He had heard of this man. 'Are you willing to take command of the brigade?' he said at last.

Gordon's eyes gleamed. 'I would, your excellency, on the same conditions.'

Tseng frowned at him. 'What conditions?'

'That I conduct my campaign without interference.'

Tseng hissed at such effrontery. 'General Ward had a commission signed by the Emperor.'

'Then Captain Gordon must have the same,' James said.

Tseng again glanced at Li Hung-chang. The Marshal now said, 'That would be impossible. Is this not the same Captain Gordon who destroyed the Yuan Ming Yuan? Prince Kung will never employ the man who burned the Summer Palace. Even less would the Dowager Empress, who wields the true power.'

'You are right,' Tseng Kuo-fan agreed.

Tz'u-hsi, James thought. The friend of his youth, now come to greatness and power – as it had been prophesied. Yet surely Lan Kuei would place defeat of the T'ai-P'ing above all other matters ... even vengeance for the destruction of the Yuan Ming Yuan.

'I will go to Peking,' he said suddenly. 'I will see Prince Kung, and Tz'u-hsi herself, if necessary. And I will procure Captain Gordon's commission.'

*

'Are you sure you know what we do?' Chang Tsin asked, as they rode into Shanghai. 'T'zu-hsi may not be at all pleased to see us.'

'Because *you* deserted her.'

'She will demand my head,' Chang Tsin admitted dolefully.

*

James went first of all to the Barrington House to report to his uncle and mother. He also had to tell Joanna the news about Ward. Sitting on the veranda with her hands on her lap, she gazed down the hill towards the river. 'I think he knew he was going to die,' she said.

'Were you in love with him, Jo?'

She half turned her head. 'I think I could have loved him.' She sighed. 'James, Frederick's dream must not be allowed to die.'

'It is now my business to see that it does not.'

*

'Will you *ever* again settle down and become the husband I thought I married?' Lucy was again pregnant.

'As soon as this business is settled,' James promised her. 'So wish me good fortune.'

*

Martin would not use a Barrington junk; he preferred to charter one. He did not know for certain what had happened in Peking following the death of the Hsien-feng Emperor. Rumour spoke of palace intrigue. But whatever had happened, he knew enough about Chinese politics to understand that while Lan Kuei – T'zu-hsi – might have attempted to seize power in the name of her son, there was no guarantee that she still held power. Caution was necessary.

Thus he disembarked into a sampan at the mouth of the Pei-ho, his hired junk having threaded its way among the barbarian warships which remained anchored in the gulf. Thence he proceeded to Tientsin, and the Barrington agent in that city. Sung-chai appeared pleased to see him, but scratched his straggly beard when he heard of his plans.

'It is very dangerous for a barbarian in Peking at this time,' he said. 'They are greatly hated there.'

'Just supply me with a sampan and a crew who can be trusted.'

Sung-chai scratched some more, but did as he was instructed. Next morning James and Chang Tsin proceeded on their way upriver to join the Grand Canal. James wore Chinese clothes, of course, but there were few people could doubt that he was a barbarian. He relied on the fact that he was travelling as fast as rumour, unless it was mounted on a very fast horse.

With every mile travelled, however, Chang Tsin grew more nervous.

*

The arrival of a Barrington at the Yun-ting-men caused some concern to the captain of the guard. But Martin carried a passport signed by Tseng Kuo-fan, and they were not detained. It was dark as they entered the city, but the streets glowed with light and hummed with noise. They proceeded towards the T'ien-an-men, and here again were halted by a guard. Again James presented his credentials.

'I come on a mission from Viceroy Tseng Kuo-fan to the Dowager Empress.'

The bemused captain told them to wait, while he sent messengers into the Forbidden City. They waited for more than hour – then a superior officer, tall and powerfully built, appeared. He ignored James, and looked at Chang Tsin. 'What is your name?'

'I am Chang Tsin,' he gasped. 'I am the favourite eunuch of the Dowager Empress. I have brought Young Barrington to see her.'

The Colonel pointed. 'You are a villain, who deserted our lady in her hour of need. Her Majesty has told me of this. I will have you flogged from here to the Great Wall and back, and then you will suffer the death of a thousand cuts.'

Chang Tsin fell to his knees in terror.

'May I ask your authority, Colonel?' James intervened.

'I am Jung-lu, commander of the royal bodyguard.'

'I can assure you it would be a mistake to arrest us. You have but to give Tz'u-hsi my name. I have been her friend for many years. I have come to see her on a matter of utmost importance to the Manchu Dynasty.'

Jung-lu's eyes gloomed at him. 'It is too late,' he grumbled. 'Tz'u-hsi will have retired.'

James realised he had taken the initiative. 'She *will* see me. Send her my name.'

Jung-lu hesitated a last time. Then he commanded that James and Chang Tsin be searched, before allowing them through the gate.

Inside the Forbidden City, James thought, as they were escorted along the great central avenue, and past the temple complex towards the palace.

They were taken in by a side door and made to wait for some

time in an ante-chamber, stared at by hostile armed eunuchs, several of whom clearly knew Chang Tsin, from the dire punishments they prophesied for him. Suddenly an inner door was thrown open. Jung-lu beckoned them inside, and they faced Tz'u-hsi.

Late as was the hour, the Dowager Empress was fully dressed, in a silk gown exquisitely decorated with a golden dragon against the green of the material. Her hair was lost to sight beneath her huge winged head-dress, save for the centre forehead where her raven tresses were parted exactly in the middle. Her face was heavily made up, her fingernails lacquered, the two outer nails of each hand grown to more than an inch and protected by fingerstalls. Only her eyes remained familiar, but these eyes belonged to a Lan Kuei whom James had never known. He had to remind himself that she was only twenty-seven years old.

She gave no sign of welcome. 'You bear a message from General Ward,' she said.

'General Ward is dead, Majesty.'

Lan Kuei's eyes flashed. 'Is it to tell me this evil news that you have forced your way into my palace with this ...' She glared at Chang Tsin, who promptly fell to his knees.

Barrington refused to be browbeaten by this girl he had once kissed. 'Your Majesty, General Ward fell in the moment of victory – just as the city of Tzeki fell to his assault.'

'Tzeki has fallen?' Lan Kuei's voice suddenly eager.

'Yes, Majesty. The T'ai-P'ing have been defeated time and again. And they have now lost one walled city. It is possible for us to think of ending this revolt. But the news of General Ward's death will spread – and quickly. His second-in-command, Burgevine, has deserted to the enemy. I am sent by Viceroy Tseng Kuo-fan to appeal to you to appoint a new commander for the Ever-Victorious Army. The Viceroy feels that without prompt action that army may disintegrate. I have a letter, Majesty.'

Lan Kuei scanned it. 'This Viceroy is a fool. He says it will be difficult to replace Ward. Why do you not take command?'

'I am not fit for the post, Majesty.'

'That is a strange admission.'

'Now is a time for honesty, even with oneself.'

'Ha! Then recommend someone else.'

James drew a deep breath. 'Captain Gordon, of the Royal Engineers. He has also served with General Ward.'

Lan Kuei frowned. 'I have heard the name.'

'That is the scoundrel who destroyed the Yuan Ming Yuan.' Jung-lu intervened.

'That wretch?'

'With respect, Your Majesty,' James said. 'Gordon is the man to lead the Ever-Victorious Army. There is none better. *He* will bring you the head of Hung Hsiu-ch'uan. Is there anything you desire more?'

Lan Kuei continued to glare at him for seconds. Then she said, 'We will talk of this matter tomorrow, when we have slept. The hour is late for such a decision. You will be found accommodation for the night, Barrington.'

James realised he had accomplished all he could have hoped. 'I thank Your Majesty,' he said. 'But what of my eunuch?'

'That scoundrel! He deserted me.'

'Let me have him, Majesty,' Jung-lu said. 'They will hear his screams in Tientsin.'

Chang Tsin, still on his knees, clasped his hands before him.

'He did not desert you,' James said.

Another glare. 'What do you know of the matter?'

'Did you not send him to save my life, when I was imprisoned in Peking? And he *did* save my life. When he sought to regain you, you had already left for Jehol.'

Tz'u-hsi looked at Chang Tsin. 'Can this be true? You would pretend to be a hero instead of the coward you really are.'

'He saved my life,' James reaffirmed.

'You may keep your eunuch, for tonight at least,' Tz'u-hsi conceded. 'We will talk again tomorrow.'

*

After being fed, James collapsed into bed; Chang Tsin slept on the floor at his feet. Next morning they were awakened early. As soon as they had breakfasted, they were marched through long corridors to Tz'u-hsi's apartments. Lan Kuei sat alone, save for a single eunuch. Thoughtfully dressed, she had not yet been made up for the day, and seemed once again the girl James remembered – although there were new lines of hardness around her mouth and eyes. But that she had not changed completely was indicated by the breach of protocol in permitting a private interview with an uncastrated male.

'Sit.' She gestured James to a chair. Chang Tsin stood nervously behind him. 'I was pleased to know you fought with Ward,' she said. 'I had not known you were a soldier. Did you know Ward well?'

'As well as anyone, I think.'

'He had the essence of greatness. Tell me of yourself, Barrington.'

James told her of his marriage, of his son, of his wife again pregnant.

'Is she beautiful, Barrington?'

There was only one possible answer. 'Not so beautiful as you, Majesty.'

Lan Kuei smiled. 'Do you ever think of what might have been – had we married? Did you love me, Barrington?'

'I have always loved you, Lan Kuei. But did you ever love me?'

Lan Kuei stared at him, and was for a moment again the girl he had kissed on the bluff above the Yangtse.

'I would have made you very rich,' he added with a smile.

'We have come a long way since we were young, James. We have seen many things, learned many things.'

'And now you have become supreme ruler of China,' James said.

Lan Kuei grimaced. 'I am merely the mother of the Emperor,' she said coyly. 'But he is a child. Thus I must endeavour to think as he thinks, and rule as I know he would wish. When he grows up, I shall be nothing more than Dowager Empress.' For a moment she was pensive, then she added, 'But that is a long time away. Tell me of this man Gordon. Tell me of him.'

James related what he knew.

'Will you fight under him?'

'Until the rebellion is crushed, Majesty.'

'And then?'

'I would hope to manage the House of Barrington.'

'That is your destiny,' Lan Kuei observed, 'as this is mine. I have never doubted that I would attain greatness. It only remains for me to bring such greatness to fruition. And for that

I must employ the best means I can find. Very well, Barrington, I will issue letters of appointment for Gordon. And then I must see this Hung Hsiu-ch'uan dragged in chains before me.'

'It shall be done.'

'As for you, Chang Tsin, are you not a scoundrel? You will remain here in the Forbidden City. I will have you whipped for deserting me.'

Chang Tsin commenced to shiver.

'Please, Majesty,' James protested.

'Then you may resume your duties as my personal eunuch,' Tz'u-hsi said. 'I have missed you.' Chang Tsin collapsed to his knees in gratitude. 'Now go and prepare my bath.' She stood, and James hastily followed. She turned to him, 'Once, you kissed me,' she said softly.

James hesitated to answer, uncertain of her mood.

She smiled. 'I liked that kiss. I have kissed other men since ...' She changed her mind about what she would say, and instead held out her hand. 'I shall not see you again. Go, James, and prosper. I shall sleep easier for knowing that the House of Barrington is in your keeping.'

*

As it happened, Charles Gordon had his own ideas on how this war should be fought. Unlike Ward, who was a supreme tactician, Gordon was more interested in the strategic aspects of the contest. Ward had defeated the T'ai-P'ing forces on twelve consecutive occasions, but so enormous were the rebel forces that they still lay within seventy miles of Shanghai, and Tzeki remained the only city of size that had been recaptured.

'The way to victory,' he assured Tseng and Li, 'lies less in defeating the T'ai-P'ing in the field, for they are like the sand on a beach, which when washed away by the sea merely re-forms itself somewhere else. It is to take away their means of existence.'

Tseng nodded. 'This is sensible. We must starve them into submission.'

The T'ai-P'ing were confounded by this change of emphasis, for suddenly the Ever-Victorious Army avoided battle, and instead slipped up the river to the southern end of the Grand Canal. The rebels had retained their control of this, and were using the country around as a vast granary; while the Canal itself provided them with a waterway for transporting supplies. This waterway Gordon now cut, by building forts opposite Chin-kiang, where the Canal debouched into the river. Meanwhile, Li was applying frontal pressure, and now at last the T'ai-P'ing began to fall back ... as their bellies rumbled with hunger.

The work was slow and unexciting. It was also extremely distressing – as they retreated, the T'ai-P'ing slaughtered as indiscriminately as when advancing. Evacuated villages too often were found to contain only corpses; and amongst the survivors disease grew more rampant than ever. However, that Gordon's tactics were proving successful could not be argued, especially when, early in the summer of 1863, an entire T'ai-P'ing division surrendered – the first time ever. Barrington sat on his horse and watched the wretched men being rounded up and herded into a vast mass by the triumphant Manchu soldiery.

'The beginning of the end,' Tseng declared.

'Yes,' Gordon said thoughtfully. 'And a huge headache for us. We can hardly feed our own people.'

'We are certainly not going to feed those scum.'

Gordon's head turned sharply. 'They are prisoners of war.'

'General Gordon, it is a business for myself, and my decision has been taken. Those men will not be fed.'

'They will resume fighting when they discover that,' James suggested.

Tseng smiled. 'It would be simplest, I agree, Colonel Barrington. As they no longer have any arms, they will die the more quickly.'

'That would be plain simple murder,' Gordon snapped. 'I will not be a party to it, your excellency. Those men surrendered to me.'

'I am your superior officer, General Gordon.'

'Not if you persist in this decision.'

Tseng gazed at him for a moment, and then bowed his head. 'That must be your decision, General.'

*

'I rather suspect he was angling for that,' James told Gordon.

'Which means that as I have not attracted the heroic reputation of Ward, I am dispensable.'

'In a sense. Ward was necessary to the Ch'ing, for the creation and maintenance of morale. He never showed them how to
win the war but, then, it is a Chinese characteristic never to win
wars, but to let them drag on until they just dwindle away. In
those circumstances, the maintenance of morale is very
important. You have come along and showed them how to win
this war – and without fighting too many bloody battles. Having
learned that, it is obviously in Tseng's interest to have the
victory gained by his own officers rather than a barbarian.'

'I've no doubt you're right,' Gordon agreed. 'Well, they're
welcome to the glory. It is difficult to decide which is worse: the
T'ai-P'ing or the Manchu.'

'I've had that difficulty myself.'

'So, what are you going to do?'

James shrugged. 'Stay here with the army.'

'You condone this massacre Tseng is preparing?'

'This isn't a very Christian country.'

Gordon held out his hand. 'I doubt we shall meet again, so I
will wish you good fortune with the brigade. You should have
had the command from the beginning.'

*

When Nanking fell in the summer of 1864, the rebellion was
officially over. The Heavenly King, preferring not to be taken
prisoner, committed suicide when he realised that all was lost.
Burgevine hanged himself. Not all of Hung's close associates
followed his example, however, and pockets of T'ai-P'ing
retreated up the river, hoping to make a last stand at Hankow –
or to escape into the mountains. Amongst them were John
Barrington and his mother.

But the pursuit, now in the hands of Li Hung-chang, since
Tseng Kuo-fan had been sent away to deal with other rebels in
the north-west, was inexorable. The T'ai-P'ing were harried
both by water and land; and in the following spring John
Barrington and Tsen-tsing, mud-stained and half-naked, shivering with hunger, were dragged before Li Hung-chang.

'Your uncle,' Li said contemptuously, summoning James to
look at the captives.

John licked his lips. 'I would ask for mercy, James,' he said.
'For the sake of our House.'

'Do not beg,' Tsen-tsing said. 'They have already decreed our deaths. Why do you not just strike off our heads?'

James looked at Li.

'That is not the death decreed for T'ai-P'ing generals,' Li said.

John swallowed. 'What is to be our fate?'

'It is the decree of the Son of Heaven that all T'ai-P'ing leaders and their families shall die the death of a thousand cuts,' Li said.

John fell to his knees. 'Have pity, I beg of you.'

Tsen-tsing looked at James. 'You will permit this?'

'It is the command of the Son of Heaven,' Li said before James could speak. *Or his mother*, James thought. All manner of reflections tumbled through his mind, but he knew he could not interfere, even if it were possible.

Tsen-tsing read her fate in his expression. Her lip curled. 'I spit on you,' she snarled.

*

After that she said nothing, even as she was stripped and encased in a steel mesh tunic which extended from her shoulders to below her thighs, then tied to a stake in the central square of Hankow. John was forced to watch his mother die first. The belts securing the tunic were tightened until bulges of flesh appeared through the links – each about an inch across. Breasts and buttocks were the first forced through, to be sliced away by the executioner, and water thrown over the victim, both to revive her and wash away the blood. Then the tunic was tightened again, and the ritual repeated. It was six hours before the mutilated body hung lifeless.

John Barrington had fainted several times during his mother's ordeal. Now it was his turn, and the water had to be regularly applied to keep him conscious. He screamed his terror and agony as the first tightening took place, his screams growing in intensity as the executioner manipulated the links to permit his castration. It took him a full eight hours to die.

*

'Tell me of it,' Joanna said.

James shook his head. 'It was barbaric. But you have been avenged.'

Avenged, she thought. She would have forgone that, to be able to see again Frederick Ward leaning on the garden gate, wearing that shy smile.

Lucy shuddered, and hugged her babe to her breast; her son clung to her skirts, hardly recognising his father after so long an absence. 'This is a barbaric country.'

'It is a great country,' James reminded her. He looked at his step-father.

'Until the next rebellion,' Lucy murmured. But no one heard her.

*

Li Hung-chang himself journeyed to Peking with the head of Hung Hsiu-ch'uan, to deliver it to Tz'u-hsi herself. The head had been embalmed, and as the Heavenly King had taken poison, looked no more than peacefully asleep. But, however clean-shaven, it was no longer a youthful face. Hung had lived life too well to permit that.

Lan Kuei gazed at it for several seconds, her features immobile. Then she said, 'Nail it to the gate. But you, Marshal Li, you deserve well of His Majesty. Be sure you will be rewarded. As will General Gordon.'

'General Gordon has already left China, Tz'u-hsi.'

'Nevertheless, I would bestow upon him the mark of His Majesty's favour. He shall have the ruby button of a mandarin of the First rank, together with the unicorn badge. We shall send these things to him, and also the yellow hunting jacket.'

'And Young Barrington, Tz'u-hsi?'

'Young Barrington is already rewarded with his prosperity. And my favour.' She inclined her head.

Li Hung-chang left the audience chamber.

'Barrington is a long-nosed hairy barbarian,' growled Jung-lu, who attended all of Tz'u-hsi's audiences. 'They are everywhere. They must be destroyed, Tz'u-hsi, or, like the weeds in a garden, they will strangle us. As they destroyed the Yuan Ming Yuan,' he added – knowing that memory would always drive Lan Kuei into a fury.

'I know,' Lan Kuei said. 'But, first, we must become stronger than they.' She half-smiled. 'And we must rebuild the Summer Palace.' She rose from her chair and walked to the window, to look down into the garden below: at Tz'u-an strolling with her ladies. 'And we must rid ourselves of the weak elements in our government, so that we alone may know what is best.' Her voice was soft. Niuhuru was her friend, and had saved her life. But she was also the senior Dowager Empress, with still the power of veto over anything her junior might propose.

Jung-lu preferred not to comment on what Tz'u-hsi might have in mind for Tz'u-an. For him there was a more urgent problem. He stood at her shoulder.

'In but a few years the T'ung-chih Emperor will claim manhood.' He faltered as he spoke, for his suggestion that the Emperor was a weak element was treason.

Tz'u-hsi brushed against him as she turned. 'He is my son,' she said. 'And will remain our Emperor.' She looked from her lover to Chang Tsin, waiting beside her chair. Not one of them was yet thirty years old. 'They say that the war with the T'ai-P'ing has cost us twenty million lives,' she remarked. 'But we have defeated them, and wiped them from the face of the earth. Do you suppose any power on earth can now oppose me, until I will it?'

Little, Brown now offers an exciting range of quality titles by both established and new authors. All of the books in this series are available by faxing, or posting your order to:

Little, Brown Books,
Cash Sales Department,
P.O. Box 11,
Falmouth,
Cornwall,
TR1O 9EN
Fax: 0326-376423

Payments can be made as follows: Cheque, postal order (payable to Little, Brown Cash Sales) or by credit cards, Visa/Access/Mastercard. Do not send cash or currency. U.K. customers and B.F.P.O.; Allow £1.00 for postage and packing for the first book, plus 50p for the second book, plus 30p for each additional book up to a maximum charge of £3.00 (7 books plus). U.K. orders over £75 free postage and packing.

Overseas customers including Ireland, please allow £2.00 for postage and packing for the first book, plus £1.00 for the second book, plus 50p for each additional book.

NAME (Block Letters) ....
ADDRESS ....
....
....

☐ I enclose my remittance for ....

☐ I wish to pay by Visa/Access/Mastercard

Number ☐☐☐☐☐☐☐☐☐☐☐☐☐☐☐☐

Card Expiry Date ☐☐☐☐

80   74